JOEBALL

A novel by

RAY AKIN

PAGE PUBLISHING, INC.
New York, NY

First originally published by Page Publishing, Inc. 2019

ISBN 978-1-68456-387-6 (Paperback)
ISBN 978-1-68456-388-3 (Digital)

Printed in the United States of America

CHAPTER 1

The Early Years

Throughout the world since time began, to own your home and the land it is on has been the desire and ambition of most people. Soon after Columbus discovered the New World, multitudes crossed the oceans to the North American continent in search of a new life and the possibility to fulfill their need of ownership. From the landing on Plymouth Rock, the western migration into the frontier continued for centuries until the late 1800s, when most of the land of Columbus's New World had been rightly or unjustly purchased or claimed.

In the south-central area of the United States, there existed a large area of land that had little or no population and was lacking in laws and enforcement thereof. This was at a time when most would say the frontier had ceased to exist, but here in an area known as the Oklahoma and Indian Territories, a small remnant of the vast frontier was still alive and well. In March of 1889, the United States government came up with a novel idea to quickly settle and populate this area and subsequently bring into it a civilization, with laws and order.

The idea was to give the land away. "Boomers" is the name given to the people that campaigned for the opening of these lands and the Oklahoma Land Rush of 1889 is what the process was called. Twelve o'clock noon on April 22, 1889, was the date and hour for this experiment to commence. This would be the largest land giveaway the world had ever seen. Six other land runs or rushes would follow the

1889 Rush. There would be three separate land runs in September of 1891: September 22, 1891, land run; September 23, 1891; and September 28, 1891, land run. The September 1891 runs involved 20,000 homesteaders that would lay claim to 976,000 acres, 6,097 plots of 160 acres. The Land Rush of April 19, 1892, had 25,000 people flock to claim three and a half million acres at 160 acres a plot. At the end of the day, when it was all said and done, four-fifths of the free land that was opened to give away, 2.5 million acres lay unclaimed. The Land Run of September 16, 1893, also known as the Cherokee Strip or Cherokee Outlet Land Run was the largest run in land, six million acres and had 100,000 participants. The Land Run of May 23, 1895, was the smallest and last land run in the Indian Territories. The 1889 Rush was considered the greatest, most magnificent of all the land rushes/runs because it was for the Unassigned Lands, considered the choicest land, and it was the first. Twelve years after the last land run, these territories became the forty-sixth state of the Union. The name *Oklahoma* comes from the Choctaw Indian language phrase, *okla humma*, meaning red people.

Howard and Mary Marshall were living west of Lawrence, Kansas, in the little town of Big Springs, when in March of 1889, they read how the United States government, from an order given by President Harrison, was going to divide up and give away some unassigned land in the Indian Territories. It was decided that it would be a race, and the first to claim would be the first to own their quarter section of land. Few rules applied: stake out the land fairly having started when the cannon fired and to homestead the land for a year to get title. Undeveloped land in the Indian Territory would have many hardships at first because of the lack of cities for commerce, schools; supplies would be slow in coming, no support (neighbors would be few and far between), and a near total lack of law enforcement or civil government. Not only the unassigned land in the rush lacked habitation, a person could travel more than a hundred fifty miles in any direction and not find the minimum of civil or civic support of any kind at the time of the land rush. Most of the area lacked any civilization of any kind. Truly it was a frontier, albeit a railroad station about forty miles away would take form of a city almost immediately.

A town not built in a day, but a town built in an afternoon. A town did not exist in the early morning hours of April 22, 1889, but as night fell on that day, there was a population of ten thousand. A few days before, at night, the coyotes and wolves howled, and deer ran freely across the grass-filled slopes of the Cimarron Valley. Now the clatter of people, the smells of fires, and night lights would drive the wildlife farther into the frontier in a matter of days as the city grew with what almost seemed to be without limits. That town, Guthrie, at first stop on the railroad line that supplied water and fuel for the steam locomotives, would in a matter of days become a beehive of activity, people, supplies, and commerce. Guthrie, in a matter of eighteen years, was a city large enough to become the first capital of the forty-sixth state of Oklahoma.

Howard would ride alone that day because he had to move fast to get the claim he wanted, high ground with a gentle slope to a creek that would supply water and trees for firewood. This was the setting that he desired and had already scouted the area days earlier, and he knew the path and direction to take at the start of the greatest race the world had ever known in a free-for-all, where the winner takes first place in claiming free land and the land of their choice by winning their race and getting there first. Howard figured to stake a parcel that was close to the center of the Unassigned Lands about twenty-four miles from the start. To cover the twenty-four-miles plus, a rider would have to have a strong, fast horse that didn't get winded easy and was able to go the distance. Howard owned just such a horse, one that he raised from a colt and had total confidence in, named Ole Sam. Ole Sam was a sixteen-hand plus, blood bay Morgan with white stocking feet and a blaze forehead, who would give a rider all he could take in a day's journey, and that was just what it would take for Ole Sam to get Howard to the land he wanted before anyone else could lay claim to it. Howard knew that Ole Sam more than likely could have been the fastest horse for the distance in the whole rush. Many Eighty-niners would run the race in covered wagons and buckboards, which slowed their pace because of the terrain and nonexistent roads that would lead to breakdowns if one pushed too fast, and making repairs would waste valuable time in a race to claim your land. Some rode plow horses, mules, and donkeys. Some folks walked to their plots, taking three to four days to stake their claims. The slower pace you made only left the land that was considered the least desirable at the time. Land that was passed over in the first days of the rush, in the years later, when oil was discovered on it, became more valuable than one could imagine on April 22, 1889. Howard knew that if he rode the fastest, no one except a Sooner could beat him to his claim, and the rumor of the day was that the Sooners were out there setting up on the borders of the unassigned land days and even the night before the rush started in an attempt to jump the line before the start time. The United States Cavalry constantly searched the area for illegal claim jumpers, Sooners, hiding out and not running the race but ready to jump out after they knew the race had started to claim the best land available. This was an impossible task for the Army to patrol an estimated two million acres with two hundred soldiers. The night before the run, the thought ran through Howard's mind of a Sooner laying claim to the land he had scouted out. It angered him to a point that he was not sure of what action he would take if confronted with that situation. It was an unpleasant thought, and Howard did not desire a gruesome start to his land ownership, so he and Mary had chosen two alternates to avoid a deadly conflict. Howard knew that after the start, if he kept his lead and rode the fastest and hardest, not seeing anyone on his left or right or allowing to be passed, taking the most direct route, he didn't see how he could be beaten to the claim he wanted, unless it was a dirty, cheating sooner.

The night before and throughout the early-morning hours before the run, at daybreak, six hours before the start, a mass of people had already assembled. An estimated fifty thousand participants crowded in to establish themselves at the starting line. Howard picked a spot in the front, on a high point at the north end of the line. As Howard positioned himself, he gazed to his left and could hardly believe his eyes as to what appeared to him to be a mass of people forming a line stretching for miles to a point he could not determine at either end with a naked eye. Howard's position at the midpoint of the line meant for him less distance to cover, for the farther south or north he placed himself increased the number of people he had to traverse and more land to cover, if not miles, mere yards, because he was going to go nearly due west and a little north. In the days before traveling as straight a line as possible from his desired stake, he figured a starting place on the line that would give him the advantage of less miles traveled. On the day of the run, it seemed to Howard that he had placed himself in about the middle where it seemed to be the most frantic and crowded area to be, even though he was satisfied with his starting position.

The plan was for Howard to be there first to drive the stake flagged with the Rocking *M* insignia and wait for Mary to follow in the wagon on nearly the same course, which they had traveled on horseback days before, until hopefully, she came upon Howard two to three days later at the place they had chosen. To reach their desired claim, Howard, being on horseback, would ford the Cimarron River, staying on the most direct line as possible. Mary, driving a team and wagon, would have to seek out a place to ford the Cimarron a little farther west, which would add a couple of miles to her trip. If for unknown reasons the original site had been claimed by someone else, Mary was to push on to the first and then the second alternative, and if Howard was still not there, wait at that spot, and Howard would find her later.

The wagon Mary drove had all the possessions they owned, supplies, building materials, towing cows, a bull and pulled by two working horses. Mary bringing up the rear and arriving safely with goods intact was more important than Howard staking out a parcel. On the wagon and with the wagon was everything they needed to survive with land or without. Howard could not leave the land unattended until it was recorded with the land agent back in Guthrie. Mary had to stay on the trail without him for two or three nights because of the slow pace she would have to travel. Along with their precious cargo, Mary was armed with a Model 1873 Winchester .44-40 carbine with a twenty-inch barrel. Mary having grown up in rural Kansas knew how to handle and fire her Winchester and liked the shorter barrel, which she could pull out from under the seat of the wagon with ease if needed. Mary also carried in an upright position, fixed in the corner of the wagon next to the hand break, a John Browning–designed breech-loading Winchester Model 1887 lever action twelve-gauge shotgun. Mary's twelve-gauge shotgun held six rounds, one chambered and five rounds in an under-barrel magazine. With a twenty-inch barrel, Mary in real close quarters could have all the firepower she needed with little or no accuracy, just point and shoot. Howard carried enough water and provisions for five days. He could replenish his water supply and let Ole Sam water in the few creeks and the Cimarron River that they had to cross. The creeks were mostly wet-weather creeks, and within the last two weeks, a few spring rains had filled them with adequate standing and flowing water that he, Mary, Ole Sam, and the livestock could take advantage of on the trip. Along with supplies, Howard carried a .44-40 Winchester 1873 and a .44-40 Colt Bisley. Howard's Winchester 1873 was a special order that had a thirty-inch octagon barrel with a twenty-inch tubular fifteen-round magazine specially equipped with a front "semi-jack" ivory bead sight, a Lyman folding leaf sight in the barrel dovetail, and a coursed knurled Lyman fold down peep sight mounted on the tang. This custom-built 1873 Winchester gave Howard the advantage in firepower and more than 150 feet more accuracy over most of the other rifles, except one just like it, then the advantage went to the best shot of the two. Howard was a good shot, not fast but accurate. His shooting experience was hunting and target practice, not shooting at people, and this was a disadvantage if he were ever in a face-to-face situation. He was sure that if someone was trying to kill or harm himself or a family member, there would be no hesitation on his part.

Twelve o'clock neared as Howard tried to steady Ole Sam, making an effort to stay well behind the starting line. He saw the smoke before he could hear the report, and he quickly loosened up on the reins to give Ole Sam his head, and with a hard heel kick in the sides, Ole Sam bolted forward. Within a few minutes, Howard knew everyone was behind him, eating his dust as he set his predetermined course west and a little north. In about ten minutes, Howard had pulled away from the frenzy of the crowd, and he backed off Ole Sam considerably to a cooldown trot, keeping a watchful eye on the nearest riders and found himself on a tack that only a few took. Most of the folks stayed due west, and the longer Howard traveled, the number behind him dwindled as they turned to the north or south to set their flags, letting everyone else know that their claim was struck. Howard let Ole Sam blow about every forty-five minutes or so and shared his water, if no creeks were available, to keep him as fresh as possible just in case a rider approached in the distance, so he could be pushed to increase the separation. When Howard and Mary made their plans, they made a map including all the landmarks they could identify, as few as there were, including keeping the sun just over their shoulder and keeping it in the general opposite side of when they laid their course back to Guthrie two days earlier.

The two landmarks that established their whereabouts were very distinctive when sighted. The first, known to all travelers passing through the territories, was maintained for assorted reasons only known in the hearts of the individual. The grave of Gid Graham. Established as a landmark in the middle of nowhere, well-known to all that traveled in those parts. The grave site was a place where sojourners would stop to rest, pay tribute to Gid Graham, add a rock on his grave, or take solace that their journey had left them unharmed so far, and that their good fortune would continue throughout the rest of their travels. The grave site carried with it a story that could become reality to any and all that passed. Gid Graham was a government freighter, which carried supplies through the territories for many years. On July 28, 1867, when he was overtaken by white outlaws, masquerading as Cheyenne or Arapaho Indians, who brutally murdered him by burning him alive while tied to a wagon wheel. This style of death would place blame on local Indians and divert attention away from them. When others found his body, they dug a shallow grave and piled rocks on top, so it would not disappear over time. His grave, twenty-two years later, still proved a direction beacon for travelers, including US marshals. Gid Graham trail was the second landmark. A northwest connecting trail that led to the Chisholm Trail. The Gid Graham trail well, used in time past, still deep cut and easy to follow, led to one of the best-known trails in the territories. Not as famous as the Chisholm Trail, nor used as much, because it did not accumulate as much land or cattle, but nonetheless, a landmark giving Howard the direction he needed.

When a traveler came upon the Chisholm Trail, it was readily identifiable. From 1867 to 1871, it was carved out by the passage of an estimated five million head of cattle crossing Indian Territory on the north route starting at the Red River Station, in present-day Montague County, Texas, and entering Kansas near Caldwell finally ending in Abilene, Kansas. In other time periods, the trail would take a different route depending on the location of the recently developed railheads. The southern end of the Chisholm Trail spanned from as far south as San Antonio, Texas, or even Donna, Texas. Small arteries of trails, like the Graham Trail, would converge from the east and west of a line from San Antonio to Red River Station at the southern edge of the Indian Territories before developing a single trail going north to the Kansas border and eventually to the railhead in Abilene, Kansas. Jesse Chisholm first blazed the path in 1864 for his wagons, hauling supplies to his two trading posts, one in the center of the territories and the other in Wichita, Kansas. The well-marked trail gave other travelers a manageable route and known hazards that could be anticipated. Although Chisholm marked and founded the trail in 1864, he never drove cattle on the famous trail that was named after him. Three years later, O. W. Wheeler and his partners were the first to drive a herd of 2,400 steers from San Antonio, Texas, to Abilene, Kansas. When Wheeler was pushing the herd north, they came to the North Canadian River in Indian Territory and found wagon tracks and just simply followed them to the end of the trail in Abilene. From first being used in 1864 and ending use in 1884, millions of cattle, thousands of wagons and travelers passed over the land, leaving a scar from south to north, of wagon-wheel ruts and tracks in the landscape that would take years for the land to heal and grow over and for the Chisholm Trail to disappear. Five years after the last cattle herd was driven on the old Chisholm Trail, through rain, hail, ice, sleet, and snow, the trail was still clearly visible with its deep wagon-wheel ruts cutting across the land going north and south so that when riders came upon it, the onlooker saw what appeared to be a nonending line of ill-kempt road of sorts that lost itself in both direction as far as one could see. Twelve miles east of the Chisholm lay Gid's grave alongside the trail that bore his name.

These were the landmarks that Howard and Mary both were looking for as they journeyed west and north from Guthrie. It was at this junction they would be able to get their bearings to alter their course more north or more south. Howard and Mary had reconnoitered the Graham Trail days before the race and had established markers that would allow them a base from which to change direction. They both hoped when they each arrived on the trail, they would have had dead reckoning and little or no adjustments in their course would be needed.

Howard and Mary both had a J. B. Le Roy compass in their possession, which gave them an advantage in staying the course. The small light black wood turned bowl with a pressed-on wood lid had within it a hand-drawn 3 1/2-inch 64-point maritime card with a white painted interior and a black rubber line. These two-small wood round boxes did not possess a look of importance but provided direction on a sea of prairie with little or no fix points or landmarks to gauge direction, where one could go in circles and not know after a day that they are making their own tracks deeper. Howard and Mary both checked their Le Roy compasses often, knowing misdirection and retracing steps would take valuable time they did not have.

The J. B. Le Roy compasses were sort of a family heirloom. Howard's great-grandfather, Charlie Marshall, was the first in his family to immigrate to America. He was reared on a farm near St. Helier, Jersey, one of the Channel Islands in the English Channel where his family farmed until being evicted by the British government. After leaving the farm as a young lad, he sought employment in the nearest city of St. Helier. He found an apprenticeship at the J. B. Le Roy Company that made nautical equipment and included compasses of all sizes and shapes. Mr. John Bosdet Le Roy was an elderly man and befriended Charlie. Charlie and Mr. Le Roy would visit while working in the shop late into the nights. Charlie would tell Mr. Le Roy that someday he would go to the American frontier and find land, which would belong to him and would provide him what was needed to exist and have a family. Mr. Le Roy gave

Charlie permission to build two compasses of his own so that when he entered the American West, he would know the direction to take. Charlie finally immigrated to America, but rarely, if ever, needed his compasses, because he settled in Stroudsburg, Pennsylvania, in the foothills of the Poconos where he owned his farm and made watches in his later years.

Howard and Mary were now using the compasses Charlie made and brought with him across the Atlantic. For Howard Marshall and his wife Mary, the first and early years of life in the territories, just outside the Nations, survival was first and foremost. Bushwhackers, squatters, cattle thieves, polecats, and downright bad evil people coming through just to kill and steal was not an everyday occurrence but happened often enough to make life more difficult. Building shelter, stocking supplies, and creating something to barter or sell for cash to get by on left enough work for every day of the year, let alone time to defend your life and property from those living life outside of the law in a time and place where lawmen did not or hardly existed to afford adequate enforcement to the settlers.

For more than a year, Guthrie was the closest place that could be called a town. Days prior to April 22, 1889, and days after, Guthrie was no more than a railroad station stop on the Southern Kansas Railway (years later, the AT&SF railway; Atchison, Topeka, and Santa Fe Railway) that ran on a north–south line, from the Kansas state line south, to Purcell, Indian Territory. Work on the Southern Kansas Railway line started in 1886 and finished in 1887. At this stop, a tent city grew that would house 50,000 souls, who would rush to claim and own, after homesteading a year later, land that belonged to them and nobody else. Deer Creek was the original name given to the railroad stop where the tent city emerged out the plains just days before the run. From 1889 to 1890, US Army troops were stationed at Camp Guthrie to keep law and order in the territories by resolving land claim disputes and bringing thieves and murderers to justice, but being some forty miles to the southeast of the Marshall claim, the Army was of little help on an immediate need or emergency. The Marshalls were on their own, not unlike everyone else in the territories.

In the later years of their lives, Howard and Mary would recount the times they would see law enforcement officers, US marshals, stopping when passing through the territories, hot on the trail of individuals wanted by the government. Usually, the desperados the US marshals were following left a trail of victims that had been robbed, murdered, or both. As the population grew and local towns developed, law enforcement improved, and crime became a lesser known evil of the prairie. US marshals would seek out information from the homesteaders to give them leads on what direction to follow or track the outlaws. The settlers of the territories kept track of everything they saw go by that was not part of their farm or their distant neighbors. When neighbors were victimized, vigilante groups would form to track down and seek out the criminal element that was taking advantage of individual farmers and take matters into their own hands if there was resistance. Most times, the vigilante farmers would find and capture and hold the perpetrators until a US marshal could be dispatched and arrive to take the prisoner into custody and back to the territorial courts for trial.

Two of the deputy US marshals that would frequent Howard and Mary's farm before statehood were Frank "Pistol Pete" Eaton from Fort Smith and John Hollinger Lowe from Paris, Texas. On many occasions, these two lawmen would stay the night at Howard and Mary's to rest their horses and themselves, have a good meal, and sleep under a roof. Because of the frequent visits, there was a misunderstanding from distant folks as to the name of the farm, thinking and not knowing, the reference to the Marshalls became the marshals. This was all well and good for Howard and Mary, for if the word in the countryside was their farm was mistaken for a weigh station for federal marshals, the more likely fleeing desperados and bands of criminals and the like would hear on the down low, that their area would be one to avoid for fear of bumping into the law.

People stayed at Guthrie after the land rush, and within a year, five thousand citizens called it home. From tents to real buildings and streets, they established a city and a trade center that was crucial to the survival of the people that settled the land after the land rush. The critical establishment of a land office on April 22, 1889, allowed legal registration of claims within a reasonable travel time for all fifty thousand legal eighty-niners as well as the illegal sooners.

As Howard came upon the old Graham Trail, he reconnoitered his position quickly and figured he had drifted about a mile south of his anticipated intersection of the trail. This was good news to not be any farther off course than he was. He knew that no one crossed his path from the south on his left, and with the fast pace he had maintained, no rider could have overtaken him from the north or his right. Being as close to the course as he was with less than a mile off, he knew that very little time had been lost, and no one could beat him to the claim he wanted. He adjusted his course a little north, staying on trail for about a half mile and hoped he would come on to the grave site of Gid Graham in a very short ride. If so, he would be claiming his land very soon. As he rode, his thoughts drifted to Mary, and he wondered how much distance she had made, hoping and praying that there were no breakdowns and the horses were healthy and pulling strong.

Just over the next rise, Howard should see the grave site of Gid Graham, and there it was, a pile of rocks with a two-foot-by-two-foot flat sandstone rock half buried in the dirt at the west end of the rectangular pile of rocks lying due east and west. The sandstone rock was probably native to the area, and someone brought it there to be a makeshift headstone for Gid's grave. The soft stone had etched in it, "Here lies Gid Graham, KILT BY MAN BURNERS, JULY 28 1874." When Howard saw the grave, he immediately started Ole Sam on a due northwest course and pushed him as hard as he could. He knew that there was only three to four miles of fairly smooth ride left with the sun starting its descent, leaving approximately four hours of sunlight left. There would be plenty for him to stake his flag and make camp for the night. Howard's excitement grew as he could see the trees that lined Turkey Creek to the west, and he would have completed his ride successfully and got his first choice of land. The closer he rode to the pin marking the 160 acres he wanted, he could hardly contain himself, until he saw the surveyor's pin had been pulled and replaced with a homesteader's insignia flag, claiming that parcel for somebody else. The stake would be next to the survey's cornerstone or a pile of rocks piled up by the surveyors on the northeast corner of each quarter section. As he approached the corner marker, Howard could not believe his eyes, no one had staked out the land he wanted. His excitement grew until he could barely breathe. Howard pushed Ole Sam as fast as he could without a soul in sight for more than a mile in any direction. Howard dismounted so fast he fell to the ground and rolled ten feet before he came to a stop. He jumped to his feet, unpacked a hammer, stake, and a cardboard with his name written on it. He added the range and township and section of the land he was claiming, a brief description of the land being claimed. He tacked the cardboard to the stake that he drove in the ground and immediately sat on the ground in amazement that it was done. This was done for a public posting and record until the land was officially recorded in Guthrie. Howard gave thought to why a Sooner had not made claim for this choice of land and then realized that as close as this was to the northern edge of the Undivided Lands, the patrols of the US Army stationed in Fort Reno would have kept any Sooner clear and unable to stake a claim, while the lands farther in from the perimeters would be less patrolled and more difficult to constantly search for squatters or sooners. Howard knew that he had claimed this land and posted it legally according to the rules, and it would be his and Mary's to defend and protect from any and all that would try to jump their claim and take away what now was rightfully theirs. As the sun was touching the horizon, Howard stopped and watched it sink into the land, and his eye caught the shadows of the trees around the Cimarron River that seemed to be pointing to him, and it gave him great relief and pride to have such a beautiful piece of God's creation to earn a living for his family and live on for the rest of his life.

This particular quarter section had a gentle slope down to the Cimarron River. The river had an eighty-foot-wide spot that ran three hundred and fifty feet long and was washed out to about four feet deep. It set on the southwest back corner of the property. When the rain stopped and the river stopped flowing, this large amount of water stayed and would serve as a pond for the livestock and a source of water, until Howard was able to dig a well that he planned to have.

Howard found a place, fifty feet inside his claim, with the pile of stones (cornerstone) and his stake clearly visible at all times to set his camp for the night. For firewood and property stakes, he found a large fallen tree limb on the riverbank, tied a rope on it, and had Ole Sam drag it to the campsite. With a hatchet he packed, he chopped firewood and started a good fire for heat and light for the night ahead. As night fell, from the high spot where he camped, he could see fires in the far distance. He knew he would have company in the morning, and he better be prepared for anything. His thoughts immediately went to Mary, and he wondered about her safety and how, hopefully, she had made good time on the first day.

Mary let the horses have a soft lead and set a deliberate pace, not too slow but fast enough. Mary did not want to push the team, but her anticipation sometimes overwhelmed her to the point to pick up the pace and hurry along and make the trip as short a time as possible. When these thoughts came upon her, she dispelled them by telling herself that placing a strain on the horses and wagon could lead to a breakdown, and that would put everything in jeopardy, and a total loss could occur. It would be better to take a day longer and arrive a day later than not at all. When Mary saw the sun start to lay low in the sky, she figured that there was about an hour of daylight left and decided this was as good a place as any to stop for the night. She watered, fed, and staked out the horses and cattle, then made camp for the night. With firewood she carried on the wagon, she made a fire, sat back, looked up at the sky, and felt a sense of loneliness that she had never felt before. At a point, Mary scanned the darkness and saw the little glimmers of light from campfires all around her. People just like her were afloat in the prairie ocean as was she. The sight of other fires led her thoughts to Howard, and her prayers and hope that he arrived safely were on her mind as she fell asleep under the stars.

As Howard waited on Mary to arrive, the anticipation was nearly unbearable. Most on his mind was filing his claim back in Guthrie. Once it was filed, it became the security everyone, who made the run desired, to finalize their ownership. To jump a claim after it was filed at the land office was nearly a wasted effort because it took the signature of the original claimant to transfer ownership, and that would take falsifying signatures on legal instruments, which was a risky business, and that practice was avoided by most of the claim jumpers.

Howard passed his time driving stakes that he fabricated with his hatchet into the ground at intervals from the cornerstones in a straight as line as possible to outline the boundaries of their quarter section. He wanted to make known to the contiguous quarter-section property owners where he thought the boundaries should be, so there would be no encroachment while his neighbors established their boundaries and/or fence lines. At the end of the second day, he saw the Eighty-niners claim the quarter sections to the north and south of his claim. Howard hoped for good neighbors and in good time would go and meet them if they didn't do the honors first. The next two days were spent continuing to mark boundaries.

Mary continued her journey at a steady pace, making a little over ten miles a day, and she, too, was full of anticipation, wondering how things went with Howard and making the claim they planned. Her thoughts were about Howard's well-being and whether she would even see him at their original planned rendezvous, or if not there, if he would be at the next place they had preplanned. At this point, Mary rationalized that she was not going to worry about what to do next if Howard was not where they intended to meet until she showed up, and he wasn't there. No more thoughts about the ifs, only the thoughts that he would be where they planned first. Thinking of what could happen made the trip longer and tiring for Mary, and it was long enough as it was. Mary tried keeping her thoughts positive, and this made the trip more bearable, which helped make the long days pass quicker, and that was fine with her. Mary checked her bearing with her compass often because she had more time than Howard did as he raced across the landscape. Mary made many small course corrections, keeping a more direct path to Howard and their reunion. Her navigation proved correct for she came upon the Graham Trail, and after joining it for a brief northwest direction on the trail, she came to Gid Graham's grave. At the grave site, Mary took a break to rest the horses and pulled out a rock that she had brought from

Big Springs, Missouri. She laid it on the grave, then gave thanks to God for her safe and accurate journey. Mary removed the chocks, climbing back into the wagon, releasing the hand brake, pushing the team forward, Mary was thrilled that she had not spent any time at all traveling in the wrong direction, and at this point, she knew as Howard did that in three to four miles, her journey would be at end.

As the sun was setting all across the horizon from as far as one could see to the north and south, a blaze of orange, red, and yellow looked as if the sky was on fire with the colors separated by strands and ribbons of clouds. With enough light left in the day, Mary could make out the figure of a horse, man, and a campsite with a fire as a beacon lighting her way on the final yards of her task that would reunite her with Howard. As the team pulled her closer, she could hear her name being yelled by Howard as he walked to her and closed the gap between them at a faster rate. Their plan to this point had worked out perfectly without misstep or flaws. As the daylight dwindled, Mary and Howard quickly staked out the cattle and placed the team horses where Ole Sam was staked. Now in the darkness of the prairie and very little light from a sliver of a waning moon, they used the campfire and a single coal oil lantern to give enough light for them to prepare their first meal of many on land that they now owned and would more than likely spend the rest of their lives on.

The morning came quickly, and the time spent with Mary seemed to be only a moment, but they both knew Howard had to ride as hard as he could back to Guthrie to record their claim. They figured he would be gone for three days. One day to get there, one day to register their claim and buy any supplies that were available, and one day's travel to get back. They discussed how many settlers would be there to register claims and knew it might take longer and that Howard would not push Ole Sam too hard on the return trip. If Howard did not show up on the third day, Mary knew not to worry because it might not go as well as they planned. In the back of Mary's mind was always the thought that led to worry, how many days out she should wait until she would break camp to look for Howard.

As Howard rode away, it was now Mary's first time to guard the claim, camp, and their possessions. Hopefully, her guard duty would only last for three, maybe four nights, alone, surviving on her wits and experience, as she was now a real pioneer woman.

The first thought that Howard had on his approach to Guthrie was that he had miscalculated and was lost. Six days had passed since Howard left on the race of his life, leaving behind him hundreds of makeshift shacks and thousands of tents. Where now stood, a virtual city of buildings with a main street full of people moving about carrying on like this town had been in existence for years. There were all sorts of supplies for sale or trade, from dry goods to building lumber piled up or in the stores ready to be packed up and taken for the right price with lines of people at every door or yard eager to make a purchase. Howard's first order of business was to record his claim at the land office. He was surprised that it was an actual building with four clerks to help with the recording, and a fifty-person line queued up to record their claim as well. Being as it was late in the day, Howard pitched camp as close as possible to the land agents' office, staked out Ole Sam, and bedded down for the night, thinking he would be the first in line in the morning. Before daybreak, Howard found a place to get a bucket of water and buy some feed for Ole Sam, then went to the land office to find a line of ten people there waiting for the doors to open a little more than an hour away. About midmorning, Howard had the land recorded, and a huge weight left his shoulders, and the relief was welcomed. Mary and Howard had discussed some food supplies, if available, that could be brought back that might later save them an additional trip to town if they ran short. Everything on the list that Howard could carry on horseback was available, and Howard left Guthrie at high noon, and he would be back with Mary before nightfall. Howard had passed several homesteaders on his trip out and back and could see the countryside changing before his eyes. As he approached his claim, he could distinguish Mary at a distance and could also see to the north of his claim another settler that hopefully would become a good neighbor, but it would be a while before they would tarry off their claim to introduce themselves.

CHAPTER 2

The Start of Life on the Marshall Farm

First order of business for Howard and Mary would be to get a garden started, for planting time was at hand. After the garden was in the ground, shelter other than the wagon had to be established for them and the livestock. As time passed, everything came together without a hitch. Howard had brought sod shears with him to build sod structures for the first year or two and hopefully not longer, until they could obtain building materials for a two-room house that had windows, roof, floor, and a door, a real house to keep them separated from the harsh weather conditions and a place to start their family. Six years passed, and Mary and Howard started to see their dreams being fulfilled. They had row crops and a large garden established; twenty heads of cattle roamed; pigs and chickens; lean-to barn; fencing; well; house; and a newborn boy, Leo, to be followed in two years by Willis. The Marshall farm was now well established, and the second generation was growing fast as well as the second generation for all the rest of the eighty-niners.

Howard saw little change from the way things were always done throughout his lifetime on the Marshall farm. Things were done the same fashion as they had been done in the beginning—hard work and long hours when needed, and rest and reflection after season work was completed. The major happening for Mary and Howard was that Leo and Willis were drafted into the Great War. They both left for about two years, and help was scarce for Howard, but things managed to get done. During the time Leo and Willis were gone, Howard and Mary reflected about their existence and ability to maintain the farm without the boys and if they would want to come back to farm life if they made it through the war. When the war was over, both boys returned, and life reestablished itself on the Marshall farm, and a legacy was started that would last at least another generation.

Howard, Mary, their sons Leo and Willis, grandsons, and their families all worked the farm. They all added contiguous land over the last half century to grow the original 160 acres to 2,560 acres before Walter was born to Willis, and before Joe, Howard's great-grandson, was added to the family.

Howard would always be proud of his participation in the run and his claim of the property where he wanted to live out his days and be buried, and that he did. In later years, when people would talk about Oklahoma being the sooner state, and that he was one of the first to settle from the land run, only a moment would pass before he corrected the conversation saying, "I'm no damned Sooner. I'm an Eighty-niner." The vehement response was followed by his explanation that he was at the starting line at high noon and claimed his stake to the letter of the law and was not part of the group that hid out and made their claim sooner than was legal, and that he was not a boomer either. They were no-good land-grabbing politicians, led by David L. Payne, who campaigned for the opening of the lands.

The only time the Marshalls left the farm was to go to war. In the Great War, Leo and Willis were drafted into the United States Army in June of 1917, fought in France, and returned to the farm January of 1919, shortly after the war ended in November of 1918. Walter, Joe's father, joined the United States Army and left the farm in August of 1942 to also fight the war in France, from Normandy Beach on D-Day to Belgium where the war ended for him. He returned to Oklahoma and the farm in April of 1945. When Joe's grandfather, great-uncle, and father returned safely, they started their families and settled in to earn a living. It was Willis's and Leo's choice and Walters's circumstance that directed them back home to the farm.

The Marshall farm was typical farm life in central Oklahoma. There were cattle, wheat crops, at times a little cotton, a few pigs, chickens, large garden, and a number of pump jacks on the southern sections. Hard work was continuous on the farm, ending one task per season starting the next. When seasonal work let up, there were lulls when feasting, relaxing, and creating memories that made life more palatable and something to look forward to. Then it was quickly back to overhauling equipment and making permanent repairs, where temporary fixes had been done because of time. Houses, outbuildings, and fences were always on the work list and usually needed immediate attention while doing other farm tasks. With the passing of years and decades, the farm grew, and more help was needed. Hired hands were commonplace as well as their families living on the Marshall farm.

As time passed, machinery took the place of workers. The population of the farm in the early years grew as acreage was added along with working livestock. Workhorses and riding horses were required to maintain the farm, and added help was needed to maintain the working herd. Horses worked to produce crops, give transportation, and were the tools used to grow the cattle herd. For Howard and his sons Willis and Leo Marshall, horses meant survival and production, food and money, for without them, life on the farm would not exist. With the end of the Great Depression, life on the farm took on the greatest change from the early beginning for the Marshalls, with the advent of horsepower in the form of a machine, the tractor. Leo and Willis both established themselves on the farm. Both married and started their families in much the same tradition as Howard and Mary. Willis met a girl from Guthrie named Juanetta, and they were married a short time later and settled in a small house on the adjoining quarter section to the north. A couple of years later, Leo met a girl named Alice from Crescent City, a town ten miles to the north and east that was started the year after Howard made his claim in 1889. Leo and Alice were married and purchased a half section a half mile east and a half mile north of Howard and Mary, where they moved into a small farmhouse on that property. Leo and Alice's property was contiguous to Willis and Juanetta's property.

Willis and Juanetta had two children, LaTrenda, born on April 15, 1922, and Walter was born on October 5, 1924. Leo and Alice did not have any children but thought of LaTrenda and Walter as their very own. Walter represented the third generation of Marshalls to farm the land and take pride in their Oklahoma heritage. Walter and LaTrenda attended grade school at the nearest rural two-room schoolhouse called Blue Creek. Walter was a fast reader and developed his reading, writing, and arithmetic to a high degree and had all the attributes of being a good athlete. At Blue Creek School, they had a basketball goal on a dirt court with a wallowed-out mudhole after a rain, which existed directly under the goal and a simple baseball diamond in a grass bare field next to the school. The establishment of rural schools soon after the territory was populated established a school district on the system of a three-mile square district. This system was designed to create four rural schools to every six-mile townships. If the schools were placed correctly, with the sparse populations, this allowed an eighth-grade education for a student within an approximate one-and-a-half-mile trip from their home to the schoolhouse. When the eighth grade was complete, there was a designated high school district that encompassed the rural schools and afforded the students the closest high school to their homes. For the Marshalls, this was Crescent High School about ten miles away.

Walter and all the country kids his age showed up at Crescent High School to start their ninth-grade year. It didn't seem as much a transition from the ultrasmall country school to the city school as one would expect because of the number of kids that lived on the farms nearly equaled the number of students that had gone to Crescent schools from the first grade. The farm kids nearly all had the same background, values, and lifestyles and understood each other without a doubt. Plus, there were more strangers in a new class than local city students.

While attending school and playing sports, Walter did well with academics but excelled in sports, and his best sport was baseball. In the spring of his junior year of high school, during baseball season in a home game, the St. Louis Pilots' scout showed up to see Walter play. Walter played shortstop and was lighting fast and seldom had an error. While at bat, to see the ball go out of the Crescent High School Park was nearly commonplace while maintaining a batting average of slightly over .400. The scout wanted to recruit Walter right then before he finished school. Walter talked to Willis and Juanetta on the phone at the school, and they told Walter to have the scout come to the house for supper, and they would discuss it over a meal. The scout accepted the offer and showed up on the porch, introduced himself as Peter Whyte, a professional baseball scout for the St. Louis Pilots Association, and that he had been a scout for St. Louis for the last two years since his retirement. Before that, he had played for the Pilots for six years. As Juanetta showed Peter his place at the table, Willis walked in from the field and introduced himself to Peter. Walter's sister graduated from Crescent High School the year before and was studying at Oklahoma Agricultural and Mechanical College (Oklahoma A&M) in Stillwater, Oklahoma. Howard and Mary now lived in a small house on the same farm within a hundred feet from Willis and Juanetta and would eat important meals with the kids and grandkids; this was deemed by the Marshalls as one of those occasions. As Howard and Mary walked through, Willis stood and introduced their guest Peter Whyte, the Pilots' baseball scout who was taking a look at their grandson Walter. Peter stood, greeted Mrs. Marshall, and shook hands with Howard. Peter thought to himself that Howard in his advanced years had an equally strong, hard-as-a-rock handshake like his son Willis. There they all sat at the long table in the Marshalls' dining room. At one end of the table sat Howard, and the other end was Willis, and on his right sat Peter with Juanetta next to him. Across the table were Walter and to his right Mary. There was no discussion about baseball while they ate the main course, but after that, Juanetta started talking to Peter about her son, the scouting prospect, as she was serving "put-up" peach cobbler with copious amounts of cold crème ladled over it. Peter started out that Walter was one of the best prospects for playing pro major league baseball that he had ever seen. Peter thought that Walter could show up in spring camp and might have the ability to play in his first year in the pros. Upon saying that, there was silence at the table. Willis let Juanetta do all the talking because he figured that Walter was still her boy, and he would not override her decision on this subject, so let her say her piece, which was, he would finish high school, and after that, it would be Walter's decision. The thought of leaving the farm and starting a new life in a big city really intrigued Walter, and it seemed to him he would really rather do that than stick around for another year. Walter's relationship with his parents was strong, good, and fulfilled, and he knew that if he chose to leave, Juanetta would agree with his decision, just not give her total approval. Walter in his heart would not knowingly do anything he could think of to disappoint his dad or mom. With but a moment of thought, Walter spoke up and told Mr. Whyte that he would honor his mother's thoughts on the matter, and if the offer was still available after he graduated from high school, he would like to try out for the St. Louis Pilots. Peter agreed with the wisdom of finishing high school and told the family that he would stop by the farm every month or so over the next year, if it was all right with the Marshalls to check in on Walter's training and coach him on some technique to help him improve his game to make him more competitive when he tried out for the team. Walter, Willis, and Juanetta all thought that would be a great idea and offered room and meals for days and nights when Peter showed up to work with Walter. Peter liked that plan and offered to pay for the lodging and meals when he showed up, but Juanetta would not have him pay for anything, so it was agreed on by all parties.

Peter Whyte stayed that night with the Marshalls and left at sunup the next morning. While he was driving away from the farm looking at a heavy haze across the blazing orange-red horizon from the rising sun, he felt good about the talk he had with the Marshalls the night before and was already looking forward to coming back and eating Juanetta's cooking and spending a couple of days and nights on the farm because it reminded him of his early life on his family farm. As Peter left the dirt road that ran to the blacktop highway, he turned his blue Ford 1940 Deluxe Coupe with a white convertible top south and pressed the accelerator to the floor as he pushed the 95-horse Flathead V-8 through the three gears to reach Highway 66, which would take him on the road, making stops along the way until he reached the Pacific Ocean in Santa Monica, California, and up the coast all the time looking for new prospects.

Walter felt good about the prospect of finishing the summer work on the farm with his dad and granddad and entering the last year of high school at Crescent with the friends he had made from Lone Elm and the last three years at CHS. Word soon got out about Walter's shot to play for the St. Louis Pilots, and the excitement for the community grew with each passing day of the summer and the fall with the anticipation that a local boy would have a chance to play big-time professional baseball. Nobody from Crescent, Oklahoma, at that time had ever had the chance to reach such a national status as this.

As late fall approached, things on the Marshall farm were working toward the slow downtime, where repairs that had piled up because time did not permit to start a project that could be put off were done as weather allowed. When the weather was bad, equipment got their due inside the barn, and work continued as always. Early December 1941 was as usual on the Marshall farm, when on Sunday morning on the seventh, when everyone was getting ready for church, it was announced the Japanese had bombed Pearl Harbor, Hawaii. As the front door opened and Mary and Howard walked in, all the Marshalls stood together, held hands, and prayed to God as to what the outcome might be for their nation and what the future would hold for the young men. The five members of the Marshall family drove to church in Crescent that day, where the only sound in the car was the soft purr of their Flathead V-8 that powered their 1936 light-gray four-door Ford sedan traveling at thirty-five miles per hour, leaving a trail of dust that could be seen for miles down a lonely dirt section line Oklahoma road. Willis could not help but think of the involvement that the United States would have and how many young American boys would give the ultimate price to preserve the freedom of the nation. On the twenty-minute trip to their church in Crescent, Willis also started reliving his experiences from combat in the Great War that he had pushed out of his mind and had not allowed in since his return from France. For Willis, it was an everyday effort to stop a memory of those days from coming to his mind, and now they were flowing in as a raging river would flood the plains and fields after days of hard rains with no constraint and a relentless surge of force that spared no boundaries. For over two decades, Willis did not entertain the thoughts of battle, and now in a brief drive, it was as though his experiences were flowing at a rate of a day in a second, a month in a minute, and a year within half the time it would take to get to church, until he pulled over and asked Juanetta to drive. As Willis opened the door and walked around to the opposite side of the car, Juanetta scooted across the seat, without uttering a word, to the driver's side to continue the drive into town. Howard, Mary, Juanetta, and Walter didn't ask what was wrong or even wanted to take notice of the change of drivers, for they knew the troubling effect the Great War had on Willis from the simple fact that he never spoke of it, and when questioned, he would always, very politely, change the subject. If someone persisted in the questioning, he would, again very politely, excuse himself and leave the room usually to stand outside by himself, notwithstanding the current weather conditions, even a snowstorm. When Willis took the front passenger seat for the drive on to church, it impossibly got even quieter than before as they all submerged themselves in thought about the immediate future. They pulled up to the First United Methodist Church of Crescent, Oklahoma, a church at that time that had a maximum seating of fifty. On a typical Sunday, the congregation would normally fill about twenty-five. Today it was full past capacity, with chairs from the fellowship hall and the Sunday school placed in the aisles and around the pulpit and choir to accommodate the burgeoning crowd a place to sit. This Sunday, there were members that had not cast a shadow on the doorsteps of the church for years and nonmembers of the community that sought out a place of worship to spend an hour this day to pray for their nation.

The return trip to the farm was as quiet as the trip into town. Willis had replaced his thoughts in the dark, quiet recess of his consciousness and was able to maintain control of them so that he resumed the driving on the trip back. Juanetta let her thoughts go back to Sunday dinner and hoped everyone would discuss their thoughts as they ate in an attempt to make sense of it all or at least make sense of the upcoming days and months of what their involvement would be, mainly concerning Walter. On this particular day, Walter was more involved in numbness, not being able to conjure even a single thought about his future, let alone have any understanding about what a world war meant to him or anyone else. As they all took their places at the table, Howard asked God to bless the meal and prayed for insight for their country's leaders, especially President Roosevelt, and all the survivors at Pearl Harbor, a place he was totally unaware of five hours ago, and the servicemen that had lost their lives in the dastardly surprise attack by the Japanese.

War was declared against the Axis powers the next day, and the entire country changed overnight. Young men from the farms and small towns all around were signing up for military service in all branches—Navy, Marines, Army, and the Army Air Corps. Classmates of Walter's chose not to finish high school and enlisted or volunteered for the draft. The numbers of farmhands all around were leaving the area to enlist, and help became as scarce as hen's teeth. Patriotism was at an all-time high, and the workforce on the small farms would be reduced by 50 percent in just a few months. Willis made no attempt to sway Walter's decision but decided to talk with him about what his options might be. When Willis approached Walt, he was surprised to hear that Walt had already made up his mind and proceeded to tell his dad that his plan was to finish high school and after graduation join the Army Air Corps. Walt explained that the way he thought another five months without him in the service should not make that much difference in winning or losing the war, and if it did, it was much to do about nothing, or the United Sates was really in trouble, and they didn't know it. After listening to Walt, Willis just nodded his head in agreement and asked if that was it and if his mind was made up, and Walt indicated it was. Willis did ask Walt why the Army Air Corps, and Walt told his dad that in his mind, if given the opportunity to fly rather than walk, flying sounded like a better way to go, and that he really couldn't come up with any other reason that sounded as good to join a different branch of service. At that point, Willis agreed and would tell Juanetta his plans, and they would leave it at that. Juanetta was glad that Walt wanted to finish high school and that enlistment would be put off until after graduation. Juanetta also thought that that would give the military a chance to catch up with the rest of the world in military strength and planning before Walt would see action. She was happy that they would all have another five of six months together before the war beckoned her boy into harm's way. For the next few weeks, all that was talked about was the war and the mention of deaths and wounded. The little community of Crescent and the surrounding farm areas already had reports of missing in action and killed in action of two local boys, one from a farm family three miles to the north of the Marshall farm and one boy from Crescent. Before Walt left to report for boot camp, those numbers quadrupled, which added much to the fears of the Marshall family and all the families of this central Oklahoma area.

About the middle of March, early on a pleasant mid-fifty-degree Saturday morning, sitting on the front porch, sipping a fresh brewed cup of hot coffee, watching the sunrise to near completion, Howard saw in the distance a plume of dust rising high into the bright-red sunlight and could barely make out a speeding blue car with a white top, adding the dust to what would otherwise be a gorgeous clear panoramic sunrise. Howard stepped off the porch to go inside the house just far enough to tell Mary and Juanetta they better make enough breakfast for one more. At that point, it aroused the curiosity of Willis, Walt, Mary, and Juanetta as they all stepped out on the porch to see who in the world would be showing up at this time in the day to visit. As the car creating the trail of dust got within a half mile, everyone was sure they recognized it as being Peter Whyte, and sure enough it was.

Peter pulled up to the front gate of the fence that surrounded the house, got out of his car to look up on the porch to see the Marshall welcoming committee, every one of them excited to see him as well as he was to see them. As Peter took the three steps up onto the porch, with huge smiles on all the awaiting faces, he was warmly greeted with hugs from the ladies and extrafirm handshakes from the men. It was as if he was a kid or grandchild returning home from an extended absence from home. Peter shared the same feeling, for it was so reminiscent of his own family and the farm he was reared on and lived for the first eighteen years of his life. After the greetings, he was ushered into the house, sat down at the table, and the questions abounded about the last eleven months of Peter's travels. Everyone wanted to know about what was really going on in the rest of the country from the West to East Coast since the war started and what his thoughts were from his observations about how things were going in Europe and in the Pacific.

The aroma of breakfast smells filled the room, and Peter could hardly wait to start eating because he had already been on the road since 4:00 AM where he had just pulled over to spend the night before sleeping in his car, next to a city park in Clinton, Oklahoma. Starting out two days before, he had just finished driving for twenty-two hours straight, after ending a monthlong scouting tour on the West Coast. With the scouting trip ending, he decided it was time to make his way back home from Los Angeles, traveling Route 66 all the way back home to St. Louis. On his trip home, there was one stop he was going to make for sure, and that was the Marshall farm, so he could talk to one of the greatest prospects he had ever tried to recruit, Walter Marshall. Before, during, and after breakfast, the questions abounded about what Peter had seen and the changes he saw throughout his travels since the war had started. His answers went from the huge number of men he saw in uniform from all branches of the service, to the restrictions on goods that could be purchased, the trains being overbooked with workers going to factories that were now part of the war-machine production, and the lines of men of all ages at the recruiting offices in every town he passed through. At that point, Peter asked about the changes in the Marshalls' rural community. The reply was that rationing had started on almost everything and that the Department of Defense had contacted all the farms in the area, wanting to know everything about their farm and what was produced from their crops, cattle, pigs, chickens, gardens, and horses. The end result, everything had to be accounted for, from the standpoint of the war effort, but the system, as far as they could understand it, would have little effect on their lifestyle, except that sale of everything produced was restricted to supplying the military first. There was little or no rationing of farm supplies or needs to continue the present or increase production levels, although there was scrutiny by the government on all purchases and the use of all supplies. Other than the checks and balances maintained by the Department of Defense and the lack of workers, they hardly knew the war was going on. Peter agreed that in all the rural interior communities, other than the rationing and less young men about, it was essentially the same. Peter made a point that life on the coastal towns he had visited on both coasts had a striking difference in that the mass number of people had increased ten times and the shipment of men, material, and equipment had all the roads and trains congested to capacity.

During the breakfast conversation, Peter mentioned that he wanted to make St. Louis by the end of the day, and he needed to be leaving within the next hour or so because he did not want to drive all night again, and everyone understood. Peter wanted to explain face-to-face that the plans and promises he had made with Walt last spring, he would not be able to fulfill. Peter had enlisted and taken a commission as an officer in the Marines. He had applied for flight school and was to report for assembly to ship out for boot camp in one week. Walt looked at Peter and explained that plans had changed with him also and laid out the direction he was going to take after high school graduation. Peter thought Walt might have opted for early enrollment at a university because he would not turn eighteen until August but fully understood the feelings and agreed with them completely. Willis and the family let Peter know that it was not necessary for him to explain himself because of the times and the war, but they appreciated his visit and the accountability and sincerity of his actions. Upon finishing a great country breakfast, Peter mentioned to Walt that if there was an opportunity after the war, whenever that might be, and they were both alive and capable, he would be back with hopes that they could start over, and Walt would have his shot at the big league. Peter said his farewells and said that he would drop a line once in a while so they could keep in touch, then took off as the Marshalls watched the dust cloud chase him until both were out of sight.

Graduation for Walt arrived, and enlistment soon followed with basic training at the United States Army Air Corps training center at Sheppard Air Field just a little north of Wichita Falls, Texas. Walt's next stop after finishing basic training was Las Vegas Army Airfield, outside of Las Vegas, Nevada, where he went to participate in radio operator school and aerial gunnery training on the newly arrived B-17s. Six weeks later, Walter was shipping out to a B-17 formation area at Great Falls Army Air Base, Montana, where he would be assigned to his aircraft and meet and train with the crew members of his B-17 as a part of the 390th Bombardment Group (Heavy). The 390th was assigned to the 13th Combat Bombardment Wing, and after formation and training was complete, they would arrive in a final staging area at Dow Army Airfield, Maine, as they prepared to transit over the North Atlantic route to their final desti-nation, a Royal Air Force station, southeast of Framlingham, Suffolk, England. The United States Army Air Force designation was Station 153 (FM). This air station also had the designation of Parham 153, and all stationed there referred to it as such. Most all Royal Air Force stations acquired their name from the closest village or ham-let that had a pub, and for Station 153 (FM), it was Parham. The 390th arrived shortly after the completion of the base, but all ground crews, supplies, and support personnel were still arriving as Walt's plane and others were landing. After arriving on the East Anglican Coast, the crew wanted to name their B-17, and that honor usu-ally went to the pilot of the aircraft. The pilot was Captain John Battle from Nebraska. John Battle was six years older than Walt and had finished his bachelor's degree from the University of Nebraska, and while there, he played baseball for the university, playing in the starting lineup from his freshman throughout his senior year. During the crew's downtimes between training and maintenance, in decent weather, the crew played baseball at any given chance. Captain John Battle did not have an inflated view of himself when it came to base-ball and his abilities. He thought of himself as being a good athlete and a good-enough baseball player to go to the professional level. As John finished his degree work at Nebraska, his next stop was to go to a professional tryout and see if he could make a team at any level. On the very first sandlot game with the flight and maintenance crew of John Battle's B-17 against other plane's crews, John saw immediately the difference in a good collegiate baseball player and a great player was as he watched Walt field, throw, and bat with a level of talent that surpassed any and all, including John, of those they played against. John did not have a lot to discuss with Walt, other than what his responsibilities of a radio operator/gunner and being a crew member that could learn other jobs in case it would be required in a combat situation. After the first intersquadron baseball game and after all training issues were done, all conversations led to baseball and about Walt's and John's life and families. In one of many discussions with Walt, John learned about Walt's grandparents, Howard and Mary, and their race for land in the Oklahoma Territories and the farm and life that they established in the western frontier against all odds. They talked about Walt's grandparents' fight for survival and to keep possession of their land and what it meant to them. The story of Howard's and Mary's determination to survive on their wits, physical and mental toughness to exist in a harsh environment always impressed John.

After they arrived at Parham 153, based on the admiration that he had grown to respect for Howard's and Mary's survival in a harsh land, John announced to his crew the name of their flying fortress, the *Eighty-Niner*. John, Walt, and the rest of the crew made it through their required twenty-five missions without a casualty. The *Eighty-Niner* took heavy damage on eight of the twenty-five missions and light damage on nine of the twenty-five missions. The downtime for repairs extended the time overseas, and it was early 1944 before the *Eighty-Niner* crew returned home for service stateside. John and Walt became the best of friends and never lost contact with each other after the war's end.

Walt and Peter Whyte kept in touch, writing an occasional letter. Peter was stationed in North Africa as a pilot flying B-24s on bombing raids over Italy and Romania. Walt sent and received a letter every two weeks until Peter's usual letter was not received. After a month, Walt went through the normal channels looking for information on Peter's whereabouts until he asked John if he could help him locate Peter. John later found out that Peter had been shot down over Italy, thought to have survived, and was a German prisoner of war. Walt hoped and prayed that someday they could get back together, and Peter would survive the war.

The crew of the *Eighty-Niner*, after a lengthy leave time in England and stateside, were sent to Pratt Army Airfield located in south-central Kansas where the entire crew volunteered for training and learning to fly the B-29 Superfortress for a secret mission that would take them back to England but not in a combat role. The secret mission was to fly the B-29 from airbase to airbase British and American to make a display to the German operatives and spies in the British countryside, who would report back to the German military that a new high-and-low-altitude, fast, heavy bomber would be deployed in the European theater, when in actuality, there were no plans for that to occur. The B-29 was designated for the Pacific theater only.

Pratt Army Airfield was 180 miles north of Crescent, Oklahoma, and that meant that Walt would be able to get home every once in a while. It was a great opportunity for any and all the crew to have a little time to spend in what used to be a normal life. John went with Walt on every trip and could not get enough of Juanetta's cooking. He enjoyed getting to help for a couple of days doing normal farmwork and lending as much of a hand to help out on the needed repairs at the Marshall farm.

The old crew of the *Eighty-Niner* received a single rank promotion across the board when they started training on the B-29. John Battle was now a major, and Walt held the rank of second grade technical sergeant. The training took longer than expected at Pratt Army Airfield because of engine problems that finally led to the Boeing engineers refitting their plane with different engines. The Boeing people wanted John and his crew to try an experimental engine that was not in full production but was considered to cure the short run times before overhauls and in-flight engine fires. The thought was that this particular plane was not considered to be used in combat situations. It was primarily to be used in short hops for show, where German enemy agents embedded all over Great Britain would be able to see and would deceive them into thinking the B-29 was going to be used in the European theater. The transatlantic crossing would be the only long flight it would have to experience, and if John and his crew would agree to the challenge, the refit would start immediately. John and his crew agreed to the plan and recognized that the risk to help the war effort was much less than any bomb run they took flying over German flak and fighter attacks. The Boeing engineers changed out the Wright R-3350 engines with the newly designed Wright R-4360 Wasp engines. At this point, the crew looked to Major Battle for a new name for the aircraft, and John asked the crew if the name *Bugeater* would be okay, and the crew agreed but wanted an explanation on the name. John explained that before the University of Nebraska was represented by the name *Cornhuskers*, they were known as the *Bugeaters*. This went well with the crew because they now associated the enemy with a bug, and they were there to devour them.

As the preparation for the transatlantic flight was complete, Walt's crew with Major John Battle sitting left seat of the plane, *Bugeater* took off from Pratt Army Airfield in April of 1944 to conduct a tour of most of Great Britain's airfields, British and American combined. This flight across the pond included a special cargo of twelve high-ranking officers from all the branches of the service including the United States Coast Guard. This cargo of personnel was picked up at the first staging area of the flight at Presque Isle Army Air Field in Maine. The air crew did not have prior knowledge of this addition to their Atlantic flight until their debriefing was complete after landing. The cargo was considered top secret, and the order was to keep all conversation to a minimum for the entire flight and to push the maximum altitude possible as they stopped at every stepping-stone along the North Atlantic route. Their first stop in Great Britain was RAF St. Mawgan in Cornwall, England. At this juncture of their trip, the special cargo disembarked the aircraft, and the deception tour began. A specially equipped ground crew preceded *Bugeater* on the same route, but in advance, so they could attend to any problem that would occur during flight, takeoff, or landing. Carrying enough parts to nearly rebuild *Bugeater* if necessary, it required an entourage of three B-17Es that had been converted to cargo planes and were reclassified as a XC-108A. The use of the B-17E as a cargo plane for parts and ground crew personnel was also part of the deception. Upon landing, the ground crew checked out *Bugeater* from fore to aft and everything in between. Although they did not expect to engage in combat, because of advanced radar giving them the chance to avoid approaching aircraft and the fact that the Allied powers at this time in the war controlled the air, occasionally, a German aircraft could slip in. The *Bugeater* was fully armed locked down and loaded for any assault that may occur. With the speed and ability to gain an altitude in excess of thirty thousand feet, it was not a probability, and the *Bugeater* was never fired upon.

As the war progressed, *Bugeater* and crew moved up and down the coast, landing at nearly every airfield that existed. Once they landed, the normal routine was to stay about a week with a few touches and goes, then exit to the next airfield. An order came through to stand down on June 2, 1945, until further notified. Four days later, at sunrise on June 6, 1944, the skies were black with thousands of Allied aircraft, and the crew knew that the invasion of Europe was underway. Major Battle and Walt carried on their mission until early December of 1944, and they were given orders to return to Pratt Army Airfield in Kansas as soon as weather permitted. On December 23, 1944, the *Bugeater* touched down, and the crew agreed, "This must be Kansas Toto." One day later on Christmas Eve, most of the crew members could reach their own homes on or before Christmas. Those that couldn't, showed up on the porch of the Marshall house to celebrate a Christmas that reminded them of home and not war. It was at this time the crew received an extended leave, and all crew members had the opportunity to go home for a few weeks and see family and friends.

During this leave, Walt helped Willis get caught up with needed repairs, and a discussion started about plans after the war. Howard was showing signs of decline in his health and for the most part was no longer able to help with the physically heavy farm duties, although he kept busy with the light duties that still needed to be done daily. Willis let it be known that his desires would be for Walt to return to the farm and make a life as Howard and he had done. Walt declared that if the opportunity to play professional ball was still available, and he made it through the rest of the war unscathed, that he would take it. Willis understood and prayed that Walt would someday return from the war and be able to fulfill his dream.

After leave was up and still being stationed in Kansas, it was decision time again for the crew of the *Bugeater*. The choice was to disband the crew and take noncombatant assignments or volunteering again to reenter the combat war for assignment to the Pacific theater to fight the Japanese. They all agreed that the fighting in Europe was winding down, and the need for combat crews was now in the Pacific Rim, and thus they agreed to volunteer. Training started again, with regrouping and staging at Palm Springs Army Airfield east of Palm Springs, California. Their time at Palm Springs Army Airfield was extended to refit and overhaul *Bugeater*. When the redo was finished, the next stop for assignment staging would be Hickam Field, Hawaii territory.

While at Palm Springs Airfield before departing for Hickam Field, the war in Europe ended on V-E Day, May 8, 1945. At the same time, the Japanese were being systematically removed from island to island. The invasion of Okinawa was in its second month as Walt and his crew were landing at Hickam Field. At this time, B-17 crews were being retrained on the B-29s. Hickam Field was a major port for the ferrying of new B-29s and was also a training field for the B-17 crews. Because of the *Bugeater*'s B-29 flight hours and the crew's extensive combat experience, John gained a promotion to lieutenant colonel for his part in the training wing. The crew was involved in training B-17 crews until V-J Day on August 15, 1945.

The war was now over, and Walt allowed himself to think more about tomorrow and the future. While in combat flying and with the knowledge that while in the military, one's life can be placed in very dangerous situations, one did not let his or her thoughts linger long about the near or distant future. Now that feeling was different for Walt for the first time in three and a half years, and he was thankful to God for allowing him to return home without harm or injury. There were thousands that didn't.

CHAPTER 3

Walt Returns Home

Training stopped within days after the Japanese ceased fighting and surrendered. By the time the official signing of the Japanese unconditional surrender had taken place on the battleship *Missouri* on September 2, 1945, troops and crew members at Hickam Field were already ferrying out and heading home. Because of combat duty and time in service, the *Eighty-Niner* crew was one of the first to get their orders to head back home to specified discharge bases to start their out-processing procedure. When they all knew their orders, Walt had a long talk with Colonel John about his plans and what direction he would now take. John had already made his decision to continue his service and try to finish a military career. John thought that the Army Air Corps' mission after the war would be changing and taking on a larger role in the US military strategy. With his experience, it would offer him a challenging and rewarding career in the years to come.

Colonel John had already guessed that Walt would head back to the farm in Crescent, Oklahoma, and see if he could restart where he had left off with a tryout with the St. Louis Pilots. Walt confirmed Colonel John's thoughts, and they talked more about baseball until they took their separate paths. Colonel John was going to report to his new duty station, and Walt continued on to Kansas City, Missouri, where he was designated to out-process. Two days after Walt's out-processing was complete, he stepped off the train in Guthrie, Oklahoma, where Willis and Juanetta were waiting to drive him home to the farm for a family reunion. From the train station in Guthrie to the front porch of the Marshall farm just outside of Crescent, which was now just a little over an hour drive, not quite like the all-day hard ride on horseback that Walt's grandfather Howard had made nearly fifty-six years ago. As Walt relaxed in the front seat of the family car, he noticed little wear in the old 1936 gray Ford from the ride that took him to Guthrie when he left nearly four years ago. The old Flathead V-8 still purred like a kitten at fifty-five miles an hour on the asphalt-paved road. Walt started thinking about the stories Howard had told him of the early days during the land rush, life in the territories, and what it took for him and Mary to just survive to see the next sunrise and sunset. Walt also thought of the stories that Willis told of the effort it took to maintain the farm in hard times, just to have food, clothing, and a place for his family to call home. Home now had a different meaning and importance when Walt thought of the millions of displaced people all over Europe and the Pacific Rim where all had been lost to the ravages of war and how there was not a place of refuge called home for countless numbers of people all over the world. As these feelings passed through Walt's mind, he felt more endeared to home, family, and farm than he had ever experienced since he left. To step back on the porch of his childhood home left him with an exhilaration that made him feel more alive than ever before.

The times during the war that Walt was able to return home on leave did not feel the same as what he was experiencing now. Everything had a distant memory, but now excitement ran through Walt's body with every sight, smell, and touch, like the freshness of a light breeze after a spring rain. As old memories had a renewed energy that gave more pleasure than ever before, it was as if all his life's past pleasures where happening at one single moment, nearly taking his breath away. When he walked through the door of the old farmhouse, Walt considered the disparity of this moment with past return trips home while on leave and acknowledged the difference was due to the fact that this time, he did not have to leave and go back into the world of war and the uncertainty of ever being able to return to the simple pleasures of family and home.

As Walt stood in the living room for a moment, everyone left him alone to let him get his thoughts in order. The family gathered in the dining room where a fresh-baked peach cobbler sat with a pitcher of fresh cold milk in the center of the dining room table. After a couple of minutes, Walt's nose led him to his customary seat at the table. The conversation and questions from Walt and family started as the peach cobbler was served. Walt now knew what home meant to him and that he was there, alive and well, to take it all in.

There was very little talk with Walt about future plans for the first two or three weeks, with the family just allowing Walt to do what pleased him. Walt, used to long days of flight and training, busied himself from sunup to sunset with late fall chores and repairs of all kinds: equipment, house, outbuildings, fence. Walt was completely taken in with the simplicity of it all. The seasons and the necessities that the seasons brought were the only boss he had, and the demands were quiet and subtle with little or no oversight except time. He had the time to get the job done if he did not hesitate. Life on the farm recognized that time was a commodity only if one used it wisely. Farmers that do usually survive and those who don't move on to something else. The change of pace from the rigid lifestyle of the military was welcomed by Walt and thoroughly enjoyed. The cool days of fall made work much easier than that of winter and especially the hot Oklahoma summer conditions. The coolness of the season took less physical effort. This allowed Walt to concentrate more on the job at hand and spend less time mentally and physically to overcome the pain that harsh weather conditions bring to working in the elements.

Thanksgiving was less than a week away, and Old Man Winter was starting to approach while life on the Marshall farm took on a slower pace, and work shifted to preparations for winter. Having the Tuesday workday over and supper finished, the telephone rang, and it was Peter Whyte. Not until that very moment did the Marshall family know that Peter had made it through the war, and they all were excited to hear his voice and wish him well. The call was to find out if there would be an extra seat at the table for the Thanksgiving meal on Thursday, and the answer was yes. Peter also asked if the

Marshall hospitality would extend for him to arrive on Wednesday afternoon and depart on mid-Friday morning. Willis and Juanetta assured Peter that it was absolutely fine for him to stay as long as he wanted, but if he did stay longer, jokingly, he would have to do work on the farm. Peter also wanted to know if Walt was back. He wanted to talk with him to make sure he would be there when he arrived, and Walt assured him he would be.

Looking up when the occasional car went by, the Marshall clan waited with anticipation on Peter's arrival, and sure enough, a dust cloud appeared on the horizon, and the closer the dust cloud got, you could start to make out a blue car with a white top. Peter pulled up in the Ford convertible that he had left in nearly four years ago. Peter did not have any family, and he was excited to spend the Thanksgiving holiday with the Marshalls, whom he now referred to as his adopted family. Talk about what had happened to him during the war was first on the question list. Peter went into as much detail as was asked to explain that on his fifteenth-bombing run with him piloting his B-24, they were shot down over northern Italy, and all his crew survived the crash landing, but all were injured, some seriously and some not. Peter had a broken leg and broken ribs and was sent to a German prisoner-of-war camp hospital and was treated with respect. Upon recovery, he was transferred to the POW camp for the duration of the war. Since he had no family, there was really no way for the Red Cross to get word of his well-being to anyone other than family members. On VE Day, the guards unlocked the gates to the prisoner camp, and most surrendered to the highest-ranking officer in the camp, who was a US Army Air Corps bird colonel. The transition of power went without incident because of the humane treatment they had been given by their German captors. He and other prisoners from other camps were detained as groups until recovery from combat injuries and general health concerns were resolved. Peter also mentioned that debriefing and transition had placed major delays from him being able to return to the States earlier. He had been mustered out about two months ago and had spent the time getting reestablished with the St. Louis Pilots Association and getting his car back. Mr. Bush, the owner of the Pilots, had allowed Peter to keep his car in an extra garage he had on his estate until Peter returned, or he received notice Peter was not coming back. Sure enough, his car was ready to go, having been maintained by Mr. Bush's motor pool staff for the last four years. It even had a new set of tires on it because the others were worn thin when he parked the car. Peter politely asked Mr. Bush how much he owed him, and the reply was nothing and not to ask any questions about how he got the tires because of the rationing programs. Peter expressed his gratitude to Mr. Bush and drove off to reconnoiter new prospects and old prospects for the 1946 baseball season.

The morning of Thanksgiving, Peter posed the question to Walt if his interest still existed in playing professional baseball. Walt told Peter that it did, but he did not know that playing baseball was the right path to take because of his age and if baseball still had a place in the postwar world. Walt also talked about going to college and getting a degree to have an education, which would give him opportunities other than continuing to earn a livelihood from the farm. Peter assured him that his old age of twenty-two did not reduce his chances of making a tryout. Nearly all the pro players that had signed up to do their part in the war were returning, and to the best of his knowledge, they were all four years older now too. The more Peter and Walt talked baseball, the old excitement of the game started to come alive inside Walt, and the more he started dreaming again of playing in the big league.

During the years of war, when there was downtime and the weather permitted, it was so easy to get a game going, and it allowed time to pass without the tedium that usually persisted when waiting to fly a bombing mission, debriefing, or training. This waiting game, which the military was so good at, hurry up to wait, when there was nothing to do, always invited mental images in, which nobody wanted running around loose, with no constraints in one's head. It was during these distraction games, wherever Walt was stationed, the flight crews and ground crews would start the baseball games, which gave Walt and everyone else a time of relief from the mental and physical pressures of their missions, which enabled them to think of something different than what might happen on the next training flight or bombing run. It was during these games that Walt would let his mind freely go to think what it would have been like if the war hadn't happened. If he had his tryout, would he have been good enough to be hired by the Pilots' organization? Walt knew when playing these games, that he was much better than anyone else by far. Although it was apparent he was the star of the all the games played around the US airfields, Walt would consider the talent, and it was hard to get a real measure of talent. Every once in a while, he would notice a player from another airfield that had the fielding ability, batting, or accuracy of throwing out a base runner that impressed him, but even then, Walt did not view them as being better than he was, maybe just as good. One physical attribute that Walt never saw with an opposing team in the military was anyone who was as fast as he was when it came to chasing down a ball or running the bases.

These idle times were brief and at times not very frequent, but it was the only time that Walt allowed himself to think of what-if, and after the war, would it still be possible for him to try out? None of the flight crews gave any thought to the future because it was really dangerous to one's sanity. Every day, it let everyone on the base know that the moment in the present day was all that one could count on, for at any time, if not in-flight, things just happened, from an enemy air raid to an accident that just would not occur in a nonwar world.

At the war's end, Walt just wanted to return home and rediscover what he considered a normal lifestyle and enjoy simple pleasures, like sleeping in his old bed and eating his mother's cooking, food that tasted like real food, and hoping that instant potatoes and instant eggs would never cross his path again, let alone eat them. After getting back to farm life and the sheer enjoyment of being with family again gave Walt a level of euphoria that he did not think was possible by just stepping a foot back on the old farm. Walt now had thoughts of an education, marriage, rearing a family, and maybe earning a living on the farm. Appreciation of this simple life that Howard, Mary, Willis, and Juanetta lived had a greater merit to Walt now than before the war. These are things he could come back too when in other parts of the world, there were millions of victims that had absolutely nothing—homes, property, or family. Walt just simply did not have an answer for Peter at that moment.

Peter understood and explained to Walt that he didn't have to make up his mind right now, and he would give Walt a phone number at the Pilots' baseball park in St. Louis where he could leave a message from which he would get back with Walt as soon as possible. The thing that Peter wanted to convince Walt was the fact that the talent he had four years ago was still there, and with the time that had passed, in actuality, he could be much better than he was four years ago. Walt listened carefully to everything Peter told him and understood that Peter was but a phone call away when Walt decided what he wanted to do.

Early Friday morning, the Marshall household and Peter were up and sitting at the kitchen table eating a country breakfast with all the tastes of home and great family conversation that made it all worth an early rise out of bed. As midmorning approached, Peter had his bag packed and in the car with Juanetta's brown-bag lunch to go along that Peter greatly appreciated. Peter started up his old Ford, told Walt to think about it, and let him know one way or the other, and he would be looking forward to hearing from him. Peter headed down the dirt road, leaving a rooster tail of dust as he made his way back to Highway 66 where he would turn west, with a dozen planned stops north and south of the old highway as he made his way back to the West Coast, looking for new prospects to recruit.

As Walt watched Peter drive away, he had a desire to talk things over with Willis and Juanetta. During the Sunday morning drive to church, Walt asked his parents their thoughts on trying to play baseball and earn a living from it. Willis and Juanetta had the same thought; Walt needed to do what he wanted to do and nothing less. The only thing they added was if he had the opportunity to go to college, that he should consider that as an option, so if professional baseball did not work out, he would have another direction to take for a career other than the farm. Walt agreed and assured his parents he was considering all options.

Baseball would not leave Walt's thoughts, and after a few days, he decided to go for the tryout and take the opportunity and chance that he would make it in the pros. He made a call to St. Louis, leaving a message for Peter, and the next day, the phone rang at the Marshalls' house in the late evening, and after the ensuing discussion with Walt, it was all set up like it was before the war. Early in March, Walt took the train to St. Louis and had his tryout and got an opportunity to play in the Pilots' organization. Walt was to report to Tulsa, Oklahoma, to play with the Tulsa Oilers, a triple AAA affiliate club in the Pilots' organization. Walt was excited about going to Tulsa to start his career because of how close he would be to home. The trip from Tulsa to Crescent was about one hundred and twenty miles, just a little over two hours, and since he had bought his first car after he signed his contract, he would be able to visit home as often as he could. This also meant that his family and friends could come and see him play while he was there.

It was in the beginning of spring of 1946, about three weeks before the season started, and the coaching staff of the Oilers liked what they saw in Walt. Everyone thought that Walt would not be in the minors for more than a year. His most impressive talent was speed and hitting long deep balls and the ability to direct his hits. He was placed in right field, the perfect spot for a good batter and a great fielder with exceptional speed. Walt lived in a small apartment in downtown Tulsa and would eat in the local downtown restaurants usually in the evenings, and one of his favorites was Nelson's Buffeteria located right off Main in downtown Tulsa. Walt was particularly delighted with their chicken fried steak with mashed potatoes and would show up there three to four nights a week. Walt was tall, lean, physically fit, and a ruggedly handsome young man with evenly cut facial features, light-brown near-blondish hair, and blue eyes. He had an even quiet demeanor about him and had a very soft quick wit that pleased most ladies with which he came in contact with. He wasn't a lady's man because he had a general respect for most people he would meet, without matter to gender, race, or any other category that there might be. Walt just plain and simple was a gentleman all the time. On one of Walt's frequent trips to Nelson's, where he enjoyed the closest thing to real home cooking, a group of young ladies spending their Friday night out in downtown Tulsa were starting out with supper at Nelson's. They were all nice-looking except for one, and to Walt, that particular one was not just nice-looking, she was the most beautiful woman he had ever seen, and he could hardly take his eyes off her. Well, it happened that Walt was sitting at the only table in the restaurant that had three empty seats. There were one and two chairs open at a few tables, and the table next to Walt's had a single seat open. When the young ladies were looking for open seats hoping to sit all together, Walt caught their eye and motioned them to his table where he offered them seating. He quietly asked for permission to sit in the empty seat at the adjacent table. This allowed the ladies to all sit together, and Walt was next to them.

Walt quickly introduced himself and engaged the young ladies in conversation. The girl that caught Walt's eye, he soon learned, was named Jane. As they exchanged tidbits of information about each other, Walt found out they were as interested in him as he was of them and especially Jane. Walt learned they were in their first year at the University of Tulsa, living on the campus in Lottie Jane Mabee, the ladies' dorm. They talked about their studies, which varied from biology majors to education majors, and they were all small-town girls from all around Oklahoma, who enjoyed living for the first time in their lives in a big city like Tulsa. After they finished eating their meal, Walt asked if he could pull up his chair to the end of their table and join them, to which they agreed. They wanted to know about Walt, and he told them everything they wanted to know. They asked where he was from originally and what he did during the war. They finally got around to why he was in Tulsa, and when they found out he was playing pro baseball with the Oilers, it made them more eager to find out more about him.

Walt wanted the conversation to continue, so he could find out more about Jane, so he offered to buy dessert on him. They all agreed to pie à la mode and coffee, except Jane, who wanted hot tea to drink with her pie and ice cream. Walt had learned to like hot tea from all the time he had spent in England over the last four years, so he told the waitress that he would drink hot tea along with Jane in hopes to gain a little edge in getting to know her.

Jane and the girls told Walt that they were going to the Majestic Theater to watch a movie after they finished eating, and they invited

Walt to join them. Not to seem overanxious, Walt asked the name of the movie and who starred in it. Jane spoke up for the group and said that it was a Frank Capra film called *It's a Wonderful Life* starring James Stewart. Walt mentioned that he would like to see James Stewart because he was in the Army Air Corps and flew in bombers, like Walt did during the war, except Stewart was a pilot and officer in a B-24, while he was an enlisted radio operator/top turret gunner on a B-17, but the experience was the same no matter what the job, rank, or plane was.

Walt also said that he was stationed in England at the same time Stewart was at an airfield about ten miles from his base. Trying to add to the conversation as they walked the three blocks from the restaurant to the movie, he also mentioned that he and his crew had actually met James Stewart on his base in England where they landed while touring all of Great Britain in their B-29.

James Stewart was a colonel and the commander of the Second Bomb Wing where Walt's B-29 spent the best part of four days and three nights. Lieutenant Colonel John Battle took Stewart and other pilots, plus the command staff on flights over the course of the four days' stay. On one flight, Stewart sat right seat with John, was allowed to take controls and pilot the *Eighty-Niner*. At the end of the flight, Stewart took the time to shake hands and talk to each and every crew member. Walt and the other crew members were impressed and surprised by the knowledge that Stewart had of their flying, bombing missions, and their combat war record. Walt added in his story that Colonel James (Jimmy) Stewart might be a movie star, but during the war, he flew combat and had an admiration for all the brotherhood that risked their lives in the skies over Germany. After Walt told the girls that he had met and talked to Jimmy Stewart, the rest of the evening had endless questions about Stewart, before and after the movie. Walt was a hit with Jane, the other girls too, but Walt was only concerned about the impression that he left with Jane.

The next day, Walt traveled over to the Tulsa University campus and into the women's dorm and left six tickets with the dorm mother at the desk to be placed in Jane Sander's mailbox. The tickets were for the Oilers home opener, to start the 1946 baseball season on Saturday of next week, compliments of Walt Marshall. Walt also left a note, telling Jane what time to arrive at the ballpark, so she and her guests could watch batting practice before the game and in the note added a phone number of the ballpark business office where a message could be left for him if she planned to attend.

When Jane checked her mailbox and found the note and the tickets, she was excited. Jane did not want to appear to be too anxious to call and leave a message, so she purposely waited until Thursday to call and leave a message that she along with other girlfriends would be there next Saturday and left the phone number at the desk of the dorm where he could leave a message for her.

It seemed to Walt an eternity until he got the message from Jane, thinking that he might have been too forward too soon but hoping every day she would be in contact. Finally, he got the message after his workout on Thursday, and he was so relieved. Now Saturday seemed like it would never get here, and the wait nearly wore Walt out. When he took the field to warm up and take batting practice and catch fly balls in the outfield, he would continually check the seats on the front row just behind the first base. At last they arrived about fifteen minutes before Walt and the team would leave the field prior to the start of the game. As Walt left the field to go into the locker room, he jogged past first base, waved to get Jane's attention, walked over to the fence, and said that he was glad that she and her guests could make it.

Walt started in right field and was batting in the middle of the order and played a mediocre game because his attention seemed to go where Jane was sitting, and maybe Walt was trying too hard to make a good impression on Jane. At the end of the game, Walt went over and asked Jane out on a date for the next weekend, and she agreed. At the end of the season in late October, Walt and Jane were married, and they were to make their home temporarily in Tulsa until Walt got called up. As winter finished and spring ball started up again, the word was that Walt could be called up at any time. The Oilers' 1947 season started, and it was just a matter of time that Walt and Jane would be relocating. Their plan was that Walt would find a small place to live or share an apartment with another player while Jane would finish the semester of summer school at Tulsa University and join Walt in St. Louis. Jane would probably enroll in the University of St. Louis to finish her degree.

Walt got the call in late August, which was good timing with Jane's school, and they both left to a new home in St. Louis. Now Walt was playing major league baseball and was being substituted, getting limited playing time. This was done in grooming Walt for the 1948 season with anticipation of 1949 being a rebuilding year when the management of the Pilots was going to make major changes in their lineup. The 1948 season was the second season in a row that in late August, the Pilots appeared to be a third-place or second-place finish at best, when the management decided that was not good enough and wanted a first-place finish like they had in the early 1940s, and that changes would have to take place, and Walt was part of the new plan for the team.

It was February 21, 1949. Walt and Jane received a call that Howard was failing and wanted to see his grandchildren. It was 11:00 AM. Walt and Jane packed and left immediately, taking Highway 66 southwest and getting as far as Claremore, Oklahoma, at seven in the evening. The weather had turned to ice and snow, and trying to drive through the night seemed extremely risky to both Walt and Jane. They spotted a place to spend the night, the El Sueno Motel that was on Highway 66 in downtown Claremore, and the Linger Longer bar-b-que restaurant was across the street north of the restaurant, less than one hundred feet away. Walt and Jane were tired, hungry, and ready to stop, and this place in the road seemed perfect, and it was. Walt and Jane would stop and spend the night in Claremore many times when traveling over the years.

The next morning, it was typical Oklahoma weather, from snow and ice to bright sunshine and warming above freezing temperatures. The weather change allowed them to make fast the trip to outside Crescent. LaTrenda, Walt's sister, lived in Stillwater, Oklahoma, and was a history professor at her alma mater, Oklahoma A&M. LaTrenda had finished her bachelor's degree at Oklahoma A&M just prior to World War II and soon after married her English professor, Steve Deem. Steve had been an officer in the US Navy reserves before the

World War II had started. Knowing that war was imminent, and it was just a matter of time before the United States would be involved, the Navy activated Steve's reserve status, and he was stationed at San Diego Naval Base at the first of November 1941, where after a short time, he would be assigned to the USS *Lexington* after it docked to load fighter planes then ferry them to Wake Island. On December 7, 1941, Steve was aboard the *Lexington* as it steamed to Wake Island. While Steve was stationed at San Diego Naval Base, LaTrenda went there to be with him and took a job working in an aircraft manufacturing plant and became a Rosie the Riveter. After Steve shipped out, LaTrenda went north to San Francisco because the thought of the day was that if the carriers needed refitting or damages repaired, Hunters Point Naval Shipyard in the San Francisco Bay Area would be the place. LaTrenda also had a girlfriend from Oklahoma A&M who had joined the Navy and worked in naval intelligence in the Bay Area. She could share an apartment with her friend Lizzie. LaTrenda took a similar job that she had in San Diego, and this also allowed her to go to graduate school at Stanford University. Steve made it through the war and was stationed in San Francisco for another eighteen months after the war, ferrying decommissioned ships to Seattle, Washington, to the ship graveyard. When Steve and LaTrenda returned to Oklahoma A&M, she had earned her doctorate in history and started teaching along with Steve.

LaTrenda and Steve only had a forty-five-minute drive to get to the farm, and when Walt and Jane arrived, they were there to greet them. Willis, Juanetta, and Mary were all in the bedroom with Howard. Howard had been sleeping a lot but was fairly clear when he would wake. With his family at his bedside, he reminisced a little about the old days and told his family he often wondered if he and Mary would be able to sustain long enough on the land to make anything out of it, hopefully enough for a living and having a family. Howard went on to explain that the land meant more than ownership. It meant belonging to something more than a job and a means to an end. Howard felt respect for the land God gave him to nurture, and in turn, he felt the land had respect for him. "If I bless the land, the land will bless me" were Howard's thoughts. In those first years,

Howard said he never imagined that he would live long enough to see his grandchildren, and yet here they were. Howard also told Willis and Walt that he thanked God every day for bringing them and Steve back from war and keeping his family safe through two world wars. Then Howard fell back into sleep, and Mary stayed by his side.

This was the first time that Walt really felt the meaning of the Marshall farm and what it meant to his grandfather and father. Walt wanted to follow his dream, and at this time, life on the farm did not fit the equation. Walt, Jane, LaTrenda, and Steve stayed at the farm for two more nights, and Howard would have more conscious moments where they could visit a little each time, but as the days passed, the time Howard spent awake grew less and less. As Walt and Jane prepared to leave, they knew that it was a matter of a few days or weeks, and Howard would be gone. Walt and Jane left early in the morning, and with good weather forecast, they would make the trip back to St. Louis in one day, knowing they would be returning soon.

Three weeks later, Howard died, and the entire family gathered at the Marshall farm for the funeral. Willis and his mother Mary decided to bury Howard on the farm and start a family cemetery on a high spot that had two big oak shade trees Howard had planted about two hundred yards from the house. Howard during his lifetime would visit this spot many times in a month, year in and year out, to sit under one of the trees to think and have some alone time with the land and nature. The family contracted with Day's Monument Company in Guthrie, Oklahoma, to make and set a black granite headstone engraved with his name, date of birth, death, and the inscription that read, "A beloved father and husband, an Eighty-niner to the end."

Walt and Jane decided that at the funeral, they would announce that Jane was pregnant, and they were expecting an addition to the family in late December or early January. Everyone was excited and wanted to know if they had chosen any names yet. Jane answered that they had not discussed a girl's name, but if it was a boy, they would name him Howard Joe Marshall and would probably just call him Joe to make it simple, and Walt and Jane liked the way it sounded, Joe Marshall. A typical late December day in St. Louis brought in temperatures in the teens with snow and ice, but it also brought in, on December 28, little Howard Joe Marshall. Walt and Jane were sure that Joe was the most beautiful baby boy ever, and they glowed with pride with the latest addition to the Marshall family. It was a great time for Jane that Walt was able to be around to help with the baby and for Walt to enjoy being a father for the first time. Off season allowed Walt to have no distractions in the caring and nurturing of Joe for the first few months before spring ball would start. Walt was not like a lot of men of his generation who didn't play a big role with infants and their care. Walt couldn't get enough of it and was the happiest guy on the planet when it came time to change a diaper or wake up in the middle of the night to give little Joe a bottle. Jane wondered at that time if life on the farm, taking care of things that were living—crops, cows, horses, farm animals, and family—played a big part in the loving, tender fathering Walt displayed in caring for his family. This side of Walt was unknown to Jane until Joe was born, and it secured the thought that the great husband Jane chose was also going to be a great father.

The 1949 season did not work the way management had thought, and the Pilots came in just below losing more than they won with a .485 record. Walt played most of the games and did gain a starting position. The management played Walt at most positions and pinch-hit with him. At the end of the season, Walt maintained a .252 batting average and played in all of ninety games and was a sure thing to start in the 1950 season.

When spring practice came about, Walt was called in to talk with the manager and was informed that he would start in right field, and they were going to place him third in the batting order, and Walt could hardly wait to tell Jane the great news. With his starting position secured, Walt was ready for spring ball to finish and the season to get started.

It was the middle of June, and the season was well underway, and the Pilots were just a little above .500 mark for the year. Management was pushing the team hard not to have a repeat of the last three seasons. Walt was batting .320 and had a great season going for him with twelve home runs under his belt. Everyone thought that Walt was a new rising star in the making, and this made Walt feel great and wanted to do even better. The Chicago Pups were in town, and there was a full house at Sportsman's Park. Walt hit a single into right field just out of reach of the second baseman. Walt on first was fast, and he got the sign to steal. He took a long lead, and as the pitcher started his delivery, he took off. The batter connected, and a hard-hit ground ball went left of a stretched-out diving second baseman who stopped the ball from going through to the outfield. As he lay on the ground, the second baseman was sitting up, turning, and slinging the ball all at the same time to the shortstop covering second base, who had to stretch out to catch an off-target toss. Concentrating on catching the ball caused the shortstop to collide with Walt as he slid into the bag. Subsequent to the collision, the shortstop landed on top of Walt's leg, flipping him over the shortstop, making his knee superextended as Walt's upper body twisted in the air, and the pain was there before Walt hit the ground. In one moment, the game and the season were over for Walt. It reminded him of flying bombing runs during the war, when in a moment of tranquility above the clouds, then in a second moment, the German fighters strafed their formation, and some planes were blown up or went down in a ball of flames, crashing into the earth below with all crew lost. The doctors did not want to diagnose the problem immediately because of the swelling and pain. About one and a half weeks later, keeping Walt's knee immobilized, the doctors called it the "unhappy triad," meaning it was an injury to the anterior cruciate ligament, medial collateral ligament, and the medial meniscus. The doctors did not know the extent of the damage and did not suggest surgery until a sufficient amount of time had passed to see what range of motion and mobility returned. At that time, they would determine what course of action to take in the treatment of Walt's knee.

With the passage of time, the swelling diminished, and Walt could move his knee, with considerable amount of pain, through a limited range of motion. The season was drawing to a close, and Walt was still having some difficulty getting around doing normal activity. The doctors saw improvement and wanted more time, hoping more healing would occur because surgery might mean an end to Walt's career. Walt was better now that it was off season, but the team had another disappointing season. Management had a growing impatience and wanted a fix to the problem immediately. Constantly checking with Walt and his doctors as to his improvement, this made Walt push his pain to gain range of motion and stability. Through this reconditioning period, Walt always thought when he tried to move his knee very slightly from side to side, it gave him the feeling his knee might give out. He was really hesitant to push himself to move his knee from side to side but continued with the exercises and training as the doctors had instructed him.

By the time Joe had his first birthday, Walt's knee was doing well, and he felt that its healing was nearing completion. A weakness seemed to come back when Walt would put pressure on his knee if he would push off when changing directions. He considered that the strength he needed would come back over time with more conditioning. Walt worked hard and followed the doctor's instructions to the finest degree and knew in his heart he would be ready to go before spring practice would start.

When spring practice came around, Walt felt confident that he could resume his place on the team and pushed himself as hard as possible. The feeling that his knee might give out at any time still plagued Walt's thoughts, but there was really no indication physically to support the feeling he had. Walt considered it was just in his head, psychosomatic, just thinking something was wrong. While shagging fly balls in the outfield in the third week of spring ball, Walt had to run down a fly ball to his right at full speed. Walt caught the ball, and while attempting to throw the ball back to an infield player while in the process of stopping, by planting his right foot from a full-speed run, his right foot slipped on wet, loose turf from an overnight rain. With full body weight pushing down on the inside of his leg and knee, Walt again went down, suffering another incredible painful knee injury.

As the doctors examined him, Walt let his mind go and started reliving the previous year and the thought of the pain and the hours, days, weeks, and months that it took him to regain his strength, and it seemed all these things started to overwhelm him until he remembered all the friends that didn't make it back from the war. The injuries that many of the flight crews suffered left them with no hope at all of living a normal life. These sobering thoughts drew back the self-pity that Walt was broaching on and allowed Walt to gain control of his emotions and just face the facts. The weeks passed with Walt starting his physical therapy again and not allowing himself to wonder, why him. Jane supported Walt and never questioned what the future held for them but continued doing what she needed to do and when it needed it to be done. This attitude was sufficient for the day and never gave doubt to the outcome. Walt, the Pilots management, and the doctors set up a meeting to discuss Walt's future with the Pilots. The consensus was that surgery at this stage would only be considered if physical therapy did not restore the flexibility and range of motion to continue with a normal lifestyle. Normal lifestyle did not include baseball or athletic endeavor of any kind. Surgery was an option but could leave Walt's knee more limited in its capacity than without the surgery. Walt's baseball career was over. The doctors told Walt that with continued physical therapy, that Walt could expect a level of rehabilitation that allowed him to carry on a normal life, but if he would injure his knee again, even with surgery, he could possibly experience a greater level of limited use and less mobility of his leg and knee. The doctors assured Walt that the future, maybe within the next ten to fifteen years, would hold a much-advanced treatment for this kind of injury. Orthopedic surgeons were in the discussion on what might be less invasive surgery for the patient and the ability to diagnose injury much better than the present-day practices.

The question of what to do next evaded Walt and Jane. Walt needed to work to support his new family, but the job market looked a little bleak for the skills that Walt had. To get a job, starting at the bottom at minimum wage was not a problem, and Walt did not know what kind of job was a good fit for him. After the war, most of his friends took advantage of the GI Bill and went to or back to college. The ones that went back to collage were at present graduating and landing jobs in fields they had prepared for over the last few years and were being hired at levels way above minimum wage and with a bright future of advancement. Walt did not know if college and the four years it would take to get a degree was an option for him at this time. Jane lacked thirty-five credit hours before she could graduate. Completing her teaching degree would allow her to find a teaching job that would help with the finances until Walt figured out what career path he would take. With all the decisions that there were to make, the greatest considerations would be the ones about Joe and his future. Walt and Jane wanted to give him a home and a family that supplied him all the opportunities to grow up in an environment that surrounded him with love and the security of a home that was no less than what their parents gave to them.

Jane and Walt decided that this was the time for the three of them to take a little time and go to Oklahoma for a visit with the folks. When Walt's knee had recovered enough to make the trip, they steered the car southwest, back down the Mother Road, Highway 66 again. They planned on two weeks for the trip, which allowed them frequent stops for Joe, and this gave Walt ample opportunity to do the exercises that would help him regain full range of motion of his knee. Again, their first overnight stop was the El Sueno Motel and the Linger Longer bar-b-que in Claremore, Oklahoma. They also planned to stay a couple of days in Muskogee, Oklahoma, with Jane's folks and stay an extended time in Crescent, Oklahoma, with Walt's folks back on the farm. Jane and Walt thought this would be an opportunity for their parents to spend some time with their grandson Joe. This trip also gave both of them a time to think in a place, the homes they grew up in, where they were protected from the cares of the outside world. They both regarded their parents' homes as a sanctuary where they could separate themselves from present day and thoughts of the future. Throughout the trip to Crescent, Walt could hardly wait to experience the feeling of coming home.

After staying with Jane's parents for three nights, Walt and Jane decided to have an early lunch about eleven and try to leave about twelve o'clock to head off to Crescent, which was about a four-hour drive. Before they left, they called Walt's parents and gave them an expected time that they would arrive so that they could plan their day to get the chores and any work done that was necessary. Willis and Juanetta were sitting on the porch when they saw off to the east a plume of dust, and they knew it was Walt and Jane. Willis and Juanetta were mostly excited to see Joe who was now pushing two and half years old and all boy, constant movement, and into everything imaginable. It was this night, after everyone went to bed, and Joe had been fast asleep for three or four hours, after having just lay down, that Walt asked Jane if she had ever thought of living her life on the farm. Jane made no hesitation with her reply by telling Walt that she had complete confidence in her husband to make the right choice, and whatever it was, it would be fine with her.

The next day, Walt was up early and knew the routine well from the years he worked with his dad and grandfather before the war. Willis didn't expect much from Walt because of his knee but was surprised how well he moved along and was a great help. After Walt shipped out for the war, Willis had an opportunity to acquire an adjoining one and a half section that was used for crops and grazing cattle. With government contracts for certain crops and cattle, Willis grew the herd and expanded the farm operation. It was hard to find help, but somehow, Willis had found some older men that were willing to work and were good hands at what they did, but they were always in need of more help. When Walt asked Willis if he could come back and work on the farm with him and the others, Willis stopped what he was doing, gave Walt a big hug, and told him he didn't even have to ask, if that was what he wanted to do, Walt would not just work on the farm, he would be a full half partner in everything they did starting the very first day, no questions asked. Willis did ask Walt if he had discussed the new plan with Jane, and Walt told him he had, and it was fine with her.

As the plans were made to move Walt, Jane, and Joe from St. Louis to the farm, they would need a place to move to. Mary was the first to speak up when she heard the good news of Walt coming back to live on the farm with his family. She talked it over with Willis and Juanetta, that there were things she was starting to struggle with, and it was very lonely with Howard being gone, and if it was all right with them, for her to take one of the spare bedrooms and live with them from now on. The plan was approved by all, and now, Walt and his family had a house of their own that they could call home.

CHAPTER 4

Joe and the Farm

Joe was a good-looking baby who grew into a fine boy who showed athletic talents as soon as he could walk. In fact, Joe did not learn to walk; he started running before he could walk. By the time Joe was four years old, anything that involved running or a ball of any kind, Joe was in for any and all activities that his parents or grandparents could come up with. No one really knows, but just after a year had passed after Walt moved back to the farm, Willis came home from a trip to town and brought back a very small puppy. It was not strange to have an occasional dog that came on the property, but the moment they crossed the line and got into something they shouldn't have, they mysteriously went missing. Willis had the thought that if you fed something and reared it, whatever it was, it had to be productive, or it didn't belong on a farm. So it was very strange that Willis brought a dog home, but he declared it was a house dog. Juanetta did not say a word, for it was a strange thing for Willis to do, and she wanted to see the why and how this was going to play out. Not only was this unexpected, the dog seemed to be a runt and in no way could it be a working dog. The family was baffled and stared at this tiny animal that was sure to have worms, for it was just near a bag of bones with not enough meat on it to grease a skillet.

While preparing lunch the next day, the dog was the main conversation while Mary, Juanetta, and Jane prepared lunch before Willis and Walt came in from the fields to eat. They started talking about a couple of phone calls that Willis had made and two trips into town over the last couple of weeks that did not seem necessary but were also not questioned by Juanetta as to their purpose. Juanetta shared that Willis said he would care for the pup, and nobody else would have to bother with him, unless they wanted to. He also told Juanetta that his name was Moses.

The gals got a laugh from the name and thought that this could be some kind of holy dog, and it had a hidden meaning to Willis. All the time the ladies were preparing lunch, Jane had noticed that Joe was not underfoot. Not really concerned, but she thought she should check on him to see what he was up to. As Jane walked from the kitchen to the dining room, in the corner was a cardboard box with an old pillow in it that Willis put there for Moses. Sitting next to the box, with his chin resting on the edge, looking down without moving a muscle was Joe. Joe had his eyes fixed on this little animal as it slept, staring at its every movement and listening to every sound it made. Joe would look as its little belly would go up and down with every breath and would listen to Moses breathing and the little noises he would make as he probably dreamed of his momma and his litter mates.

Jane wondered what Joe must be thinking, but whatever it was, Joe was devoting all his attention to it. Jane quietly moved toward Joe as not to startle him and then sat next to Joe on the floor. As they sat next to each other, quietly looking at this little dog, Jane wondered what this addition to the family would mean and how long it would keep Joe's attention, but for now, Joe was totally consumed with this tiny animal. After a couple of minutes, Moses woke up, and Jane picked him up and told Joe to come with her as they took Moses out into the yard to let him move around in the grass and see if he would do his business, and he did. Joe wanted to hold Moses, and Jane said he could but had to careful because he was just a puppy. As Joe held Moses, he was so delighted with himself; he started laughing and could not stop. Mary instructed Joe to put Moses back in the box, and after lunch, they would take Moses outside again, and Joe could hardly wait until lunch was over. At this moment, Jane figured out the reasoning to Willis's madness.

The entire family would always eat meals together, sometimes at the folks' house and sometimes at Walt and Jane's. That evening it was at Juanetta and Willis's, and they sat with bated breath as Willis decided to answer why he brought a dog and not only a dog but one that looked like a wet rat. Willis said he had contacted a breeder from Oklahoma City to bring the best of his litter to Crescent, and if he looked all right, he would buy it from him, and Willis did just that. The first trip was for the breeder to bring the male and female, so Willis could see the stock the pups were coming from, and they passed muster. Along with regular trips to town, Willis would stop at the city library and read up on different dog breeds, and after much research, he decided on this particular breed, a Jack Russell terrier.

The next question the family had was the name. Willis explained in his opinion such a little dog had to have a name that gave you a sense of big and powerful, and it just seemed to him it was a good fit. The next family question was why. Willis said in his research that he found out that the energy level of a Jack Russell terrier was greater than most of the other breeds of dogs, and they needed a master that had the time to spend with the dog and had to have a lot of energy to keep up. Willis said it would be interesting which would wear the other out first, Joe or Moses. Willis also added that in England, the Jack Russell was originally bred for fox hunting, but as it turned out, any vermin that was not wanted on the farm, from rats to possum, the Jack Russell terrier would find them fair prey. Willis said he had never seen a child with as much energy as Joe, and he knew Joe had enough to wear all of them out, so the fact of the matter was, Willis brought home a working farm animal and a companion for Joe.

Moses was the perfect partner for Joe. Joe was a quick learner on how to throw a ball. Moses, on the other hand, was also a quick learner on how to retrieve a ball. Willis gave Joe a small rubber ball, a little larger than a golf ball, and as a three-year-old, he was a little clumsy at throwing it. Likewise, Moses, not very large at eight weeks old, but he was already game for chasing anything that was thrown. At first, it was Joe chasing Moses with the ball in his mouth, and then it was Moses trying to catch Joe with the ball in his hand. After a while, Joe's awkward throw quickly became fluid, and Moses found out the more obedient he was in returning the ball to Joe, the ball would be hurled again for him to chase down and return. This rudimentary game had only a beginning without an end. The repetition of toss and return, this cycle, was slow to repeat only by the length of the throw. The shorter the toss, the faster the cycle happened, and another throw was on its way for Moses to run down.

Most of the time, Joe attempted to throw the ball as far as he could for the immediate fetch by Moses, running back to Joe and dropping the ball for Joe to try to throw farther on every attempt. The only short throw was when Joe would play a mean trick on Moses. Joe would feign a long throw and throw the ball short, only to watch Moses do a somersault when he abruptly stopped to come back to the ball. Within a year, everyone was amazed at the distance Joe could pitch a ball, a larger ball at this time, and how fast Moses could return it. Amazement was also expressed by first-time visitors on how endless this throw-and-return game was. One session of throw and return might consist of a hundred throws, to the disbelief of any and all watching. When Moses and Joe played, they played hard, and when they rested, they rested hard, a real pair.

The September after Joe turned six years old, it was time for him to start school. Joe would attend the same school that Walt attended more than twenty years before. Approximately three miles away was the Blue Creek School, a two-room school that went from the first grade through grade eight and had a total of fifty-five students in all grades. First through fourth were in one room, and fifth through eighth were in the other classroom. The number of students in each class would differ from year to year; some years, there would be three in a class, and the next year, there might be ten. The interesting thing was that the distribution of the number of students in a room was nearly always equal throughout Joe's years at Blue Creek, and it always seemed to work out that way.

Because of the combined class size and an attempt to keep the class sizes equal in each room, the fifth grade might be added to one side and taken from the other. At times, when the one to fourth side became the first to fifth side, the fourth graders were always disappointed because crossing over, as the Blue Creek students called it, meant you weren't a little kid anymore. You became one of the big kids when you crossed over. The second student-to-room balancing act was advancing the placement of the really smart kids. The two teachers at Blue Creek worked as a team and knew when a student needed to have their learning accelerated, and this was a simple task. They moved to the upper-grade side and would normally be seated by their age in a class placement of the first row on the right would be first graders, the second for second graders, and so on. If you were a fast learner, a second grader might be in the fourth-grade row. In the two-room school environment, the students that needed the repetition would be able to hear the material for four years if they wanted to or not. For the students that caught on quick, they were exposed to fourth-grade material in the first grade. Most of the students that were in the Blue Creek School knew their three *r*'s with an utmost efficiency.

There was so much interest in the students at Blue Creek School by the teachers and parents that on the rare occasion when a brilliant mind became apparent, the two teachers, Mrs. Sutherland and Ms. Lemons, would both stay the hours after school that were needed to prepare those rare students with studies much more advanced for Blue Creek, even advanced for high school in Crescent. One student that Mrs. Sutherland and Ms. Lemons tutored, Joe Akin, a student that Joe knew but was three years older, left Blue Creek School and went directly to the university in Stillwater, Oklahoma A&M, and studied chemistry and biology. Joe Akin, who Mrs. Sutherland referred to as a prodigy once, continued his education and later earned his medical degree, plus other postdoctoral degrees in medical research.

Blue Creek School was the perfect place for Joe Marshall to go to school, learn, and have fun. Joe was athletic at a young age and also very quick to learn and had a maturity to learn years beyond his age. Blue Creek did not have a gym, but they had a basketball goal on the playground with a dirt court, except when it rained, then the goal had a mud court. The playground also had a well-worn backstop for a carved-in-the-dirt baseball diamond and a pasture for an outfield. A plastic plate for home base and a piece of wood, a rock or a cardboard box for bases, and enough kids, girls and boys, to make up two teams that could play each other made Blue Creek School complete for a kid growing up on a farm in rural Oklahoma.

What made the Blue Creek two-room school a great place for a little kid was the inclusion because of the number of available players. If half of the students all ages were boys, there were twenty-six or twenty-seven boys. Of twenty-six boys, half are first to fourth graders, and that leaves twelve or thirteen to make up two nine-player baseball teams. The older boys had to have the participation of the younger boys to constitute a real game. Then there had to be a proper division of the available players; it would not be fair to have all the older boys on one team and the other team made primarily of the younger boys. Mrs. Sutherland was a better judge of athletic ability than Ms. Lemons was, so Mrs. Sutherland assigned players according to their ability, not just age, to play on each team, and when the roster was set, it stayed the same for the entire school year. The school mascot's name was the Mustangs. When other two-room schools played each other, Mrs. Sutherland set the roster again with the best players, not just the older players. Most of the time, the team that represented Blue Creek School was composed of the older boys; only once in a great while would a fourth grader make the school team, but it did happen. Usually, third and fourth graders supplied the playground teams, and the first and second graders got to practice with everyone, but not play in a game. Joe didn't make one of the playground teams when he was a first grader, and this gave him the opportunity to watch the older boys more closely, so he would know how good he had to be so he could play on one of the playground teams come the next year. In a lot of aspects, Joe, at the Blue Creek School, could play better than most of the boys two grades ahead of him, and maybe in a school that had fifty or sixty first graders the same age as Joe, he might not be more talented than everyone in his class, let alone the two classes ahead of him. At Blue Creek School, that was not the case.

As the first-grade year came to a close, Joe had a glove and a baseball in his hands literally all the time. In the evenings before Willis and Walt came in from the fields, Joe had played throw and retrieve with Moses an hour, and when Jane would start to feel sorry for Moses, although he never slowed down, she would go outside and play catch with Joe for thirty minutes before setting supper on the table. Joe would take a little time off to wash up, eat, and then be excused from the table to go back out with Moses to start the process all over again. After about an hour, Walt would go out and play catch with Joe, and by this time, Moses needed a little relief to rest and watch the ball go back and forth for nearly another hour.

Walt had occasional problems with his knee, but for the most part, him being careful not to put a side pressure on his knee while lifting a heavy load or trying to kick or move something with the inside of his foot that would place outside pressure on his knee, he could avoid most of the pain and immobility from his knee. Most days, his knee might be a little sore from time to time after a long day's work, but this was manageable and did not inhibit his daily work or lifestyle. Walt would look forward to the good weather days after supper, seemingly never too tired to play catch or teach Joe something about the game. As Joe grew older, batting, fielding, and even pitching were all part of the evenings, holidays, and Sundays when only the basic chores were done on the farm.

During the earlier years of these days of Walt and Joe playing after supper, Willis was the first to make an observation about Joe and his speed. Quite often, Willis would join the pair and even bat the ball to one of them, similar to an infield practice where you threw the ball back to the one shagging the ball for the batter. Joe loved to do this with his dad and his grandpa because to him it felt like he was throwing a runner out at a base. One day, after Joe was six years old, Walt would throw the ball wide to make Joe run to catch it, or when Willis would hit the ball a little left or right, and Joe would move to make the catch. Willis made the observation that he seemed faster than Walt was at the same age. When Willis shared this with Walt, Walt thought that his dad was seeing something in Joe that really did not exist. Walt remembered how fast he was but could not really see the comparison with Joe. This running comment from Willis continued for a couple of summers without any agreement from any of the family.

When summer break was over and everyone, except last year's eight graders who graduated and started school in Crescent, was back at the Blue Creek School makeshift baseball field, it was as exciting to Joe as a childhood Christmas Day. He was able to play a real game, not all at one time, because the kids kept the inning count and started back with the same count on the batter of the same inning, from recess to recess until all nine innings or extra innings were completed so they could declare a winner. During Joe's first-grade year, because of the age difference of the students at Blue Creek School, it was hard to see the talent in Joe, but it was there and visible when you compared Joe with a kid within one or two years of Joe's age.

When the summer break was over and Joe started the second grade the first day back, the playground baseball started, it then became apparent to Mrs. Sutherland as she made up the rosters to make two comparably talented teams. Mrs. Sutherland noticed that Joe was playing at a higher level than her fourth graders, and his coordination was remarkable for his age. When she made up the rosters, she thought that the older boys might complain as they did when she played a girl who played better than most boys. The older kids would say it's not fair to have a girl on their team until they found out they had a good player, even if it was a girl. Over the years, Mrs. Sutherland had seen great talent in the young girls and their ability to play baseball, but unfortunately, at that time, girls' sports, other than basketball, were not developed in their rural community. Much to her surprise, when the rosters were handed out to see who was on the two teams, the older boys that had Joe Marshall placed on their team did not say a word but rather seemed delighted. Then it dawned on Mrs. Sutherland that they too saw this talent in Joe, and it was not just in her imagination.

Three weeks into fall classes, Mrs. Sutherland and Ms. Lemons had a parent-teacher conference at Blue Creek School. This conference over the years became more of a social event, and it always packed out the little school cafeteria and classrooms. Nearly all parents that could show up did, and there was a meal served that consisted of the meat and sides cooked in the cafeteria by Edna "Big Ed" Lucas, the Blue Creek School cook. Anytime the school had an event, and a meal was included, for a small charge, nearly the entire community would show up, if you had a child in school or not, just to eat Big Ed's cooking. Mrs. Lucas's cooking was known throughout four counties, and when an event was scheduled within a thirty-mile radius, Big Ed got the call. During the fall teacher-parent conference, Mrs. Sutherland took extra time to talk to Walt and Jane about Joe. She asked if they had noticed his unusual athletic ability. Since no one in the family had an experience to compare Joe to other kids his age, they had really never given it a thought, except Walt mentioned that his dad Willis was convinced that Joe was much faster than Walt was at the same age. Walt told Mrs. Sutherland that he had discounted his dad's observation because Walt knew that he was faster than the other kids he came in contact with as a kid, including Blue Creek School under Mrs. Sutherland's tutelage. Mrs. Sutherland told Walt that her memory was still sound and had not forgotten Walt as a student and his baseball talent and was fully aware of how much faster he was than the other students at that time, and with that being said, she told Walt that she would confirm Willis's thought. Joe was faster than Walt at the same age.

Walt left the conference with Jane and Joe that evening with a thought in his head if Joe had an exceptional ability, he wondered as Joe got older, if he would slow as other kids his age matured. Walt still did not believe there could be that much difference in Joe and other kids close to his age. In early fall, Mrs. Sutherland would set a single roster and schedule to play the other two- and four-room schools nearby. The parents would volunteer to transport the school team in half a dozen cars to make the five- or six-mile trip. The local small schools did this in an effort to give rural students experience in meeting and interacting with more kids than the fifty or so they would be in contact during their eight years at Blue Creek School. The other small schools had the same thought in mind for their students. It was at one of these games that Mrs. Sutherland wanted Walt to see Joe play and asked if he would take a carload to the next game. Walt agreed. Walt, June, Juanetta, and Willis took two cars and half the team. The other parents also volunteered to take the other half of the team to play another two-room school team, the Justus Wildcats.

Walt remembered the same kind of game when he was a kid, if not the same game at the same place, as they were going to play that day. Approximately every six miles, north, south, east, and west, there was another small two-, three-, or four-room rural school. By far, the majority were two-room schools just like Blue Creek School that allowed the students to compete in whatever sport was possible with the limited funds that were available in the small rural communities. For most of the students, it was the only time they ever ventured out from their home area. They could easily spend their entire lives hardly knowing much of an outside world. These small-school activities and games exposed most of the students to an outside world literally unknown to them were it not for sports like baseball, basketball, and track.

Walt and Jane were excited to see Joe play and had no expectation of how well he might do. The Justus Wildcats team, as far as age of players, had the same composition as Blue Creek Mustangs. The older kids, sixth, seventh, and eighth graders made up most of the team, but because of not enough older players to make a complete team, every once in a while, the school might have a fourth- or third-grade boy make the team at any of the small schools. Some schools would also let the girls fill out the roster to make a team. Hardly ever did a fourth-grade boy make a team when an older girl could play better and was more of an asset to the team. In the larger schools that had a high school, like Crescent, there were enough students, and the schools had the facilities, so they would have complete girl and boy teams in most sports out of each grade. This was not the case with the less-funded two-room schools; they had to make do with or without the facilities and the combination of grades to have the number of players needed.

As a second grader, Joe didn't have the ability of the older kids but competed with some of the fifth graders on their team or the opposing team. Joe's throws and fielding were better than any player within two years of his age. Joe had an understanding of the game that far exceeded his years. As Walt and Jane watched, they were amazed at the level of play that Joe displayed. Joe's batting compared with any other seven- to eight-year-old was also advanced for his age, but not as much as his speed, throwing, and fielding. For the first time, Walt could see what Willis had been talking about when comparing Joe's speed to Walt's. After the game, Walt and Jane agreed if Joe continued to have an interest in baseball and matured his abilities at the accomplished pace that he was playing now, he could very well become an excellent athlete and a great baseball player. Only time would tell.

Time and age added greatly to Joe's baseball skills. Moses, with each passing year, had to run longer to retrieve a toss of the rubber ball from Joe and continued to bring back as many as Joe threw. The practices with Walt each evening intensified as time rolled along with Joe never getting enough workouts with his dad. By the time Joe was in the eighth grade, Joe worked his dad so hard in a practice that Walt would tell Jane that he might be in the best physical condition he had ever been in his life. The kids that Joe went to school with would get together during the summer, whenever they had a chance, to play a game of sorts. The friends that Joe had from school always wanted to come to the Marshall farm because Walt, when he had time, would work with and teach technique to any kid that showed desire and would show up. Just getting to a friend's house in that part of the country was a long walk, bike ride, or run because hardly any of the parents would drive their kids anywhere, unless it was to some kind of doctor in town. As with all of Joe's friends, they lived or worked on the farms with their parents, helped with the work, and did not go into town to play organized baseball in the summers. The kids that lived closer to town in the other small schools could have played Little League summer ball, but this was not an option for the kids who went to Blue Creek School. The summer before the rural kids showed up to enter the town schools, the kids that were good enough and had the parents to take them into town was the first year they had an opportunity to play on a real Little League team. Playing with the town kids the summer before you started school in town gave the rural kids indoctrination before the first day of school and allowed the kids a chance to develop some relationships beforehand.

Joe's last year at Blue Creek was exciting for Joe in baseball and academics. Joe was now one of the upperclassmen and was finally part of the oldest kids' group in the school. The eighth graders were sort of celebrities of the school, and Joe wanted to make the most of his last year there. Joe's skill at baseball was probably good enough to make the high school varsity team in Crescent, but that was still a year away and eagerly anticipated. Because of Walter's tutelage with Joe and his classmates over the last eight years, the overall talent on the Blue Creek School's baseball team made them a force to contend with in the realm of two-room and small-school teams.

Walt had spent a lot of time teaching baseball with any and all the students at Blue Creek School, but most of the time spent in practicing and refining skills was with Joe's three best friends from Blue Creek School: Paul, Mike, and John. These three were better than average players that were still improving their game with each passing year of maturity and physical strength. They weren't the level of talent as Joe but were solid in their throwing, fielding, and batting and complemented each other when playing in a game. Mike and John were younger by one year, and Paul was the same age and grade as Joe. When not doing farm chores or going to school, the four of them and others would get together at Wycoff Corner where they could throw and hit the ball and make as much of a game situation as possible depending on how many showed up.

Wycoff Corner was an area that was as centrally located between Joe, Paul, Mike, and John, which made the travel time equal to the four of them and a place that was flat and level without trees or structures that would be in the way of play. Years before Joe's time, there was a house and a couple of buildings where the old trails crossed, forming an intersection of sorts. From 1880 to around 1910, the Wycoff family originally lived there and ran a stopover station for the travelers. The Wycoffs supplied the necessities for their horses, a supply of basic goods, livery, horse courier, water, and wagon repairs.

Now, decades long gone except for a few fence posts, the remnants of a storm shelter and a hand pump over an old water well, which the locals maintained with new leather cups so you could still pump water through it, made the perfect spot for a bunch of young kids to play baseball, have a good time, and refresh themselves with fresh water on a hot summer day. Every time Joe made the trip to Wycoff Corner, Moses was along, and everyone there appreciated the extra help in finding an errant hit or throw that wound up in the tall grass or weeds. The Wycoff Corner field that the boys maintained was surrounded by unkempt land. The land was a thicket that not man or beast wanted to travel or invade, except for Moses. He would sit patiently awaiting the opportunity for the command to fetch, for he kept his eye on the ball at all times. When one of the guys would yell "Fetch ball," Moses would take off from the shade of the truck that Joe would drive and enter the land where no man would go and always bring the ball back to the one that gave him the command. All those that played at Wycoff Corner gave Moses the vote of most valuable player, Moses MVP. The rationale was that if Moses didn't bring the ball back, they couldn't continue to play. They only had one ball.

To get to Wycoff Corner, the boys would drive an old farm truck, tractor, rode a bicycle, or walked, unless it was just after a rain, and the road would be too muddy for half a day or more. If it did rain, most everyone knew not to go, or if the party lines were open, they could call to cancel or make new arrangements. Once in a while, only two would show up, and that was perfect because two was all that was needed to play. Wycoff Corner was more central to most of the boys whereas Blue Creek School was farther away and not as handy unless they put together enough players to have a real game, then the school field was used. As the years passed, most of Joe's friends had left Blue Creek School. When all the boys drove cars themselves, not just to play baseball, Wycoff Corner remained the gathering place for Joe and his friends to get away and meet for any and all reasons.

The last year for Joe at Blue Creek School, the Mustangs beat any and all comers. Mrs. Sutherland arranged double the games that year, knowing the potential of their team and wanting exposure for the boys to get them more prepared for their transition to Crescent High School. The games gave little competition to their team because of the higher level of play that Joe, Mike, Paul, and John provided. The four of them overwhelmed, without question, all the teams that they played. Mrs. Sutherland enjoyed the notoriety of the success for her little-known school and relished the opportunity for her young athletes, students, and the families and their participation. Mrs. Sutherland often wondered where the raw talent that Joe possessed would take him and the success it would bring him if channeled properly and always wished the best for him.

CHAPTER 5

Crescent High School

For his first day as a ninth grader at Crescent High School, Joe stood in front of the house waiting for the school bus to arrive with all sorts of thoughts going through his head. He wanted to fit in with everyone, but he had been informed that the transition from the rural schools to the city school was tough on most kids. The rural kids were not used to strangers, and Crescent High School was full of them. Not only the kids from Crescent, but all the other rural schools descended on Crescent High School from all over Logan County and some of Kingfisher County. Some of the rural schools Joe had never heard of before. The rural schools west and south of Crescent, Joe and his classmates were familiar with, but not the rest. To the majority of the students in Crescent High School, Joe and his class-mates from Blue Creek School were unheard of. Crescent schools was a small Oklahoma school system in comparison to other state schools, not the smallest by any means, but not the largest either. Before the rural students were introduced for their ninth-grade year into the Crescent schools, there were about eighty students per class year. After the addition of rural schools, the ninth-grade class grew to about one hundred students. Six rural schools, with three to eight students per school, attended Crescent High School for the next four years. Basketball was the only athletic opportunity for the rural girls, along with the city girls, at Crescent High School. The girls' bas-ketball team at Crescent High School, if not for the rural students, probably would not exist for a lack of interest from the city girls.

The combined talent of all the rural schools along with the numbers, allowed Crescent High School girls' basketball to be a force to contend with in their conference.

For the rural boys, there was a sport that rarely a rural farm boy had played, football. Public school football was introduced in the seventh grade, and the ninth graders from the city already had two years of experience, training and coaching in football that left the rural boys at a huge disadvantage and intimidated most of them to not join the team. Sports in the public schools' systems were conducted on the last hour of the school day, and practice usually carried over the end of last hour at a minimum of an hour and most times an hour and a half. The school buses ran at the end of the last hour of classes, and if you played sports, you had to provide your own transportation home. Most of the rural students lived on farms, and when they arrived home after school, they had chores to do that would take one to two hours most every day according to the weather. The work the children did after school was necessary on most of the farms and not just a duty their parents dreamed up to keep them busy. The greatest part of the rural community had just enough to live and get by. To maintain this in all the little farms and larger ones, all members of the family did their share of the work that was needed to survive.

Joe's situation was different than most of his classmates because the Marshall farm had added land over the years, and the family was blessed to have health and success in their crops and growing herds of cattle. After Joe graduated from the eighth grade at Blue Creek School, Mrs. Sutherland retired, and Jane, who had finished her teaching degree when they lived in St. Louis, took over for Mrs. Sutherland and maintained her teaching position until Blue Creek School was closed down years later. The extra income for Joe's family was always an extra bonus for the family and allowed them benefits that most families that Joe knew did not have. One of these benefits was the ability of the family to provide Joe with a vehicle that would allow him to transport himself back and forth to school. This decision was reached by all the family as it was with Walt twenty years earlier when he was the recipient of an old worn-out farm truck for the same purpose. Willis gave Joe his 1948 F-1 Ford truck that was bought new by him at that time, replacing a 1934 Ford that Willis had bought used in 1936 and had worn out over the war years and a few years after. The 1948 truck had been partially retired a couple of years ago when Willis had the thought that before he completely used it up, it might be an item that Joe would be able to use, and he was right.

Joe knew the old truck well and had helped his dad and grandfather work on it many times and had driven and ridden in it more times than he could count. Even after the truck had been set aside, its use was still valuable for light duty and transportation. Being old enough to have a driver's license was not an issue in the far reaches of the Oklahoman outback farm country. The section line roads were seldom used by anyone else except the people that lived on the farms and hauled crops and livestock. The young kids started driving in the fields, helping their folks and hired hands as soon as they could reach the pedals and look over the dash at the same time or close to it. Joe was not an exception to the rule along with all his friends and acquaintances.

Joe had thought when his grandfather had not sold the old truck when he bought the new one, that it might be his in a couple of years but knew not to ask, just hoping it might work out that way. Many times, he was allowed to drive the old truck to Wycoff Corner to play baseball with his friends. Now it was official, and Joe named his truck Nellie Belle like Roy Rogers named his jeep on the television show. The 1948 F-1 truck was a neat old truck and had been well maintained. When not in the fields working or being driven, it was always parked inside one of the outbuildings out of the sun and weather. Like all the other pieces of equipment on the Marshall farm, the feeling was if weather, time, rust, and sun don't take a toll on the equipment, they should last longer and give longer service without breakdown, making them more productive over time than equipment left out in the elements. Most farmers did not have the luxury of having enough outbuildings to cover their equipment because of cost, or they did not deem it necessary. Even if the Marshall clan was not correct on this item, all the family agreed the machinery looked better and made them feel better working the equipment than having things rusted beyond the point of recognition. This was the case of Joe's truck with the body of the truck being mostly intact and not just a bucket of rust. Over the years, it had been cleaned and waxed on occasion with the green paint still in fairly good shape.

Nellie Belle was a 1948 Green Ford F-2 3/4 ton (5,700 GVWR max.), with a 239 CID 100hp Flathead V8. The shifter was on the floor (Ford didn't move the shifter to the steering column until 1949), and it had an option that was critical to being able to travel in all weather conditions, the Marmon-Herrington all-wheel drive. This made Nellie Belle almost unstoppable on the muddy or snow-packed section line, gravel dirt roads that they had to traveled on most of the time. This was a great asset to Joe because if school was in session and the buses could run, so could he. The fact that Joe was not old enough to have a driver's license and drive was not that unusual for farm country kids. All the kids in the rural area learned to drive in the fields and down section line roads, helping their folks or neighbors in all conditions. The most common thing to drive first was a tractor, not in working the fields, but transporting the machinery from one place to another. Just bringing a tractor or truck to the field being plowed, cut, bailed, or harvested usually saved a trip and made things go smoother and quicker. For Joe, it freed up his family from driving into town twice a day and on weekends, plus to drop off and pick up Joe using a lot more fuel and causing wear and tear on a vehicle.

Joe was on the way to school in Crescent and was headed to pick up Paul who lived one section line to the east. Like Joe, Paul was a farm kid, and his folks owned and maintained a half-section farm and leased another section for grazing their herd. Paul's folks were smart farmers, and his great-grandparents were eighty-niners also. It seemed to Joe that Paul's folks did better than most, but his grandparents had died and were not there to help by giving Paul a truck, as were Joe's. When Joe told Paul that his grandparents gave him the old truck to drive, it was great news because Paul knew he had a ride back and forth with Joe, and this would allow him to be in sports also. Although Joe and Paul got home later in the day, the chores were still there to do, and through the winter months, the chores were usually done in the dark. The young boys never gave it a thought about what their responsibility was to the family and their work on the farm, nor did they complain or ask why they did things that the town kids didn't have to do. They just did it. The unknown factor to Joe and Paul and other farm boys that did the same thing was they toughened up more with the physical work added to their day after the workouts at school. From the ninth grade on, the boys got stronger and leaner than most, just from the fact they did a lot more than the city athletes.

Not until his grandparents gave him the truck did Joe ask if it would be all right to go out for football. Walt and Jane did not object and reminded Joe that his work on the farm would still need to be done, and maintaining good grades was most important, and Joe agreed with them. Walt also discussed with Joe the understanding that once he started something and committed to it, to be sure and weigh out the obligation for the season, to finish it, and not quit until that obligation was complete, which Joe understood. Joe discussed with Paul about playing football, and Paul agreed that if Joe would go out, so would he if his parents agreed, which they did.

Joe in the ninth grade was 5'11" tall and weighed one hundred forty-five pounds and could have been the fastest athlete in the entire Crescent school system, let alone the ninth grade. Paul was always big and quick on his feet at 6'1" and one hundred and seventy pounds. There were only two kids in the whole school taller, no matter what their age. The seventh, eighth, and ninth all played together and shared the same locker room but were separated from the high school athletes. The sophomores, juniors, and seniors all practiced at the high school practice field, and their locker room was at the high school football stadium.

Not many of the rural students went out for football strictly because it was intimidating to kids that had never played organized football and had little or no experience in playing football. Unlike in basketball and baseball, a lot of them knew about the games and how to play. They were immediately comfortable on the court and entered the school population with less harassment than most of the other rural kids. Acceptance for the first few weeks with the town kids was a little harsh in one or two cases a year, but for the most part, any hazing disappeared after the first two weeks. In most cases, the rural students would befriend each other first because of the things they had in common, and after a while, all the students matriculated, and the initiation as it were was over. Some of the rural schools had a gym or something that resembled a gym, and if they had a facility, the students, boys and girls, played basketball all the time from the first grade through the eighth, literal gym rats. Some of these gym-rat rural kids could play a level of basketball that a Crescent Junior High city kid had not yet experienced or seen that level of talent before. The good rural school basketball players were accepted faster than all the rest because of what their talent would add to the school team.

The most difficult program for a rural kid to start was ninth-grade football. The initiation was by far the harshest of all to break into. First thing, lack of playing experience, the second, the rural kids had not gone through the rite of passage, two-a-days for the upcoming season. Most of the other kids had the experience of playing in their seventh and eighth grade years, and all the boys on the ninth-grade roster at the time of the first day of school had just completed the dreaded summer practices. From all the six different rural schools that descended on the Crescent Junior High ninth-grade class, there were only seven boys that made the decision to go out for football, including Paul and Joe.

Those seven boys all related to each other because of their common background and the uncertainty of what they were getting involved in. One of the common things they all possessed was their toughness. Many hours in the fields and the long summer workdays that farm life demanded seasoned these kids with the physical ability to do whatever the coaches asked them to do, no matter what the temperature was or the weather conditions. It didn't take long for the rural boys to show the others what they were made of, and they were there to compete to play and not sit on the bench. Even though Joe and Paul did not know the other five rural boys, when the occasion did arise where a town kid wanted to haze or pick on a rural kid, automatically, the rural boys would gather to protect their own, and it would be seven of them to pick on not just one. Quick to realize, the Crescent city boys would have to take on seven tough kids, not just one. The hazing ended, and they all became a team.

Paul was put on the line, playing tackle on offense and defense; he caught on fast, learning his responsibilities and plays and became a starter on the first team. Joe was placed in the halfback position when the coaches saw his speed and natural athletic ability. The more comfortable Joe became with the game and understood how the plays in football developed, he could utilize his speed to outrun most defenders and gain yards each time he touched the ball. Joe got to start with the first team on the third game of the season and became the most productive halfback in Crescent Junior High history. Joe also demonstrated his ability to throw the football, and as soon as he was comfortable in his halfback position, the coaches started working Joe into a quarterback position during the weekly practices. When the season was half over, with the game well in hand with a comfortable lead, the coaches would get Joe in the game as a third team quarterback to give him some game experience in an effort to groom him as a backup quarterback. Joe made it look easy and really enjoyed the quarterback position and the control of the game that a quarterback had and the difference he could make while playing that position.

The ninth-grade year where Crescent School played in an athletic conference, Joe had his first opportunity to play against many other athletes from ten different schools from all over four different counties. It was at this time that Joe realized he possessed a talent that most of the other athletes he encountered did not have. This physical and athletic difference made Joe want to develop his talents even more and compete as much as was possible in as many sports as he could. Joe's passion was competition in athletics, but his love was still baseball.

Crescent Junior High won all their games that year and set a school record for most wins. Joe and Paul were no longer Mustangs from Blue Creek School; they were now known as Crescent Tigers. As football season finished, basketball season was already underway where most of the basketball team was made up from the football players. In a small Oklahoma school of one hundred students per class, most of the athletes play all sports to make the teams large enough to compete. It was not unusual for seven to ten boys to play in all four sports offered at Crescent: football, basketball, baseball, and track. All the teams in the conference had the same situation, and it made the competition fairly equal. Joe made all the teams and made a difference in their win/loss success. Joe was successful in basketball, track, and baseball, but in baseball, his talent was far in excess of any ninth-grade player in Crescent or in the teams that made up the conference.

The Crescent High School baseball coach caught wind of Joe and was told that he could play a level of baseball that exceeded most of his peers. Coach Yost thought he would take a look at Joe during a home game when he was dazzling everyone while playing in his first year on the ninth-grade football team.

Coach Yost was the high school line coach and the Crescent High School head baseball coach. A hardline WWII Marine who served in the South Pacific with the Third Marine Division, he was feared by the players, students, administration, parents, fans, and the opposing teams. Coach Yost came by his hardness naturally from his dad, a worker in the steel mills in Pittsburg, Pennsylvania, from there to playing football for Oklahoma A&M and then to the United States Marine Corps when WWII started. When the war ended, Coach Yost finished his bachelor's degree in education at Oklahoma A&M and began coaching football as a career. About the only person that did not have the fear that most felt was the head football coach, Coach Smith, who had a similar background as Coach Yost. The only difference was that Coach Smith took a backstage to Coach Yost when it came to discipline because Coach Smith informally appointed Coach Yost as the enforcer while Coach Jensen played the role of the peacemaker, a duo play they both got the maximum out of with each and every player that came their way.

CHAPTER 6

Ninth-Grade Baseball

Yost was a real competitor, and he had been exposed to and competed with high levels of gifted athletes at Oklahoma A&M. While playing intramural sports in the Marine Corps, he had also encountered great athletes that had skill levels that most humans did not have. The two most common skills of these gifted athletes that Coach Yost had observed were speed and quickness of their hands and feet. As Coach Yost studied Joe, even at this young age, he noticed these factors immediately. Once Coach Yost saw Joe take the handoff on an end-around play, and at the moment the defensive end made a play to tackle Joe, at that very moment, Joe turned on the afterburners and left the would-be tackler, grabbing thin air, and into the end zone went Joe. After that, Coach Yost couldn't take his eyes off Joe. Coach Yost was there looking for an extra man out of the ninth-grade class to fill out his baseball team roster because of a small sophomore and junior class. This left the team a little weak in having enough players to build a lineup with backups and enough pitchers to rotate through the games. Having a ninth-grader play with the high school was not unheard of but rarely done because of the great disparity of athletic ability that existed between the older and younger players. Most of the time, it was hard enough for a sophomore to compete with juniors and seniors, but a freshman normally really stretched the physical maturity and strength difference. A freshman most of the time lacked the maturity to be at a competitive level with two- and three-year-older players.

After seeing Joe play, the next day, Coach Yost was on the phone calling people that could give him a little insight about Joe and what kind of person he was. Coach Yost was trying to find out if Joe was mature enough to play one year up on the high school baseball team. Coach Yost wanted somebody to tell him that Joe had the maturity to handle the level of play and would be all right around the older players. If Coach Yost could confirm Joe's maturity and ability on the baseball field, he would offer him the chance, if Joe wanted to, to play with the high school team. The first to get a call was the ninth-grade head coach Sam Webb. Coach Webb told Coach Yost that Joe was older than his years, tough as nails, and had speed that he had never witnessed or been able to coach in all his life. Coach Webb also told Coach Yost that Joe also had an unusual gift for an athlete his age, sports smarts. Coach Webb explained how Joe could fit together in his head almost immediately all the other position assignments along with his assignments and could see the strength and weakness of the defensive set and would know what play to run against it for the most yardages. Coach Webb told Coach Yost that Joe Marshall had an understanding of the game that exceeded veterans of a decade of involvement. This was more than Coach Yost expected to hear and became excited to make his next phone call. Coach Yost's next phone call was to a longtime friend, Joe's Blue Creek School teacher, Mrs. Sutherland. Not only a longtime friend, Mrs. Sutherland was an educator that Coach Yost had great respect for and knew that he would receive a detailed objective report on Joe that he could count on.

When Mrs. Sutherland answered the phone and after Coach Yost identified himself, Mrs. Sutherland inquired why it took so long for her to get a call from him about Joe. Coach Yost explained that Coach Sam Webb was his first contact and did not realize until that phone call that Joe was a Blue Creek School product, but he was glad that Mrs. Sutherland was part of Joe's history and one that Joe would always be proud to reflect back on. Coach Yost had many students that excelled academically and as athletes from Blue Creek School and knew the care that the teaching team of Sutherland and Lemon took in developing young adults to succeed and not to fail, and most succeeded in all aspects of their lives. Mrs. Sutherland began to explain to Coach Yost that Joe had no equal in all her past and present students. Mrs. Sutherland felt like Joe could attain any level of any discipline that she knew of in academics, sports, or both. She could not think of any limit that he could not achieve. Mrs. Sutherland told Coach Yost he had better smarten up and handle this youngster with regard to guidance and goal setting because Joe only knows one way to train and learn, and that is all out, all the time, nothing held back. Mrs. Sutherland, with great respect for Coach Yost, explained it very simply, not to let himself inhibit or get in Joe's way. He needed no prodding, just guidance.

It was at the moment after the conversation with Mrs. Sutherland that Coach Yost wanted to visit with Joe. Coach Yost waited until the end of the ninth-grade football season to visit with Joe. The ninth-grade season ended two weeks before the senior high season, and this gave Coach Yost, with the permission of Coach Smith, an opportunity to talk to Joe with his ninth-grade Coach Webb, to discuss the possibility of Joe joining the senior high team for the last two games of the high school season and maybe more games if they made it into the playoffs. Coach Webb agreed to letting Joe have the opportunity if he so desired. All the coaches knew that the difference between ninth grade and senior athletes was immense, and there was the danger of Joe getting hurt during practice or in a game if he was allowed to play. When asked, Joe accepted the challenge immediately, based on his parents' approval.

When Joe arrived home that evening, it was already dark, which was normal, and supper was on the table. Willis, Jane, Juanetta were at the table, and Moses was under the table, patiently waiting for scraps, when old Nellie Belle pulled up, and Joe came through the door. Joe waited for supper to get underway and Moses to get his first treat from the table from Willis before he brought up the subject of him playing a couple more weeks of football. Everyone knew the last ninth-grade game had been played, and all present asked if the season or practice sessions had been extended. Joe then explained about the conversations with the coaches and the offer to play and practice with the varsity till the end of the season. With that out on the table, everyone got quiet and waited until Walt spoke up before anyone else made a comment. Walt asked Joe what his thoughts were about this opportunity, and Joe simply said he would like to try it. Walt wondered about the size of the older players compared with Joe's and if that could be a little dangerous. Joe wanted clarity from his dad, dangerous to them or him. Everyone at the table laughed at the comment, and Walt agreed to let Joe try his hand with the older players.

That Monday came around really fast for Joe, and he could hardly think of anything else all weekend and throughout his classes on Monday. The next to last hour finished, and Joe had all his equipment in Nellie Belle waiting to take him to the high school football locker room. By this time, Joe was friends with all the ninth graders on the football team. The fact that he would have an opportunity to practice with the varsity was next to unbelievable to all of them. When Joe got to Nellie Belle, the truck was loaded with his football teammates while Paul had dibs on riding shotgun. With four in the front seat and eight in the truck bed, another teammate driving had six, three had motorcycles with a passenger on the back that accounted for the entire ninth grade team going to see Joe at his first senior high practice.

When they arrived at the locker room, it was busy with the high school team hustling around to get on the field before the half hour. The high school locker room was next to the high school and the football field, whereas Joe had to drive six blocks to get there. He was already running behind the other players when he and his unofficial entourage all walked into the dressing room. No one knew what to think about all the visitors, and when Coach Yost came out of his office ready to go to the practice field, he stopped abruptly and asked what in Sam Hill was going on with the gaggle of kids invading his locker room. Joe and all the others stood like deer in headlights until Coach Yost told them, except for Joe, to get the H out and go to the practice field if they wanted to hang around. Coach Yost asked Joe if the others were his personal cheering squad to which Joe replied, "Yes, sir, they are." Coach Yost explained to Joe he better be on the practice field on time and left to get the practice started. Joe was moving as fast as he could to get dressed out and get on the field when he looked up to see Coach Smith, the head coach, standing there looking at Joe. As Joe was fumbling around, obvious to Coach Smith he was getting dressed as fast as he could, Smith explained to Joe to take his time and get buttoned up good and tight because the practice did not start until he got on the field. With that, Coach Smith also said if Joe was in front of him as they approached the field, he would be on time, and so that was the way they left the locker room, Joe and behind him Coach Smith. As Joe reached the other players, the captain of the team yelled out to circle up to do warm-ups and calisthenics. Joe had gained an inch and fifteen pounds since the start of school and the ninth-grade football season. He did not appear to be that much smaller than all the rest. In fact, he was larger than most. As Paul and his friends watched with anticipation from the sidelines, they would watch every move of Joe and the other players. In each of their minds, they were thinking that next year in August, they would be on the same field ready to start two-a-days and their varsity years.

After some warm-ups, the team separated into the backs and linemen, and Joe was now the center of attraction among the backs. None of them would say anything to Joe and instead just walked past him when moving about while they were doing drills; Joe would get the shoulder bump as they passed. Joe was all right with that because he knew he was the new guy, and he probably was a threat to them and their playing time. Joe kept up with all of them while they went through the drills, which were the same ones they did in the ninth-grade practices. The first thing Joe noticed was the greater agility and speed the older players had compared with his ninth-grade teammates. Joe was hoping as the team came together to scrimmage, that he would get a chance to run a play and/or carry the ball.

Most of the practice went by as Joe waited for an opportunity to carry the ball, and for a moment, he thought that the first day might pass, and he would have to wait for another day to see what he could do if handed the ball. At that very instant, Coach Smith yelled Marshall, and Joe jumped into the huddle like a bolt of lightning had struck a spot right next to where he was standing. Coach Smith leaned into the huddle and told the quarterback to hand off the ball to Joe on an end-around running play. Joe had run the same play with the ninth-grade team and knew exactly what to do. As the quarterback took the snap and turned to hand Joe the ball, Joe nearly left his position before he took the handoff. A split second passed, which seemed to Joe as a whole minute, before he secured the ball enough to run, and the defense was already coming through the line. Joe ran a little deep into the backfield to avoid the fast-approaching defensive tackle and guard, and that was when his speed kicked in more than he had ever experienced before. He rounded the end of the line and was running down the sideline as the defensive backs were taking an angle of pursuit to overtake Joe. At the moment he would be tackled, Joe went against the grain, and the would-be tacklers overran him. He ran into a clear space until Coach Smith blew his whistle to end the play. Players and coaches thought it was a fluke and could not take in the speed that Joe had just displayed, all except his ninth-grade teammates standing on the sideline at the moment Joe broke the run into the clear. They started yelling, screaming, and cheering Joe on. They clearly understood what had just happened and knew without a doubt it was all Joe and no fluke.

Coach Smith and Coach Yost thought that play would be the last of practice for that day, but now they wanted to know what Joe could do with another carry. Again, Joe carried the ball with a different play, but the same results ensued. By this time, Paul and Joe's other teammates who made the trip were going nuts on the sideline with excitement for Joe's success. Because of a lack of good athletes in the smaller schools, most of the first team players played both ways, offense, and when the ball exchanged hands, then played defense. That meant when Joe ran the ball, the first team offense was blocking against the second team defense. After Joe ran three plays into the open with Coach Smith blowing his whistle to end the play, Coach Smith and Coach Yost decided to let Joe run the ball on the same plays, but now with the second team defense playing as second team offense. The big problem now for Joe, everyone on the field knew the three plays that he would run. As Joe got the handoff, this time for an end-around run, the handoff from the quarterback was smooth and clean, and he was at full speed on his second step and made it around the end but now with an ever-faster speed that took him straight down the sideline, outrunning the angle of pursuit of the first team defensive backs into the clear, and Coach Smith blew his whistle to end the play.

The ninth-grade teammates and Paul did not yell and scream for Joe on that play. They just stood there with their mouths agape in disbelief at what they had just witnessed for the first time. They had seen Joe's speed but not what he just showed on that play. When Joe broke away and ran the ball unopposed into a clear field, Coach Smith blew the whistle and signaled to Coach Yost to start the wind sprints and end the practice. After the boys had showered and left the locker room, Coach Smith and Coach Yost stayed behind to discuss what had just happened on the practice field, and they still could not believe what they had seen. Coach Smith and Coach Yost were not reared in the Crescent area, but both of them knew of Joe's dad Walt and that he had played professional baseball and was a great athlete in high school and after the war. Anyone they would talk to would tell them what salt of the earth the Marshall family was, and that they were well established in the community as being an honest, hardworking, and a smart business family that lived by their word.

The football season ended, and Joe was given the chance to play in the Friday night game as a substitute which allowed the senior players their playing time in their senior year. Joe dazzled the crowds by scoring touchdowns and gaining as many yards per carry as any player in Crescent High School history. The night after the last game of the season, Coach Yost pondered what kind of baseball player Joe was. He had heard from many parents who had seen Joe play the rural school teams and told of his batting and fielding ability, but against what type of opponents was Yost's question in his head. Then he thought of Joe's exploits on the football field and his speed. At that moment, he could hardly think of anything else and could not wait till baseball season rolled along.

Winter did not allow many days outside because of the cold and wet conditions, so Joe played basketball to have something to do and stay in shape. Joe again, because of his speed, did very well in any athletic endeavor that he participated in. Basketball, like football, was not where his true desire laid. Joe added a dimension to the basketball team that made them successful as in football, but this was all in anticipation of the start of baseball season. Coach Yost had Joe show up on the first baseball practice of the season. The Crescent School did not have a ninth-grade school sponsored baseball program, so if Joe was going to play baseball his first year at Crescent School, he would need to make the high school varsity team. Coming out to play with the high school baseball program was much easier for the older players to accept Joe because most of them were also the high school football players, and Joe had gained their respect. When Joe stepped on the field, the players wanted to see if Joe had the baseball magic that he had on the gridiron. As the first practice got under-way, all eyes were on Joe. There was a greater interest in the town and school about the first practice of the season than Coach Yost had ever seen before. The bleachers were nearly full, and that was an accomplishment that rarely happened even in a winning season during a scheduled game. Coach Yost knew the word had traveled around about this ninth grader who made the last two games of the football season exciting and filled the stands, which was also a rare occasion in Crescent High School and especially on an away game. Now Joe had engaged the town and school with anticipation about seeing what some would call a phenom athlete.

As practice progressed, Coach Yost called Joe over from some warm-up drills and told him to join the other players in the outfield to take some fly ball outfield practice. Coach Yost was ready to see what skill level Joe had. At first, Coach Yost placed the ball to their positions and then started hitting shallow fly balls then deeper. Joe moved up and back with ease and snagged every ball. Then man by man in the outfield, Yost moved the ball a little farther from each man's position, making them hustle to make the catch. As each fly ball became harder to reach, the ball would hit the ground beyond the player's ability to catch the ball, except for Joe. As Coach Yost pushed the ball farther and farther away, Joe was able to chase every one down and make a successful catch. Yost finally pushed the ball until in a game Joe would be running over the other outfielder's posi-tion to make a catch, and at that point, Yost motioned to Joe to come in. Coach Yost wanted Joe to start the rotation for batting practice and told his batting practice pitcher to toe the mound.

Coach Yost was eager to see if Joe could handle the bat as well as he could field the ball. Joe was right-handed and stepped up to the plate, batting right just as Coach Yost thought he would. He told Joe to hit away on any pitch he could connect without overdoing it. The batting practice pitcher placed a controlled ball in the strike zone with a little speed, a pitch Joe could see all the way to the end of his bat. Joe connected with a solid hit and the sound that everyone recognized as a long fly ball, and that it was flying over the right center field fence. Watching the ball take flight, Coach Yost's initial thought was how effortless Joe's swing seemed to be to hit a ball that far. The next half-dozen pitches took the same path as the first. At this point, Coach Yost approached Joe and asked if he could bat left as well as he did right, and Joe's reply was to simply step to the other side of the plate to set up for the next pitch. This time was the same as the first six pitches, out of the park close to center field. All eyes were on Joe by this time, and Coach Yost wanted to see more from Joe. Yost stepped over to the batting cage, asked Joe to move the ball around by starting to hit the ball to the left field regardless of where the pitch was thrown. Joe nodded his head in agreement, and the next six pitches were hit to left field. Then Coach Yost directed Joe to hit the next round to center and after that, to right. Coach Yost then asked Joe to bat right and take a couple of pitches to right, center, and left, and Joe did as suggested. After that first practice, Joe had earned a respect from all on the field, coaches and players and those in the stands. No one was disappointed.

After Coach Yost ended practice that day, he asked Joe to stay to talk some things over concerning Joe's performance in practice. Coach Yost told Joe that he was humbled at practice that day by Joe's ability, and his hopes were that he could bring his coaching talents up to a level that would equal or at least not hinder Joe's growth and potential. Joe again just nodded because he realized the sincerity that Coach Yost was expressing to him. He replied to Yost that he would give him 100 percent of his focus and ability every time he stepped on the field, no questions asked. Before leaving Coach Yost, Joe asked if it would be all right for him to request a favor. Yost agreed, and Joe pointed to his truck, and in the front seat was Paul waiting on Joe to finish, so he could get a ride home. Joe told Coach Yost about his friend, and that he would be here every day with Joe sitting in the stands or in the truck because Joe was Paul's ride home. Joe wanted to know if Yost would allow Paul, also a ninth grader, to try out for the team. Ninth-grade athletes could only come out for varsity if asked by the coaching staff. Coach Yost asked Joe what his last name was and if he was any good. Joe replied Paul's last name was Pixley, and he could play shortstop or second base as good as Joe had seen. Coach Yost stared at Joe for a moment and said he did not have to try out, to just have Paul on the field tomorrow ready for practice. Joe's recommendation was good enough for him. What Coach Yost did not tell Joe was that he was glad Joe had someone with him his own age and a person with him each day as he traveled the long ride back and forth from home to school and back again.

CHAPTER 7

Joe's First Season of Varsity Baseball

B aseball was a true love for Joe, and other sports seemed to be a means to an end. Joe knew he had to condition his body on a year-round basis, which other sports gave him the opportunity to do. Now Joe was playing structured baseball with structured practices, not just a workout between him and his dad, but competition with which he could hone his game. The scheduled games with other high schools also provided him with comparisons of his skills with those skills of others and identify where he needed improvement. Walt was the best influence on Joe for the development of his game. Walt knew from his own experience, learned and natural, what Joe needed to work on and what would come with time and physical maturity. If there was one element of Joe's game that he did not possess as a ninth grader, it was what nature would add over time, bigger muscles and strength that would come with age.

The first game of the season was an away game with a larger school, the Guthrie Blue Jays. The season opener for the surrounding high schools was usually a sacrificial lamb for a small school to play a larger school, and such was the case for Crescent. The first game for Crescent High School was always with Guthrie High School at Squires Field. The game was always a rout for Guthrie but usually worked as a barometer for Crescent. If Crescent stayed in the game and put runs on the scoreboard, it normally meant a good season for Crescent without concerns on how lopsided the game turned out. Crescent rarely had a balanced team offensively and defensively. Because of the few players that the population of the high school supplied, they might have good pitching/fielding one year with weak hitting and the next year strong hitting and weak pitching/fielding. This could be the season that had good pitching and fielding. From graduation last year, the two above-average hitters were missing from this team. Joe was an unknown quality, how he would do with stronger pitchers than the ones he practiced with.

To make things worse, this home opener, compared to other years, had two Guthrie seniors that had gone through a huge growth spurt since last season and now were one and two in their pitching rotation. In the game last year, played at the same time of the season, the Blue Jays held Crescent to one run and a 14–1 loss. Although the Crescent Tigers were not happy with that outcome, their season worked out to be better than expected, winning over half their games.

The weather could not have been more perfect for the start of the baseball season, when at three o'clock in the afternoon on March 2, the sky was clear and brilliant blue, sixty-five degrees with just a hint of a breeze out of the north. Coach Yost noticed there was a larger crowd than normally traveled with the team from Crescent. They were in the bleachers to see the first game of the season, and the coach hoped they would not be disappointed on their ride home. Coach Yost had placed Joe batting fourth in the batting rotation because he had proved himself to be the best hitter on the team. From the start of the season through all practice sessions, Paul Pixley had proved himself to Coach Yost that he was the player Joe had described. Coach Yost had placed Pixley on third base because of his strong arm and quickness and second in the batting order.

With the excitement building, the Tigers batted first as a visiting team. With one out, Pixley was at bat, and a 3–2 count, he hit a ground ball down the left baseline just out of reach of the third baseman for a single. The next batter struck out, bringing Joe to the plate with Pixley on first and two outs. The senior Blue Jay pitcher had heard about the freshman from Crescent and had considered it nothing but hype because in his mind, nobody could be that good and be a freshman. With that in his head, he decided to show Joe his stuff and burn a fastball right by him, watching as it flew over the plate into the catcher's mitt or seeing Joe as he takes a big swing and hitting nothing but air. Surprisingly, Joe was extremely calm and had not considered anything about the day, him being a freshman, his performance, or anything else except the chance he had to play ball at this very moment in time. As Joe stepped into the batter's box, swung his bat to relax, looked at the pitcher, and got into his stance, the first pitch was on its way. Joe took a full swing, never feeling the impact of the ball on the bat, but hearing the collision, and as he took off for first base looking a little to his left, seeing the ball going over the fence in right center field. The Crescent fans were wild with excitement when Joe hit the ball out of the park, and the crowd could hardly contain themselves from yelling as loud as they could. As Joe started to round the bases, just before he got to the first base bag, he noticed his family in the bleachers and caught a look at his dad with a big smile on his face and giving Joe a thumbs-up. Before Joe had made his trip around the bases, he had a feeling that his memory of this event would always be etched in his mind, and he was correct. As the years passed, Joe would often recall this picture in his memory with great fondness.

That eventful day for the Crescent High School baseball and Joe Marshall didn't turn out to be a victory on the scoreboard, but a victory in the hearts of the Tiger fans and players. The final score was 3–2 in favor of the Blue Jays, and Joe had three hits and a walk for four at bats. It came out to be the closet game in the school's history, and Joe faced their best pitchers without being struck out. At the end of the day, everyone in the town knew that this was going to be a great year for their high school baseball team, and with great anticipation, they were looking forward to the next game on the schedule.

Joe's first high school baseball season worked out to be one of the best ever. Joe's play inspired the team to do better and want to win. As the weeks passed, Joe grew stronger, and he learned to play with more intensity, and his teammates followed suit in intensity and focus. The year finished with the Tigers winning their conference and going to the quarterfinals in the state playoffs. The Tigers finished the season twenty-two wins and three losses, with Joe batting a phenomenal .632 average, the highest season batting average that any and all could ever remember. The large schools always received the most ink in the newspapers. Difficult to get even weekly notice of a small school's season, no matter how successful it was, Joe had articles in both the Tulsa and Oklahoma City papers nearly twice a week giving praise to this young kid's ability and his accomplishments. Joe listened to his dad to not pay any attention to what the papers had to say about him good or bad. Walt explained to Joe that the praise and popularity could turn on a dime to scorn and ridicule; to take stock in oneself stays with you while praise from others can be taken away in a mere moment.

At the end of the baseball season, a huge interest in the baseball program grew at Crescent High School and in the city of Crescent. The great season led to improvements being started on the baseball field and stadium, and donations from individuals and community business provided money for equipment and new uniforms. The high school team's success also stimulated the baseball programs in the rural communities and the town's summer youth teams. Baseball in Crescent and the surrounding area had a new enthusiasm because of one player making a difference and being a driving force to winning instead of losing. Next year's baseball season was the talk of the town and the school. The high school baseball season brought a close community even closer together. The talk of the town centered on Joe Marshall and his exploits on the baseball diamond and what another year of growth, physically and mentally, would bring to his game and the success of the team.

The school year ended with the junior/senior prom and graduation. The graduation included four of the baseball team's starters and positions that would be hard to fill with upcoming classes. There were enough underclassmen to fill the gaps, but the talent of two- and three-year starters always left a gap in experience.

The summer offered Legion baseball, and nearly all the high school team participated and played through most of the summer in this program. Legion ball provided countywide participation for the players, and each had to earn his position on the team. The teams in the different Legion programs provided a higher level of skilled play-ers and more intense competition than high school ball. Joe had to do work on the farm nearly every day during the summer. A day that included a practice or a game for Joe started before sunrise and usu-ally continued into the night. Even after a game, Joe might need to help Walt finish a repair or chore that needed to be done before the start of the next day. Weather and time were a blessing and a curse for farm life. There existed a time, a window, to get a job done, and when that time had passed, the opportunity to complete the task at hand passed also. Work in the fields or working the herd, keeping the farm machinery working, and daily chores in the summertime was in itself a full-time job without distractions. The entire family sup-ported Joe's participation in the Legion baseball, and they all pitched in to finish the daily work when it extended the day into the night. Game day was a great event in the Marshall family even if it meant hustling around and starting earlier than normal to attend a game. It was great fun to watch Joe play, and game day broke up the daily routine which made the workday pass faster than normal.

Legion baseball came to a close with Joe being more successful than his first year of high school ball. The baseball community of the surrounding counties now knew about Joe Marshall and how tal-ented he was. With each and every new team that Joe played against, his notoriety preceded him. Joe Marshall was quickly on his way of becoming a young superstar legend in Logan County, Oklahoma.

CHAPTER 8

Joe's Sophomore Year

The sophomore year was near. When summer practice and two-a-day drills started for football, Nellie Belle would make the rounds on Joe's way to school. With the addition of Paul in the front seat, three more Blue Creek School graduates were in the truck heading for Crescent so that they too could play football as ninth graders. Joe would make an additional stop to drop off and pick up the younger kids before and after his and Paul's practice. The ninth graders in Crescent played and practiced at separate facilities, and Joe did not mind going out of his way to help anyone who wanted to play football or any other sport. All the students at Blue Creek School knew of Joe Marshall, from the first grade to the eight. Joe was now a local hero to the little two-room schools throughout the district that sent their students, after eighth grade graduations, to the Crescent school system to complete their secondary education.

Joe and Paul went to the dressing room for the first summer practice, expecting a little hazing from the seniors, but were surprised when his teammates from the two weeks last year and the baseball teammates from last year were all smiles as they came up to Paul and introduced themselves. The atmosphere was not hostile for the underclassmen; it was extremely friendly, leaving all the sophomores with an air of acceptance and an immediate feeling of being a part of the team. Joe had brought to the team last year a new level of competition that had not been experienced before his arrival. With Joe in the arsenal of running backs on the team, it meant there was a possibility for a great season on the horizon, and all the upperclass-men knew that for a fact. As class leaders, the seniors had a meeting before the summer practices had started and decided not to start any hazing of lower classmen and not give the country kids extra grief as the season started. The senior members wanted the season to start on a positive note, not isolating anyone for any reason. The seniors had voted to have Ronnie Johnson be a spokesman for the senior players to tell everyone that went out and stuck it out for the summer practice and two-a-days would be a valuable part of the team. That everyone would be able to make a contribution to the team. They would all work together to make a difference for the team to become a contender for the state championship. Ronnie assured the juniors and sophomores that if any one of them needed help in anything, the whole team would be there to give assistance and support. As Ronnie continued, he wanted all the players to know that this team was going to be compared to a chain and would be built by making the least and most insignificant part as strong as possible, for the chain is only as strong as its weakest link. So the weakest link had to be strong, and it would be made strong with the help of the entire team. Ronnie let the underclassmen know that the team had to develop from the least to the most to have a winning season.

Joe admired the senior class players and saw in them a commit-ment that in his thinking was the cornerstone to making a good team great. He liked the fact that all were included from the start without ill will or bad feelings between the older players and the youngest. Joe also knew in his heart that everyone on the team had to play to his absolute potential, challenging each other to develop a focus that was based on the team playing as a unit taking on all challengers.

Joe, from the first practice on, had a different feeling from the year before with his teammates and coaches. From the very first scrimmage, there was a concentration from all on the field to get everything out of a practice and more if possible. There was no com-plaining or asking why something had to be done that the coaches asked for. If one of the team would start talking negative, two or three of his teammates would go over and discuss the situation quickly and let it be known that now was the time to pay attention, and whatever the problem was at that moment would be discussed after the practice, and everyone on the team would help to get it resolved as soon as possible. Full concentration and focus seemed to be demanded by all the players during the entire practice, and anything else would have to wait until after practice.

This new attitude was recognized by the coaches within the first ten minutes of scrimmage. Coach Smith and Coach Yost noticed the lack of mental errors when the plays were being run, and they could tell that it was an all-out effort on every practice play that was run. Both coaches accomplished so much more than they expected the first day that the practice plan was accomplished twenty minutes early. When Smith and Yost realized they had accomplished their goals for the first practice session, Coach Yost blew his whistle for the team to form a line and start running wind sprints to end the practice.

The first practice was indicative for the entire football season. With Joe leading the way as a running back, the Crescent Tigers went undefeated and were state champions for the first time in school history. Paul and Joe were awarded all-conference honors, and Ronnie "Toe Joe" Johnson was picked for "all state" honors, again a first for Crescent High School football. Ronnie Johnson had it right at the first of the year when he could see a great season, if everyone bought in and gave their all, in an effort to reach the ultimate goal, win them all. Joe savored his sophomore football season and learned that when even the least talented person on a team goes all out on every play at every practice, it sets a tone to achieve, which infects the thoughts of all the teammates, even the most talented, to reach higher and accomplish more than they could even dream was possible.

With the football season ending three weeks later than normal, Joe and a few others on the football team went directly into the basketball season. The state title football game was on a Saturday night, and the first basketball game was on the following Friday night. The football players that also played basketball missed the first two weeks of basketball practice and a scrimmage game. Coming into the season late was not a problem for the members of the team that did not play football, nor was it a problem for Coach Beach, the basketball coach. All the students, teachers, administration, and the people of

Crescent followed the success of the football team, and the excitement of winning all the games of the season made all the football team local celebrities, and they could hardly do any wrong.

Coach Beach was also a big football fan and could not be happier that part of his basketball team was not at his practices but would soon be. Coach Beach saw the difference in support and enthusiasm from the community and school from the success of the football team and hoped that it would carry over into his basketball program. When Joe played with the high school team for the last two games of his ninth-grade season, Coach Beach watched the athletic ability that Joe displayed. Like Coach Smith and Yost, Coach Beach also knew Mrs. Sutherland from Blue Creek School and knew to call her and find out about this incredibly talented young man. Coach Beach took great interest in Joe's ninth grade basketball season, not missing a single game and could hardly wait until he had Joe on the high school basketball court playing for him.

Because of Joe's speed and his ever-increasing physical size and strength that was developing naturally as he aged and grew, Joe was well above average on the basketball court. The ability that Joe had was not all physical; it was also in his presence. When Joe walked into a room, it felt more like twenty people walked in. He just seemed bigger than life. Joe was smart, aware of his surroundings, and had a natural humbleness that drew people to him who couldn't get enough of his company at any one time. When after a rain, you feel a slight breeze against your face, and as you inhale, you feel and smell a sweet fragrance, you want to immediately exhale so you can experience the feeling again. That was the way people felt with Joe.

With Coach Beach as well as other coaches and players, they did not resent Joe's popularity or his success; his association gave others a confidence that their desires and goals could become reality.

Basketball season was similar to football season, with great success and a winning season that went deep into the playoffs. Basketball was always good at Crescent High School because of the smaller schools that supplied all the extra talent. The most prevalent game of the two-room schools was basketball. The boys and girls started playing in the first grade and continued to the eighth grade. At home and school, summer, fall, and spring, the farm kids played basketball. Coach Beach had his pick of talent and always had a strong bench that was full of younger players that could hardly wait their turn to take the court. Joe was talented at basketball, but his true love was always baseball.

Like any great athlete, Joe played 100 percent at any sport that he participated in, but in baseball, it came so naturally, it was like second nature, and improvement came without effort. What Joe picked up from other players and coaches about technique or skill improvement in football or basketball, he could quickly apply to his game and abilities with little or no effort. In baseball, with Walt as his coach, there were very few around Crescent that had something to share that would improve Joe's game. Coach Yost knew immediately that Walt had done a great job in being Joe's mentor in developing skill and knowledge about baseball. Not very many players had a former professional to coach them over the years with a major league level of expertise that Walt had. Walt not only could play the game, he knew how to coach and develop players. Walt also shared the strategies of the game with Joe throughout his lifetime, which in essence filled in all the blanks about the game for Joe.

As another successful basketball season came to a close, the town and school started buzzing about the upcoming baseball season. The same senior group that understood how important it was in football to develop the entire team from the least talented to the most took the lead from the football team and at the start of the season had a team meeting. This team meeting brought the baseball team together with a total commitment that included everyone that made the team. The team all agreed that anyone who needed help would get it from another member of the team or the coaching staff. It was agreed that there would be no exclusion of any players that made the team, and that any and all effort would be toward building a winning team and successful season.

The preseason opener with Guthrie would be the telltale sign as to how the Tigers' season would develop. Ronnie Johnson played catcher, and Pixley was on third, and a kid, Henry Bockus, who came from Lone Elm, a two-room school, to Crescent at the same time Joe did, was a pitcher. Ronnie was a great catcher and had a tremendous arm along with being a better-than-average hitter. Mi, standing at six foot one inch, a sophomore like Joe, took on a growth spurt over the last year and had added a lot of strength and muscle to an already-tall frame, which added speed that was lacking the year before. Now the team had three strong sophomores and five seniors that were dedicated to whatever it took to make the team as competitive as they could possibly be. The coaches and team knew that if there was a moment in time that the Crescent Tigers could beat the Guthrie Blue Jays, this was the year.

The Crescent High School versus Guthrie High School was not a home-and-home series. The game was always played in Guthrie because of the larger stadium, and it was a favor from Guthrie to play a small school like Crescent to open the season. To find a non-conference team for Crescent to play to open the season with would mean a long road trip and would be expensive, whereas Guthrie was a short drive with very little cost associated with the trip. This was good for Joe and his teammates because they were very familiar with the field, they were not tired from a long bus ride, and there would hopefully be a lot of Crescent High School fans at the game because of its close proximity.

The bus ride from Crescent to Guthrie was extremely quiet, and Coach did not have to say a word to anyone to calm down and think about the game. This was not the normal for an away trip because there was usually a little rowdiness going on between the players and always a little "grab ass" as the coaches would say. This trip had each and every team member deep in thought and concentration about their play and what they would do in the different scenarios of the game. Even the players who would normally sit on the bench were in deep thought just in case their number was called for whatever the reason. Nobody wanted to be the weak link in the chain that broke and allowed the winning run to cross the plate.

The younger players bought in to the idea that everyone counted, and at every practice, they gave it their all, to give the older players and would-be starters all the competition they could handle. The young kids, the benchwarmers, knew the harder it was for the starters to beat them, the better the starting players would be prepared to face the competition when their season started. In practice, they enjoyed the intensity and hoped they could maintain that level for the season, hopefully winning all the games.

As Crescent took the field for warm-up and batting practice, the bleachers were half full with game time about an hour away. On this March 1 game, the temperature was 82 degrees with a south wind of five to ten miles an hour pushing across the diamond to the left field with scattered clouds, but mostly sunny. This was not the perfect day as last year proved to be for weather, but nonetheless great weather for Oklahoma because the wind could be twenty to thirty miles an hour, making it miserable for both teams and fans included.

Coach Yost had worked the team in scrimmage with the batters facing Shelton at the mound two times a week. Coach Yost would give the batters a 2–2 count and would have Shelton throw at or about 80 percent. Yost wanted all the team to see a level of pitching that they might face this season so that they could be prepared and know how to react against real speed and a good breaking ball. Shelton had both with a natural talent that needed little coaching just like Joe. Joe was more developed than 95 percent of the players he would encounter throughout the season. Joe at the age of sixteen was easily in the top of the top 5 percent of all the high school players in the state of Oklahoma. Shelton would be there very soon as time passed; growth in strength and muscle would be the additive to the improvement of his skill level.

When the pregame batting practice was wrapping up, Joe noticed a constant noise that filled the air, which had escaped him throughout the warm-up. As Joe looked into the stands, every seat was taken, and there were people two and three deep around the entire fence line. Behind home plate, people were standing four and five deep. The stadium was overflowing with fans to the point they could hardly move about. Just the talking between them amounted to a low roar. It was an activity at a baseball game that none involved, including Coach Yost, had ever experienced before. Not only had Crescent showed up in force, the Guthrie Blue Jay followers equaled or exceeded the number of Crescent fans.

The two star pitchers from Guthrie that had beat the Tigers at this time a year ago were still in the Blue Jays rotation and were expecting another victory this year. The interest in Guthrie was not only in their team, but also in the young phenom, Joe Marshall. The word had been around in the four-county area, even statewide, about a baseball player that had the potential of being great and some-day could star while playing in the major leagues. Not only from Crescent and Guthrie, there were those in attendance from the Tulsa and Oklahoma City areas with an interest in seeing a great player, Joe Marshall, in his developing years before stardom. Some folks from the four-county area knew about Joe's father, Walt, and the great ball player he was in high school and the injury that ended his career. Knowing what was in Joe's background helped along the popularity and added to the fan base that Joe was acquiring.

The crowd got into the game with the introduction of the play-ers. At each name, a roar arose that probably could be heard a mile away. The experience was more intense than it was at the state play-offs the preceding year for either team. When Paul was talking to Joe in the dugout just before the game, he told Joe that the hair on the back of his neck stood up when he was introduced. Joe thought that was funny and laughed out loud. When the other teammates heard and saw Joe laugh, in that moment, it broke the intensity and brought into the dugout the desire for the game to start, to put runs on the scoreboard and play the Guthrie Blue Jays into the ground and go home with a victory.

When the umpire yelled play ball and as Allen Walker, the first in the batting order, approached the plate to start the game, the elec-tricity and excitement in the park was so great, you could feel it all over your body. Players on both teams felt the adrenaline surging through their bodies, which gave them less control and more action and reaction. As the first pitch came from the mound, looking for an inside corner of the plate, it went wide and struck Allen in the side. With a little pain, he took his position on first base and was relieved that he was not the first out. The second in the batting order was Pixley, and Paul was feeling confident that he could hit the ace from Guthrie. Paul was 2–2 on the count and had the go-ahead to take a swing if he had a pitch that he thought he could hit, and sure enough, Paul took a swing at the next pitch and pushed a ground ball through the gap between third and short. Allen advanced to second, and Paul was safe on first. The next batter was Ronnie "Toe Joe" Johnson. Toe Joe could hit the ball and had natural baseball talent. Toe Joe, a senior, was one of the two black players on the team and had thoughts of getting a baseball scholarship so that he could attend college and get his degree. If he was able to do that, he would be the first in his family to attend and hopefully graduate from college. Toe Joe and Joe were the most talented players on the team and could have played at any school, no matter what the size.

As Toe Joe saw the first pitch, he thought it was a little wide but took a swing and drove it just out of reach to the left of the first baseman, landing in short right field, advancing both runners and finding him safe on first with a single that loaded the bases. At this point, the Blue Jays' coach called time and approached the mound to talk with his star pitcher. The gist of the talk was to pitch to Joe, which was a mistake on their part. The wise thing was to intentionally walk Joe and not give him a chance to hit, but pride got in the way, and the pitcher was given the go-ahead to pitch to Joe. The thought of Crescent beating Guthrie was, in the coach's mind, not even a possibility, and why should they be scared of some country kid that thought he was a big shot? The Blue Jays' pitcher was gaining a little control and was keeping the ball just out of the strike zone, but Joe was not biting. With the count at 3–0, the next pitch was a fastball and approached going a little inside. Joe took a full swing and connected with the ball, sending it out of the park over the left center fence. The crowd went crazy as Joe rounded the bases with a grand slam and the score 4–0.

The rest of the game played well for the Tigers with the first inning derailing the Blue Jays who continued to be rattled for the rest of the game. The final score was 7–2 with the first game of the season being a victory for Crescent High School, the Tigers having beaten the Guthrie Blue Jays for the first time in school history.

The sophomore baseball season for Joe Marshall and the other team members put Crescent High School in the history books for having the first undefeated season in Tigers' history, and one of the few undefeated seasons of all high schools in the state of Oklahoma in state history. The season brought a lot of news coverage to Crescent, and the television stations covered many of the games as the Tigers continued to win through the end of the season. The interest in baseball all around the center of the state, including Oklahoma City, was at its highest level ever. Throughout the state, everyone knew about Joe Marshall and the Crescent Tigers' success. The Tigers even had a pictorial and article in the magazine *Sports Illustrated*, featuring Joe Marshall as a phenomenal high school baseball player that would be drafted by the pros right out of high school. The major leagues gained a little interest in Joe at the end of the season and had scouts present during the state playoffs. Most of the major league teams had a scout at one or more of the Tigers' games toward the end of the season, and all were impressed by the rare ability that such a young player as Joe possessed. The main comments behind the scenes and off the record by the pro scouts were about Joe's speed and his ability to see a pitch and turn it into a hit or a home run. Because Joe was a sixteen-year-old sophomore, still in high school, the pro scouts maintained their distance, and there was no contact between them, Joe or his parents.

As the season ended, Ronnie "Toe Joe" Johnson was voted on as an Oklahoma all-state baseball player and got his full-paid scholarship from Oklahoma State University to play baseball and become a Cowboy. Toe Joe was the first all-state baseball player from Crescent High School and the only black player to ever receive a full scholarship from a major university in school history.

With Joe's sophomore school year over and Legion ball getting ready to start, the Marshall family was entertaining all sorts of interest in Joe's career. Joe being mature beyond his years did not let any of these things or his athletic success go to his head. Joe was still Joe, and when there was downtime between school, chores, and practice, he and his friends would still gather at Wycoff Corner to play a little sandlot ball just for fun and to have a good time without any pressures from parents, coaches, or otherwise interested third parties. The Wycoff Corner became a popular place to go for all the players of all sports at Crescent High School because of Joe and his rural school friends. Wycoff Corner also became the meeting place for most classmates and teammates. High school friends, girls and boys, teammates from basketball and football, would gather together and plan an outing to go to Wycoff Corner to play a game and just have fun. A lot of the times, they would meet and play touch football or just pass the football, and then there were times they would just circle the vehicles, put blankets on the ground, drink a beer, and talk. There was always someone that had a connection to buy beer or one of the seniors that had turned eighteen would make the short trip to Kansas, just north across the state line, where it was legal to buy beer at eighteen and then meet everyone at Wycoff Corner. This gathering would take place a dozen times during the school year and three of four times during the summer break. These gatherings provided a good time for all who attended.

CHAPTER 9

A Promise from a Son to His Dad

Three weeks after the high school baseball season ended, Joe's sophomore year was finished, and Legion baseball practice was in high gear. The Legion ball was a full step up in competition because the best of the area and county baseball players participated in the program. The other Legion teams were formed from major school systems in the state and from counties that had much-larger populations than that of Logan County. Joe now played with the best players from many of the teams that he played against while playing for Crescent High School. Joe thought it was odd at first making friends from the teams earlier in the year that he tried to beat, but as new teammates on the same team and from the respect that most had for Joe and his gifted play, Joe made new friends quickly.

Walt and Jane tried to attend most of Joe's games and would miss a game only when time-critical work at the farm had to be done. Walt and Jane had enjoyed all the sporting events that Joe participated in and gave Joe all the support that they could, hardly ever missing a game or a team function. Joe excelled in every sport he played, and that just made attendance at the games more exciting for Walt and Jane.

For Jane and Walt, the most enjoyable moments that they experienced watching Joe play came from baseball. From watching Walt play, Jane had allowed baseball to enter into her life and become a vital part of her and Walt's relationship. Before Jane had met Walt, going to a baseball game was an excuse, on a hot summer night, to get out of the house and gather with friends to visit and have fun. During grade school and junior high summers, it was peewee baseball, and during the high school summers, it was Legion baseball where Jane and her friends would get together at the local baseball parks. During these years, Jane was not well versed on baseball, and her trying to carrying on a conversation about baseball would have been the equivalent of the old Abbott and Costello routine wanting to know Who's on First. For Jane, going to a baseball game in the pre-Walt years was a social setting where young boys and young men played a game that was a sideline activity to getting together with friends and acquaintances. When Jane went to watch Walt play, she could hardly remove her eyes from him and still did not have a clue to what was happening on the field of play. The more she was around Walt, before they were married, the more she was around baseball. The people Walt associated with were involved in baseball, and the people Jane and Walt would meet at parties, dinners, and outings were also involved in baseball, let alone the many nights and days Jane spent at the ballpark not really knowing what was going on. She started to ask questions. Jane first found out that she had to learn a new language before she could even start to learn the rules, and learning the rules were key to understanding the conversation after she learned the new language.

Jane found out that if she really wanted to learn baseball, there were people all around her that were willing to give her lessons and teach her everything she wanted to know. It was during her time in Tulsa, sitting with fans devoted to baseball, that she started feeling the heartbeat of a game that people loved and were willing to share with anyone that asked. The more she learned, the more she wanted to learn, and before the end of that first summer in Tulsa, Jane would count the minutes until she could be at the ballpark, not to just watch the game, but to feel the crowd, hear the distinct baseball sounds and chatter, having the smells of fresh-cut grass, hot dogs, and popcorn tingle her senses. Not only did Jane fall in love with baseball, she fell in love with a baseball player, Walt. Jane had a sharp intellect and picked up on all facets of the game from player's abilities to coaching styles and strategies. By the time October arrived, Jane had the game in her blood and not only knew the language, she also knew who was on first, what's on second, and I don't know is on third.

Jane might have matters to attend to, but when it came to watching a baseball game Joe was in, she would be in the bleachers between home plate and the dugout on the third baseline, at the start of warm-ups and batting practice, until the last out of the game. Jane liked watching all baseball, but when it came to watching Joe play, she couldn't get enough. Sometimes on an away game that was an hour or more away, Jane and one of the other parents would travel, and Walt would tend the farm and stay home. It was a rare occasion that Walt would miss a game, but many times, he would show up later than Jane, but before the game started.

During the summer after Joe's sophomore year, at sixteen-years-plus old, while Joe was starting to play Legion baseball, he weighed in at one hundred eighty-five pounds and was six feet one inch tall. At the end of Joe's sophomore baseball season, Joe was the biggest player on the team. Now playing Legion ball, there were few players that were taller than Joe and still none as fast. It was during the first Legion game of the summer between Joe's sophomore and junior year when Walt was watching Joe play that he noticed a difference in everything Joe did. With Joe's extra weight and height, there was more speed and power. Joe threw the ball harder and faster, had more bat speed, and hit the ball harder and farther. Walt thought Joe looked more like a full-grown man during the first game of that summer and could hardly believe the improvement in Joe's game.

As Walt continued to watch Joe, he told Jane that it looked as though Joe was a man playing among boys on the field. Until this time, Walt knew that Joe was a gifted athlete, and compared to his teammates in high school, there was an obvious difference in talent, ability, knowledge of the game, and maturity, but now it appeared to Walt that the disparity in talent between Joe and his teammates and the opposing players had grown to a point that everyone could see, hear, and feel the superiority of play that Joe humbly possessed. Walt asked Jane if she had noticed an extreme difference in Joe's play, and she agreed. Jane also mentioned to Walt that Joe seemed more intense and serious about his play than just one month before, and

Walt said that he could see that also. Sometimes it was hard to see the intensity with which Joe played. Because of the influence Joe had on his teammates, they became more intense and serious as Joe did, which also changed the mood in both dugouts.

Walt started to see the level of Joe's play being equal to his play when he played professional baseball. Walt on the first game of the summer saw in Joe professional talent that was unequal to anything he had seen, and then Walt realized that Joe could probably play at a professional level now. The thought of Joe's ability and talent being at a professional level at sixteen years old had never entered Walt's mind until now. Joe became a stellar player, and fans that wanted to see a young phenom who would someday play in the major leagues came from all over the state to see a kid before he became a national celebrity, so they could say that they saw Joe Marshall play when he was still in high school. From the start of the summer of Legion baseball, reporters from all the big and small papers showed up at home and away games to take pictures and write articles about this outstanding young baseball player from Crescent, Oklahoma. Through all the attention that fans, kids, college scouts, and sport writers gave Joe, it never seemed to bother him, and he just went along about his business of playing the game.

Joe was the kind of young man that reporters loved to write about. Joe always had a smile on his face and had the thought that all the notoriety and fuss around and about him was silly. Walt and Jane would ask Joe about his feelings on his popularity, and Joe would reply with the statement to them and anyone else, that if it wasn't for his eight teammates on the field with him during every game, he wouldn't be the star of anything. Joe never let it get by him that it always takes a team to play team sports, and no one person makes a team. Joe had a handle on popularity that very few celebrities had that were twice or three times his age. For Joe to have the maturity not to let attention go to his head, Walt and Jane were very thankful.

Walt and Joe had talked to each other all the time. They would talk about all sorts of things, from farmwork, Walt's experience in the war, girls, and even what the future might hold. Television reception in rural Logan County, Oklahoma, in the sixties left a lot to be desired and was not the center of attraction in the Marshall home, so family conversation was a mainstay and a daily event on and around the farm. The normal conversation between Joe and Walt was about little things in life and daily experiences. What was said hardly ever carried a correctional tone or a direction in life theme. Most of the time, talk was what was being thought about today, from Walt or Joe.

Walt had just finished watching Joe play a Legion game in Kingfisher in which Joe went three for four, three runs batted in and runner thrown out from deep right field to end the game with a win, where Joe was the outstanding player of the game. Jane and Walt had driven together for that game while Joe rode with the team in a small bus that a local church had donated for use in away games. On the way home, Walt asked Jane what her thoughts were about Joe when he finished high school and the prospect of Joe playing in professional baseball. Without hesitation, Jane readily replied that her desire would be for Joe to go to college and get his degree and after that do whatever he desired. Jane also qualified her response with saying that it was his life and what he decides to do after finishing high school would be his choice, without regard to her thoughts. Likewise, Jane posed the question to Walt, and he replied with the same thoughts, except adding that if Joe decided to go to college, Walt would like to see Joe completely dedicate himself to his studies to receive the highest level of understanding in the discipline he chose. It was Walt's feeling that Joe dedicating himself to his studies in his career field would enhance his possibility in his endeavors of employment for life after baseball, if he would make a choice other than farm life. Walt and Jane both agreed there would be no problem with them if Joe chose farm life with them, rather than seek out a life elsewhere. They both wanted the best for Joe, and both agreed it would be his decision, not theirs.

It was on Walt's mind how he came back to the farm to seek out a life and brought his family with him. He often wondered if he made the right choice when his baseball career was over, and he returned to his home, the Marshall farm. At the time, going to college and using his GI Bill benefits to help with the cost of tuition and housing was an option, but he quickly dismissed it and chose to stay on the land and make a living out of it, as did his dad and grandfather. Walt never thought that returning to the farm after his baseball injury was the wrong decision, but one that limited future choices.

Walt expressed these feelings to Jane, and she agreed their career direction had been taken when they returned to the farm, and that she could not be greater pleased with the life they now had and could not imagine any other life that would have pleased her more. Walt cherished that conversation and trip home with Jane and revisited it in his mind often.

That night returning home from Kingfisher, Walt and Jane agreed it would be all right to discuss and ask what Joe's thoughts were about his future and the direction he saw himself taking after graduating from high school. Jane also shared with Walt that she thought it was Walt that should have the talk on a one to one between him and Joe, a man-to-man talk. Walt disagreed with Jane and said it should be a family meeting between the three of them.

Later in the week, a late-evening thunderstorm gave the area better than an inch of rain, and the rain continued on through the next morning and early afternoon. There was some equipment that needed some maintenance work and a tractor that needed an oil change and grease, and the rain gave Walt and Joe an opportunity to get these items off their checklist. After the work on the tractor and equipment was complete, Walt and Joe headed into the house for lunch with Jane and Juanetta.

With the soft sounds of the rain and a cool breeze coming through the house and the absence of heat, it made lunch a relaxing and enjoyable meal. No one felt an urgency to finish the meal and go back to work. It was one of those rare times that came along, once in a great while, where the thing to do was to take as long as you wanted for lunch because everything else you could do was placed on hold because of the rain. To add to the freshness of the air, the smell of a blackberry cobbler was drifting from the kitchen to the dining room, nearly making their mouths water before they ate lunch. The blackberries had come into season a couple of weeks earlier than normal, and Jane had made a blackberry cobbler with fresh-picked blackberries that a neighbor the next section over had given to her. Having a cobbler to eat in the summer was an infrequent delight because of the heat added to an already-hot kitchen.

The wind of the thunderstorm had pushed through, and now the only noises about were sounds of raindrops as they hit different and sundry objects in the yard and around the house, from the hood of the car to the washtub that covered the garden tiller to keep the motor dry and weather off it. With just a light breeze left from the storm, all the windows in the house were wide open, and the cool breeze felt good as it slowly meandered through the house. Normally, in the middle of June, the Oklahoma summer had already arrived, and it was more pleasant to eat on the front porch or on the back patio in the shade of one of the largest elm trees in Logan County. But for this day, the dining room being cool, the wafting smell of a blackberry cobbler, and the pleasant temperature made it the perfect place for a sandwich and potato salad lunch, with ice-cold sweet tea to drink.

Lunch finished, everyone picked up their dish and silverware from the table and placed the items in the kitchen sink, then lined up to dip up a large portion of cobbler with ice-cold half-and-half poured on top and return to the dining room to sit and enjoy dessert. As everyone indulged in their first bite, Walt felt moved to bring up a talk with Joe about what his feelings were on the next few years and what he might do after high school. Joe first mentioned that since the start of summer break and with the start of Legion baseball, he had given the next two or three years more than one thought, and the more he thought about it, the direction he should take did not become clearer, but became more clouded. Joe explained to his folks that most would think there wasn't a choice, that he would surely play professional baseball as soon as he graduated from high school. As Joe continued talking, it was clear that he had an understanding of his options, which showed a maturity well past his age, which was typical Joe. Joe told his folks that he knew they loved him and would never tell him what choice to make about his future, for the simple reason they did not know the future for themselves, let alone anyone else.

Joe wanted Walt's, Jane's, and Juanetta's input to help him figure out his feelings and to take a direction that would give him the best and greatest of life's experiences. Sitting around the table at mealtimes with his family was always a treat for Joe, and he had great memories of the food, the company, and conversations as far back as he could remember. During these times, Joe had garnered direction, moral thought, how to handle problems, maturity, and above all, wisdom. As a young child, he gave ear to business dealings and how to handle different personal contacts in buying and selling, trading, borrowing, and helping others in need. At the Marshall family dining table over Joe's sixteen years of life, he had a front-row seat to listen to things that worked and those things that did not work. He heard about life and life's decisions of friends and family that had bountiful and happy, harmonious results. Joe also heard about bad decisions of family and friends that led to death, calamity, and uncertainty. Joe learned that these life stories were true and had real-life situations that often repeated themselves with happiness and success and with repeated sadness and despair.

The greatest lesson Joe learned at the Marshalls' dining table was that not all the choices made from the Marshalls' discussions had the desired results. Some resulted as fruitful and had the expected desired outcome, and at times, in some choices, the desired outcome was the reverse of expected with undesirable results. In the decisions that did not go as planned, they were in themselves not a mistake, but a teaching moment of learning what did not work and hopefully were not to be repeated. The main lesson learned by the family and Joe was the second time you made the same decision and received the same undesired result, that was when a mistake was made.

Before the cobbler was finished, Joe told the family he wanted them to tell him their ideas and what was on their minds. Joe explained if they did not speak up, he could not read their minds or hear their thoughts. Joe felt like his decisions were just like all other matters that were dealt with on the farm and in life. The family's combined experiences far exceeded Joe's, and he wanted their input so that he could figure things that were not even in his thoughts, let alone in his experiences. Joe explained he did not want them to make decisions for him, but for them to help him explore different options that would present themselves over the next two years. Joe had absolute respect for his family and their concern for him and his life.

Most of all, Joe relied on his father to discern matters that Joe had little or no understanding of. Joe saw in his dad a gentle spirit coupled with wisdom that desired for Joe to grow physically, mentally, spiritually in an ever-maturing manly being. Walt knew that Joe had to exercise his ability to make choices as much as he had to exercise any other muscle in his body that he wanted to make stronger.

In learning answers to life's questions, one started with the basics of life, and one improved. Hopefully, improvement comes as one continued and grew older. The members of the Marshall family had a belief in God and at family meetings would frequently go to what they referred to as "life's lesson number 101." This was when in doubt about a decision, go reread Psalm 101:2, "I will behave myself wisely in a perfect way" or as Walt put it, "Walk with integrity, and in the fact, you made the right decision harming no one."

Jane and Juanetta shared with Joe their desire for him to finish high school, and from there, they had little or no other input. Joe asked Walt if he had anything to add. Walt thought for a moment and asked what his thoughts about college were. Joe explained that college was something he wanted to do but didn't know just when and how. If offered an opportunity to play professional baseball, it would work out. Joe also added that as far as he was concerned, living his life out on the farm and doing what his family had been doing for the last seventy-five years would be okay with him. With Joe to finish high school, graduate from college, play professional baseball, then return to live out his days on the Marshall farm would probably be the most complete life that he could think of. Joe added that at some point in that list of things he would like to do was also find a young lady to fall in love with and get married.

Jane and Juanetta were well pleased that Joe considered having a love interest in his life someday among the other desires of his life. Jokingly, Juanetta asked Joe on the point of getting married if he had already picked out a bride. Jane and Walt knew that only a grandmother could ask a question like that. If a parent asked, it would not seem as amusing. Quite to everyone's surprise, Joe told Juanetta, in fact, there was a girl from Crescent High School that he was sure was going to be the next Mrs. Marshall. Walt, Jane, and Juanetta were taken aback and told Joe that they were unaware that he had even started dating someone and wanted to know what her name was. Joe explained that he hadn't found the right time to ask her out just yet, but from the way he felt, he knew that she was the one, and her name was Louise.

Walt laughed and said that if Joe was planning on marrying this gal, he better hurry up and ask her on a date before someone else does. Walt asked how long he had known Louise, to which Joe explained that she was a year younger than him, and he had known her since the second grade. Jane wondered if Joe had known Louise since the second grade, then she must have been a first grader at Blue Creek School, and Joe confirmed it. Juanetta then piped up and asked Joe if he had just discovered in the last year that Louise was a girl. Joe told his grandmother that was exactly right. At the end of Joe's eight-grade year, he knew Louise as a classmate and after not seeing her through his ninth-grade year at Crescent, this very attractive girl bumped into him in the hall at the start of school last year and said hello. Joe told his folks that he said hello back and then asked her if they knew each other. Joe said that she answered by calling him silly and that they had known each other for years, and at that moment, Joe asked if she was Big Ed's daughter, Louise Lucas, and she said yes. Joe told his folks that he was just flabbergasted, that he could not remember the last time he had seen or even thought of Louise, but for sure the last time he had seen her, she was a skinny little kid, and now he can't think about anything else. Walt, Jane, and Juanetta got the biggest laugh at Joe and absolutely knew that Joe was smitten and might not ever get over it.

Walt was happy with what Joe had said and felt within himself that this was a good moment for him to mention his thoughts about Joe and his decisions in the near future. Walt began by telling Joe that he was proud of him and that he had taken a big step from the start of his last high school season to the start of his summer Legion season. Walt explained to Joe that in his opinion, Joe could be picked up by the pros now, and that he would do just fine, but until just now, that was not the case, and this was the reason to be talking about Joe's future, even if to others it might seem a little premature. Walt saw a major difference in power and ability over Joe's teammates and the members of the teams they played. Walt thought that by the end of the summer, they would be getting visits and phone calls from scouts from the pros and colleges, and if that was the case, it would be best to get his mind in the right place and know without question what direction he would take before an offer was tendered. Trying to make up one's mind at a time when things could go to one's head, thinking that one was important, when one was really not, that kind of thinking throws an influence into the direction that one would have not taken, if one had thought through it beforehand. Walt wanted Joe to fully understand that they were not telling a right or wrong way to go, only to think it out thoroughly beforehand.

As Walt explained to Joe about his own experiences, it was more about completely focusing on one's mission, single-minded focus, without letting other factors deter oneself, is how one was successful at any endeavor one did. Walt told Joe he did not realize what a single focus was until he was in World War II during his first bombing mission. From takeoff until landing, thinking about nothing else but one's job and completing the work at hand was what made their bombing mission successful and returned their plane to the field they took off from. It was the complete focus from the pilot to the tail gunner on his B-17 that allowed them to return home to family and loved ones. Walt also explained that this was the same talk Willis had given him before he left home to go into World War II. Willis also explained to Walt that single-minded focus was what brought him and his brother back from the Great War in Europe. That same focus allowed Howard and Mary to survive in the middle of nowhere after they claimed their land after the Land Rush of 1889.

Walt told Joe that when he came home from World War II, he was considering going to Oklahoma A&M to get his college degree in business, when at that moment in time, his old friend Peter Whyte, the baseball scout, contacted Walt, and they started over again where they left off four years ago with Walt trying out for professional baseball. After Walt's knee injury, he considered going to college again but was responsible to support his family and pay the bills, so at that moment, he decided to work with his dad on the farm and make a living out of it. Walt said that he did not think he made the wrong choice, when he chose to play professional baseball and not to go to college and then again, when baseball came to an early end, there was the choice of going to college or work on the farm. To work on the farm was not a mistake, but one Walt fully committed to, and when the option of going to college was not considered, Walt focused solely on the work at hand with total commitment, and success naturally followed.

Joe took all the comments to heart from his family and then asked Walt what he thought, in reflection, was the most critical qualities an individual can have in his or her life. Walt stared into Joe's sky-blue eyes in silence for a few seconds before he answered. Walt answered Joe's question with, for an individual, first being truthful and respectful to family, friends, and other people, and second, knowledge through education. Walt was not saying anything new to Joe, but more or less was reiterating what he always said and lived as an example to Joe. Walt, Jane, Juanetta, and Willis, when he was alive, respected people for what they were as opposed to who they were. The family, to Joe's memory, treated people they had interactions and dealings with, not by hearsay and the experiences others said they had, but by the outcomes of their own firsthand dealings. Joe consistently had the subtle teaching of "A man is no better than his word," with the added "A simple yes, I will, or no, I won't" is all that it takes, then doing what you said you would do.

Having education so one could follow their dreams, having respect for oneself, and honoring one's word to others will guide them as they take their first step and continued steps in one's journey of life was as simple as Walt could put it. Walt then continued with focusing on one thing at a time so you can get it right the first time and not have to go back and try it again. Achieve the highest level of accomplishment that was possible so that one absolutely knows what one knows, and know in absolute terms what one doesn't know the first time through. Walt said in his way of thinking it was better to take steps forward and no steps back. It was a better use of time.

Joe had the maturity to recognize the love that his family had for him and that they wished the very best for him and his future.

Joe also knew they would not tell him what to do, and they would allow him to make his own choice, and they would not let him know if they agreed or not with the direction he would take. Joe also knew that they were not pressuring him to respond immediately or even respond at all, but to put it simply, they were there if he wanted to talk things over.

With this in Joe's mind, he intended to assuage his folks' feelings to let them know exactly what was on his mind. Joe was not typical, from the fact that he was sixteen in age pushing forty-five in maturity. He told his family that he was going to finish high school and hopefully graduate at the top of his class and gain an academic scholarship to Oklahoma State University (Oklahoma A&M changed to Oklahoma State University on July 1, 1957) and live with his aunt and uncle that were tenured professors at OSU. Joe then asked Walt what his thoughts were about playing for the university baseball team.

Walt spoke immediately to say that was not his decision, but Joe's. Joe asked his dad what he would do if it were him. Walt, still being a little evasive to Joe's question, asked what Joe wanted to study at OSU, and Joe replied without hesitation, finance and accounting. Walt, still shuffling around not wanting to answer Joe's question, asked how long he thought it would take him with those majors to get his degree. Joe paused briefly and then said three and a half years. Walt then asked Joe if that were so, how many hours a day it would take to accomplish that goal, and Joe said nearly all the awake time that he would have that wasn't involved in sleeping. Walt looked at Joe and said it looked like he already had his answer. Walt then spoke directly to Joe and said that if professional baseball was in his life, that his skill set was good enough now, yet if he gets picked up by a team just after his twenty-first birthday, and he had his degree in hand, it would please Walt greatly, but if things change and Joe changed his mind, that was his choice, not Walt's.

Joe told his dad, mom, and grandma that he keeps in touch with Toe Joe, who took a full-ride baseball scholarship to OSU and talks a lot about his experience at OSU. Toe Joe told him that time management was critical, and he had very little spare time after baseball, classes, and studying to relax and call his own. To keep his grades up takes him late into most nights and that he looks forward to breaks to just rest his mind and body. Joe knew that playing for OSU would be a lot of fun, and the competition would be great, and that he could contribute to the university and team in a big way, but he also knew that the commitment in time was a major factor. Joe made it clear to his family that he was going to take his dad's advice, to do one thing at a time, high school, college, and then pro baseball if the opportunity was still there.

The next morning, as Walt and Joe drove out to the river to check on some fencing, Walt asked Joe for a promise. Joe asked what his dad wanted him to promise and why he was so serious. Walt explained to Joe that he knew that Joe had real talent. The lure to play ball before Joe was ready could become a real temptation to change his mind. Thinking the change could take him down a road that might not turn out as anticipated, Walt explained to Joe that his injury that ended his baseball career also ended some dreams he had and made him rethink some of his decisions as to being right or wrong.

Walt said that he wanted to play baseball more than anything else in the world, and that in the end, he was content with his choices, and there was no blame to be had. He had followed his heart, and he had the chance to live his dream for at least a couple of years. Walt also wanted Joe to know that returning to the farm was always the plan when baseball was over. Walt told Joe that during the war, inside the plane before the German fighter planes attacked and the flak started, he calmed himself by thinking of the simple life he had on his dad's farm, and desperately, he wanted to be part of the Marshall farm again. The farm was Walt's heritage, and he knew he would return to a life that was established by his grandfather and father. Walt wanted Joe to promise him that what he chose to do would come from his heart, responsibility to family, and his desire to play the game. Not from anyone else.

As Walt came to the river where some fence needed to be repaired, he stopped the truck and turned off the motor. With the windows rolled down, there were only the sounds of the outdoors and the cattle grazing. For a moment, they both paused and listened to nature, a calming and relaxing sound, one that Howard, Mary, Willis, Juanetta, Walt, Jane, and Joe had heard many times at this exact place on the farm. As the sounds of nothing quieted their mood, Joe looked at his dad with all the respect a son could have for a father and promised Walt that without regard to the pressures and promises the future might hold, he would be responsible to family and would always try to follow his heart in all matters and to play baseball as long as he could for the both of them.

CHAPTER 10

Commitment to Family and Honoring Your Word

With every game played, Joe's popularity grew around the state. Joe had articles written weekly in both papers in Oklahoma City and both papers in Tulsa. Occasionally, one or two of the six major television stations in the state would cover a Legion game Joe was playing in. His baseball skills and abilities were getting attention in the border states all around Oklahoma and even some national attention. Walt could see Joe's growing interest soon after the first game of the summer season. This was the spark of the concern that started the conversation with the family and Joe about his future, and Walt was correct in his assumption.

Scouts from professional and college teams would show up at games, and the few that could find the Marshall farm would show up on the front porch. Most of the Crescent city and rural folks, who had people asking for directions to the Marshall farm, knew that they were not invited by a member of the Marshall family, and their presence was not wanted by any one of the Marshall family. It became a game when the area people gave directions to the Marshall farm, to give the most accurate, opposite, wrong way directions as possible. Most of the area residents knew how to drive to the Marshall farm. Some folks in town might have a general idea of the location and could find it with little or no difficulty, but only a few knew the farm's exact location, but all the residents knew it was an invasion to the Marshalls' family privacy to have strangers showing up all the time of the day or night.

Joe's popularity drew a variety of writers for the newspapers, newscasters, scouts, and people that just wanted Joe's autograph. The only time that a problem would occur is when they were persistent to get a story, and they became an interruption to getting work done. Sometimes, when Walt and Joe where working in the fields, Jane and Juanetta had a hard time running them off after they did not direct them to the place on the farm where Joe was working. Most of the time, the real journalists were polite and would just return later in the day or evening, and the Marshalls would have a guest for supper, wanted or not. Walt had just purchased a quarter section of land that was contiguous with the original land rush property that Howard and Mary had laid claim to eighty-three years ago. This quarter section lay square west with the one hundred sixty acres Howard staked during the land rush, where the west edge of the river was Howard's west boundary. The new quarter section's east property line was the Marshall farm and the river. This extended the original property another half mile to the west and gave the Marshall farm both sides of the river. The property purchased had changed hands a few times over the last eighty years and at this time had wound up being landlocked when Walt bought it. The last owner of the property had won it in a card game, and for ten years had leased it out to a farmer that owned the land to the south of the landlocked parcel. The farmer who had leased the property was getting a little older and was reducing the size of his operation and did not need the land any longer. The absentee owner needed to raise some money quick and made Walt a cash offer, too good to turn down.

In the half mile of river that ran through the Marshall farm, there were a couple of places that you could ford when the river was down. There was a rock bottom, which allowed a person to drive a truck with four-wheel drive over the river. The land on both sides of the river had a gentle slope, an advantage when the river would come out of its banks during a flood. At these times, the livestock could seek higher ground and escape the floodwaters of the river without taking fence down. Down river from the Marshall farm, the land flattened out, and when floodwaters rose, the neighbors of the Marshalls would take the fence down to allow their livestock to escape to safety.

Howard and Willis had both in their time added a north/south half section of property to the original land, one parcel to the south and the other parcel to the north of the original claim. The river ran the complete width of the original claim but meandered into the southwest corner of the north addition and meandered away at the northwest corner of the south addition. The river ran into the land from the west, flowing north and south for a half mile. Then the river flowed west away from the land. In the first two additions of land, there was about two hundred feet of river access as the river flowed into and then away from the Marshall property.

There was little to do to the new property to make it ready for use. This would be additional pasture so that they could increase the size of the herd. There was about a half of a mile of fence that needed to be replaced and a half of mile of fence that needed to be repaired. Other than that, it was a well-maintained pasture that could support about twenty-five heads of cattle. Joe and Walt worked for the best part of two weeks getting the west quarter section fence in order to move the twenty-five head on to it for grazing. The twenty-five select cows that were to calf in late October were going to be the herd that Walt moved to the new pasture.

When the herd was moved into the new pasture, it was the last week in July, and Joe had his last game of the summer on Saturday night of that week. The game was for the Legion State Championship and was going to be played in the All Sports Stadium at the fairgrounds, which was the home of the Pacific Coast League Oklahoma City 89ers. This was the biggest game Joe had ever played in, and it had a five o'clock start. The Guthrie Legion team would be in Oklahoma City the day before the game to see the 89ers play the last game of a three-game home stand with the Tulsa Oilers and would stay overnight, making the last game of the season a two-day event. This was a real treat for the boys and a very special time for most of them. To be in the city on an overnight stay was a first time for nearly all the team members, and the excitement was high. Jane was a designated driver and drove Joe and three of his teammates to the city.

She would go to the 89ers game and stay overnight to participate as a chaperone for the team. Walt had to finish getting the herd moved to the new pasture and would drive himself down to the city the day of the game to be there before the start of batting practice to meet up with Jane.

The night was perfect for a big game, and the stadium was near capacity because the favored team was the Oklahoma City Legion team made up of hometown players and was the perennial favorite to win the game. It was the David vs. Goliath game, the small rural team from Logan County pitted against the best team in the state of Oklahoma.

Game day provided perfect weather for a typical Oklahoma late July afternoon baseball game. The stands were covered, giving the crowd a little shade from a setting sun, and a light breeze from the south gave a soothing comfort from the late afternoon ninety-six degrees. The last five innings would be played under the lights as night covered the stadium, giving the players and fans relief from the heat and glare of a summertime sun on a cloudless clear day.

The Logan County Legion team batted first, and in typical style, Pixley was batting third in the order with two outs. He made contact with the ball and got on first base with a Texas leaguer that just went over the outstretched glove of the second baseman. Joe stepped up to the plate and on the first pitch made full contact with the ball, and it sailed over the center-field fence and out of the park. The crowd went crazy as they witnessed a feat that few professional players had done over the years at the All Sports Stadium. Even the fans of the opposing team cheered Joe as he ran the bases because they were there to testify that they actually saw a high school junior hit a ball that traveled 440 feet in the park, over the center-field wall, and landed in the parking lot behind the stadium. If someone in attendance had not heard of Joe Marshall before the game, they now knew of him and what he was capable of doing.

Walt and Jane stood up from their seats when Joe hit the ball, and Walt knew from the sound of the bat going through the air and the hard click off the sweet spot on the wood of the bat when it made at contact, it was going to be a long hit ball, and it was. Walt knew that with each game, Joe was taking a step up in his game, and hits like this would soon become commonplace at this level of competition. This one hit, a home run, in a minor league professional park would be more noticed than a total of all the plays, hits, and games that Joe had played up to this point.

As the game continued, Joe and his teammates controlled the game from the start to the finish while containing a late rally by the Oklahoma City team in the seventh inning, to finish the game 12–7 with a victory and the State of Oklahoma Legion Baseball championship. Joe went 4-for-4 at the plate and played an errorless game, making spectacular catches on the run that seemed out of reach for anyone except Joe.

After the game, while still on the field taking it all in, Joe was approached by all the sports newspeople and some college and pro scouts. It seemed as though everyone wanted to talk to Joe. Joe was happy to talk to everyone that wanted to hear him say something about the game and his teammates, not just about him. When asked a question about a play or a hit that he had made, Joe would not make a comment about what he did but what one of his teammates did. Joe knew in his heart, no matter how good one player was, it still took a team where each member can trust and count on each other, to do the right thing at the right time. Joe had learned from Walt and his coaches that the successful team worked as one unit and not as nine individuals. So when the sports newspeople wanted to talk about Joe's feats, he quickly changed the subject as to how the team worked on that particular play, giving the credit to the team and not just one person.

Walt and Jane met Joe on the field to celebrate with him, the team, and family members present. When the excitement of the celebration settled down, the trophy was awarded, and the season was officially at an end. The parents, coaches, and players decided that it would be appropriate for the team to have supper in the city before heading home to extend the celebration as long as possible. It was decided to go to Beverly's to eat the best fried chicken in the Oklahoma City area, and it was in the same direction as Guthrie from the stadium. Walt and Jane were as happy as they could be for

Joe and the team for such a great season. Walt looked at Joe as he talked and joked with his friends and teammates. For Walt, it was a moment that he could see Joe in the future doing and accomplishing anything he set his mind to. Walt, while sitting with Jane in the restaurant, could feel it in his being that Joe was capable of guiding his own life, and that pleased Walt to the core. Walt silently thanked God for the mature, understanding, caring, and good-hearted son that he had been given. At that moment, Walt whispered in Jane's ear that he had just prayed. Jane looked at Walt with big tears in her eyes and told Walt that she wholeheartedly agreed with his prayer and thanks be to God.

With the celebration meal finished, it was time to head home and start a new day of work and training for the upcoming year of sports at Guthrie High School. Walt had driven his pickup truck and had the front seat half filled with tools and fence material, and he would drive home alone and let Joe drive home with Jane, so he could visit with Paul and his other teammates on the drive back. Walt knew that the boys were still excited and wanted to talk and relive as much of the game and season as they possibly could, and the trip home would give them that opportunity. Jane needed to drop off the other players in town and at their homes if they lived in the rural area. She and Joe would be in about an hour later than Walt. Walt wanted to get an earlier start than Joe, letting him sleep in the next day. Walt told Jane he would probably be in bed by the time she and Joe got home, and he would see her for breakfast in the morning.

As Jane was loading everyone in her car and saying goodbye at the restaurant to the other moms and dads that drove the other team members to the game, Walt walked over to Joe, gave him a big hug, and told Joe he played a great game and that he loved him. Walt then left the group to head home and was well down the road before Jane and Joe left Beverly's.

CHAPTER 11

Life Can Change in a Moment

Walt would take Highway 74 due north out of Oklahoma City until he crossed the Cimarron River. On the north side of Cimarron City, he would turn west on Cooksey Road. Cooksey Road would take Walt about six miles west before he would turn north and then west again to arrive at the Marshall farm. All the roads were bar ditch dirt with a little gravel and traveled through the countryside passing very few farms and houses, mostly uninhabited land that without a bright moon would be pitch-black with nary a light to be seen.

Jane would drive Highway 74 due north as Walt did, except she would continue north through Crescent and to the high school where she would drop two of her four passengers off where their cars were parked. They would drive to their homes from there. Jane would then take Dover Crescent Road west to County Line Road, then south dropping the two other boys at their respective houses as she and Joe worked their way back home. Walt had a more direct route, and Joe and Jane would take about an hour longer because of fifteen more miles to drive and three additional stops. Walt left Beverly's restaurant at nine and Jane with Joe and the other boys at nine thirty.

The night sky was clear without a single cloud and one of the brightest full moons that Walt had ever seen. The brilliant full moon made the trip home a more relaxing trip than driving home in the pitch dark of a moonless night. Walt was relaxed as he turned off the highway and started his drive down the section line dirt road. Walt had driven this road many times and was quite familiar with the surroundings and could see nearly as well as a sunlit day except without a glare. At nine forty-five in the rural country of central Oklahoma on any night of the week, you had the road to yourself. Walt could see lights on a vehicle, at least a mile away when the land was flat. Walt always thought that driving at night on the isolated section roads was like being at sea, in the middle of the ocean, looking across the water without seeing a thing but the glimmer of the moonlight on the water. Walt was thinking of the day and evening, thinking about Joe and the game that night and how proud he was of Joe. For a moment, he pondered where Joe would go from here and the paths he would take in his life.

In the last moment thinking of Joe, while crossing through the third section line intersection, a tee intersection, a truck approaching from the south ran into Walt, hitting him center of the driver's door. Walt did not see another vehicle, had no time to react, and in a moment's passing, Walt died instantly.

On this intersection, the east west road that Walt was traveling had a higher elevation than the approaching road from the south. As the road from the south intersected with Cooksey Road, it rose sharply, hiding traffic traveling north, obscured from cars moving east or west on Cooksey Road. The dust from fast-moving cars was not as apparent in the moonlight as it would be on a sunny day, and Walt did not see the headlights because there weren't any. Three cousins from two families staying with their grandparents for a month in the summer had decided to take one of the old farm trucks for a joy ride after the grandparents had gone to bed. The twenty-year-old truck was just used for rough work on the farm in the fields. The brakes did not work well, and the lights did not work at all, but it was in good-enough working order to drive up and down the deserted section line roads. Not knowing the roads that well and not paying attention, with the fast incline to the intersection and with the low approach, by the time the driver saw Walt's pickup lights, stomping the brake pedal as hard as he could, the brakes failed, and the old pickup careened into Walt's door at fifty miles an hour. Walt never saw the truck approach, and the impact was vicious, literally smashing Walt's body against the far side of his truck, with death occurring from massive head trauma. All three boys were injured, broken bones, but not life-threatening. Fifteen minutes after the accident, a man and his wife had gone to the Legion game to watch their nephew play and had eaten afterward. They were traveling the same path as Walt did to head home. If they had not been on Cooksey Road that evening, it could have been hours before another traveler would have passed by so that help could arrive to assist the boys and identify Walt. The couple knew who Joe was and were familiar with Walt and the Marshall family.

Jane and Joe were north of the farm on County Line Road, dropping Paul off, and that was their last stop before heading home. It was now an hour and a half since they left Walt at Beverly's restaurant in Oklahoma City and were about ten minutes from getting home. As Jane and Joe were approaching the driveway, the porch lights were on at the house, and the headlights of Jane's car caught the reflectors of the patrol lights of an Oklahoma highway patrol car and the Logan County sheriff's car. Jane and Joe both knew the area highway patrolman, Charlie Reece, and the sheriff of Logan County, Amos Ward. Jane and Joe both knew something was wrong and first thought it had something to do with Juanetta and at the moment had not noticed that Walt's truck was not in the driveway next to the house.

Jane and Joe got out of the car, and Amos and Charlie slowly approached. Jane asked if Juanetta was all right. Amos, being an old friend and a high school classmate of Walt's, paused and looked square into Jane's eyes, held both of her hands, and told her it was not Juanetta, but it was Walt. Joe quickly asked where his dad was and wanted to know if he was injured and how bad. At that time, Juanetta opened the screen door of the house and walked down the steps where Jane and Joe were and said that Walt was gone. Amos explained to Jane and Joe that an accident had occurred about an hour ago and that Walt had died on impact, and there was nothing anybody could do. Charlie told Jane they had transported Walt's body to the Crescent City hospital by ambulance, and he would take her and Joe there when they felt like they wanted to make the trip. Amos said he would also wait around until Jane and Joe were ready, and he would go with them to the hospital and, when finished at the hospital, accompany them back to the farm.

Joe, Jane, and Juanetta went back into the house and sat in the living room, not making a move or a sound as they took in the enormity of what had happened. After a few minutes, Juanetta stood up and walked toward the telephone. She paused for a moment and looked at Jane, staring past her for a moment and then said she needed to call LaTrenda and Steve, Walt's sister and her husband, to tell them what had happened. Jane nodded back at Juanetta and said she agreed, and Juanetta was right in calling as soon as possible. Joe was silent, not moving or noticing anyone, sitting in a corner of the living room fixated on a picture of a large sailing ship hanging on the wall directly across from him. At that moment, Joe heard a car pulling down the driveway from the section line road. Joe stood up and looked out to see who it was coming to the house this late at night. As Joe moved slowly to the front door, he could see it was Paul Pixley and his mom, dad, and two of his little brothers. Word gets around fast in the rural part of the county when tragedy strikes. Joe met Paul on the front porch and walked over to sit with him on the porch swing as Mr. Pixley and Mrs. Pixley went into the house. Paul's little brothers stayed in the car and went to sleep as everybody else was in the house.

Mrs. Pixley sat down with Jane and just held her hand without saying a word. Mr. Pixley walked straight through the living room and dining room to the kitchen where he found the percolating coffeepot and coffee and started brewing some coffee. Juanetta soon joined Mrs. Pixley and Jane in the living room and sat down, saying only that LaTrenda and Steve will be at the hospital in Crescent in about an hour and will wait there until they arrived.

Paul did not say anything to Joe, deciding not to say a word until Joe wanted to talk. Joe would make the swing go back and forth with a little bit of motion from his foot but did not move a muscle. Paul did not want to make any small talk with Joe and really did not know what to say, if in fact there was anything to say. Paul just sat there trying to imagine what Joe and his family were thinking about and the pain they were going through at a moment like this. Paul considered Walt a friend of his as well as Joe, although he was much closer to Joe than Walt, but nonetheless, he really liked Walt and always enjoyed his company. As Paul started to think of Walt and all the time he had spent with the Marshall family working, visiting, practicing baseball, and eating meals when his heart became dark and sad and tears piled up in his eyes. Joe sat stoically, not showing any emotion at all, and Paul wondered if Joe even knew he was there.

After a few minutes, Juanetta stood up and, like someone that had faced trials and tribulations before, while living on the edge of the frontier, told Jane that they needed to go with Charlie and Amos to the hospital to see Walt. Jane stood up slowly with Mrs. Pixley at her side and walked with them to the front door. Mrs. Pixley said that she would stay over, and Mr. Pixley and the boys would go back home then pick her up tomorrow in the late morning. As Jane and Juanetta walked out on the front porch, Jane looked at Joe and told him it was time to go to the hospital to see his dad. Mrs. Pixley told Paul to go back home with his dad. Joe got up from the swing and moved to the porch steps. When Joe took the first step down, he stopped, turned around, and asked Mrs. Pixley if it would be all right for Paul to go to the hospital with him and stay the night, if that was okay with her. Mrs. Pixley looked over to Mr. Pixley, and he nodded his head that it was fine. He would pick Paul up in the morning when he came to fetch Mrs. Pixley.

Until that moment, Paul did not really know if Joe was aware he was sitting next to him on the swing, but now he realized that Joe was fully aware of his presence and wanted his company. Paul walked over to Charlie's patrol car and opened the door for Jane, Juanetta, and Joe. Charlie turned his patrol car around in the front yard, followed closely behind by Sheriff Ward as they drove to the hospital in Crescent.

After a couple of miles, Jane asked Charlie about the details of the accident, and he told her exactly what had occurred with the names of the boys and their relatives' names where they were staying. Charlie also added that Walt died on impact when his head hit the frame around the door of his truck. After Charlie gave Jane a full explanation, Jane only asked the condition of the boys and if they would be all right. Charlie explained that their injuries were not life-threatening and that they should not have any long-lasting physical effects to deal with. Jane mentioned to Charlie that she was glad that the boys did not suffer severe injuries and that they would recover without any disabilities. The only other comment Jane made on the trip to the hospital was that one or two seconds earlier or later, it would have been nothing more than a close call, with no harm or foul. Jane asked Charlie, without expecting an answer, what he thought the odds were, at that time of night, on a back-road section line intersection, that there would even be two cars on those two roads at the same time, let alone converging at that intersection at precisely the same time. Charlie did not answer Jane, only nodded his head in agreement, that he understood what Jane was saying. Juanetta was sitting in the front seat next to Charlie and said, without turning around, that people never know how many times in their life that God separated them from harm or loss by the same one or two seconds. Most of the time, the only awareness we have of that separation is when He does not.

Nothing else was said during the trip to the hospital. When they arrived at the emergency room entrance to the hospital, there was a pause, and everyone sat silently not wanting to exit the car. Juanetta was the first to open the door and get out as the others followed her through the emergency entrance of the hospital. The trip to the hospital was not necessary for the family to do, but the confirmation was needed by all, Jane, Juanetta, and Joe.

Not knowing what to expect, Walt looked as though he was just asleep and could wake up at any time. Paul, Charlie, and Amos stayed in the waiting room while the family was in the emergency room. Dr. Anderson was the physician on call and attended to Walt when he arrived at the hospital. Dr. Anderson was checking on some of his patients when the Marshall family arrived and was coming back to check on Jane, Juanetta, and Joe when he was told they had arrived. Dr. Anderson passed by the waiting room and went directly into the emergency to talk to the Marshalls and answer any questions they might have. In a few minutes, LaTrenda and Steve arrived, and Amos directed them into the emergency room with the others.

Dr. Anderson came out of the emergency room and walked to the nurses' station and made a phone call to the Musgrove Funeral Home and talked to John, explaining the circumstances. John asked him to tell Jane they would be there in a few minutes. When John Musgrove arrived at the hospital emergency room entrance, he backed the hearse up, and he and his assistant brought in a gurney, moved quickly and calmly into the emergency, and in two minutes were back through the doors and driving off.

Steve and LaTrenda drove a station wagon, which had enough seating for all of them, and Jane thanked Amos and Charlie for their help and concern and that they would ride home with Steve and LaTrenda. Upon arriving home, Mrs. Pixley had the lights on and had changed the sheets and made ready LaTrenda's old bedroom for her and Steve. Mrs. Pixley laid out sheets and pillows on the sofas for her and Paul to sleep on and set some things out in the kitchen for in the morning. Joe had not said a word except when he asked if Paul could go with him to the hospital. As all were ready to go to bed, Joe looked at Paul and thanked him for being around and staying the night. He would talk to Paul in the morning.

When Joe was in his bed, all he could think of was his dad. Joe, being more mature than most who were his age, started to accept the fact that Walt was gone but wanted it all to be just a bad dream, and when he awoke in the morning, all would be back to normal. In his heart, he knew that it was not a dream, and life for him would not be normal for anytime in the foreseeable future. Joe had a melancholy feeling that ran deep into his innermost being and would not release him no matter how hard he tried to think of something else or go to sleep. After two hours, Joe finally fell asleep, weary and exhausted from the loss of his dad.

Mrs. Pixley was up early the next morning to help around the house, trying to do things for the family, doing whatever she could to make things comfortable for them in their time of grief. Mrs. Pixley had a fresh pot of coffee on, and Mr. Pixley had done an inventory on breakfast food the night before and had already made a run to town and back out to the Marshalls' farm with four sacks of groceries for the family so that Mrs. Pixley would have something to prepare to meet the needs of the family for a couple of days. Steve was the first up, and he joined Mrs. Pixley at the kitchen table at seven thirty and had a cup of coffee to read *The Oklahoman* that Mr. Pixley had dropped off with the groceries thirty minutes earlier. The daily newspaper that the Marshalls subscribed to was delivered by the rural mail carrier and was a day old when received at the farm. *The Oklahoman* that Steve was reading was the current paper, and it was nice to read before it became old news. Steve was accustomed to reading the current copy on a daily basis because he lived in Stillwater. Walt had two farmhands, brothers Darrell and David Ward, coming by to help work some cattle and complete moving part of the herd into the new west-quarter section. They arrived at the farm at about the same time Steve got downstairs and poured his first cup of coffee. As Steve saw them pull up, he knew Walt had made arrangements for something, so he went outside to tell them what had happened and find out what plans Walt had made with them. Steve had been around the farm on weekends, summer breaks from OSU, holidays, and during leave during World War II. Steve was very smart, and his perspicacity allowed him to be quick on the uptake, and along with his familiarity of farmwork, especially on the Marshall farm, he understood what Darrell and David were going to do. He told them to go ahead and that he would check with them later in the day. Steve was also familiar with the Ward brothers and knew they were good hands and competent in their ability and needed little or no oversight in their work. Darrell and David both knew that Walt had died and were showing up and hour and a half later than normal to let everyone sleep a little later from being up late last night and were very sad at what had happened. Darrell and David knew the work still needed to be done, and that was why they were there. They also asked Steve if it would be all right at the end of the day, when they had finished, to stop by and pay their condolences to the family. Steve agreed and said it would be fine and the right thing to do. Steve returned to the kitchen. Mrs. Pixley was half finished with making breakfast for him and Juanetta, who had joined them while Steve was outside with the Ward brothers.

Within the next thirty minutes, Jane, Joe, Paul, and the rest of the family had awakened, and all were downstairs having breakfast, but little was mentioned about Walt not being there, and little was said about what needed to be done in making arrangements for Walt's services. Steve asked Jane if he could help or even take care of the items that needed to be addressed to make the final preparations for Walt. Jane said that it would be appreciated if he could handle all the arrangements, and after they were finished, let her know the details. Steve left the table almost immediately, cleaned up, and headed into Crescent to make the arrangements with Musgrove Funeral Home, the pastor at the church, and the cemetery.

Mr. Pixley came around about ten thirty, expressed his condolences to the family, and told Mrs. Pixley that he would stay until she had prepared something for lunch for the family, then take her and Paul home. Paul went to his dad and asked if it would be okay to stay if Joe wanted him to, and Mr. Pixley said that he had brought him a change of clothes, anticipating that might be the case. Paul went to Joe and asked if he wanted him to hang around through the next couple of days. Joe told Paul that he would really like it if he would stay longer.

Paul stayed with Joe until the day after the funeral after which he went home with his folks. Joe and Paul throughout those five days did the daily chores around the farm and handled business as usual except Joe said hardly anything, and Paul never once pressed him for a response. Two days after the funeral, Paul went by to see Joe; Jane directed him to the new quarter section west of the house. Jane said that Joe had driven Nellie Belle early that morning and did not know what he was doing, but if Paul wanted to, he could drive the small tractor out to check on him. Steve and LaTrenda were still at the house because they were in the summer break at OSU, and it wasn't necessary for them to go back for at least another month, and if necessary, they could commute for as long as help was needed around the farm. Steve saw Paul going over to the small tractor and motioned to Paul to pull the tractor over to the fuel tank because it was low on diesel, and it needed to be filled up. Paul followed Steve's instructions, and Steve asked Paul if he knew were Joe was. Paul said that he thought he was in the west-quarter section. Steve said he would find Joe at the extreme west fence line where Joe was finishing up some fence work that Joe was helping Walt with before the accident. Paul drove the tractor straight to Joe and started helping Joe as soon as he got off the tractor.

Paul knew what to do to repair the fence, and direction and talk were not needed, and Joe didn't offer any. When noon came around, Joe finally spoke and asked Paul if he was hungry, and Paul said he was. Nellie Belle was parked under a grove of trees close to the riverbank, and that was a good a place to take a break and eat some lunch. Jane had packed some sandwiches in a small ice chest, along with some soft drinks and water. In a cardboard box, Jane had included some potato chips and a couple of apples, enough food to make two meals for Joe, in case he stayed out all day and into the evening.

When Paul dropped the tailgate of the truck to sit on, Joe brought the small ice chest with the cardboard box balanced on top and placed it on the tailgate next to Paul. The day was typical for a late July afternoon in Oklahoma with the temperature creeping up to ninety-nine degrees and probably past one hundred by midafternoon. The salvation from the heat for Joe and Paul was a nice five-mile-an-hour breeze out of the south and occasional cloud cover that would deliver a little relief from the sun, on and off through the day. Halfway through his sandwich, talking to Paul for the first time since Walt died, Joe looked over at Paul and told him he felt like he was totally lost in his thoughts. He could hardly keep his mind on anything for longer than a few minutes until his mind drifted back to thinking about his dad. Paul did not have a clue on what to say to Joe and above all did not want to say the wrong thing that would make Joe feel worse than he did. Paul paused for a moment and then asked Joe what memories of his dad came to him most often. With tears welling up in Joe's eyes, he told Paul the first and most often reoccurring memory of his dad was when he would hug him and tell him he loved him, which Joe could not remember a day when that did not happen.

Paul made the comment to Joe that it was a great memory to have, and more than likely, Joe would have it for the rest of his life.

Paul felt like Joe wanted to talk about Walt, so he asked Joe what other memories he frequented about his dad. Joe told Paul, second to his dad's hugs was more of what his dad would tell him. Be a man, do what you are supposed to do when you are supposed to do it and how it was supposed to be done, were one of Walt's most-often-repeated axioms. Paul laughed when Joe mentioned that "Waltisms," and he told Joe that Walt had shared that saying with him on more than one occasion. He probably should have said it more often but didn't, not wanting to hurt Paul's feelings. When Paul said what he did, they both had a good laugh and started sharing stories about Walt and all the times that they had experienced with Walt in work, play, and just visiting. Paul also shared with Joe that afternoon that of all the grownups Paul knew, Walt was his favorite and that he missed him so much that it felt like there was a black hole in his life. Paul also told Joe that Walt always treated him like an adult and not like a kid. Paul liked that and never wanted to let Walt down when he had a job to do for him and would work extra hard at doing the best he had to offer to gain his respect.

For the next couple of hours, not a lot of work got done, and it didn't really matter because the boys talking started a healing process for Joe and Paul both. Later in the day, when Paul and Joe returned to the barn to drop the tractor off, they went into the house and asked Jane if it was okay for them to go to town for a while. Jane was in agreement as long as Paul would call Mrs. Pixley and get permission also. Paul was lucky with nobody on the party line, so he was immediately able to ask his mother, and off to town they went, giving old Nellie Belle a good run.

It was about five o'clock when Joe and Paul got into Crescent and directly went to Gentry Drug Store because they had a soda fountain, and it was one of the few businesses in Crescent where they could go in and sit in air-conditioning. Joe wanted a root beer float, and Paul wanted a cherry vanilla Dr. Pepper with an extra squirt of cherry syrup. It was a special treat for them both to be in town on a summer weekday. There were three booths in Gentry Drug that the town folks and mostly teenagers used to meet and visit and just take an occasional break to get a snack or soft drink. Joe started to tell Paul about the last real conversation Joe had with his dad about doing one thing at a time and what Walt's thoughts and concerns were regarding Joe going to college and not taking professional baseball seriously until he finished high school and probably not until he received his degree. Paul asked Joe what he had told his dad, and Joe explained that he had told Walt not to worry, that he would take one thing at a time and not entertain baseball as a career until everything was in order. Joe told Paul that when they were discussing the issue, he had not paid it the serious attention that his mom and dad had. There would be plenty of time to talk it over the next couple of years. Now as Joe explained to Paul, the next couple of years to talk it over with Walt did not exist, and Paul agreed, but added that Joe would do the right thing. It was his way since the first time Paul had met him.

Ten minutes had not passed when three of the guys Paul and Joe played football with walked into Gentry's and were surprised to see Joe and Paul there. Pulling up an extra chair, they sat down together, all telling Joe they were sorry about his dad and giving Joe all the support they could muster. Two of the guys, Steve Neely and Steve Clark, were Crescent kids in Joe and Paul's class, and the third, Mike Simpson, was a rural kid in the class above them, who had a job at one of the feed stores in town and had just finished work. Clark got up and went to the payphone and called a couple of their teammates and told them Joe and Paul were in town at Gentry's Drug, and by the time word got around, Mr. Gentry had a full house of paying customers with nearly all the high school athletes in town buying a cold drink or ice cream. Mr. Gentry knew the Marshall family and Walt very well. Walt had been one grade behind and played sports with Bud Gentry. Mr. Gentry had gone to college after high school, and when World War II had started, he finished his first year and joined the United States Army Air Corps as Walt had done and became a pilot flying a P-47 Thunderbolt, flying out of Great Britain as Walt did. After the war, Mr. Gentry and Walt discovered that Mr. Gentry had flown fighter support for a bombing mission that Walt had flown in. Mr. Gentry and Walt had mentioned many times that two kids from Crescent, Oklahoma, could have been flying next to each other over the channel and France and Germany and never knew it.

Mr. Gentry was happy for all the noise and kids, boys and girls alike, being in his business and all of them wanting to talk to Joe and trying to make him feel better the best they could. Joe, being an incredibly handsome and polite young man, this allowed him to make the acquaintance and befriend in a gentlemanly manner most of the young ladies in Crescent High School, and quite a few showed up at Gentry's to visit with Joe. Mr. Gentry also wanted Joe to feel at home and was glad that Joe had picked his place to come to on his first trip to town after his dad's death.

This was a moment in time that Joe would keep in his memories and reflect back on many times throughout his life. These young men and ladies, teammates and friends of Joe, showing their concern for him and bringing his spirits up at a time when he needed it left an indelible impression on Joe of the meaning of relationships and what they are made of: people caring about other people.

Of the twenty-some kids that showed up at Gentry's Drug to talk to Joe, one stood out more than the others and was of special interest to him, Louise Lucas from Blue Creek School. Louise had a summer part-time job working in the bank that her uncle owned. Louise had a good mind for numbers and showed a talent for bookkeeping, recording, and filing that her uncle recognized and put her to work in what might be a career for her after high school. Gentry's was across the street from the bank, and when Louise had finished work that day, it was her routine to go across the street and drink a Pepsi and eat a bag of Lay's potato chips, relax a little in what was normally a library atmosphere, before driving home. Louise could see the abnormal activity before she opened the door and was surprised to see all her classmates there and especially Joe. Louise caught Joe's eye the second she walked through the door as it diverted all his attention to her. Joe stood up from the booth and immediately walked to her and asked if she would like to sit with him at the center of all the commotion. Louise agreed but made mention that there was not an extra seat at the booth where he was sitting, and Joe assured her there was. When they got to the booth, Joe asked Paul to move and give Louise his seat, and with little argument and quick on the uptake, Paul gave Louise his place.

As Louise talked to Joe, Paul noticed that Joe talked more in a few minutes to Louise than he had said to him in three weeks. Joe hung on every word that Louise said, and she had his undivided attention until she had to leave to go home. Shortly after Louise left, the gathering broke up, and everyone left to start home. As Paul and Joe walked around the corner to where they had parked Nellie Belle, Paul noticed a distinct difference in Joe's mood and behavior. Joe had a little lift in his step and was a little more talkative, and his demeanor was not as heavy as when they arrived at Gentry's. Paul had the feeling the healing process just started, and Joe was being his old self for the first time since Walt's death, and he thanked God for it.

CHAPTER 12

Joe Deciding What to Do

Driving out of town and heading down a section line road with a plume of dust following behind Nellie Belle as Joe made his way to take Paul home, the conversation between the two was much different than just a few hours before during the trip into town. The first item to be discussed was Paul's question of what the deal was with him and Louise. Joe told Paul that he thought that Louise was the girl for him. Of course, she was, was Paul's reply, and he asked how he knew this. Joe told Paul that he just knew it, that's all; he just knew. Joe also explained that he had told his dad that he thought that Louise was the girl he was going to marry. Paul laughed and said that he ought to go out on a date before they got married, and Joe, with a big smile on his face, said that was probably right. Nonetheless, Joe said he would ask Louise out one of these days, and Paul said he better hurry up before someone else beats him to it. Joe agreed that if it was okay with her parents, that he might just ask her out next week. Paul thought that was a good idea, especially if he planned on getting married soon. Joe looked at Paul and said it wouldn't be that soon because he was going to take one thing at a time.

Paul asked Joe what he meant by one thing at a time. Joe explained that the one thing he had to do now was make sure the farm can run without his dad, with him filling in to take up the gap. Paul asked what the next thing to do was. Joe replied to finish high school. Paul asked after high school what he was going to do. Joe told Paul he didn't know until that time came, and he would figure it out then, but until then, he would apply himself to helping his mom with the farm and finishing high school. Paul explained to Joe that he knew that it wasn't any of his business but wondered about money and finances with his dad being gone. Paul was a very close friend and did not talk out of turn or about other people's business, and Joe thought that Paul's question was one out of concern and did not mind giving him an answer. Joe asked if he knew Richard Streeter and what he did for a living. Paul said he knew Mr. Streeter and figured he sold some kind of insurance. Joe told Paul that he was correct, and that he sold mainly farm insurance but also sold life insurance. Joe said that Richard was also an old friend of Walt's, and after the war and after Richard finished up college at Oklahoma A&M, he came to Walt as one of his first customers and asked Walt if he would help start his business, allowing him to write the insurance coverage for the farm and for Walt to take out a life insurance premium also. Joe said Walt was not happy to do the life insurance part but being a friend, he understood the value of the life coverage and took it out anyway.

Joe went on to explain that there was no debt on the farm, and things had gone well for his dad and granddad for ten years, and after his granddad died, things had gone well for his dad the last five years. Joe also mentioned that his mom still had her teaching job, and all that put together, financially they were strong, but it still needed to sustain itself to continue. Paul told Joe that as the summer continued and into the fall, if Joe needed any help, that he would be there to give a hand. Paul also explained if he needed to, he would show up in the evenings if he had to do something on their farm during the day, but he would show up when he finished his work and give a hand anyway. When Joe dropped Paul off, he told him he cherished their relationship and felt like Paul was a brother more than a friend, and if he would ever need something, he could count on Joe. With that, Joe thanked Paul and headed for home, pushing old Nellie Belle through the gears.

Joe did not know all that Walt did, but he knew that what he did not know, Juanetta and Jane knew enough to get the job done, and Joe was willing to do whatever it took to get it done. Joe picked up where Walt stopped and kept everything going without a hitch. Hay was cut, bailed, and hauled to the barn, cows worked and ready to calf in November, crops harvested, fence kept up, and fields worked. Joe kept it all in shape and even hired help when needed. Typically, the Ward brothers were the go-to for help, but when they were committed to other work, Paul would come over and pitch in to get things done in a timely manner. Sometimes, Jane would be there to help, and Juanetta would take care of the garden and housework. Like always, it took everybody at times, and work was always on the time clock. Mother Nature did not care if you had the time left to get the job done, for time and weather didn't wear a watch or mark off days on the calendar. Time just passed, and the weather just happened without regard to a piece of machinery breaking down or you being ready or not.

As the middle of August approached, on an evening when Paul was helping Joe fix a tractor, Paul asked Joe what his thoughts were about football practice starting. Joe hadn't said a word since Walt died about sports or him participating in sports. Joe told Paul that he would not be going out for football, and more than likely, he would not participate in basketball or baseball when the respective seasons came up this year. Joe explained to Paul that he did not see how he would have the time to practice and/or play the games with the work he needed to do at the farm. He also told Paul that his heart just was not in it anymore, and the desire to compete and be aggressive and to practice hard to win the game did not exist at this time in his life. Of all the sports Joe played, baseball would be the only game he would miss.

Joe explained to Paul that he still thinks of baseball and the last game they played in Oklahoma City the night Walt died. Baseball was a major part of the Marshall family life. Not involving the ball and glove in the family routine left life unfulfilled for Joe. The absence of Walt and Joe throwing the ball, Juanetta and Jane sitting on the porch watching the ball whiz by and hearing the snap of the ball hitting the glove, it was as though two people died that night, Walt and Marshall baseball.

It was about seven o'clock when Paul and Joe finished the repair job on the tractor, and Paul was invited for supper as was usual when

Jane called out to the boys that supper was ready. Paul asked to be excused the minute he finished supper and said he would be gone just a minute if that was all right because everyone else was still eating. Juanetta told Paul to get up and do whatever it was he needed to do. Paul ran out to his car and came back to the table as fast as he could. The Marshalls looked at Paul and could not figure out what he was up to. When supper was finished and the table cleared with dishes done, a cold glass of ice tea in their hands, they headed for the porch. Paul had gotten his glove and sat it on the porch swing and then told Joe to get a ball and his glove and that they throw the ball. At first, Joe said no, and Paul insisted, at which Joe gave in. The whiz of the ball and the snap of the leather was a healing sound to the family and greatly appreciated by all. Paul and Joe threw the ball to each other that evening until they could not see the ball, and Joe still did not have enough because it felt so good. A feeling was back that Joe had not felt for over a month, and he did not think that he would ever have that kind of feeling ever again. Part of Walt had returned to Joe and the Marshall family that night, which had been missing far too long.

A typical Sunday on the farm started with an early breakfast, milking, and the light chores. After that, you cleaned up and headed to town to go to church. Joe had quite a few friends that went to the First Methodist Church in Crescent, and that day was the same as usual. When Joe, Jane, and Juanetta sat down, in front of them, Joe could see Steve Clark, Steve Neely, and three or four more of the guys Joe knew and played sports with. After the service, they all got together outside, and Neely mentioned to Joe that Paul had contacted them and a bunch of the other guys to get a game going at Wycoff Corner today at two thirty and wanted to know if Joe was in for it. They told Joe that Paul, who went to the Catholic church, would be by in a few minutes and tell them all who was going to show up. Before Paul arrived, Joe asked Jane if it would be all right to play a little baseball later that day, and Jane was fine with the plan. Within a couple of minutes, Paul showed up with his parents and told Joe that the word had gotten out, and almost all the guys that play sports with Joe were going to show up, and Paul thought it would be a great time.

Joe, Jane, and Juanetta got in the car and headed home, and as soon as they arrived, Joe changed clothes, got his glove, bat, and a couple of balls and headed to Wycoff Corner. When he arrived, he could hardly believe his eyes at the crowd that had already gathered. Besides the guys being there, about fifteen young ladies who were classmates of Joe's and the others showed up with soft drinks and sandwiches for a picnic of sorts. It was quite the gathering and the largest crowd that Wycoff Corner had ever seen.

After a little conversation, the boys started a game that included four of the girls, two on each team, so that all would participate. The rules were changed for the girls so that they received pitches that were thrown underhand and were allowed to play whatever position they wanted. Louise was there and was chosen as a player. Unknown to the rest of the crowd, Louise did not need to be pitched underhand and could play third base with the best of them. This became quite evident on the first pitch. She hit the ball through the seam between the second baseman and the first baseman with a solid single.

Joe and Paul were given the duties to be team captains, and as soon as the teams were selected, the game started. The teams were matched up fairly equally, except for Joe, which made it lopsided when he stepped up to bat. Before play started, everyone started joking about leveling the playing field with having Joe bat one handed, to give the other team a chance. Joe agreed in an attempt to make everything fair, but Paul said nobody was serious about having Joe bat with one hand. They all wanted Joe to hit the ball as solid and as far as he could. There was something about seeing Joe do things that nobody else could do, and being there to witness him at bat and play made the event meaningful and memorable for the bystanders, fans, and other players. If you knew Joe, you would have to make an effort not to like him or be jealous of him. Joe was a great athlete and a person that wanted everyone to do the best they could, and if he could help somebody else to reach their goals or play their best, he was all in to help, and help he did. In baseball, you could hardly be envious of Joe because most knew he was so much better at the sport that he could not be compared to anyone that you knew, including yourself.

Being with or just around Joe, playing against him or watching, it was fun to see his abilities displayed and the mastery of the game that he possessed at a level that one had, in person, never seen before. Joe took his first pitch of the game and hit the ball solid and hard, to drive it so far, that it landed in the tall grass past the mowed outfield, and it suspended play for ten minutes to find it. The rest of the day was fun to everyone that had made the effort to come out to Wycoff Corner, if you played or just watched. When the game reached the bottom of the ninth inning, Joe was in right field, playing deep, and shifted a few feet to the first baseline. Joe shifted to his left because Paul was batting with two outs, and Joe knew that Paul could hit the ball well, and sometimes, he would hit the ball a little late, driving the ball to the right field corner. Paul saw where Joe was set, and he took the first pitch and hit a high fly ball deep into the right center field, absolutely center of the center fielder and Joe. Everyone thought Paul had the perfect hit, out of reach of both outfielders. The moment the ball came off the bat, Joe knew he had positioned himself too far left and made the catch almost impossible. Joe on a wide-open full speed run, glove extended, never taking his eye off the ball, on the tip end of the web of his glove, snagged the ball to the amazement of all those present. No one could believe what they had just seen but had to attest that Joe did what did not seem possible to do, and the game was over.

There was a half-dozen very large trees that stood between the remains or, better yet, what was left of two old buildings, remnants of the old wagon stopover and stagecoach station. The size of one of the relics, basically foundation stones, made one think it could have been a livery or barn for the horses, and the smaller remains looked to be a house. The trees were clustered closer to the smaller structure and probably planted there by the owners at the turn of the century. It was there, closer to the footprint of the old house and what remained of the storm cellar, where the hand pump stood. The hand pump had lasted all these years, more than likely seventy-plus years old, and still worked. It sat on a base or slab of concrete approximately four feet by four feet, which was nice because it kept one from standing in mud, from splashing and overfilling buckets when pumping water up to the spout. Rusted from top to bottom, but one could still see the raised letters on the sides of the pump base and on the flat area of the handle, where it read "F. E. Myers & Bro." The old pump stood a little over four feet tall and had a handle three foot long to pump with. Wired to the main housing of the pump above the spout was a tin box, and inside the tin box was another but smaller tin box, and it held leather cups for the pump. There was also a bucket, hung by the bail, over the spout. The basic idea was that the last user would fill the bucket up in case the pump needed priming for the next user. Seldom, if ever, did the pump need priming because it was used by the area residents for fresh water all the time. Some farms did not have good drinking water, and they would travel to Wycoff Corner and fill up barrels of water to replenish their cisterns during dry months. The spare cup leathers were there so that anyone could repair the pump if needed, but the only thing that needed to be repaired over the years were the leathers. The idea was when the last leather was used, that person would buy three more for the tin, so this way, the pump stayed in operation.

As everyone moved to the shade the trees provided and where the cars were parked, the line started at the water pump. Everyone would take turns at the pump handle to keep a continuous stream of ice-cold water going through the spout. Some of the guys would take the old bucket and half-fill it, to pour the cold water over their heads, and others would get on their knees and stick their heads under the spout and then turn their heads to get a big drink of water. Louise and the other girls would simply wet a towel to hold over their face and wipe the dust off their arms and legs. The girls also had a glass that they would fill for drinking water. But nonetheless, the old hand pump was the center of attraction after and sometimes during an afternoon game.

Joe's grandfather Willis leased Wycoff Corner in the early teens, during some hard times, and made a deal with the present owners, distant relatives of the last folks that occupied Wycoff Corner, to have first rights to buy the property if they ever decided to sell. Walt continued to lease the land with the same arrangements after Willis died. It was Willis that had installed the Myers pump and poured the concrete at its base, with proof being his initials and date scratched in the concrete, "W.M. 5-1-1913." Every time Joe drank or cooled off with the water from that pump, he thought of the story his grandfather had told him that when he converted the old hand-dug well, which had a cylinder bucket and a rope to draw water with, to be modern with the times. Willis had told Joe the water table was high at Wycoff Corner, and the well was hardly thirty-five feet deep, but the top of the water was less than fifteen feet from the top of the ground. Willis also told Joe that you could pull water all day long and not lower it a foot. It was surely the best well in the county.

When everyone was cleaned up and refreshed, they backed up all the trucks to form somewhat of a circle, dropped the tailgates, spread out some blankets on the ground, and the picnic started in full swing. The guys and gals brought things to make sandwiches with, fried chicken, barbequed ribs, cookies, potato chips, soft drinks, and even some beer. When the food nearly ran out, and everyone was full, it was time to lay back and enjoy the cool late-afternoon breeze and the conversation of friends and teammates. The big trees provided plenty of shade and about the only shade within the four contiguous full sections of land. Joe always figured the water that supplied the well also provided a source of water for the trees to survive over the many years, and the well was the reason to locate the stopover station when this area was on the fringe of the frontier.

It was at this time that Joe decided to talk about his feelings and thoughts about playing sports, mainly directed at the athletes he played with at Crescent High School. Joe was sitting on the tailgate of Nellie Belle with his legs slightly swinging back and forth as he looked into the faces of all those seated around him as he told them that sports would not be part of his life for the next few years for a couple of reasons: one being that most of his time would be used helping his mom run the farm, and second, his heart, at this time, was just not in it anymore. Joe mentioned that playing baseball today was the longest time he had not had thoughts about his dad. Getting ready, driving out, and playing throughout the afternoon, thoughts about his dad had not entered his head, and he appreciated everyone getting together to make this a special afternoon and memory for him.

No one there expected Joe to say more than he did because Joe just did not talk much about anything, let alone his innermost feelings about the death of his dad. It became very quiet after Joe said his piece when Paul spoke up and said loud enough for everyone present to hear that whatever Joe decided was fine with him and did not need to be discussed any further. After Paul spoke up, others made nearly the same comment to the group and Joe. They all understood, and whatever Joe decided was the right course for him to take. He would have their support and understanding, and nothing else needed to be said by Joe on the matter. Before the crowd broke up, Joe mentioned that it would be nice, every once in a while, to get back together when possible, repeat the good time that they all had today, with which everyone was in agreement.

As everyone was leaving, Louise told Joe that she would like to see him next weekend if that was okay with him. Joe agreed without pausing and said he would call and set a time, and that it would be nice if he could bring her out to his house to visit with his family and have a meal. Louise thought that would be perfect and would be waiting on his call.

Almost everyone that lived in the rural country area drove alone to Wycoff Corner, and the town kids got as many in one or two cars as possible to make the trip. As Joe was going home alone in his truck and alone in his thoughts, he considered his love for sports and especially baseball and what he was giving up. These thoughts and feelings were quickly displaced by Joe, knowing what his responsibilities were to his family and what he needed to do as a man to take responsibility in the situation. With that in mind, he knew there would be no extra time for daily participation in sports. He could also hear Walt's words in his head, saying to do one thing at a time, not to divide his thoughts, to do the best as possible to whatever the task was at hand. Walt's old saying of "Do what you are supposed to do when you are supposed to do it and how it is supposed to be done to the best of your ability" was the reoccurring memory that repeated itself over and over in Joe's head until he pulled up to his home.

Juanetta and Jane were in the living room when Joe walked through the door, and the first thing to be asked was if he had a good time. Joe told them all about the game and the great time he had, and he hoped they would all get together again as much as possible. Joe also mentioned what he had told them about not being involved in sports, that he would be helping on the farm. Juanetta and Jane both said it was not necessary for Joe to give up sports, that they, meaning all of them, would be able to get things done, and Joe would have the time to practice just as he had done before. As Joe discussed the situation, he agreed that they would probably get along all right, but he knew that the more time he spent on the chores and duties of the farm, things would go much more smoothly and be less of a burden on all. Then Joe mentioned that his desire to play, at this time, was gone, and his heart was not in it, just as he had told his teammates a few hours before. Juanetta and Jane felt bad in their hearts that the toll of Walt's death would involve Joe not playing sports, but they also knew that Walt would want Joe to follow his heart and do what he felt was the right thing to do, no matter what he had to give up. Jane knew that Joe had made up his mind, and if he did change it, time would have to pass. Jane and Juanetta told Joe that they supported what he chose to do and that things would work out when he was following his heart, as they always did.

CHAPTER 13

Last Two Years of High School

Middle of August, when two-a-day football practice started, Joe was on the tractor in the field turning the soil, getting it ready for planting winter wheat. Early that morning, Joe let his thoughts go to what he would be doing if his dad was still here. Although the heat was already in the mideighty degrees at 7:00 AM with a humidity level of 68 percent, making the work on the tractor very uncomfortable with the heat of the engine blowing back on Joe. He knew on the practice field at Crescent High School, calisthenics was just now starting, and no matter how hot, dusty, and uncomfortable it was on the tractor, on the football practice field, it was much more so. Within an hour, the morning sun would be taking its toll on the physically weaker players, and being able to concentrate would be an increasing problem as the practice and heat of the morning drew on. Joe started imagining how thirst in the next hour would start to be distracting and energy level would start to diminish with each degree hotter it grew.

Joe had a section to turn, and this was the first day of about three he would spend in the fields, and then it would be planting time within a week. As Joe lingered in his thoughts, he started to get a drink of cold water out of an insulated one-gallon water jug of Walt's, which he carried on the tractor just as Walt did. The common practice was to drink straight out of the jug, and just as Joe placed the spout on his lips, where he could already feel the moisture that the jug afforded him, a feeling of guilt came over him. Joe started thinking of Paul and all his other buddies that by this time, one and a half hours into the practice, they could think of nothing else but a drink of water. At Crescent High School, as was with most high schools in Oklahoma and other states, in the midsixties, having water available in the heat of the summer was not an acceptable practice of the coaching staffs. The idea was, the longer you could go without water in the summer heat, the tougher you became. Even the best of well-conditioned and in supreme physical-shape athletes, as a summer two-a-day practice approached two and a half hours, the only thing on your mind was water. With this thought in mind, Joe sat his water jug down, firmly snapped the lid closed, and decided he would not refresh himself until his teammates would at the locker and dressing room after their practice.

Joe had to check his thoughts all through the day because they would drift to football practice, then to his dad, and eventually Louise. When Joe was starting a project or a routine chore, he could concentrate and didn't have a problem letting his mind drift. It was later on when he would be involved with a job that he and his dad had done many times before working as a team, where Joe would be waiting for Walt to hold something down or hand him a tool. As Joe held his hand out and the end wrench was not placed in his hand at that precise moment, he would stop, look for his dad for a split second before reality set in. For in that brief moment, Joe's mind could virtually see Walt, and he could feel the wrench in his hand, and he would pause as the thoughts would flood in as water rushing through the open flood gates of a great dam that holds back an ocean of water. All through the day, a multitude of things triggered his memory, and sometimes, the feelings were so strong that Joe would stop what he was doing for a few minutes as he mentally brought himself back together, and he would proceed on.

In these times when Joe struggled to redirect his thoughts, there was a feeling that seemed to overwhelm him to a point that labored his breathing and rendered him feeling as if his surroundings were closing in about him. Although these feelings were brief, they reoccurred many times a day when Joe was alone, and no matter how hard he tried, something would trigger a memory, and the discomfort would regenerate itself, leaving Joe lost in his fields of memories. When Joe was by himself or with Jane and/or Juanetta and was struck with one of these episodes, his outward reaction was to simply stop what he was doing, stare aimlessly ahead, not saying a word and not moving for one or two minutes, then continuing on with what he was doing. While eating supper one evening as Jane, Juanetta, and Joe were conversing and enjoying the meal and the evening, with a degree of normalcy, Joe started to tell a story that related to a job he had finished on the farm earlier in the day that made him laugh. As he turned his head to the right to see Walt's reaction, the dark feeling grabbed him once again. Jane and Juanetta knew to wait, for they had had the same experience and knew that in the moment, nothing said would give any relief to its victim.

On this occasion, Jane and Juanetta decided to share their feelings with Joe about how they were dealing with their own grief and how much they missed Walt. Juanetta mentioned melancholy to Joe and asked him if he knew what it meant. Joe told his grandmother that he had never heard the word and had no idea what it meant. Juanetta told Joe that it was a feeling of sadness that started in your mind and fell onto your spirit. When that dismal feeling moved from your mind onto or into your spirit, it really took hold of you and gave you the feeling that nothing will ever be the same again. Juanetta told Joe that it was easier to deal with something in your head, but your spirit grieved harder than your mind, and rightly so when you experience a loss of someone in your life that was as important as Walt. If one did not grieve in their spirits at the loss of loved ones, the meaning of life would escape them, and life would be equated to material things, and of such things can be replaced, but loved ones cannot. Joe understood what his grandmother was trying to explain. The melancholy feeling he was experiencing was a good thing because it brought with it the greater meaning of life that objects don't possess. Juanetta told Joe as time passed, the feeling of loss would fade and give way to great memories that will last for one's entire life.

Joe's presence on the football practice field was sorely missed in more than just carrying the ball and making big plays. Joe had the ability to lead and inspire the other players to play hard and play smart. When Joe was on the practice field or game field, all his teammates did not want to be the one to let the team down or to let Joe down. When Joe was around, everyone gave it all they had and left everything on the field at the end of the day. But the fact of the matter was that all the team knew Joe to the very last man, and they felt his pain and respected his decision not to play. Paul had shared with the team and the coaches what Joe was going through, and that he did not have the desire to play at this time, and for as much as Paul knew, Joe might never play sports again. At the time that Paul talked to the team and as he was saying that Joe may never play sports again, in the recesses of his mind, Paul wondered how Joe would ever give up baseball for the rest of his life. Paul knew deep down because of his love of the game, at some point in Joe's life, he would return to baseball. He just didn't know when.

The football coaching staff knew that Joe was a player who showed up once in a coach's lifetime, and without the play-making ability that Joe created, a repeat of a season like the one before might be hard to do, if not impossible. The team looked good, and the coaches knew that they would be competitive. Joe's competitive spirit gave everyone a higher level of expectation of one's self. This greater expectation fell on each and every member of the team, and everyone had the feeling that nothing was impossible, and the only way to lose was not to play every down with a 100 percent effort.

Coach Yost and Coach Jensen felt bad for Joe but still wanted him on the team. They both had great respect for Joe's father and family and did not feel like they should ask Joe to reconsider and come out and join the team. They also knew that Joe was much more mature than any kid his age or even ten years older, and that he would not be swayed when he had his mind made up. Yost had mentioned to Jensen that the best approach was to let time take its course, and if Joe changed his mind, you would look up one day, and he would be on the practice field ready to go.

At the start of second semester last year, the football coaching staff added an assistant backfield and backs coach, Coach Bird. Coach Bird was a good-enough coach but was not very popular with the players. He was young and cocky and pretty much knew that he was right about nearly everything, and if you didn't believe it, just ask him, and he would tell you. There was one thing that Coach Bird did not try to correct, and that was the way Joe ran the ball in spring practice. The first time Coach Bird saw Joe run the ball, he knew, as well as everyone else, that he or they, had nothing to add to, let alone try to correct, the way Joe ran a play. Joe also understood the offense and everyone's assignment along with the defensive set and what to adjust offensively against any defensive set. When Yost or Jensen had a question about a play, they weren't embarrassed to call Joe over to the side and ask what they needed to do, adjust, or change the play. Yost and Jensen both knew that Joe, if he desired to coach after he finished college, that he could be a great coach. There might be a point in time when they would be asking Joe for a job.

When summer two-a-days were coming to an end, Coach Bird approached Paul and told him that he was going to talk to Joe and convince him to come back out and play football. Coach Bird was telling Paul that Joe just did not understand that he had an obligation to the team to play, and if he didn't come out and play, he would be a disgrace to the team and school. Paul explained to Coach Bird that he did not know Joe well enough, and with his short tenure at Crescent, he did not realize the force he would face in dealing with Joe. He would be setting back any decision that Joe would make in the future. Paul finally tried to tell Coach Bird that his approaching Joe with that attitude would be an egregious insult to Joe and his family. Any and all that knew Joe would never even think, let alone say, something like that to Joe. Coach Bird explained to Paul that he was just a kid and did not understand what needed to be done to get Joe back on the team.

Paul went to the other team members and told them what Coach Bird was planning to do. He did not want to be the lone one to talk to Coach Yost and Coach Jensen to explain what he felt by leaving Joe alone to make his own decisions without any outside influence or pressure. Everyone on the team agreed because they all respected Joe, and they all agreed that it was none of their business what Joe decided to do. It was not said, but all thought and knew that if the roles were reversed, Joe would not involve himself in their business and would only, and chances are that he would not, give his opinion if asked. The whole team thought it would be embarrassing and would reflect poorly on them if Coach Bird would carry out his plan. All players on the football team wanted Joe to be left alone and not be bothered by anyone, if they had anything to do with it.

The team had a meeting after practice that the coaching staff was not aware of. At that team meeting, Coach Bird's plan to contact Joe was discussed, and the team took a vote of all present, and the entire team was there including the managers, and all voted for Joe to be left alone. Joe was to decide without outside influence if he was ever going to play again, let alone this season. After the vote by show of hands raised was taken, it was decided that Paul would approach Coach Jensen and Coach Yost, tell them of Coach Bird's plan, and that the team had a unanimous vote not to approach Joe at all. It was solely Joe's choice to play or not to play. Paul agreed that he would approach the coaching staff, but he thought that each class should be represented. Paul agreed that he would represent the junior class, Jackie Roberts and Buzzy Tacker would represent the senior and sophomore class respectively.

At the team meeting, it was also agreed that if they were going to object to Coach Bird contacting Joe, it should be done immediately before any harm could be done. Paul knew it would not do any good to attempt to dissuade Coach Bird, after how well his first effort had gone. In his opinion, this team action was the avenue they had to use to intervene. Paul was not sure at how this team intervention would be taken by the coaching staff, and he had a little trepidation as to the outcome of students-kids telling coaches-grownups what they should be or not be doing. Paul also had it in the back of his mind that this action might appear as being disrespectful and that it might not turn out favorable for the team, let alone for him, Jackie, or Buzzy. Paul's final thought about this objection that might be deemed a protest or a threat to the coaching staff was that he did not want his friend to be put on a guilt trip of having to think through a decision that he had already made. Paul's mind was made up that Joe, his friend, did not need to be bothered by somebody who did not know him or what made him think.

The meeting was called just outside of the locker room as everyone was going home, and be it that the coaches were still inside their office that was located within the locker room, Paul, Jackie, and Buzzy went back into the locker room. Paul, with a little hesitation, went up to Coach Yost, with Jensen and Bird watching, and asked him if they would mind discussing an issue that the team had. Coach Yost got real quiet, not saying a word for at least a minute, which seemed to Paul like half an hour and in that time period nearly stared a hole through Paul. At one moment, before Coach Yost said a word, Paul was certain he could see smoke coming out of his ears, and then Coach Yost slowly stood up in the "diplomatic" way he was well-known for. He addressed Paul screaming, "What in the heck do you mean by a team issue?" Paul thought that this would be the initial reaction from an old US Marine veteran that had fought through the Second World War from island to island in which you never questioned authority, and you never brought an "issue" up that the men had. You just did what you were told to do, no questions asked, or you were put into the brig or shot. Paul braced himself, looked straight ahead as the yelling continued with Coach Yost in Paul's face screaming as loud as he could, which felt to Paul like a tornadic wind with a slight rain included. Paul knew not to flinch or look away or even move the slightest because it might be misconstrued as backing up or trying to move away from the monsoon torrent that was taking place right in front of him. To give the impression that you were trying to avoid the eruption would be a sign of weakness, and that would very easily triple or even quadruple the magnitude of heat that Coach Yost was displacing.

Before entering the coaches' office, Jackie being the senior and Paul the junior knew the possibility of what could happen, and they knew that Buzzy, the sophomore, was unaware of the pending outburst at the mere thought of having an organized team issue and how it would be received by the coaching staff, in particular, Coach Yost. Buzzy was instructed to not move at all, not even shift his weight from one foot to the other, not move his eyes, no eye movement at all, but to look straight ahead, and above all, not to say a word at any time, even when leaving, if they came out alive. Jackie already knew that the only one to say anything, even if asked a direct question, was Paul. One person talking was the only way to make a case and defend your position, if there was any chance at all.

Paul did not mind the way Coach Yost took objection with the mere mention of a team not agreeing, or in this case, perceiving dissension from the team as a whole with the coaching staff and the fact that Coach Yost would take it personally. In actuality, it was the exact reaction Paul and Jackie expected from past situations with the coaches at Crescent and the other coaching staff that they had encountered while playing sports. It was the way things were handled for decades, if not forever. Paul knew in his heart that not only in the military in time of an all-out global war, but when Coach Yost was a kid playing sports, his coaches handled like things in a similar manner. Knowing how not to react as well as how to react was the key in how to minimize the losses or the punishment. Typically, once the infraction was handled and punishment met, life went right back to normal, and the situation was not revisited again, and nothing was carried over. About this situation, Paul was not sure how things would be handled and if it would be forgotten in the end.

When things were finally put in order and Paul, Jackie, and Buzzy for sure knew who the boss was (at least Coach Yost was convinced that he had convinced the three of them who the boss was), Coach Yost, after a few moments of quiet, regained a frame of mind that would allow him to hear, took his seat, looked up at Paul, and asked, "Now what in the hell is this team issue you want to tell me about?"

Looking squarely and straight ahead, conscious of not making eye contact with any of the coaches because they all objected to being "eyeballed" and always asked the question to an individual they were mad at, if they were eyeballing one of them, meaning casting an angry glare at them, this they didn't like, and Paul knew it. Taking this in to account, Paul started out by saying "sir," showing respect and then softly saying that it was the team's position that they thought Joe Marshall was a tremendous athlete and a huge asset to the team, and he could mean the difference between winning and losing if he was not part of the team. Paul continued that it would be the desire of the team, all members, no dissenters, that they would appreciate

Joe Marshall on the team not only because of his talent and football skills, but his leadership also, and with that, his absence would create a void that may not be able to be filled by any other player. With full knowledge of the difference Joe Marshall would make in their team and maybe a state championship at stake, it was in the opinion of the entire team, all teammates, that Joe Marshall not be contacted by any of them or anybody else, in an attempt to convince him to rejoin the team. The decision to play was his and his alone. Paul also explained that the members thought that it would look bad and be an affront to the relationship that Joe had with each and every one on the team not to honor the standing decision Joe had made, and that his decision was already well thought through by himself, and he would not change his mind on the new direction that he was taking. Paul then explained that this was the feeling the team had on Joe Marshall's participation, and the team for sure wanted the coaching staff to know how they felt.

Coach Yost looked a little puzzled at Paul's remarks and asked if that was all he or the others wanted to say. Paul said he was speaking for Jackie and Buzzy, and that was all there was. Coach Yost told Paul he appreciated them conveying the team's thoughts on Joe, and he hoped that the team didn't think that their thoughts were any different than his own. Paul thought for a moment before he replied and considered that a degree of diplomacy was in order. He told Coach Yost it was an opinion of the team that the coaching staff needed to know the absolute attitude of the team considering Joe's absence, and the team was solidified on this matter.

Coach Yost explained to the three of them that this wasn't necessary for them to address such an issue because he felt the same way. He knew the Marshall family and grieved with them on their loss and had nothing but a complete respect for Joe Marshall and the memory of his father Walt. Coach Yost went on to tell Paul and his comrades that he had lost his father and had to make choices involving sports and work to help support his mother and their family. From his own experience, people trying to change his mind was not appreciated, and that he had a resentment for the people who told him that he did not know what he was doing because he was a kid. They were not living in his shoes. Coach Yost told Paul that he and his coaching staff could not agree more with the team about Joe Marshall. Joe was a mature young man way beyond his years, and his situation was his alone, and that he felt Joe would have to figure out things the best he could, given his situation.

Paul thanked the coaches for their time and apologized for keeping them as late as he did. Paul turned slowly around, and Jackie and Buzzy followed suit. Paul made sure that he did not make eye contact with Coach Bird because he did not want to encourage any ill feelings between the two of them, but on this issue, he could have cared less what Coach Bird thought of him. Paul considered that Coach Bird just wanted to win and viewed Joe as a way to accomplish his goal so that he could move on and upward with his career. Joe was not Coach Bird's friend. Joe was a means to an end for himself, and Paul knew that. He did not give it any consideration what the fallout with Coach Bird and himself would be.

To Paul's amazement, after football practice the next day, Coach Bird called Paul over to the side and told him that he appreciated the way Paul handled the dispute between them, and that Paul probably saved him an embarrassing situation with Coach Yost. Coach Bird also complimented Paul on being a good friend to Joe. He admired the way Paul protected his friend's feelings, and it had taught him a valuable lesson in being a friend, to stand up for the people that are important in his life. Coach Bird took another coaching job right after the end of the season, and nobody around Crescent ever heard of him again.

As time passed, the thoughts of sports would have a continual recurrence for Joe at which time he would set his desires aside and continue with what he felt was the right approach for the well-being of his mother and grandmother and the ongoing operation of the family farm. The time of year that Joe struggled with the most was the start of baseball season. Joe's heart and mind were part of his love for baseball, and no matter how hard he tried to separate himself from the feeling of wanting to play and be part of the game, he could not do it. It proved to be a constant item on his mind all through April and May of his junior and senior year, and Joe would constantly have to readjust his focus during those months to get any-thing accomplished, be it studies or work.

The one constant in Joe's life after his dad's death was his rela-tionship with Louise. When Joe found himself struggling with his thoughts and the things he wanted to do, as opposed to the things he felt he should be doing, they would all sort themselves out with one talk with Louise. Joe would talk to his mom about what he was dealing with in his head at times, and Jane was a great listener, if not the best ever, but she knew that her telling Joe a way to deal with his feelings was not what Joe wanted to hear. Joe felt that Jane would address a solution for Joe that was for his benefit, not hers, and he was right. Jane wanted Joe to be free from the responsibilities that he took on and follow his dreams and desires. Jane also knew that the way Joe was built, he would never be at peace with himself if he did not address what he perceived was his responsibility. Jane thanked God for Louise being in Joe's life and for the person she was and how dearly she cared for Joe.

As busy as Joe was going to school and working the farm, he still found time, once or sometimes twice a month, weather permit-ting, to get together with his classmates and friends to play baseball or touch football at Wycoff Corner, typically on Sundays, which Joe kept for a day off from normal duties. When Joe was with his friends and Louise during these times at Wycoff Corner, it was as if every-thing was perfect, and his mind was at ease. In later years, Joe would attest that he could remember nearly every minute of every day that they would gather at Wycoff Corner. When questioned by the people present on one of these gatherings, Joe would bring up details of who did what and what was said that made everyone laugh or a play that was made and who made it. Most of the time, these memories of Joe's would be validated by the collective listeners, much to their amaze-ment of the details Joe remembered. What they did not know was that those events, activities, and the people present at Wycoff Corner gave Joe so much pleasure that he played them over and over in his mind as he went through the routine of long workdays.

Joe did not waver from his commitment to his mother, work, or his high school studies over the next two years. Joe was gifted academically and excelled in his studies as he did in sports. Jane was always proud of Joe's achievements in school and marveled in his ability to equally understand math and science along with having a high-functioning level of a literary and art discipline. Joe continued to maintain a four-point average throughout high school, and when graduation time arrived, he was class valedictorian with the highest grade-point average in his graduating class. Joe did not return to sports for his last two years of high school, and no one, teammates, coaches, or classmates, had any animosity for his lack of participation in sports.

Paul was a constant companion to Joe and was around the Marshall house most of the time, either helping on the farm as an after-school paid job or at night studying with Joe. On a weekend or school holiday, the Marshall house was the gathering point for a host of Joe's friends. Jane loved to have as many of Joe's classmates and old teammates as the house would hold. As with the gatherings at Wycoff Corner, at the Marshalls' house during a weekend or holiday, everyone brought their baseball gloves, baseballs, and a couple of bats winter or summer, weather permitting. Jane would cook lunch or supper when the group showed up. Not knowing beforehand how many would show, she stocked large supplies of spaghetti, red sauce, and white sauce fixings and baked homemade bread, making plenty of it for the kids to eat.

These get-togethers kept Joe's baseball skills tuned up, and he never lost the competitive edge throughout his last two years of high school, thanks to his close friends, buddies, and associates. As graduation approached, Joe would occasionally gather his thoughts and wonder about his future and remaining on the farm after high school graduation. After thinking through it a few times, on different occasions, Joe would come full circle, coming back to the fact, if Jane agreed with it or not, he needed to be where he was to run the farm, and there just was not an alternative direction to take. This was not upsetting to Joe because he loved farm life and the Marshall farm, and if he ever left, at the end of any such adventure, it was in Joe's mind that he would return and live out his days on the Marshall farm, just the same, as three generations of Marshalls that preceded him.

CHAPTER 14

Off to Oklahoma State University

C rescent High School graduation came on the last Saturday of May, and Joe's Aunt LaTrenda and Uncle Steve came to the farm on Thursday to stay over the weekend and join in the celebration of Joe's graduation. Throughout the years and especially since Walt died, LaTrenda and Steve would typically show up for Sunday lunch, staying about three hours before heading back to Stillwater. On the major holidays, they would always stay over one night if not two, and it was always fun for them to be there with the family. Joe was a source of continued questions about the university, the students, what Steve and LaTrenda were teaching, and what the happenings were on the campus.

Occasionally, Joe and Jane would travel to Stillwater and go to a function that LaTrenda and/or Steve were involved with that they thought Joe would be interested in. On all these trips, Joe's interest was high, and he loved being involved as a guest and could not get enough of the university atmosphere. On some trips, Steve and LaTrenda would provide tickets to a sports event that was scheduled on the same day, and that meant a double bonus for Joe. Steve and LaTrenda were aware that Joe could not get enough of the feeling of being on the campus or attending whatever was going on while he was there. As graduation drew nearer, Joe had resigned himself to the thought that being able to attend Oklahoma State University and be a Cowboy was not in his near future plans, and the dream of going to college might have to be placed on the back burner for some time to come, if ever.

Early Friday morning, the day before Joe's graduation, there was a heavy rain that had persisted throughout the early-morning hours followed by a thunderstorm from about twelve o'clock midnight, the night before. Other than basic chores, work was put on hold until the rain let up, and even then, it could be too muddy to get anything done. Because of the sound of the rain and the unusually cool temperature, Joe slept in past his normal 5:00 AM and awoke at 5:30 AM. As Joe descended the stairs, he could smell the coffee and could hear voices when he reached the middle of the stairs and before he reached the last step. As he passed from the living room, dining room, and into the kitchen, he was surprised to see everyone at the kitchen table all reading a section of yesterday's newspaper that Steve and LaTrenda had brought with them. Steve and LaTrenda purposely did not read their copy of the Stillwater afternoon paper so that they and others would have something to read in the morning at the Marshall farm. The daily newspaper arrived a day late at the farm with the current day's mail, and it was not a thought to make a trek into town to pick up a newspaper the day it was printed, so Steve and LaTrenda supplied a day-old newspaper to have something to read in the morning, not wanting to wait on the rural mail carrier.

The normal early morning had Jane and Joe arriving in the kitchen at about the same time, within one or two minutes of each other. The unspoken rule was the first to arrive in the kitchen made a fresh pot of coffee because the day could not start in the Marshall house until the first cup of coffee was finished. As Joe walked into the kitchen, his surprise led to wondering why the whole household was up already, starting the morning routine. Juanetta always slept in an hour later than Jane and Joe, while Steve and LaTrenda viewed an outing to the Marshall farm as a mini vacation, and they would have a tendency to sleep in late and not arise until six thirty, an unheard-of late hour to the residents of the farm, about which Steve and LaTrenda would receive a lighthearted ribbing from the other members of the family for missing out on the best part of the day.

Joe passed by the family, wishing everyone a good morning and went straight to the cupboard to get his favorite cup, placing it on the kitchen counter, then reaching over Jane's shoulder, excusing himself as he retrieved the half-and-half. As Joe poured in a portion of half-and-half followed by the coffee, he noticed that he was nearly being ignored be everyone, like they were reading something in the paper that had their whole attention. Joe took his first sip of coffee, and he realized that the sports section or the front page might demand full attention, but the classifieds and entertainment sections, no way. So Joe asked what was up with them and what was so interesting that they could hardly say good morning.

Sort of in unison, the sections of newspaper, which until this point was covering their faces, slowly came down to rest on the kitchen table. Not one of them was making eye contact with Joe, and this action conveyed to Joe that something was definitely up, and now he was anxious to find out what it was. Steve then broke the silence to tell Joe that they, meaning everyone but Joe, had been working out a plan that until now did not concern him, but at this juncture, the plan needed his input to be continued.

Steve had complete respect for Joe and his thought process and the choices he made. Steve wanted Joe to know that he nor anyone in the family would counter a decision or try to change his mind after he had given the necessary thought to the situation at hand. Steve also explained that a discussion had been ongoing for the last five months between Jane, Juanetta, LaTrenda, and himself about future plans from this point forward for himself and LaTrenda. Steve continued to explain that he and LaTrenda were considering changing their work life just a little in a preretirement plan. This plan would go into effect, starting at the first of the upcoming fall semester at Oklahoma State University. Steve's initial plan would involve him taking a sabbatical, which he had already applied for and was granted by the administration, starting from the first day of class of the fall semester. Starting immediately, LaTrenda and himself would be moving into Juanetta's old house doing remodeling as they lived there, starting with the bathrooms and kitchen, eventually redoing most of the old house and the additions that had been done over the decades. When the move for both of them was complete, LaTrenda would start commuting from the farm to Stillwater through the summer and from that time on for the years to come.

Joe knew that Steve and LaTrenda had a master plan that would bring LaTrenda back to the farm. Steve loved being on the farm, and during holidays when he was not teaching or doing research, he would come to the farm and help Willis and Walt when they needed it. Steve's childhood was spent living with his grandparents on a dairy farm in Missouri, and he had working experience with crops and dairy cattle. Steve's parents were killed in a car accident when he was four years old, and almost all his memories involved farm life. Steve's parents had an estate that enabled and provided him with funding to go to college, graduate school, and allowed him to complete his doctoral work. His grandparents were on his mother's side, and along with his mother's two brothers, Steve's uncles, worked the dairy farm until he left to go college. Steve had shared with Willis, Walt, and Joe that living on his grandparents' farm was the best possible outcome for him after his parents' death, and it was a lifestyle that he missed dearly.

When Steve first met LaTrenda and on the third or fourth date found out that LaTrenda was born and reared on a farm, it was easy for him to understand why he felt they had common views on most things, and LaTrenda felt the same about Steve. Joe had been aware of Steve and LaTrenda's feelings for a long time and was just a little intrigued by the sudden time line of their direction. Joe came right out and asked if Steve and LaTrenda were feeling all right and wanted to know if there was some health issue he needed to know about. Steve continued to speak for the group and assured Joe that LaTrenda and he had no issues health-wise and that was for sure not the reason why all this was coming up so suddenly, which as a matter of fact, it had taken five months to get to this point.

There was another set of information the Steve wanted Joe to know, which was that LaTrenda had been appointed to the head of her department, and that he had been awarded an additional grant to do research. As head of his department and after his sabbatical, he would have more of a flexible schedule that did not involve many classes. Steve pointed out to Joe that this was a main point of him and LaTrenda making the move back to the farm this summer. Along with this news, Steve told the group that he had put in for his Navy retirement as a captain, after a combined active and reserved service duty of thirty-two years, which had involved him in World War II and the Korean conflict.

Steve, having said all of this, told Joe that they were now at the point that could involve him. This piqued Joe's interest, and he was anxious for Steve to spit out why he would be involved in this plan. Joe felt a little confused about Steve's explanation as if he was trying to defend his and LaTrenda's decision because he was very pleased that his aunt and uncle had an opportunity to move back and be more involved with the family and the farm. As Steve continued, he told Joe that they had been granted the perfect day to explain all this with the heavy rains interrupting the work of the day and not have interruptions to deal with, which allowed them time to explain in detail their whole plan.

Steve now addressed the point that could possibly involve Joe. Having said all this to Joe, Steve began to address the real purpose of the early-morning meeting. Steve explained to Joe that they were not selling their house in Stillwater at this time, and it would be available for Joe to use if he were a student at OSU, plus with the time off that Steve would now have, he wanted to run the farm in Joe's absence. Along with the house being available, having three bedrooms, two would be available for Joe, and one to rent. The third bedroom that had its own bath would be reserved for the rare occasion that he or LaTrenda might need it if they had a late-night function with the university or needed to spend the night in Stillwater. Also added to the plan was the fact that, unbeknownst to Joe, he had been awarded an academic scholarship from a foundation that Steve and LaTrenda founded and funded for the last twenty years. Steve and LaTrenda had also checked with a friend about the possibility of Joe receiving a four-year United States Air Force ROTC scholarship, and the answer was a high probability with the fact that Joe's grandfather and father served in World War I and World War II respectively along with Joe's grade point and high scores on his ACT and SAT. It would nearly make him a shoo-in for the scholarship.

No one present knew how Joe would respond to the information that was suddenly dumped onto him. Jane felt that it might upset Joe because of meddling into his affairs or how he would view his uncle's involvement on the farm if he was not around. With all this in Joe's court, he stood silently for a few moments, staring at the kitchen table while he processed all this information. After a few moments of silence, Joe first mentioned that it would be his heart's desire to be able to attend OSU in the fall, and before this moment, he could not figure out how it would be possible. Joe next asked a question of LaTrenda and Steve if their decision to move to the farm was solely about him. Steve and LaTrenda both chimed in and told Joe that this was absolutely a plan they had for years, and the time to pull the trigger was as good now as it would ever be.

Joe listened without saying a word and did not take offense at what Steve had said. Joe held his coffee in one hand and pulled out the remaining chair from the kitchen table. As Joe took a seat at the table, he slowly gazed at each of his family members in deep thought about what had just been said, and the first thought that came into his mind was that his family was making a major sacrifice that only he would benefit from. The second thought was his commitment to his family and if this would be what Walt would want him to do. All present did not say anything, allowing Joe to focus on his thoughts and on what he had been offered. After a few moments, Joe asked his family if they were all right with him talking about this plan they had come up with, and they agreed that it was up for discussion.

First thing Joe wanted to address was the effect that this move would have on Steve's and LaTrenda's career, and second, what their thoughts were about this being a selfish move on his part, not being responsible to his mother and grandmother. Without pause, Steve and LaTrenda spoke out and said again that this was a plan long before Walt died, and it had absolutely no effect on their career in the slightest. Then Steve explained to Joe that as soon as he came back from the Navy in World War II, he and LaTrenda had planned to build a house and live on the farm after Walt made the move to reestablish his opportunity to play professional baseball. The plan that Steve and LaTrenda were working toward living on the farm and commuting to Stillwater for a couple of years before they built a house, changed when Walt had his injury and was returning to the farm. They bought a home in Stillwater where they both worked for the university. Steve explained it to Joe that now with Walt's absence, their original plan of twenty-two years ago was now proceeding forward, and that it consisted of a return to farm life that had long been a desire of his, and he was anxiously looking forward to. Steve also mentioned that if Joe took their deal or not, LaTrenda and he would be moving to the farm during their summer break starting within the next few weeks. Steve added one last detail to the plan. If Joe wanted to have Paul as his roommate, it would be fine with them.

After Steve finished, Jane looked at Joe and asked Joe if he really thought that Walt would object at an opportunity for him to study and earn a degree and follow his dreams as much as Walt followed his. Up to this point in time, Joe had not given too much credence to the possibility of him attending OSU in the fall, or at any time in the foreseeable future. Inside Joe wanted to tell everyone that he was in full agreement, and he liked every detail of the plan that Steve and LaTrenda laid out, but he resisted the temptation to reply without giving it more thought. Joe thanked Steve and LaTrenda for their magnanimous offer and asked them if they would mind to give him a day to think it over and give them a reply the next day. They said that not a single one of them thought they would get an answer today, and Joe should take all the time he needed to make a decision. Joe got a big smile on his face and asked Steve if he minded to do the early-morning chores, and if he didn't mind, there was some business he would like to take care of in town this morning. If the rain would stop, he would be back in time to help Steve get other work done. This was okay with Steve, and Joe immediately took off in Nellie Bell and headed down the muddy section line road straight to the bank where Louise worked.

Steve, LaTrenda, Jane, and Juanetta thought that all went well, and their plan was well received by Joe, and the consensus of their opinions was Joe's "business" was to talk it over with Louise, and if she agreed, Joe would be a freshman at Oklahoma State University in the fall. At this point, they all made bets on Joe's next stop, but no bets were actually made because they all agreed that the next stop would be Paul Pixley, and Paul would be the second to know Joe's plan, and the family would be the third to be informed, which was fine with them.

Crescent High School had finished the spring semester on Thursday, and Louise was working at her part-time/summer job at the bank. When Joe pulled up to the bank, it was still raining, and the bank had just opened its door for business. Louise was at a desk in the corner away from the lobby of the bank and could see Joe when he walked into the bank lobby. She was surprised but delighted to see him. There were only three people in the bank when Joe walked through the gate of the spindled rail-fence-like divider that separated the lobby of the bank from the five or six desks where the employees of the bank worked that were not tellers. The rest of the bank staff did not arrive at the bank for another thirty minutes, and with the rain, there were no customers in the bank when Joe arrived, which gave him an opportunity to visit with Louise and tell her about what his uncle and aunt had offered to do for him.

Joe and Louise sat at her little desk, about as far away from the front of the bank as one could get and still be in the same building, when Joe started to explain Steve and LaTrenda's plan of moving to the farm to live and work while commuting to Stillwater. Joe was telling Louise in a matter-of-fact way, showing little or no expression as to how he felt about the plan, good or bad. Joe just wanted to give Louise the facts of what was said to him and did not want his feelings or desires to affect her thoughts about the matter at hand. When Joe had finished, he paused and just stared at Louise for a moment, waiting for her response. Louise's face turned from a serious look to a smile from ear to ear and told Joe that she was overjoyed at the opportunity he had and what a blessing from God to have a family that would support him in his endeavors to go to college. Louise then asked Joe if his family was excited for him to going to school and to live at Stillwater. Joe told Louise that he wanted to talk to her first before he accepted the offer, and she asked why he would think he had to check with her first. There was another long pause before anything was said, and then Joe explained to Louise that from this point on, in his life, and he hoped their lives, that any decision made would be about them and not just him. He would hope it would be the same for her, and when he finished his degree, he wanted Louise to marry him.

There was silence between Joe and Louise for a couple of minutes, and Joe was not going to say a word. It was Louise's turn to say something, and Joe would endure the pain of nothing being said until she spoke. Finally, Louise told Joe to go back home and tell his family that he was excited to accept the plan and yes. Joe confirmed that the yes was to his proposal of marriage, and Louise confirmed. At that point, Joe leaned over the desk and gave Louise the biggest kiss on her lips that you could imagine to which Mrs. Andrews, the head teller, yelled back at them and told them that she would have none of that in her bank.

Joe let Louise go back to work, and the next stop was Paul's house. Paul was up visiting with his grandparents that were staying at his house until graduation on Saturday when Joe walked in. Joe told Paul that they needed to talk about this fall and going to Stillwater. Joe told Paul what the plan was, and he was excited to a high degree and was really happy for his good friend Joe.

Paul was awarded a books-and-tuition baseball scholarship from Oklahoma State University along with a job with the university that involved about ten hours a week and was already enrolled for the fall semester. Joe asked Paul if he had made arrangements for housing, and if he hadn't, there was an extra room at his aunt's house for a reasonable rate, and Paul would be welcome to it, if he wanted to live with him. Paul wanted to live with Joe for more than one reason. The first would be less expensive to live with Joe, and the second, Joe would keep Paul on the straight and narrow with his studies and less goofing around. Paul had visited with Joe on many occasions about the scholarship but never brought it up or tried to convince Joe to enroll with him, but deep down, he always knew that Joe wanted to be in Stillwater when September rolled around. Paul asked Joe if his aunt and uncle would give him some help with the administration so that he would not be required to live on campus for his freshman year. Joe told Paul he had already asked, and they agreed to sponsor Paul so that he could live off campus his first year. Now they were going to live together, and it would make the experience all the better for the both of them.

Joe and Steve worked the farm until one week before classes started. Jane and Juanetta were glad that LaTrenda and Steve were around and very happy for Joe to have this opportunity, but they were sad that Joe would be leaving home. They both knew that twenty-five years earlier, at this same age, Walt and his classmates and friends were heading off to war in far-off places they or their parents had never heard of. That the parents of those young men had to accept the fact when they left home, there was a good chance they would never see their sons again. With that in mind, Jane took solace in the fact that Joe was less than forty-five miles from home, and Joe would be back on the holidays and would be there when Steve needed help on the farm. With that in mind, it was still not easy for Jane when Joe took off, but at the moment, Joe was backing out of the driveway, the thought of Joe coming home for a holiday gave her a smile and something to look forward to.

Steve and LaTrenda were great help with getting Joe and Paul acquainted with the campus and the different buildings. Paul really did not have an idea on what he wanted to major in or what kind of classes to take when he enrolled earlier, so he decided to change his class schedule to match Joe's, thinking that if they had the same class schedule, and they both were good students, they could help each other study and review for tests. Joe was in favor of Paul doing this because he felt the same way, thinking there were mutual benefits and savings taking the same classes. Joe hoped Paul would enjoy business as much as himself or as time went on and would appreciate the business side of life. Paul was also eager to take the United States Air Force ROTC class.

Steve, Paul, and Joe walked the campus with the list of classes Joe was enrolled in and took them to the designated buildings and specific classrooms that were listed. Steve and LaTrenda also helped Joe and Paul pick their classes and the instructors for them and even helped with what they needed from the bookstore. Paul went along with Joe and Steve and stayed at their house for the week before classes, and Steve and LaTrenda helped them along with advice on study habits and time management. With the start of the fall semester, Paul would not live in the athletic dorm on campus with the other athletes at the university, but he was allowed to eat most of his meals at the athletic dining facility, which would be a great cost savings and reduce the financial burden for Paul to eventually earn his bachelor's degree.

Steve and LaTrenda asked Joe before he enrolled if he knew what major he wanted to study, and without hesitation, Joe replied business, accounting, and finance. The Marshall family had always had a good business sense, and Joe knew that was the reason why their farm had run profitably when others didn't. Howard stressed to Willis the business side of farming and Willis to Walt the same and then Walt to Joe. Handling business was as important, if not more important, than the farming itself. Business of any kind was intriguing to Joe. When Joe heard of a business failing or going bankrupt, Joe wanted to know why and on his own had taken his high school accounting class further than anyone had ever dreamed of. At a very early age when Joe would read the business section of the paper, he would ask Walt and Jane all sorts of questions on what the different stock listings meant and what the meanings of the different terms meant, from IPO to selling long or short. Earnings per share was the single item of the stock market that held Joe's interest more than anything else at the time he graduated from high school. The money on the farm that Joe earned from twelve years old was invested in a stock portfolio that Willis had helped set up for Joe through a friend of Willis in Oklahoma City. At eighteen years old, Joe would invest his money in the stock market centering his choice of purchase on the highest dividend paid per price of share, and with this strategy, Joe had success with his investments. For the little money that Joe had invested over the last six years, he had developed an impressive value for his portfolio and at his young age had a better understanding of how the stock market worked than most adults that dabbled in the stock market.

The choice of majors that Joe wanted to study was confirmed by him by the time he finished the eighth grade. Joe wanted to know as much about business as Oklahoma State University could possibly allow him to absorb in the four years he planned to be there. Joe enrolled in eighteen hours for his first semester, primarily taking required educational classes, except for his first business class, Accounting I. Steve and LaTrenda questioned Joe about taking such a heavy load his first college semester, but Joe assured them he knew what he was doing. One thing pushed Joe to take more than a full class schedule. He only had four years to complete his bachelor's degree, which was the maximum length of time that his 2-S deferment allowed him before he had to enter the military.

Paul and Joe had both reported to the Selective Service Board's office in Guthrie when they turned eighteen to register for the draft and apply for their deferments. On a weekend in May before they graduated from high school, they were told to report to the Selective Service Board in Guthrie, along with eighty or so Logan County seniors to be bused to Oklahoma City to the Selective Service Induction Center for a preinduction physical, so that the US military would know the number of physically qualified draft-eligible inductees that could be counted on if drafted. The Vietnam War had been going on since they were in the ninth grade, and Paul and Joe both thought that they would like to finish their college before entering into military service, and the 2-S deferment allowed them to do that if they maintained a 2.0 grade point on a minimum of thirty college hours completed a year. They both passed their preinduction physical with flying colors, which made them draft eligible when their 2-s deferment ran out in four years.

Steve and LaTrenda moved out of their home in Stillwater before Joe and Paul started moving in. Steve and LaTrenda left their bedroom and bathroom intact, and this was off limits to everyone else in the house. They also left all their kitchen utensils, towels, cleaning materials, and most of their furniture so that Joe and Paul would have very little to purchase to start keeping house. All this was greatly appreciated by Joe and Paul and would always be remembered by Joe as an act of kindness that he really didn't know how to repay or that he would ever have the chance to repay them.

CHAPTER 15

Life at the University

As the first day of class arrived, Joe and Paul woke up at six for their first class at eight, which would give them two hours to get ready and walk to class. Where they lived was three blocks from campus, and it only took a few minutes to get to any class they had. When they enrolled in their classes, Steve and LaTrenda instructed them to take the earliest class they could find, preferably an 8:00 AM class because that would start their day early, and they wouldn't have the luxury of sleeping in late and losing valuable time that would be more productive. Joe and Steve did as Steve and LaTrenda suggested because if anyone knew how the academic world worked, they did without a doubt.

Joe thought of what Steve and LaTrenda had told him about making a routine of study, and if he wanted things to go smoothly, he would approach academics and college life like a job. Joe gave this some thought and decided that he did not have the free time he originally thought he had. On the farm, Joe would wake up at 5:00 AM when there were things to do, and most of the time, there was more to do in the summer months than a normal day of work could finish. Joe decided that his approach to studying would be the same as his job on the farm. The study day would be like a workday and would start early and finish late if something needed to be done.

By the end of the first week, Joe realized that the class work and material were no more difficult than a new class in high school except that there was a lot more of it. Now he had double the classes that he had in high school, plus the volume of material to study was more than double. Joe also found out that in high school, his classes did not have a fourth as much work after class as his college classes had. The accounting class Joe and Paul enrolled in required work to be handed in the next class for every class attended along with the required reading. Every class had a reading assignment, and most had at least a paper a week to be finished and handed in by the end of the last class of the week. Steve and LaTrenda explained that the measure of work needed academically would run close to three hours for every hour enrolled. If that ran true with the classes Joe took, that would be fifty-four study hours and eighteen class hours for a total of seventy-two hours a week.

Joe hoped that it would not take as many study hours as the rule of thumb that Steve and LaTrenda outlined, but if it did, Joe's thoughts were that was only ten hours a day. Paul had his baseball practice time to add to his schedule. In the off season, it took about one and a half hours a day, and this would change when the season started in the second semester and would take a longer commitment of time.

After a couple of weeks, Joe and Paul developed a routine that LaTrenda and Steve would be proud of. The 5:00 AM start time was established, and by 5:45 AM, they were out the door heading to campus so they would be at the library at 6:00 AM sharp. Joe had told Steve it would be nice if he and Paul could have a place to study early in the morning so that they could maximize their study time and be close to their first class. Because most of the classroom buildings did not open until 7:00 AM, and they wanted a place that was close to their classes and already be on campus by that time, they thought about the library. Steve knew the head librarian, Mr. Shell, and knew that he arrived at 6:00 AM Monday through Friday to start his day at the library an hour before the library officially opened. Mr. Shell was the first person to show up at the library and unlock the door and immediately relock the door as he went to his office to get things started for his workday at the library. Steve had asked him for a favor, and he agreed that if he would vouch for them, and they would be there at the time he opened the door, he would let them in. He explained to Joe and Paul the very first day that he would not wait on them for even a second. If they wanted in the library early, they needed to be there when his key entered the lock, and they explained they understood the terms.

As their day and week proceeded, they found quiet places and empty rooms in the buildings where their next classes were, so that when class time came, they were only one or two minutes away from the classroom that they needed to attend. A part of their routine was to have the assignment to be handed in ready before they hit the sack the night before, sacrificing sleep time to ensure their best work and not waste time redoing things that were done in a rush just before class. Another part of their routine was to start an assignment as soon as possible, which sometimes was immediately after class in one of their quiet areas before their next class. Joe and Paul also took the advice of Steve and LaTrenda to not set classes immediately after each other, if possible, maintain one-hour intervals between classes. This routine gave Joe and Paul the opportunity to study notes from the previous class, and if they had questions from the lecture, to go by their instructor's office before they left campus and to review their assignment for the next class.

Getting to know Mr. Shell, the head librarian, was a big plus for Joe and Paul. He was a no-nonsense individual, and you had to prove yourself to him before he would give you the time of the day. He warmed up to Joe and Paul after nine weeks of being there to greet him at the library door at 6:00 AM without missing a day. Mr. Shell was a first-generation German, born and reared in the New York City borough of Brooklyn where his parents had immigrated to before the Great War in 1914. Mr. Shell was born there in 1915 and given the all-American first name of Dallas. Mr. Shell did not speak English until he entered the first grade and went on to receive his doctor of philosophy from Columbia University.

When Joe and Paul went into the library, they were all alone, and the silence was deafening. They located a little spot on the first floor over in a corner where they set up shop to study, and nobody knew they were even there until ten minutes before the hour of eight o'clock when they left their seats to head out for their first class, reaching their classroom seats two to three minutes before the professor entered the room. They would return to the library at least once a day to study where they would see Mr. Shell, and he would sometimes stop and ask how Joe and Paul were getting along, or he would ask if he could help them with anything. After Mr. Shell had asked three or four times over a few weeks if he could help them, Joe in a bold moment of his told him one day that he could use his help, and he quickly agreed to assist Joe and Paul with their request. They needed help in how to use the library for a couple of term papers that needed to be turned in at the end of the semester. Mr. Shell asked Joe and Paul if they could meet him on Saturday morning at 8:00 AM and have in hand their topic for their term paper, he would give them a lesson in library science and how to look up research material for their term paper.

Saturday was a day off for Mr. Shell, and Paul and Joe were well aware that he was giving off his free time to help them. Because of this, they gave him 100 percent of their attention and made sure that he did not have to repeat anything. They were all ears. Mr. Shell excelled as an instructor, and he made everything easy to understand. He knew from past experience where students had a hard time understanding and would pause, ask a question about what he had just discussed, and if you answered correctly, he moved on. If not, he backed up, went over the material again, followed by another question and so on until he finished the material he wanted to cover. By the end of the first morning, Paul and Joe had a working knowledge of the Dewey Decimal System and had a good understanding on basic data research in the library. As the years passed, Joe and Paul would look back on the Saturday mornings they would spend with Mr. Shell in the library. The lessons they learned at his tutelage were invaluable and played a great part in the success they had in academics at Oklahoma State University. Mr. Shell would always speak of Joe and Paul as his star students and the fastest learners that he had ever instructed.

The relationship with Mr. Shell continued long after the Saturday mornings wherein he taught Joe and Paul everything he could about library research and the inner workings of a major university library. At the point where the teaching stopped, the Saturday morning routine shifted to a local café for donuts and coffee. The café where they met was owned by a second-generation German that would prepare a small batch of Spritzkuchen just for himself and Mr. Shell. This fried pastry was similar to doughnuts, except Mr. Defenbaugh would use rum instead of lemon for the liquid in the glaze. Mr. Shell called them crullers and delighted in them because it reminded him of his mother and home when he was a child. Joe and Paul enjoyed the crullers more than the doughnuts, and outside of being in a German community in the States or in Germany, it was a treat you generally could not find in an American town. As time passed over the next four years, not a week went by that Joe and/or Paul missed a Saturday afternoon or evening German meal at the Shells. Mr. Shell's wife, Paula, was a great cook, and the meal on Saturday was a culinary delight compared to the meals Paul and Joe had throughout the week. Along with developing a great friendship, Joe and Paul learned German. When it came time to take a foreign language, Joe and Paul enrolled in German, and along with help from Mr. Shell agreeing not to speak English, only German in his presence, the classes of German I and German II were two classes Joe and Paul excelled in with very little effort and were enjoyable to take.

The end of every class day would take Paul accompanied by Joe to the gym at two thirty where individuals and small groups of baseball players would informally work out and on good days finish their workout at the baseball field, working in pairs or foursomes but not necessarily as a team. There was little or no coach guidance given to these workouts, and seldom would you see a baseball coach after these informal workouts started. There was always a graduate assistant or a trainer from start to finish but not a coach. This was where Paul would spend his afternoons working out with the university's baseball team, and most of the time, Joe would just tag along.

The study system that Paul and Joe had worked out was just near perfect. By the middle of the afternoon, using nearly every moment of their non-class time and starting their study day at 6:00 AM gave them a full workday by the time they went to the gym. Joe would work out with Paul and the rest of the team until about five thirty, and by the time they showered up, they were heading for the house by a quarter till six, ready to eat supper.

Most of the time for supper, they had fixed something the night before that they would finish off the next night, or LaTrenda stayed over in the middle of the week and filled the refrigerator with food from the farm, enough to last three or four days. LaTrenda typically scheduled meetings on Wednesday afternoons and evenings and, instead of driving back to the farm late on Wednesday night, would just stay. LaTrenda was good company, and Joe really enjoyed the nights that she stayed over because he could catch up with everything that was going on at the farm. Steve would seldom stay the evening unless he was attending a sporting event, and LaTrenda would be with him so they both would spend the evening.

When Steve did stay the night, nearly all the talk was about the farm. If Steve wanted to talk to Joe about a decision that needed to be made at the farm, he would show up in a hallway outside one of Joe's classrooms or meet him at the gym. Steve knew Joe's schedule, and not often but when the occasion came up, Steve would find Joe. Joe knew Steve's schedule also, and if Joe had not talked to Steve in a couple of weeks, he would drop by Steve's office for a chat. Joe and Paul stayed in Stillwater and did not go home unless it was a holiday.

After supper, Joe and Paul would study for two to three hours and get everything ready for the next day. One piece of furniture that Steve and LaTrenda did not leave was their television. Television reception on the farm was very poor, and because of this, neither Paul nor Joe ever developed a habit of watching TV. Steve and LaTrenda both thought that they did not want to contribute to the boys developing a habit that would waste their time and not have anything to show for it. Their thought was if you were at the house, one should be sleeping, eating, studying, or getting ready to leave to do something, not sitting around watching TV.

Where Joe and Paul lived was a short walk from campus and a short walk from the campus corner where it seemed most of the OSU students that were not studying spent their time eating, drinking, partying, and having a good time. A couple of times a week, when they were ahead on their studies, between eight thirty and nine, they would head to the strip for a break and enjoy college life. Most students did not have the self-discipline that Joe and Paul had, and heading down to the strip in the middle of the week would spell disaster for most young men. More than likely, it was the campus corner that led to the strip, which was the downfall for a lot of students and contributed to them struggling with their classes or flunking out, which subsequently headed them back home or into the army with a trip to Vietnam.

Paul and Joe were not twenty-one, but they both enjoyed beer. Not being of the majority age was normally not a problem on the strip for most students. Joe and Paul both had a manly appearance and had the swagger to go with it. They found out that if they did not cause a problem or get involved with someone who was causing a problem, they were served a couple of cold beers and went on their way. Joe was determined to succeed and pull as much knowledge from the university as possible, and his drive rubbed off on Paul, and he became as determined as Joe. Not many students had the spartan life or the rigors of their study routine, but the more rigid Joe and Paul stayed with their daily regime, the free time they had increased; no wasted time gave them extra time.

Saturday was an off day of the routine. Saturday all day and night was a free day to do what you wanted to do, and they did not want to think about studies unless there was something pressing, then they would make an exception. Saturday did have a routine: cleaning house, shopping for groceries, and doing laundry. Neither of them wanted LaTrenda to see her house a mess, and when she stayed overnight, they did not want her taking her time cleaning the house. They had respect for LaTrenda and the house, and when LaTrenda and/or Steve came to the house, Joe and Paul wanted them as comfortable as when they lived there, and it always was.

Sunday was a little different than Saturday in that the morning was the same as the day before, but the late afternoon and evening was dedicated to study and reading. If something was left over from the week before, four or five hours on Sunday caught them up, and they started Monday morning at the library with Mr. Shell ahead of the study game.

The study, workout, and break-time routine were set and worked flawlessly. The best part of the day for Joe was when he accompanied Paul to the baseball team workout. The very first workout that Paul and Joe attended they bumped into Toe Joe, who was a junior and a starter on the baseball team. Toe Joe was glad to see Joe, and the first question asked was if Joe was going to play ball at OSU. Joe explained that he was there just for the academics, and that participating or going out for the team was just not in the present plan. Toe Joe respected Joe and his choice and knew that he had not played out his junior and senior year at Crescent High School. Toe Joe also knew that if Joe had played through his senior year, that he would have been one of the top picks by the professional baseball scouts and wouldn't be at OSU to start his freshman year. There were a few others on the OSU team that Joe had played against over the years that he recognized, and they recognized him. Those few players that knew Joe from the past would make their way over to visit with him to find out why he dropped off the radar over two years ago and also wanted to know if he was on the team and would be playing with them in the spring.

When Joe was approached by someone that he used to play against two-plus years ago, one of the first comments would be about his size and how much bigger he was than the tall, skinny kid he was two years ago. The last time Joe was seen by these opposing players, Joe was around six feet one inch tall and weighed around two hundred and ten pounds. Now Joe was six feet three inches and weighed in at two hundred forty-five pounds, all muscle and about as lean as he could be. The thing they would ask about was if there was a chance he would be playing with the team. These players remembered the talent that Joe had possessed two years ago, and they knew that at the level Joe played at then, he was good enough to play and start with OSU baseball as a true freshman, which had just been allowed by the NCAA for the 1968 season in baseball. When Joe explained as he did with Toe Joe, they respected his decision but truly did not understand why a gifted athlete like Joe would not play.

Joe was known throughout most of central Oklahoma and around the Tulsa area in northeast Oklahoma when he stopped playing, and just like everything else, the hot topic he was quickly cooled off when he was no longer in the picture. There were a couple of articles in the Oklahoma City and Tulsa papers where their sport writers wrote articles that questioned the absence of the Crescent High School star at the start of the season, but as time progressed, the memory of Joe and his unbelievable talent quickly faded. By the start of Joe's senior year, Joe was unknown, and most of the general public knowledge of him had vanished. It was only in Joe's teammates and the opposing players' memories that Joe now existed, and those memories could possibly last a lifetime with those individuals.

The workouts that Paul attended had other nonteam members with them, and the coaches never mentioned it to any of the players that were on the OSU roster. Through the first semester, Joe would take the time to work out with Paul and the team, and it was something that he truly enjoyed and looked forward to every time. Joe kept his glove and a ball with his books, and when they went to the field, he would be ready to throw the ball and play catch. During these workouts, Joe immediately noticed the higher level of talent that these players had from the level he last played against high school–age players. Joe also felt a surge in his own ability that was sparked by the higher level of competition that these guys possessed. Whatever level of ability Joe played against or with, he would bring out of himself a higher level of play that would exceed that of those around him. This feeling of asking more of himself and receiving it gave Joe a rush and exhilaration that he had not felt in a long time, and he liked it.

The fall semester was off season, and organized workouts for the team did not start until second semester in late January. Because there wasn't an overview of the practices by the coaches in the fall semester, Joe mingled in with the other players, and his talent was noticeably higher than the other players, scholarship or walk-on. When the assistant baseball coaches would check in on the informal practices, when they noticed Joe, they thought he was part of the team.

This changed at the start of the spring semester, where team practices and team meetings were scheduled to start at a certain time, completely organized and attended by the full coaching staff. When these meetings took place, Joe would just blend in and sit in the back, not participate, and if it was a closed meeting, Joe would find a quiet place to study until Paul was finished. When the team took to the field for practice, Joe would hang around on the sides of the field on the outside of the baselines, throwing, catching, and playing around with the other players on the field, shagging the occasional errant ball. At a certain point, after everyone was warmed up and the practice got into full swing, Joe would fade out of the scene and head back to the house, and Paul would show up a couple of hours later.

The head coach of the OSU Cowboys baseball team was new on the job, hiring on just before the end of the fall semester. The head coach that had recruited Paul developed a heart condition during the fall semester and resigned because of his health condition, and the university replaced him with a hard-core, no-nonsense coach named Ron Robinson. Coach Robinson had played in the major leagues from 1928 through 1938. After finishing his playing career, he coached baseball at all levels of the minor leagues and had actually retired from all coaching in 1965 at the age of sixty-two. The OSU athletic director in the middle of December was having a difficult time finding a replacement so close to the start of the season. Most of the assistant coaches at that particular time were fairly new to their positions and early in their coaching careers, and none of them had head coaching experience that the university or the athletic director thought was sufficient to take the helm of the team.

The thought was to get a seasoned head coach that would assure the team had the leadership they needed to get them the most successful season possible. At that point, the administration talked to Coach Ron Robinson to come out of retirement and bring the team together for the start of the season. It did not take much enticement by the university because Coach Robinson missed the game, and after three years of retirement, he jumped at the chance to move to Stillwater with his wife and take up residency.

Robinson was originally from Retrop, Oklahoma, a tiny community south of Elk City and west of Sentinel. Robinson, being reared on a farm close to the little community's two-room schoolhouse, knew what hard work was and was used to it and how to get by on next to nothing. Retrop was not much more than a wide spot in the road, which was originally named Porter. When the community leaders found out that there was already a town established with a city charter in Oklahoma that had the name *Porter*, they just reversed the spelling and renamed the town *Retrop*. Other than the small school, a small grocery store, and a gas station, there wasn't much to the town. Nearly everyone in the community did some type of farming, and the Robinson family was no different from the other families in their area.

Ron Robinson's father, Horace, claimed his land in the third land run in Oklahoma, on April 19, 1892. Ron was living on his family farm when he got the call from Oklahoma State University to be their head baseball coach. Ron had lived all over the United States when he played and coached professional baseball but always considered he would retire and return to Oklahoma on the land that was part of his heritage. After his parents died, he retained the land and the old house and, upon retirement, built a new house where he thought he would live out his days.

The legendary baseball coach Casey Stengel was, without a doubt, the mold that Ron Robinson came from. The old saying that they broke the mold when that person was born, in this case, was not strong enough, because with Ron Robinson, the saying continued with, "They might have broken the mold when Ron was born, but they are still looking for the mold maker to kick his ass."

To the point, gruff, surly, hard to please, and maybe mean are but a few of the words that one would describe Ron Robinson if you were one of his players. He wasted no time in redirecting and/ or correcting a player, and he did not like repeating himself. He had the opinion that if you could hear him when he spoke in a normal tone, that when he yelled, you had no excuse because he knew you heard him and just did not do what you were told, or at least you did something different when he corrected you to save yourself from being confronted. To make the same mistake after a correction from Coach Robinson was nearly bringing down upon you hellfire and damnation. Not many people ever said they liked Coach Robinson, but those who played with him played under him, and those that coached with him did everything within their means to please him and always maintained the highest respect for him. Of those connected with him, he demanded their best effort and 100 percent focus at all times.

Coach Robinson had a theory that not many people truly had a mental deficiency that inhibited them from learning, but laziness, lack of direction, no desire, and an unperfected and directed focus were the culprits that robbed people of their success. This success might be on a job, school, or in the field of athletics. Coach Robinson had noticed in his playing and coaching career that in his opinion, there were three levels of players that he had been associated with that separated successful baseball players: (1) physical abilities, which included natural strength, reaction time, speed, durability, and above all, eyesight. Some of these physical abilities could be improved, but a player could only go so far before his parents' genes became a limiting factor that rendered them unable to compete; (2) desire, the player that would put themselves through whatever it took could trump a more naturally gifted athlete; (3) focus, Robinson noted two levels of focus in his time in baseball. The first focus, all the really good players had developed, and superhuman focus, which the great players had developed. Robinson felt like the great players could nearly will the ball to do what they wanted, and when the great players were in the game, time ceased to exist because it had no meaning or effect on their play. In the major league, Robinson felt that all the players that made it to that level were the best in the nation. Of those incredible athletes that played in the majors, about 5 percent would be the greatest to ever play the game. With all their attributes that got them to the major league, Robinson felt that the separating ability was the superhuman focus that took all the rest of the world out of the park except for the ball and their reaction to it.

Coach Robinson felt those were things he could minutely improve with a player at a division 1 level and gain a measurable competitive improvement, but the one thing he knew he could improve by a large margin was focus, a mental toughness that could drown everything out including yourself. Coach Robinson knew that if a player in any sport started thinking good or bad of what just immediately happened, it would be impossible for them to completely focus on the next play, and that was to him the difference between winning and losing. Robinson never felt that he could bring a player to the superhuman focus. In his opinion of what he called superhuman focus was already in the greats, and at some point, they just allowed it to take over their conscience, and at that very moment, they did things other players could not.

Coach Robinson had been successful throughout his playing and coaching career, and when he had retired, he felt that it was the right time in his life to seek out a life that had less stress and tension than what he had done for the last forty years. When he received the call from his old-time friend at OSU to coach the baseball team, it did not take him long to make up his mind to go with the offer. After two years of sitting on the bleachers, for the last three months, it had dawned on him that he might have stepped out of the game four or five years too soon because he was still mentally and physically fit to do the job, and he missed the game more than he could have ever imagined. When the last two spring seasons started without him participating, he could hardly contain himself with his desire of being involved in some way. He could not read or watch enough baseball to satisfy his need of wanting to be in the game at any level. He wanted to be in a place where he could smell the baseball smells and hear baseball noises, and the only place that could happen was being on the field during a game in a baseball park.

Coach Robinson talked things over with his wife, and she was glad to spend her time in Stillwater and was actually excited to leave the solitude of country living where neighbors were about a mile apart, and it was a twenty-mile round trip to find a grocery store. The Robinsons closed up their farmhouse, rented a house in Stillwater, and Ron was excited to get started with his new team.

CHAPTER 16

Joe Meets Coach Ron Robinson

Coach Robinson arrived on campus at the end of December with the players on Christmas break. When they returned to campus, they would be involved in test week. This all meant that he would not be able to check out his team for another three weeks, but it gave him an opportunity to meet his assistant coaches and access the strengths and weaknesses of the team from their viewpoint. Coach Robinson knew that arriving on campus as late in the academic year as he did, he would retain the present coaching staff and not make any changes until next season if he was still around.

When Joe and Paul started their second semester, it was like a repeat of the first semester. They employed the same routine as the fall semester because it worked out very well for both of them. Joe and Paul both had a four-point average at the end of the semester and hoped that they could continue with the great success during the spring semester. Again, in the spring semester along with their required basic education classes, they took more classes in their major field. This time, it was Accounting II and a finance class. They had enrolled in another eighteen-hour load, but as disciplined as they were, many classes did not seem to bother them. Joe had considered that Paul would be spending more time with the baseball team this semester than last, and he would have less time to study than before. With them taking the same classes at the same time, Joe knew that he could tutor Paul if he got a little behind, and Joe was sure that with his help, Paul would do fine.

At the end of their first day, just as last semester, if the weather was cold and inclement, they would go to the dressing room and work out in the gym for a couple of hours and head home. During these workouts, Joe would hang out with the other members of the team and do whatever they were doing and would hardly be noticed. The assistant coaches who knew Joe was not a member of the team did not mind him working out with the team. They didn't mind because they could readily see the talent Joe had and the work attitude he had around the other players. The coaches also noticed his positive attitude rubbed off on the other players, and everyone got along with Joe. One of the assistant coaches knew from watching Joe that he could easily make the team. He asked Paul about Joe and wondered why he did not try out for a position on the team. Paul explained that with the talent Joe possessed, he could not only start on this team but any team in the nation, but the simple fact was Joe Marshall had his reasons and was simply not interested at playing ball at this time, end of discussion.

When Coach Robinson arrived and got his feet on the ground, he took a hands-on approach to learn about the assistant coaches and players as soon as he could. In his mind, he was already starting behind the eight ball, and time was not an ally. On the very first practice, he took a hard look at his assistants to see how they operated and if he could see any weaknesses in their style or abilities. The first thing that Coach Robinson would take note on was if they were they self-starters and if they did have in their own mind how they wanted to develop the players and what they wanted to develop the team into. At the end of the day, Coach Robinson was more than pleased at what he had seen and felt that the quality of coaching that he had inherited was much higher than he had expected and more than he originally could have hoped for. Coach Robinson would continue assessing his assistant coaches, but he felt there would be no problems in the future and without needing any corrections at the moment in the coaching staff. This gave him an opportunity sooner than expected to look and appraise the athletic ability and playing level of his team.

Coach Robinson had contacted his assistant coaches the day he took the job to do a write-up, including stats, on each player on the team and to mail the papers to him in Retrop, so he could be familiar with them and their background before he had a chance to meet them. Coach Robinson wanted to know as much as he could about his team so that when he arrived on campus, he could hit the ground running.

The first week of the second semester was a bitter-cold, sleet-driven week that kept everyone in, and all the workouts were in the gym. Coach Robinson continued to do his evaluation of the coaches and players without a lot of contact with the team. The weather, which was typical for Oklahoma in the winter, suddenly turned nice with warm sunny days where the ground dried quickly, and the temperature went into the low fifties, and the team moved outside onto the university field where the team would start some real baseball workouts. Coach Robinson then started directly working with the team and his assistant coaches. During the cold weather, Joe would still accompany Paul, freely working with Paul and the other team members, and when the weather broke and the field dried out, Joe went along with Paul to look and watch the team go through infield practice and batting practice and planned to head home a little earlier than Paul.

Joe was standing a little past third base about ten feet outside the field, in the foul ball area with some of the outfielders that were rotating in and out of the outfield. The outfielders were taking fly ball practice, shagging the balls from the people taking batting practice, with his hand in glove. When the players would rotate out of the outfield and queue up for batting practice, Joe would play catch with them to keep warmed up and fight off a little bit of a chill the wind gave at fifty-two degrees as the sun disappeared and the shadows elongated. Joe thought he would leave a little early and did not dress in his sweat clothes like the other guys.

Coach Robinson was standing halfway between third base and home plate about ten feet outside of the third baseline watching the swings of the batters and the fielding of the ball when he noticed a guy in blue jeans and a tan Carhart work jacket. He immediately turned to Coach Hennessey, the batting coach, and asked why the kid standing just off the left field in the foul ball territory was not dressed out. Coach Hennessey looked over and casually identified the kid as Joe Marshall and that he was not on the team. At that moment, the bulldog in Coach Robinson erupted, and he asked Coach Hennessey if he was not on the team, what in the hell he was doing on his practice field. Before Coach Hennessey could say a word, Robinson took off like a lion that had targeted his prey. That day was the day the Tulsa and Oklahoma City news stations had decided to cover the first outdoor practice of the Oklahoma State baseball team. They were filming the new coach working the team on the field and planning an interview with him after practice about his thoughts on the upcoming Cowboy baseball season when, all of a sudden, he took off going down the third baseline with a full head of steam.

Joe was standing with Toe Joe talking about how nice the day was and the opportunity to get to play some ball in the last week of January. While Joe was facing the outfield, he did not notice what was happening to his right and at the moment did not realize that he had caught the attention and ire of the new head coach, let alone his pending immediate ejection from the park. A lot of things started to happen at about the same time that Joe finished his conversation with Toe Joe. Joe noticed as he turned to his right to leave the field that someone was yelling, and Joe realized it was Coach Robinson yelling at him. Why Coach Robinson was yelling at him, he did not know, but he felt for sure in a few seconds, he would find out why. At that precise moment in time, the batter taking batting practice, batting left, swung a little late and hit a line-drive ball that was heading straight for the back of Coach Robinson's head.

In his exuberance to personally throw some deadbeat intruder off his practice field, Coach Robinson could only focus on Joe and was deadened to any other sights or sounds. Coach Robinson at the crack of the bat was at the third base bag, and Joe another thirty feet beyond straight ahead of the approaching Robinson, with his glove still on his hand. Quickly he saw the danger of the moment and with full focus on where the ball heading, Joe charged directly at the coach. As Robinson realized that this six-foot-plus, two-hundred-plus young man was charging right at him and braced himself for the collision, he thought that if it was a fight this kid wanted, a fight he would get. As their bodies crashed into each other, Joe kept his eye on the ball, snagged it with the power of the ball slightly pressuring the back of the web against Coach Robison's head, unnoticed by him. The two of them fell to the ground. It was like watching a linebacker tackle a back that made it through the line with a squared up, heads up, unassisted tackle.

As they hit the ground, Coach Robinson, having spent as a youth some of his time getting into and out of some brawls and fights, was on top of Joe as fast as a duck on a June bug. Briefly giving Joe a once-over, they were speedily separated by the coaches and teammates. Coach Robinson was infuriated that someone would attack him without cause, and he wanted Joe removed and never be allowed to come back. Everyone present tried in vain to explain what had happened, but to no avail. With his dander still up, he had Joe removed. With the excitement over, but everyone's hearts still beating fast, Coach Robinson demanded that the practice resume, to stop the talking about the incident, and get things back to normal.

As the practice came to an end, there was still the planned interview with the TV stations and talking to the TV sports reporters. With the cameras recording for all four stations present, the first and only questions were about the incident earlier on the field with the nonmember of the team and the coach's reaction to it. Coach Robinson explained that people not associated with the team were not and should not be allowed in or around scheduled meetings, functions, or practices, and if they do show up, they will be removed immediately. That did not satisfy the reporters, and Robinson insisted that was enough of an explanation, of which the reporters did not agree. Robinson was confused and did not understand the interest in someone that was not supposed to be there being removed. One reporter mentioned that was not what they wanted to know about, but the incredible play the kid made that could have saved the coach's life. The question did not make sense to Robinson, for all he could see was a big young man attacking him without cause or reason and him defending himself against the unprovoked attack. At this point, Coach Robinson removed himself from the interview, a little perplexed at the insistence of the reporters to go over something that they were clearly wrong about and did not have their facts in order.

By this time, all the players had left the field, showered up, and had headed out as Coach Robinson and Coach Hennessey were walking back to their offices to go over the practice schedule for the next day. While they were walking, Robinson asked Hennessey what his explanations of the incident were, and Hennessey told Robinson if he wanted to believe it or not, the kid saved him, if not from death, for a certainty of a severe injury. Robinson did not argue with Hennessey but could hardly believe or agree that at the distance that separated Joe from him, how he could close the distance so fast and make such a catch to save him from harm. Hennessey explained that if he had not seen it for himself, and someone would try to explain what happened, he too would say it was impossible, but for a fact, he saw it, and it did happen.

Later that evening, just before going to bed, Coach Robinson was watching the news, and the sports anchor started off his program about the fireworks that started off the first field practice for the OSU baseball program. In the sportscast, they had the whole incident on film, and at first, Coach Robinson was totally embarrassed until he saw the reaction time and Joe catching the ball directly behind his head and still had a hard time believing that Joe could have had the time to do what he did. Coach Robinson knew that a couple of the news crews stayed the night in Stillwater for an early-morning interview with the head coach of the basketball team because OSU was starting Big 8 conference play the next night. Coach Robinson made a few calls and located one of the sport news crews enjoying the evening at a restaurant bar down on the strip close to the campus. The entire news crew of Chanel 6 Tulsa was there, and they did not mind talking with Coach Robinson. He just wanted to get their perspective on what they saw before they edited the film for the broadcast. To his surprise, they said they ran it just as it happened, no editing. As Coach Robinson started to leave, he asked if when they got back to Tulsa, if they would mind sending him a copy of the tape they showed on the air, and they said that would not be a problem. They could have a copy brought up tomorrow night with the crew that was going to cover the basketball game. Coach Robinson told them that he would pick it up from them at Gallagher Hall just before the basketball game, and they said the tape would be there.

Coach Robinson was at Gallagher Hall an hour before game time and, as agreed, picked up a copy of the tape that had captured himself and Joe Marshall. He took the film back to his office that evening, loaded it into his projector, and played it over and over again, making himself believe what he was seeing, and after thirty or more replays, he was convinced. The next day at practice, he started asking the assistant coaches about Joe and who his friends where and what they knew about him. The consensus from everyone was that Joe was a tremendous athlete, and from what they could tell from the limited workouts that they had done with him, he was also a very talented baseball player. If he wanted to know more about Joe, Toe Joe and Paul were friends of his from high school.

When Coach Robinson asked Paul and Toe Joe about Joe, he was surprised to hear from them that Joe was the best athlete, and on top of that, he was the best baseball player that they had ever played with or against. The other thing Paul and Toe Joe added about Joe was that he knew exactly who he was and what he was about. Basically, a nineteen-year-old pushing forty in maturity. Paul said that he lived with Joe, and he would tell him that Coach Robinson was asking about him. Coach Robinson asked Paul if he would invite Joe out to the next day's practice, and Paul said it wouldn't do any good for him to ask Joe because he would not come back out after what had happened the other day. Coach Robinson asked if Joe was upset with him, and Paul said that wasn't the problem at all. Joe was more embarrassed that he had unknowingly broken a rule about being at a practice session. Coach Robinson then asked Paul where they lived and what time in the evening they were normally at home. Paul replied with every night of the week from after practice to ten o'clock. Coach Robinson then asked if they ever left the house on a weekday, and Paul said sure, after ten o'clock when their studies were done, for an hour or so.

That night, at ten o'clock, Coach Robinson showed up on Paul and Joe's porch with a hot peach cobbler and a half gallon of vanilla ice cream and knocked on the door. Joe went to the door wondering who in the heck would be showing up at ten o'clock, and when he answered the door, he was really surprised to see of all people, Coach Robinson. Coach Robinson was holding a sack in his left hand and holding the cobbler from the bottom of the bowl with his right hand. Joe looked at the coach and mentioned in a joking tone that he was not going to worry about the coach taking a swing at him since his hands were full, and Coach Robinson grunted a laugh and told Joe that was not going to happen again, and Joe invited him in.

Coach Robinson stepped inside the house, and as he looked around, his first impression was that these young guys really kept a nice, neat house. As he walked further through the house following Joe, there was Paul at the dining room table with his three books stacked neatly on top of each other, one open with some accounting worksheets next to it. On the other side of the table, where Joe sat, was a similar look with a table study light at Joe's end and one at Paul's end. Coach Robinson asked if he was interrupting, and both Paul and Joe said they were just now finishing with their studies for the night and that Coach Robison was not bothering them at all.

Coach told Joe and Paul that when he got home this evening, his wife was preparing a peach cobbler with some peaches they had picked and canned last summer in Retrop for their dessert after supper, and it had given him the thought to bring it over to Joe and Paul's house for a peace offering of sorts. Coach said that his wife had agreed to his plan and had changed her baking time so that it would still be hot when he left the house and yet warm enough at ten o'clock to melt the vanilla ice cream that he had bought earlier to go with it. Joe without hesitation told Coach Robinson that he should not have been on his practice field to start with, and that he was sorry for what had happened, and if anything, it was he that should be making a peace offering to him. When Joe finished, Coach Robinson said that if there were no hard feelings on either side, that they had already spent enough time on that issue and that they have some hot peach cobbler and ice cream, to which Joe and Paul heartily agreed because their mouths were watering at the smell of the cobbler.

Paul went into the kitchen to get the bowls, knife, forks, and a spoon while Coach Robinson started talking with Joe and asked him when he realized that the ball was going straight for his head. Joe paused for a moment and then told Coach Robinson that as he was turning to his right, out of the corner of his eye, he could see the ball come off the bat at contact and knew the direction it would take without a doubt. Joe told the coach that it might be hard to believe, but that was the truth, and he had to instantly go with his gut instinct, not giving pause to think, or it would be too late. Coach Robinson explained that he had looked at the TV film thirty times, and as he looked Joe in the eyes, he told him that he knew it for a fact also.

Coach Robinson told Joe that the great baseball players of all time that he had personally asked how they were able to get the jump on the ball and make the unmakeable play would tell him the same thing that Joe had just explained, that they could tell where the ball was going just as it came off the bat. Coach told Paul and Joe that he wanted to talk more about them and baseball, but it was time to dish up and eat the tasty treat. In a few moments, the cobbler was covered with melting vanilla ice cream, and all three of them were enjoying Mrs. Robinson's award-winning cobbler.

After they finished the first serving, they all had seconds, which finished off the cobbler and the half gallon of ice cream. Joe started a pot of coffee and poured three cups for them to sip as they settled into a conversation about Joe and baseball. Coach told Joe that he had visited with Toe Joe Johnson about Joe, and that all he could do was sing praises about Joe and that the incident on the field was a huge misunderstanding. Coach also added that they had a common friend in Peter Whyte. This intrigued Joe about what Mr. Whyte might have said about him. Coach Robinson told Joe that when he had talked to Peter early in the evening, the player that he had the scuffle with could possibly be, if he chose to play again, the greatest baseball player of all time. Coach Robinson explained to Joe and Paul that a statement like that from somebody else would go in one ear and out the other, but not from a person that had a great nose for talent like Peter Whyte. Coach Robinson said laughingly that Peter

Whyte was what you got when you crossed a lion with a parrot. You really don't know what you get, but when it talks, you listen.

Joe told Coach Robinson that after his father died, that baseball was not in the cards for him because of his responsibilities on the farm and filling the void left with his father's untimely death. Joe also mentioned that his close friend Paul would keep baseball alive with him anytime there was an opportunity and told him about the games organized at a sandlot field at a place called Wycoff Corner that was north of the Marshall farm. With the efforts of Paul and his other high school classmates at Wycoff Corner, the thoughts of baseball and playing the game remained alive in him over the passing of time.

Joe talked to Coach Robinson about his dad's thoughts about getting an education, and that if his dad had it to do over, that he might have gone to college right out of the service and then professional baseball. Joe also explained that his dad talked to him just before he died about desires and goals and what a person wanted out of life and not to start to go about doing things without a full commitment and a halfway approach in his accomplishments. Joe said that his dad wanted him to concentrate on one thing at a time, regarding his major decisions in his life, and to achieve the greatest reward for the work and time involved in his endeavors. Joe felt that his dad at that time was telling him to go to college, get his degree, and if professional baseball was an opportunity at that time, it would still be an opportunity after he graduated.

Joe told Coach Robinson that he really wanted to play, and it was hard not to be around the game, and when he would show up with Paul, it relieved most of his desire to be on the team and to be playing as a member of the team. Joe explained that he couldn't say what his dad's thoughts would be if he were alive today, but Joe felt that as long as he was comfortable with his choice, for the time being, then he was trying to honor his promise to his dad that he made nearly two and a half years ago, and he would continue on the course that he had planned for now. Joe also explained that when he had finished his academic requirements and graduated with his bachelor's degree, he would at that time reevaluate his desire and the possibilities for him to play baseball, and if both facets existed after three and a half years, he will bring his whole body, mind, and spirit to playing the game wherever he could. Joe hoped that Coach Robinson would understand his feelings about his promise to his dad and what the game meant to him. Coach Robinson understood and was glad that Joe had fully explained the situation and his desire to fulfill his commitment to his father.

Coach Robinson told the boys that it was getting late, and the wife would probably start to worry about him if he did not get home soon, and that they would have to wrap it up for the night. Coach also mentioned that his practices were closed, but he wanted Joe to be there as much as Joe wanted to be, and he hoped that they could spend a lot more time on and off the field together, if Joe wanted to. It would be the start of a long-lasting friendship. As Coach Robinson started out the door, he told Joe that he understood that Joe had his reasons for not continuing to play baseball and that he had the ultimate respect for his reasoning, not to be changed or questioned by him or anyone else, but if Joe loved the game and just wanted to be around, to have that great feeling that only a baseball park and the game being played can give, Joe was welcome any and all the time to be on his field and work out with the team. As Coach Robinson was walking down the two steps from the porch, he looked back at Joe and said he would see him at the next practice.

Joe did show up at the next practice, and when his eyes met Coach Robinson's, the coach just waved Joe over to where he was watching the players take batting practice. As Joe approached, Coach Robinson motioned for Joe to just stand by his side and then asked Joe what he thought about the swing of the batter at the plate. The batter at the plate was Phil Wright, and Joe watched for a few minutes and a dozen swings and told the coach that the only thing he noticed was that Phil had a very slight and barely noticeable step away from the plate on an inside fastball, but other than that, his swing looked solid. Coach Robinson shook his head up and down a time or two and then told Joe to just blend in and participate wherever he wanted and stay as long as he wanted. Coach then suggested that if Joe wanted to, he could start by hitting some fly balls for outfield practice and to make them stretch to make the catch. Joe agreed and would place the ball at the extreme edge of their ability and speed to make the play. As Coach Robinson watched Joe work the outfield with absolute precision, Phil just finished his time at batting practice, and the coach called him over and told Phil the next time at batting practice, if he would make a conscious effort to step straight ahead, he might get a better rotation and a little more power in his hitting.

The season pressed on, and Joe showed up to every practice, and Coach Robinson would direct Joe where to or who to work with. Coach Robinson noticed that Joe's ability to play the game at a higher level was equaled to his ability to coach and instruct the players. There was not a coach or player on the field that Joe had worked with that he had not gained their trust or respect. The only question they had when Joe helped or coached them that went unasked was, Why aren't you playing?

Most practices, Joe would stay about an hour working out with the team at Coach Robinson's discretion, helping out where directed, all the time finding an area to hone his skills. Joe began to notice that he might have a slight adjustment that he himself needed that he would discover when working with the individual that Coach Robinson had directed him to. Coach Robinson might notice a slight tweak in Joe's game that Joe himself would become aware of when he would help someone else correct the same flaw. Coach Robinson could see minor improvements in Joe over the weeks and months while Joe was out with the team, and he knew the correction had to be subtle, and it would take someone with a higher skill level than his to correct, so why not let Joe correct himself, and he did, at no surprise to Coach Robinson.

Coach Robinson had a great first season with the Cowboys, and the administration offered him a five-year contract, and he signed it, thinking that if he made it for another five years, it would finish his coaching career for sure. Along with the weekly visits with the Shells, Paul and Joe would also have a weekly meal and an evening visit with the Robinsons. Paul would always be amazed that on every visit with the Robinsons, he would visit with Mrs. Robinson, while Joe and the coach would talk baseball all through the meal and afterward until Mrs. Robinson put her foot down and said that it was enough about baseball, and the conversation would finally change, typically to another sport, usually football, to Mrs. Robinson's dismay.

The relationship and the weekly meetings with the Robinsons and the Shells continued throughout Joe and Paul's time at Oklahoma State University. Through this relationship and coupled with LaTrenda's and Steve's position within the university, Paul and Joe had exposure to all facets of sporting events, lectures, meetings, and the different parties given to visiting dignitaries of the university that the normal student did not have access to. There was not one single event on the campus that they did not have a ticket to attend and usually enough tickets to invite a friend along. Having an extra ticket came in real handy when it came to having a date, and Joe and Paul would sometimes be the only students there with a date, much to the envy of the other faculty and administration. By the time Joe and Paul graduated, they knew most of the faculty and administrators by title, first and last name, and in turn, they knew Paul and Joe.

The great thing about having the tickets and invitations from the Robinsons, Shells, and Steve and LaTrenda was they did not cost Paul and Joe anything, and most of the time, food was included. When they were able to take a friend, it meant a cheap date or an inexpensive night out with friends. Most importantly, the experience of associating with people in the research and academic culture and the development of their etiquette, social graces, and their refinement of being able to handle themselves at any level of social engagement would prove to be invaluable in the years to come. The opportunity to extend their education beyond academia, which their close friends gave them without expectation of repayment, was greatly appreciated and never forgotten by both Joe and Paul.

CHAPTER 17

Graduation and Marriage

The last season and the last semester of their senior year was at hand, which found Paul and Joe thinking constantly about life after college. They were both set to graduate in May, and most of their decisions for after graduation were taking different directions, except for one. They had both decided to get married immediately after graduating. Paul had met a young lady from Tulsa, Beverly, during his sophomore year in an accounting class, and they had been dating ever since. Beverly was going to graduate at the same time as Paul, and their wedding ceremony was set the week after graduation. It was nice that Paul had found someone to date on a steady basis that he really liked in his sophomore year because that was the same year that Louise came to OSU, which nearly occupied all of Joe's spare time.

The big difference was that Paul had decided to go into the United States Air Force after graduating and become a pilot, and Joe had not made up his mind as clearly as Paul. Joe's 2-S deferment would expire immediately after graduation just as Paul's would, and they both knew that being drafted was a surety because their draft numbers were both well below the high of 180 that the government did not expect to eclipse by the end of the year. If your draft number was higher than 180, you would probably not be called up. If your number was less than 180 or a lower number, the chance of being drafted would increase. Joe's draft number was seventeen, and Paul's number was thirty-six. It guaranteed them to be drafted shortly after graduating.

Louise's freshman year, she enrolled in as many classes that her advisor would sign off on, took a course between semesters, and took classes through the summer. Louise wanted to be able to graduate in three years if possible and if not, three and a half. She wanted to be able to marry and to go with Joe after graduation wherever the military or his career would take him with her degree in hand. This was also a requirement of her parents that she would have graduated from OSU before they would give their blessing to marry Joe.

Joe had worked hard to get out of school as much as he could. Paul and Joe both were graduating in the top 10 percent of their graduating class, and if not for their military service pending, they would have had job offers from many of the major businesses throughout the nation. Joe was still unsettled about his career, and in the back of his mind, he still felt a desire to play baseball when he finished at OSU. As the spring semester started, Paul was involved in organized baseball workouts with the team, and Coach Robinson and Joe tagged along as usual. On one of the earlier workouts, Joe stayed for the entire practice and walked back with Coach Robinson to his office. As they walked, Joe started asking the coach what his thoughts were about him being able to play in the major league and being able to get a tryout with a team.

Coach Robinson told Joe that if he really wanted to play professional baseball and play in the major leagues, that getting a tryout was not a problem in any way. All he had to do was ask, and it would happen. Joe then asked the coach if he thought he had the talent to make it. Coach Robinson told Joe of all the talent he had ever seen, his abilities exceeded all others, and if it was his desire to play in the major league, again, he did not see any problem. Coach Robinson explained to Joe that over the last three seasons, he had given Joe a workout that kept his skills honed, and anything he thought was lacking, he had Joe instruct other players in those techniques so that Joe would figure out and perfect his own skills while helping the other players correct their deficiencies, and that plan worked. Robinson also mentioned to Joe that in his participation with the team in their practices, he had noticed an increase in his level of play, and that he was probably more ready for a tryout than he had ever been in all his life. Anything lacking with Joe would be lacking with any rookie, and a year with a team's minor league club would bring him up to speed and, in Joe's case, maybe less than a year. Coach Robinson had never once mentioned or asked Joe what his plans were about playing baseball at any time, with his team or professionally, and now that Joe brought it up with him, he wanted to take the opportunity to tell Joe what he really thought.

Coach Robinson told Joe that in his opinion, he could not be more pleased if Joe would give it a try. His thoughts were that if Joe did not give it a shot, it would be in the back of his mind as a what-if the rest of his life. Coach also explained that he always thought it was admirable of Joe to honor his father and to concentrate on one thing at a time, not letting baseball be a factor during his education so that he could get out of school all that he could. Joe was in shape and had maintained a top level of fitness at all times, and Robinson told him that over the next season, when he worked out with the team during the first hour as he normally did, that if he wanted to stay longer or for the entire practice, it was fine with him.

Joe had talked to Paul a lot about plans to join the Air Force and go to flight school, and the fact of the matter, that would be a five- or six-year commitment with the Air Force, and if Joe wanted to play professional baseball, that would not work for him. Paul told Joe he should check with the US Air Force Reserve and see what their active-duty requirements were, and if there would be a possibility to work out his active-duty requirement after the season, if a pro team picked him up in October. Joe thought that was a great idea, and he would talk it over with Louise. Joe thought if Louise would agree, they might have a plan in place if Joe decided that he really wanted to have baseball back in his life.

Joe met with Louise later that evening, and he wanted to know what her thoughts were concerning plans after graduation. Joe and Louise would both graduate at the end of May, Louise with her degree in accounting and Joe with a double major in accounting and finance. Louise had finished all her requirements in three years so that she could graduate at the same time as Joe and which would allow them to get married and start their grand adventure of life together at the same time.

Louise explained to Joe that now was the time to go back to baseball if he so desired before he started into a career of finance. Joe and Louise also discussed his military service, and together, they decided if he could join a United States Air Force Reserve or Guard unit and delay his active military until after baseball season, all based on Joe being picked up by a professional team to play at any level, that would allow him to play and satisfy his military obligation. All Joe needed now was an opportunity to try out for a big-league team, and if he got that chance, he felt sure he could play at an A or maybe an AA club to start with.

A couple of weeks had passed, and Joe checked with different Air Force Reserve and Guard units and finally got a chance to talk with a recruiter at the Air National Guard unit in Tulsa, Oklahoma. From that visit, Joe found out everything he needed to know about how and when he could join, and that the plan Louise and he had developed would work just fine after they had graduated.

Their plan was to graduate, Joe join the Air Force Reserves or an Air Force Guard unit, get married, get a tryout for baseball, and start their life together wherever they landed. Now Joe needed to get a major league team to invite him for a tryout, and the two people to help him do that were Ron Robinson and the family's old-time friend, Peter Whyte.

The Saturday night following Joe's appointment with the Air Guard unit in Tulsa was supper night at the Robinsons, and Joe had asked Mrs. Robinson if he could bring Louise with him for supper, and she told Joe it was absolutely fine to bring Louise any time he wanted, that Louise was always welcome. Mrs. Robinson told Joe they would have a house full because Paul was also bringing Beverly, and she thought, the more the merrier. Before they arrived, Joe had Louise's approval to announce their plans to everyone present, and with Paul and Beverly planning to attend, it would be a perfect time because they as of yet had not told Paul their final plans. During supper and just after they had finished eating, just before Mrs. Robinson and Ron started serving dessert, Joe stood up and said that he wanted to make an announcement. When Joe started talking, everyone thought that Joe was going to announce their wedding date, and those close to Joe or Louise knew that it would be sometime in June following graduation but did not know the day. It was with mild anticipation as they all listened to Joe expecting to hear the date. Then Joe surprised them all by saying that he had decided to play baseball again, and that he wanted to have a tryout as soon as possible. It was at that point that Joe asked Coach Robinson to work with Peter Whyte and use their contacts to get him a tryout. Coach Robinson was excited to be of service. Then Louise said there was more to the announcement as she added that they had set the date of June 22 to get married. This was great news, and they all celebrated about the news for the rest of the evening.

Once a year, before and after Walt died, at Christmastime, Peter Whyte would call and check in on the Marshall family and get caught up with the goings-on. Jane, Joe's mom, was always glad to hear from Peter and find out what was new with him also. Every time Peter spoke with Jane, he always inquired about Joe and how he was getting along in school and if he was married yet. Jane filled in all the blanks, and Peter was satisfied till the next phone call. Before Peter would hang up the phone, he would invariably ask Jane if Joe had decided to start playing baseball again, and for five years straight, Jane would tell Peter that Joe was staying the course he had set and was not playing with a team. Jane would also explain to Peter that Joe was still working out about an hour a day with the university baseball team, and that Coach Robinson had taken an interest in Joe and his training over the last three years. Peter had been around Ron Robinson and knew that he was a good coach and had a really good eye for talent. He was confident that Robinson understood the immense talent Joe possessed, and he would want to be a part of encouraging and directing Joe in his career to play at the highest level the game could offer him.

Peter Whyte had witnessed and had been involved with some of the greatest talent that baseball had ever had, and he knew that under the tutelage of a great coach like Ron Robinson, that Joe's game would not diminish but would continue to improve with every workout that was under his purview. Peter would give Jane the current telephone number that she could use to contact him if there was ever anything she ever needed, and that once he got the message, he would return her call as soon as possible and with that would say goodbye.

Joe gave the number to contact Peter Whyte to Coach Robinson, and the coach placed a call to Peter the next day. Peter was the head scout for the San Diego Sand Dogs of the American League, and although he was older than most of the scouts, he was still revered by his peers and owners as having the best eye for talent in the game. Peter was in the Seattle, Washington, area when he called in his home office in San Diego and got the message to return a call to Coach Ron Robinson. Peter had the feeling and suspected that the call was going to be about Joe Marshall, and that Joe wanted to resurrect his baseball career, but he did not know for sure because he had coaches from all over the United States contact him about future prospects including Coach Robinson years ago. Deep down in his thoughts, Peter was hoping as he was making the call that it was about Joe and found himself getting excited about the possibility it was about Joe.

It was close to the end of the day for Coach Robinson when the phone rang, and when he answered the phone with the dry "Robinson," more or less saying, "This is who you got, and what do you want?" without saying another word, Peter Whyte identified himself, and Robinson's whole demeanor of "I could care less who's calling" to one of exhilaration approaching an eagerness to talk. Whyte explained that he had gotten his number from the home office, and that was all he had to say before Robinson knew that it was about Joe, and as he told Whyte, it was only a matter of time before Joe would want to get involved again. Coach Robinson could hardly get a word out before Peter asked what he wanted him to do and when he wanted it to happen.

Coach Robinson started by giving Whyte a complete account of Louise and Joe's plans. He started with the time line of Joe wanting a tryout, to graduation, progressing to marriage, and in the fall, to Joe's enlistment in the Air Force Reserves or Guard. Coach Robinson also explained that Joe would have six months of active duty starting in early October. Peter with great interest took notes on the dates of Joe and Louise's plan and then asked Coach Robinson when Joe wanted a tryout. Coach Robinson told Peter that Joe was open to a tryout as soon as possible. Peter came right back to the Coach Robinson and wanted to know if Joe had his form and was in good-enough shape to take an early tryout. Coach Robinson communicated to Peter that Joe was in superb shape, and his game was tuned in, and he added that Joe was even faster than he was a year ago. Coach Robinson talked about Joe's level of maturity, being that it was well beyond his years, and that he had never met anyone that had a greater clarity of a thought process and mental tenacity of focus that Joe processed. Peter mentioned that the apple didn't fall far from the tree, meaning that Joe got a lot of that quality from his father and grandfather. Coach Robinson said that he had met Joe's dad once but wished he could have had the pleasure to know him better.

Peter asked Coach Robinson to do him a favor and ask Jane Marshall for a number to contact General Battle, Walt's B-17 pilot from WWII. Peter had met General Battle when he was still a colonel, at an event a few years back, and Peter had remembered that he was Walt's commander through the war. General Battle and Peter visited that evening, and while they were in the same area for a little while, Battle and Whyte would get together and became better acquainted with each other. Peter told Robinson that at the time, he had his contact number, but after he was promoted, General Battle was transferred overseas. He had lost contact with him. Whyte knew, that like him, General Battle stayed in touch with a call at least once a year and never missed sending a Christmas card to Jane, giving her new or existing contact information. Peter needed a good contact number for General John, and he would see if they could get together to work something out with Joe's enlistment and tryout. Coach Robinson agreed and told him that he would have that information to him before the end of the next day.

Peter received the phone number that would get him in touch with General Battle and made the call as soon as he could. When Peter left the message to ask the general to return the call, he found out that General John was now serving in the Pentagon in Washington, DC, and held the rank of major general. Peter was told that General John was busy and had meetings scheduled nearly nonstop for the next couple of days, and that was fine with Peter. The number Peter left was the home office of the San Diego Sand Dogs' office at the ballpark, and Peter was going to be in town for the next week doing paperwork and looking at the local talent. Peter was hoping that General John could find a place for Joe close to where he would be sent after his tryout.

Peter had seen Joe play during his sophomore/junior summer when Walt died. Peter was on a scouting trip in southern Kansas when he found out where Joe would be playing. He drove out of his way to see Joe play in an out-of-town game. He did not have any extra time to spend with the Marshalls before or after the game and really did not want them to know he was even looking at Joe. Peter's trip was just to look and not to contact Joe, and that was the way he wanted to keep it. That night, he saw Joe run down a deep hit fly ball and make a catch that he had only seen top pro athletes pull off. That same evening, he saw Joe knock the ball out of the park two times and watched Joe being intentionally walked on his other two trips to the plate. The first of the two home runs that Joe hit that night landed in the street that was in front of the houses that backed up to center field of the ballpark. Everyone in the stands that night, home fans and visitors, stood up in disbelief of how far the ball traveled.

When the game was over, Peter drove through the neighborhood that bordered the outfield of the ballpark to see if there were any witnesses to Joe's home run. On the opposite side of the street from the houses that backed up to the baseball field, Peter saw an older couple sitting on their porch, enjoying the cool summer breeze while sipping iced tea. Peter pulled up to the curb and got out of his car, stood in the lawn next to the curb, and asked the man and his wife if earlier in the evening if they had seen any baseballs come over the houses across the street from them. It was a bright night lighted by a full moon, and the light from the baseball park illuminated the neighborhood. Peter could see their faces clearly from the forty feet of yard that separated them, and it seemed by the couple's expressions that he was an unwanted visitor.

In typical Oklahoma fashion, the old man asked Peter what business was it of his, whether he had seen a baseball come his way lately or not. Peter understood the old man completely and knew that more of an explanation was needed about his presence, for him to get anything out of the old fellow. Peter introduced himself and explained, still standing forty feet from the front porch, that he was a baseball scout for the San Diego Sand Dogs, and he knew of a kid that was playing that night and wanted to see him play and watch a good Legion game. At that, the old man introduced himself as Bill and his wife Betty. He then asked Peter if he would like to come up to the porch, have a seat, and if he would like some iced tea to cool down. Peter walked up to the porch and made himself comfortable. About the time Betty served him a glass of iced tea, the old man told Peter that there was something he wanted to show him. The old man reached behind him and retrieved a baseball that earlier he had placed on a window ledge behind the porch swing. Balancing the ball in his hand with his palm up and with his fingers outstretched, as if you were holding your hand out to see if it was raining, was perched a fairly new baseball. Peter asked Bill if that was the ball that came over the houses earlier in the evening, and Bill said that this was the one. Bill with a little bit of a grin and a gleam in his eye asked Peter if he wanted to know where it landed, and Peter with an excited voice asked Bill if he actually saw it hit the ground. Bill replied with a yep and answered Peter's question with, "I sure do." Bill led Peter off the porch and halfway across the street where he stopped and pointed to a spot in the middle of the street and told Peter that was the spot. Bill saw Peter looking at the outfield fence and back down to the middle of the street when he told Peter, 525 feet. Peter asked Bill how he figured 525 feet. Bill told Peter this was simple. The center outfield fence was 385 feet. The lots in his neighborhood were 125 feet deep, and halfway across a thirty-foot street was 15 feet. Bill then looked Peter in the face and made the statement that it was a hell of a hit for a high school kid, and Peter agreed. Bill then told Peter to hold out his hand, and Bill placed the ball in Peter's hand and told him to date it and write the kid's name on it and keep it for a souvenir, that the kid might be famous someday. Peter did keep the ball and stored it away with his most meaningful possessions.

Peter Whyte, with what he previously knew about Joe and with the report that Coach Robinson gave him about Joe, he was assured that Joe would earn a position after his tryout with the Sand Dogs. What he did not know was how long they would keep him in a farm club playing minor league ball. Peter knew in his heart that Joe would not stay in a minor league team for more than a season and maybe less.

Peter got a reply back from General John, and he was assured that the general would do all he could to help Joe find a guard or reserve unit that would work well with his location and give Joe the flexibility he would need when moved from one team to another. Knowing that Joe would be able to stay in the States serving his military obligation by getting into a guard or reserve unit, Peter started lining up a tryout for Joe during his spring break in March.

Joe was in his last semester of college and was in the top 5 percent of the business school. He was in line upon graduation to receive most of the academic honors awarded to the business majors. Louise was also slated to graduate in the top of her class at the end of the semester, and the wedding date was set for June. Joe had his tryout set for March. All was in order, and Joe had taken one thing at a time like he had promised his dad that he would do. Joe felt that now was his time to go back to the game that he loved so dearly, and that he had followed his dad's wisdom by getting the most out of an endeavor that was possible.

Paul also was set to enter the US Air Force in June as soon as he graduated, and the baseball season was over. Paul had completed his ROTC requirements and, upon graduation, was commissioned as an officer in the USAF. Paul's first assignment was pilot training, and he was planning to make a career in the Air Force.

CHAPTER 18

The Tryout

Peter secured a day for Joe's tryout during his spring break. It was a time just before the start of the season when there was a transition downtime from spring camp to the start of league play, and the practices for the Sand Dogs were at their home park Eaton Field in San Diego, California. Peter and Coach Robinson had made numerous calls to Hambrick, the manager of the San Diego Dogs, about Joe and the caliber of athlete that he was. Hambrick thought that Whyte was crazy at first for trying to set up a tryout for a kid that had not played organized baseball for the last six years, since he was sixteen years old. Hambrick was also suspicious of a guy that his highest level of competition was small-town backwoods Legion ball. Hambrick did not like the idea. He was set on not giving Joe a tryout and saving a waste of his time. Hambrick's attitude changed when he got a call from Ron Robinson praising Joe Marshall. Hambrick had seen enough "Dreamers Division" players to last a lifetime and did not like the idea that his top scout was bringing him an unknown and better yet an unknown that hasn't played since he was a sophomore in a tiny high school in rural Oklahoma. Hambrick was in his late forties and had been at all levels baseball had to offer. He had coached with Ron Robinson twenty years ago and had great respect for his ability and his nose for good talent. Hambrick knew that Whyte had a connection with this kid's dad, and he also remembered Walt Marshall when he played professional baseball. Hambrick had it in the back of his mind that Whyte was doing a favor to the Marshall family, and though he respected the gesture of giving a kid his shot to play in the majors, he did not want to waste his time. Hambrick had to give the tryout to Joe a little more thought when Robinson told him that he better not pass on this kid because it would haunt him the rest of his life. Ron Robinson had sent Hambrick a couple of players through the years that were great players and went on to have an extended career in the majors and had never wasted anybody's time, let alone his own. Now Hambrick had two voices in his head telling him to see what this young man from nowhere had to offer. Hambrick agreed to give Joe Marshall a tryout, but it had to be in front of him in Eaton Field, San Diego, California. Joe now had his opportunity.

Joe's tryout was scheduled in the third week of March, which gave him two and a half months to fine-tune his craft. Coach Robinson worked out a training schedule and a workout routine that allowed Joe to carry on with his studies and to go over the specifics of what he would do in his tryout. Joe was already in excellent shape, and his participation with the OSU team throughout the last few years allowed his game to improve steadily and kept him sharp. Coach Robinson wanted Joe to take additional time playing at each position and taking more batting practice. Coach Robinson knew a couple of retired major league pitchers that owed him a few favors, and he decided that this was the time to collect on them.

Coach Robinson wanted to see what Joe could do with a 90 mph-plus fastball and some junk. Joe could hit the high 70 mph and low 80 mph fastball that his Cowboy pitchers could deliver, but he wanted Joe to see some real speed before he left to San Diego. He also wanted Joe to see some real breaking balls and especially a major league curveball before he made the trip.

For two months, Coach Robinson worked Joe really hard with his team. He worked him at each position around the bases and the outfield and allowed his best pitchers to throw to Joe during the week and on weekends. After increasing the intensity of Joe's training and about two weeks before Joe was to report to San Diego, Coach Robinson brought in two longtime friends that both had successful twenty-year careers in the major leagues and loved the game. Mike Shelton drove to Stillwater from Kansas City, Missouri, and Steve

Clark drove in from Broken Arrow, Oklahoma, to take a look at Joe and give Coach Robinson the help he needed.

Shelton and Clark were physical specimens and, while in their midforties in age, had the look of a thirty-five-year-old. They both could deliver close to their best performances on any one given day but could not keep up with the pace, frequency, demands, and length of season that a major league pitcher had to live to be in the game day in and day out. They both retired while still on top of their game before injury made the retirement decision for them. When Robinson called them, they jumped at the opportunity to try their stuff on a kid that Robinson thought was really good. Shelton in his prime could throw a fastball over the plate in the strike zone at a 97 mph plus. Clark could throw professional junk balls when he was in high school and, in the pros, could back the most seasoned of batters from the plate with his curveball. According to Coach Robinson, Clark's curveball dropped the most of any curveball he had ever seen.

Coach Robinson had told Joe that he would have a couple of his old friends drop in Stillwater to pitch him some balls that he might see when in San Diego during his tryout. Joe did not give it a lot of thought about who Coach Robinson might bring in to help get him prepared and did not ask Robinson who they were. Joe thought that if Coach Robinson wanted him to know who they were, he would have already told him. Joe had just assumed that it would be a couple of guys who played in the minors and were in the Oklahoma City or Tulsa area with a little more speed than the Cowboy pitchers had and then did not give it any more thought. Joe also did not know exactly when these two friends were going to show, but he thought that it would be within the last two weeks before he had to leave for his tryout, and he was correct.

On the Saturday prior to the Saturday that Joe was to report to the Sand Dogs' stadium in San Diego, Coach Robinson dropped by Joe and Paul's house and told them that they would have a work-out scheduled when the sun came up on Sunday the next morning. Coach Robinson made Joe and Paul aware that there would only be part of the team present and not to tell anyone about it. Coach mentioned that he did not want any distractions, meaning reporters from the university or local papers present and for sure no TV reporters around to take up time. Joe and Paul agreed to be there about 6:30 AM, thirty minutes before the sun came up. For the most part, early on Sunday morning, most of the students that stayed in Stillwater over the weekend would not be up that early after a long Saturday night. In fact, they could be just coming home about that time and would only be interested in going to bed, let alone be interested in a bunch of guys on a baseball field. Most of the locals would be sleeping in, and the others would be getting ready to go to the Sunday school or their church service and would not be running around the campus.

What Paul and Joe did not know was that Coach Robinson wanted this workout to be known to as few as possible people. It was Robinson's plan that Joe show up to his tryout with little or no distraction and without any questions from the press or notoriety that Joe would have to deal with. Coach Robinson knew that if anybody got wind of Mike Shelton or Steve Clark coming to Stillwater, that alone would generate interest among the public as well as the press, and the first question asked would be, Why are you here? Not wanting to create a false cover story, Coach Robinson wanted the workout to be on the quiet and to let the minimum number of people know what was going on.

Early Sunday morning, Paul and Joe were at the university's ballpark where they met up with ten of Paul's teammates. One of the managers was there and brought the equipment and immediately started bringing things out of the bags. There were enough players there to field a team at each position. As the sun started to come up, long shadows crossed the field, and without a cloud in the sky, the sun brightly illuminated the early morning. About the time the guys had the bags in place, they had taken the field, getting ready to do some warm-up exercises when Coach Robinson pulled up in his car with two passengers. Paul and Joe knew that the two men with Coach Robinson were the two pitchers that were going to pitch to Joe, but they hadn't recognized them as of yet and really did not recognize them until Coach Robinson introduced them.

When Shelton and Clark were introduced, the entire team was overwhelmed with excitement and awe because Shelton and Clark were the first major league players they had ever met face-to-face and had shaken hands. The guys asked why they were here, and they replied with a simple answer of, "To help an old friend and the love of the game." Coach Robinson knew that his guys would want to visit and ask all sorts of questions to Shelton and Clark, and he knew that all the questions would be well received and welcomed by both of them. In turn, Shelton and Clark would ask them questions about their parents, studies, brothers and sisters, hometowns, and where they went to high school and who their current favorite major league team and players were. Shelton and Clark, when possible when in a crowd of players, would always ask, What was the most memorable game you had ever seen or had played in? Shelton and Clark had both learned that players of all skill levels and fans that truly loved baseball could always recite, nearly play by play, what they had seen or played in.

Coach Robinson had to finally break up the question-and-answer session and the stories being told by Shelton and Clark to get to the reason they were all there. Coach Robinson had kept it a secret about Joe getting a tryout with the San Diego Sand Dogs. When he told the team he had assembled that morning, they were all super-excited to help Joe in any way they could. To take the field with two of the major league's best pitchers of the last twenty years was a treat they would never forget.

By the time everyone was warmed up, the sun was shining brightly, and the anticipation was at a high level for everyone on the field, not just Joe. Shelton and Clark were hopeful that Joe would do good, but they were not going hold anything back. Their feeling was, if Joe was all he was cracked up to be, and he was the player Ron Robinson had touted him to be, he would do just fine, and if he wasn't, they would save him a trip to San Diego.

The best pitcher the Cowboys had that year was Bob Wadley, a kid out of Claremore, Oklahoma. Coach Robinson had asked him to be there that day and wanted him to start things off pitching to Joe. He had pitched to Joe many times before with little or no success of getting a pitch in the zone by him. Once in a great while, Bob would throw a change up and get Joe to take a swing and hit nothing but air. A few times, Bob threw a slider, and Joe would not get good contact with the ball, and the ball would be fielded easily, which would result in throwing Joe out. Bob also knew that if he tried the same thing twice in a row with Joe, he would get to see the ball go over the fence and out of the park. Bob knew that at this point in his career, he was competitive and was a winning pitcher at the college level, but being honest to himself, he knew that he was not in the same league as Joe, and as a matter of fact, he did not know anybody that was. When Coach Robinson stopped Bob after pitching to Joe, and it was time for Shelton to throw some heat to Joe, Bob was about to come out of his shoes with excitement to see what Joe could do against an all-star pitcher like Mike Shelton.

Shelton had been warming up while Wadley was throwing to Joe, and when he approached the mound, he wanted to throw a few more and get a good feel from the mound before he got into his rhythm. After about ten throws, he motioned for Joe to step up to the plate. Shelton threw one right over the plate in the high eighties. Joe was pumped and took a full swing, made good contact with the ball, and it went over the fence at right center. Shelton took a long look at the ball and watched it until it went behind the fence. Shelton kept pulling the trigger, inching up the heat a little with each consecutive throw and experienced the same results, Joe nailing a fly ball over the fence. It was at this point that Shelton decided to bring on the heat. No more than Joe saw the ball leave Shelton's hand, it went past him with a hiss followed by a swish of Joe's bat, and then a pop from the ball in the catcher's mitt. Joe stared at the ball in the catcher's mitt for a second while he was trying to process what had just happened. Joe found it hard to believe that the ball got past him so fast. In his mind, he was trying to remember if he even saw the ball go by and wondered if he had just swung the bat like a reflex action without even seeing the ball. Bill Beard was the Oklahoma State catcher during the season, and he had agreed to come out and help Joe at Coach Robinson's request. Bill was a tough farm kid with hands as hard as Joe's, and when Shelton's ball popped in the center of Bill's mitt, you also heard him give a little groan from the pain of a 105-mph fastball.

Bill hesitated before throwing the ball back to Shelton and asked Joe if he saw the ball. Joe told Bill that he didn't know, and Bill said that he didn't know if he did or not but felt lucky he had his glove in the right place. At that, Bill threw the ball back to Shelton who had a smile that stretched from ear to ear. As Shelton stood on the mound, and before he threw the next ball, he declared to Joe and Bill that they had better pay attention and keep their eye on the ball, or it would get by them before they knew it. With that remark, Shelton started laughing and looked over to Ron and yelled that his boy had now seen a major league pitch but didn't know if he saw it or not. He had to ask his catcher if he saw it and laughed some more.

With a huge smile still on his face, Shelton wound up and blazed another hundred-plus fastball right into the strike zone, thinking as he released the ball, that Joe would still be looking for the ball when he heard it hit the catcher's mitt. This time, Joe saw the ball, but his swing was a little late, and the ball went foul just outside the first baseline. Bill looked up from behind the plate and told Joe he was sure glad that he hit the ball because he was not sure he could have moved fast enough to catch it if Joe missed and did not make contact.

Ron threw another ball out to Shelton and with a laugh told him he sure saw that one. Shelton, who had a great sense of humor, looked over to Robinson and said he had made fun of Joe too early. As Shelton stood with one foot on the rubber looking down at Joe from the mound, Joe realized that things just got serious. Shelton was going to deliver all he had, so Joe had better give it all the focus he had, or things wouldn't be pretty when they were through. Joe looked intently at Shelton and just nodded his head, not saying a word, but agreeing that he heard the warning and for Mike Shelton to bring it on, and that he did.

The old pro in Mike Shelton was aroused, and the competition was on. Shelton's focus clicked in, and for all intents, getting a pitch by this kid Joe Marshall was the equivalent of when he pitched in the last inning of the 1959 World Series with the winner of that game taking home the prize. Being competitive and having total focus didn't have degrees to guys like Mike Shelton and Steve Clark. When the joking and kidding around was over, and they decided the game was on, nothing else had meaning. The only thing that mattered at this point in time was for Mike Shelton to leave Joe Marshall swinging at thin air, and that he was as serious as it got.

Joe standing at the plate had the same level of focus, and his was a focus that was tied to a natural talent that put his entire being into motion. At that same moment, a moment of total focus that Mike Shelton was in, so was Joe. At the end of about twenty pitches, Coach Robinson stopped the action and called for a break. Joe had missed six pitches, fouled six, knocked two out of the park, and hit six that could have been hits, if in an actual game. They went to the dugout to take a break. Joe and Mike sat in silence for a couple of minutes as they backed out of their zone mode and then started discussing the events of the workout.

As they were sitting in the dugout, Mike looked over to Joe and asked him if he knew how many pitches he had thrown. Joe thought for a moment and guessed that he had swung at or hit about ten pitches. They both agreed that was probably correct, and they both wondered why Coach Robinson had stopped them so early. When Ron walked over to the dugout, he wanted to know what Mike thought about Joe's ability to hit a fastball. Mike told Ron that he thought that Joe had one of the best swings he had ever seen. Mike went on to say that the strikes Joe made contact with, those same pitches, when he was still playing in the majors, went by the best that played the game without ever being touched, and the fact that Joe made contact with most of the pitches was truly amazing for a kid not ever before seeing pitches that fast. Joe and Mike both asked Coach Robinson what the tally of hits and misses was, and when Ron mentioned that Joe had a probable eight hits out of twenty pitches, which included two home runs that cleared the right field fence easily, Mike and Joe both couldn't believe there were twenty pitches. Ron Robinson looked at both of them and told them that their intensity had let the whole world outside of themselves stop, and time stood still, and they didn't even know what had happened.

As Mike and Joe cooled down, Steve Clark started warming up, throwing pitches to Bob from the mound. Joe, looking at the pitches Steve was throwing, quietly mentioned to Mike that the zone he went into while he was batting wasn't the first time that had happened to him, and as a matter of fact, it had happened countless number of times before. Mike told Joe he understood because it had happened to him all through his pitching life. Mike also added that when he did not get into what he called his "dead zone," batters would knock him out of the park. Mike told Joe that he could even take it so deep that someone would have to tell him the game was over when he was sitting in the dugout in the bottom half of the ninth inning, and his team had the lead. Joe told Mike that he had similar experiences in baseball and even when working on the family farm.

When Steve was finished warming up, Coach Robinson called for Joe to come to the plate. It was about nine o'clock when Steve was ready to start. Around the field, the activity had drawn some onlookers, and Coach Robinson wanted to get finished before any of them got brave enough to come up and start asking questions. Robinson was eager to get Joe at bat and get things finished up as soon as possible, but he was not going to rush Joe or Steve. Steve started with fastballs over the outside corners. While Steve was painting the corners, he would place one a little high then one a little low, both just barely out of the strike zone. Steve was testing Joe's eyes and ball selection. Then he would take one outside and then one inside, seeing what Joe had a tendency to go for. Steve was amazed that Joe only took a swing at the pitches in the zone and made great contact with the ball nearly every time. Now Steve started to enter his zone where any and all thoughts disappeared, except for throwing the ball into the catcher's mitt. Bob Wadley didn't have the fastball in his arsenal, but he could throw all the breaking balls. His nickname was Junkman. He had a great curveball, the best in the Big 8 Conference, and Joe was used to hitting it out of the park, but most batters that Bob faced could not connect when Bob threw his curve. The first curveball that Steve sent over the plate that had double the drop of Bob Wadley's curve and the most by far that he had ever faced.

Steve would throw Joe a curve, and he would miss. Then he would deliver a slider, slurve, screwball, palm ball, and a changeup, and Joe handled them all. Steve would mix in throwing a curve, and through twenty pitches and five curveballs, Joe had only missed the curveballs. Joe stepped out of the box for a couple of seconds while he rotated his head and shook his shoulder and stretched by arching his back while holding his bat in both hands straight up over his head. Joe then stepped back into the box, and as Steve delivered the next pitch, Joe slowed the ball down in his head, and as the ball dropped, Joe caught it perfectly, and out of the park, it flew. Steve threw five more curveballs with the same outcome, and with that, he called it quits and said he had enough.

Mike Shelton and Ron Robinson were watching from the dugout, and when Ron heard Steve say he had enough, he called everybody into the dugout. Mike Shelton looked over to Steve while laughing all the time and said, "He sure kicked your butt." Steve fired back and told Shelton, "He did the same to you, only you weren't watching yourself." Mike and Steve looked in the direction of Joe and Robinson and said in unison, "He's ready for San Diego."

Coach Robinson called everyone in and all those present gathered in the first base dugout to take a break and visit for a little while before going in their separate directions. Joe was the center of attraction while Mike Shelton and Steve Clark started asking all sorts of questions directed at Joe. As Shelton and Clark asked Joe varied questions about his family, background, when he started playing sports and baseball, and then came the question why he stopped. Joe answered that he loved his dad, and that his dad was a major part of him playing baseball. Joe wanted to please his dad as much as he wanted to play the game, and when his dad died, that part of the equation was gone and was replaced with the responsibility of running the family farm and helping his mom. Joe also mentioned that one of his last conversations with his dad that concerned Joe's future, his dad wanted him to go to college and get his degree, to concentrate on one thing at a time so that he would receive the most out of his education. Walt felt that if baseball was in Joe's future, there would be plenty of time for it after he received his degree.

More of a final question for Joe, Shelton and Clark both wanted to know what Joe saw when they released the ball while pitching to him. Joe thought it was a trick question and told them he saw the ball. Then they pressed him for more of a description of the ball he saw at the release. Joe looked at them and asked them not to laugh, but he could actually see the stitching and the rotation of the ball from the moment it left the pitcher's hand, until he hit it, or it went by him. As Steve and Mike listened to Joe's answer, looking intently at Joe, not saying a word, they slightly nodded their heads as if in total agreement or understanding of Joe's reply.

Joe asked Mike and Steve why they stopped playing when they did because from the pitches they threw today, it appeared to Joe that they could still be playing in the pros. Mike spoke first and told Joe that throwing twenty, thirty, forty pitches at any one time, once or twice a month at his age, was not a challenge, and there was plenty of time for recovery because he would choose when he wanted to throw again. He also mentioned that when playing in the pros, when they tell you it's your turn at the mound, the choice was not yours to pitch or not, and 162 games in a season took away recovery time between games. Steve said that it was the same for him, and that with each additional year of age as he approached forty years old, each turn at the mound took more out of him physically than the year before.

Just before they headed out and all ears were still turned to Mike and Steve as they told Joe that they both were still involved in base-ball, in a backstage way, not playing competitively, but their involvement in no way replaced the feeling of being in a game and facing down a batter at the plate. Steve and Mike both agreed that it would be great if there was a team out in the world that needed a pitcher for one or two batters once every two or three weeks, and if there was such a team, they would apply for the job and more than likely do it at no charge, but they both knew that job did not exist. With that, Mike and Steve wished Joe the best at his tryout, and from what they saw, he would have no trouble in getting an offer to play.

Everything was now set, and the arrangements for Joe's trip were booked. Jane, Juanetta, LaTrenda, and Steve all pitched in to provide the money for Joe's trip. Joe didn't want his family to pay for his expenses, that he could take the money out of his savings and investments, but Jane insisted that the family would help him out, and that he needed to save his money for after he married Louise. Joe agreed and was happy that he had his entire family's support.

The plan was that Joe would leave Oklahoma City Will Rogers Airport on Wednesday morning early and arrive in San Diego around three o'clock in the afternoon, catch a cab from the airport, and check into a downtown hotel. The following day, Thursday, the plan was to take the day off for Joe to look around San Diego, take it easy, and have a little downtime before his tryout on Friday. Then, on Friday, he would take a cab to Eaton Field, giving himself plenty of time to arrive before his 11:00 AM tryout.

Paul, Coach Robinson, and Louise took Joe to the airport and saw him off to San Diego. This was the first time Joe had been on an airplane, and it was his first time to fly. It was all a little confusing to him at first, but once he got into the plane and found his seat, he started to relax. The stewardess, a very attractive lady, who Joe thought was just a little younger than his mom, came by his seat. Joe seemed a little nervous, and she asked him if it was his first time to fly. Joe asked her if it was that noticeable, and with a smile, she said yes, it was. The lady introduced herself as June and asked Joe if he lived in Oklahoma City, and he replied that he was a senior at Oklahoma State University living in Stillwater. Joe's answer made June smile really big, and she told Joe that her oldest son was living on campus and was just finishing his freshman year at Oklahoma State University. Joe asked June what his name was and what he was majoring in, and June replied with "Steve" and that his declared major was business. At that point, June told Joe it would be just a few minutes, and they would start their departure. She would come back again just before takeoff and check on him.

About five minutes later, the same stewardess came by and asked Joe to come with her and for him to bring whatever he had with him, and he did so. She guided him to the first-class section where she directed him to sit in an aisle seat. She then told him that the first class was only half booked on this flight, and since it was his first time to fly, she thought he would be more comfortable here, and the attendants would be able to take care of him better than in the coach section. Joe really didn't know what the difference between first-class and coach was but could tell the seats were bigger, and he had more room in this seat than he had before he was moved to first class.

He thanked June for taking care of him, and her effort was much appreciated. She told Joe that she would be able to visit a little longer after they were in the air and for him to sit back, relax, and enjoy the flight. Joe's flight landed in Phoenix, Arizona, briefly, allowing passengers to disembark if their destination was Phoenix and to allow new passengers to board, but passengers continuing on to San Diego would remain on the plane and not disembark. Joe thought this was a great way to spend his first airplane flight, very comfortable, eating all the great meals he wanted and drinking whatever pleased him.

After the plane took off, Joe started thinking about his dad and what his first flight was like. As Joe thought along the line of his dad's first experience, it was probably in an aerial gunnery school at Nellis Air Force Base, Las Vegas, Nevada, during World War II. Joe considered the disparity between the two experiences and in his heart thought that if Walt was with him now, he would think it was comical and would probably be laughing out loud. June checked on Joe a couple of times during the flight and gave Joe directions on leaving the gate, picking up his luggage, and where to get a cab to take him to the hotel. Joe was very appreciative and got June's son's name and what dorm he lived in. He told her when he got back, he would look him up and introduce himself. June was happy to help Joe and hoped they could meet again someday, and Joe agreed.

Joe was staying in the US Grant Hotel in downtown San Diego. The US Grant Hotel was a neat hotel with an interesting history, being built by Ulysses S. Grant's son, Ulysses S. Grant Jr. It was a very nice hotel and was the first real hotel that Joe had ever stayed in. When Joe went with his mom and dad, they would camp out or stay in a motel. So far, the whole experience was more than Joe had ever envisioned. The next day was calming for Joe as he took his time to visit downtown San Diego and look at all the shops, department stores, and restaurants. The largest cities that Joe had been in were Oklahoma City and Tulsa. San Diego was much larger in size and in the number of people moving about. Coach Robinson insisted that Joe take an extra day before the tryout, and Joe resisted, thinking he would be ready to go the day after he got there. Now as Joe moved about taking his time and enjoying the sites and the seventy-degree weather, he was glad that Coach Robinson prevailed, and Joe had an extra day to wind down.

Joe woke up on Friday morning at his normal time of around 5:30 AM, which was 3:30 AM California time. He tried going back to sleep, but to no avail, so he decided to go ahead and get up and start the day. He started by packing his duffel bag that he was going to take to the stadium, making sure he had the things he was going to need. He decided to wear his street shoes, baseball pants, an undershirt that had three-quarter-length sleeves, his OSU Cowboys baseball hat that Coach Robinson had given him just before he boarded his plane, and he would wear a light workout jacket over his shirt because it was a little cool early in the mornings. In his bag, he placed his cleats, glove, a towel, blue jeans, a polo knit shirt, socks, and a change of boxer shorts. Joe thought if possible, they would allow him to shower and change after his tryout, and this way he would be ready to go as soon as he could change into his cleats.

On his walk around the day, before Joe had discovered a little restaurant two blocks from the hotel that stayed open twenty-four hours a day, and since he was up so early, when it turned five o'clock, he decided to go get breakfast and jog the two blocks to relieve some energy that was piling up. Joe took his time with breakfast and read the entire newspaper that he brought from the hotel. It was close to seven o'clock when he got back to the hotel. Coach Robinson had told Joe when he was ready to go to Eaton Field, that he should check with the concierge at the hotel, and the concierge would know how long it took. He would direct Joe to the doorman of the hotel to hail Joe a cab. The concierge was very helpful to Joe and advised that Joe allow thirty minutes longer than the normal fifteen-minute ride because of traffic.

Joe wanted to be at Eaton Field forty-five minutes early, and he was allowing forty-five minutes for travel and traffic, so he wanted to be in the cab at nine thirty, and that would get him there in plenty of time. Joe caught his cab at nine forty-five, and he was on his way for his 11:00 AM tryout. The traffic was a little heavier than normal. Joe arrived at Eaton Field at 10:20 AM, and he still had plenty of time to get where he was going. As he entered the stadium, he was directed to a corridor that would take him directly to the field through the locker rooms and up through the dugout. When Joe started to go under the stadium, he noticed two older gentlemen trying to load some barrels onto a flatbed truck. As Joe approached, he noticed that they were struggling to lift the loaded barrel to the height of the bed of the truck, which was about thirty inches high. The closer he got, he realized that they might need some help because it was six inches higher than they could lift. As Joe walked next to them, he could tell their ages a little closer, and Joe thought they were both in their late forties. Both were trim and fit looking, and Joe could tell that they were used to working, and they reminded him of the farmhands that worked on the Marshall farm back in Crescent, Oklahoma. The shorter of the two had dark-tan skin with a full head of thick black hair and reminded Joe of a Mexican family that lived two sections over from the Marshall farm. The other gentleman was a black and had a powerful build, and he reminded Joe of great athletes that he had met over the years.

Joe had a few extra minutes before he would be late for his tryout, and Joe decided that he would ask them if they needed his help. When he was close enough, he spoke up, introducing himself as Joe Marshall. The dark-tanned man immediately introduced himself as Benito Rodriguez while pulling off his glove and extending his hand to shake Joe's. As Joe shook Benito's hand, again he was reminded of the rock-hard, thick, rough hand with the thick muscular fingers of his dad and grandfather and the other farmers that he was acquainted with and had shaken their hands in the past. Then Benito introduced the black man as his friend C. D. Jones. CD did not say a word as he slowly extended his ungloved hand, and as Joe placed his hand in CD's, he felt more than a firm handshake from an extremely powerful hand. Joe, without pausing, increased his grip and squeezed equally as hard not to let up, but to match the pressure level that CD applied. Joe knew he was being given a challenge, and this had happened before, something of a manly thing, and knew to give it his all and not let up, but to measure his pressure with that of CD's. Joe did not know why this guy was wanting to measure his steel, but Joe was obliged and would take it all the way if necessary. CD and Joe stared at each other without any movement, not even a blink for at least five seconds, when Benito laughed out loud and said it was enough of that and asked Joe how they could help him. At that very moment, CD and Joe released their grip simultaneously. He asked if he could help them get the barrel loaded. Benito, with a big smile across his face, replied saying that he never turned down a helping hand and would appreciate all the help he could get. Benito leaned the barrel over slightly where all three of them could get their hands under and, with one motion, lifted it onto the bed of the truck.

The weight of the barrel was more than Joe expected and could hardly believe that the two of them, Benito and CD, would even attempt to load the barrel by themselves. With the barrel loaded, Joe picked up his bag and said he was happy to help and started on his way when Benito asked Joe if he could spare a little more of his time. Joe explained that he was here for a tryout and just had a few minutes before he would be late. Benito asked Joe if he could help him and CD to load ten more of the barrels, and with the three of them, it would just take a few minutes, and if Joe did not help, they would not be able to get their job done. Also, Benito mentioned to Joe that he knew the manager of the team, and it would be all right if Joe was running a little late. The manager, Hambrick, got there late most of the time and assured Joe that it would not be a problem. Joe paused for a moment, feeling concerned for these two older guys trying to do a job that could hurt them because of the weight, and finally said okay, if it only took a few minutes. Benito, CD, and Joe went through a doorway next to the truck and pulled ten more barrels out and loaded them as quickly as the first, and the job was done.

Joe asked Benito the directions to the field, and Benito gave him specific instructions, and with that, Joe said his goodbyes, picked up his bag, and quickly ran to his tryout. Now ten minutes late, as Joe ran down the corridor, he could hear Benito yelling at him, saying, "Don't worry, it will be fine!" Joe started thinking that one of the biggest moments in his life, he was now late and hearing one of the maintenance workers at the ballpark telling him that everything would be just fine. Joe hoped Benito was right.

Joe followed Benito's directions, continued through a corridor that led to a wide hallway, which eventually took him past the locker room and a hallway that led to the dugout and then to the field. When Joe was on the field, he was in awe at the size of the ballpark when standing on the playing surface. It seemed so large that Joe felt a little intimidated for a few moments as he scanned what seemed to him the enormity of the place. At that moment, he heard a voice that reminded him of his first encounter with Coach Ron Robinson. The voice he heard was asking the same question he was asked four years ago, "Who the hell are you, and what are you doing on my field?" As Joe fixated on the voice and who of the fifteen to twenty people on the field that it came from, he moved slowly to the person that was moving toward him.

As the two narrowed the distance between them, Joe was taken aback a little when it seemed to him that he was approaching Ron Robinson's younger twin. The resemblance between Coach Robinson and whom he guessed was Coach Hambrick was uncanny. The way this individual walked, talked, gruff speech, and basically moved was a mirror image of Coach Robinson. At a distance of ten feet, Joe thought he should identify himself, and no faster than Joe said his name, he was greeted with what seemed like a growling barking dog, telling him that he assumed as much.

Then he identified himself as Coach Scott Hambrick and that he had been waiting for fifteen minutes, and that when the person he had been waiting for finally arrived, he was not dressed out ready to go. Coach Hambrick then continued that he was doing a friend a favor, granting Joe a tryout, with a player that he had never heard of and could care less if he ever saw him, and it added insult to injury to wait on a player that didn't know how to tell time or didn't care. Coach Hambrick then continued that he didn't wait for a player that he knew of and wanted to see. So having said that, the next barking command to come from Coach Hambrick was for Joe to get off his field and out of his ballpark as quick as possible or be removed by security.

Joe knew that he had made a mistake and, in his mind, had a resolve that there would be another chance, if not here, somewhere else. There was also an instant feeling that he had let a lot of people down including himself. As he turned to leave, another thought occurred that if he had to do it over, there still existed the probability that he would stop and help the two maintenance workers lift the heavy load. As Joe was walking away, he was dealing with the disparity of the euphoric feeling he had just a few minutes prior when he walked on to the field, to that of a numb, or no feeling at all, void that left him with little or no sensitivity for just a moment. Then Joe decided that there was nothing he could do about the situation, and he had better do what Coach Hambrick had told him to. Joe walked briskly to the dugout along the same path he had arrived, followed closely behind by Coach Hambrick. As Joe approached the two steps in the dugout that stepped down from the field level to the floor of the dugout, the phone on the wall to his right began ringing. Coach Hambrick followed Joe step by step into the dugout and quickly reached over to answer the phone as Joe continued on.

Joe continued walking from the dugout into a hallway, more of a tunnel, that echoed sounds, and he could hear Coach Hambrick on the phone in a grumpy tone repeatedly saying, "Yeah, yeah, okay, yeah, okay, you're kidding," Then an "Okay, I got it." Then Joe heard Coach Hambrick ask him to hold up for a moment, and then he wanted confirmation that he was Joe Marshall. Joe stopped and affirmed he was Joe Marshall. At that point, Coach Hambrick told him to go into the locker room, dress out, and be on the field in ten minutes, and if at all possible not to be late. Joe did not hesitate or even say a word but jumped into the locker room and changed as fast as Superman in a phone booth.

Joe was back on the field in less than ten minutes and located Coach Hambrick the moment he stepped up out of the dugout and started his way. While he was jogging over to where Coach Hambrick was standing, he wondered why or what had changed his mind about letting him try out and then deciding it made no difference because what he had come for was now going to happen.

Joe knew that this was not a normal tryout where a bunch of hopeful players showed up, listed their name, and stood around until their position and name were called. Everyone waited their turn to show their stuff. Joe was the only one trying out, and the rest of the players currently on the roster of the San Diego Sand Dogs were working out and doing drills. They were also there to assist the coaching staff in Joe's tryout.

There was another coach standing next to Coach Hambrick as Joe approached. Coach Hambrick told Joe to go with Coach Pickup, and he would take him through stretching and warm-up exercises and explain what the first element of the tryout would be. After forty-five minutes with Coach Pickup, Joe had developed some heat and was perspiring all over his body. He wanted to tell Coach Pickup after twenty minutes that he felt that he was fully warmed up and was ready for the next event. Thinking that Coach Pickup said nothing but what he wanted Joe to do, not making any casual conversation at all, Joe figured he had better not open his mouth unless he was asked a question, and he knew the answer, if not, keep his lips sealed. Joe knew that this was all business at a higher level than it was at Oklahoma State, and the coaches and players present did not want to waste a moment, let alone a minute.

Coach Pickup motioned to Joe to follow him, and they met up with two other coaches along the foul ball line in right field. They explained to Joe that he would be running a timed sixty-yard dash. They said that Joe would be in a slightly open stance, feet in line with the direction that he will run with his chest perpendicular to the direction he would be running, as though he was on base getting ready to run to the next base. He would start at the right foul line and run past the coach standing sixty yards out in the right field. As they were setting Joe up to start, Coach Hambrick came close by to watch. Coach Pickup told Joe that he wanted him to run half speed on the first run from start to finish and not to push it, and it was not timed. Joe understood. Joe waited and got the go from Coach Pickup and ran half speed past the coach in the outfield without timing it. This was repeated three times. Then Coach Pickup told Joe to start out fast as though he was running a twenty-yard dash and jog out the last forty yards without putting on the brakes, just like when you run through the finish line, and they did that three times without a time. Really no one was paying any attention to what Joe was doing except for Coach Pickup.

When Joe jogged back to the foul line where Coach Pickup was, he was told to catch his breath, walk around a little, and let his heart come to a resting heart rate, and that he would be with him in a few minutes. Coach Pickup walked away from Joe and went to talk to Coach Hambrick while Joe caught his breath and let his heartbeat slow a little. Coach Pickup quietly told Coach Hambrick he needed to take a closer look at this unknown. Coach Hambrick asked why, and Coach Pickup said that when Joe pushed the first twenty, it seemed as though he was shot out of a cannon. "Explosive" was how Coach Pickup explained it. Coach Pickup told Coach Hambrick that if Joe didn't peter out at the forty, this might be something to see. Hambrick walked over to Joe, and they asked Joe if he was ready, and he nodded. Coach Pickup told Joe the command would be ready, set, then blow his whistle to go, and again, Joe nodded that he understood. The coach at the finish line acknowledged he was ready, and the whistle blew, and Joe took off. Coach Hambrick and Coach Pickup standing at the starting line knew in an instant that Joe ran a very fast time, but watching from his backside, it was not apparent how fast he ran.

Coach Hambrick yelled at Coach Henning to shout out his time, but Coach Henning remained silent to the dismay of Coach Hambrick. Then, with Coach Hambrick getting more irritated by the second, Coach Henning started jogging toward Coach Hambrick and Pickup with stopwatch in hand. The first thing Coach Hambrick asked Coach Henning was, "Can't you read a stopwatch?" Coach Henning said that his must be broken or not working properly because it read 6.1 seconds. As Coach Hambrick looked at the stopwatch, he told Coach Henning to throw that SOB away and get a new one. In the meantime, he told him to use his, which he pulled out of his front pocket. Then Coach Hambrick told everyone to get ready and encouraged everyone to get it right this time before they wore the kid out. Again, the whistle blew, and Joe took off, and as Joe crossed the finish line, Coach Hambrick was yelling at Coach Henning for his time. Again, no reply, and Coach Henning started back to Coach Hambrick. This lit the fuse on Coach Hambrick. What in hell was the matter this time? Coach Henning did not say a word but just handed the stopwatch to Coach Hambrick with the needle on it just below the 6.1 second line, meaning something less than 6.1, maybe a 6.09 or lower. Coach Hambrick at this moment was madder than a hatter.

He told Henning to give his stopwatch back and made the statement that if he wanted something done right, that he did it himself. He also told Coach Pickup to come with him, and they would both time Joe's next run. Joe rested a few minutes, and when he was ready, he took his stance, and the whistle blew, and he was off. Coach Hambrick and Pickup hit the button on top of their stopwatches as Joe ran by, and they both stared at their respective watches, not moving or blinking for the longest time. This time, both stopwatches had the needle just shy of the 6.0 mark, a time that was near unbelievable.

A crowd had developed around the coaches and Joe just before he ran his last sixty-yard dash. Players, other coaches, and even the ground personnel on the field that day had seen the speed displayed by Joe, and it drew their interest and comments. Even at a distance, the speed Joe had was visible. One of the Sand Dogs on the field this day commented that Joe was as fast as a big cat chasing his prey and that Joe ran like a deer in the wild. All this was true, and the events of this left indelible memories in the minds of all that were present.

After staring at their respective stopwatches, Coach Hambrick and Coach Pickup stood silent for a few seconds, pondering the level of talent that was in their presence. Once the reality set in, Coach Hambrick looked directly into Joe's eyes and directed him to start warming up his arm, and the next thing would be working in the outfield because Coach Hambrick wanted to see Joe's arm strength to see if Joe could really air the ball out. Coach Hambrick took a position to the side of the home plate, and Coach Pickup took a position at the outside edge of the infield by first base. Joe was in the shallow center left field, and his outfield work started with grounders where Joe's fielding and accuracy throwing the ball back to home plate could be judged. Coach Hambrick wanted Joe to field about fifteen grounders and would increase the distance so that Joe would have enough easy throws to home to warm up his arm thoroughly. After the initial fifteen throws, Coach Hambrick would move Joe back fifty or sixty feet every two or three throws, where Joe would only be fielding fly balls, until he was fielding balls deep in right field next to the warning track.

On each throw, Joe's accuracy was perfect, and Coach Hambrick was getting real excited to see a deeper hit ball returned with the same accuracy as a shallow hit ball. Hambrick wanted to know when Joe would reach his maximum and motioned for a cutoff man to line up with Joe when he caught the ball and home plate. Coach Pickup yelled at Joe to hit the cutoff man if he could not get the ball to home plate. As Joe was getting deeper and deeper into right center field, Coach Hambrick told the player hitting the fly balls to move Joe around and make him chase a few, and on all catches, the ball came back to home plate in the air or maybe a short hop in front of the catcher. Before they wore Joe out, Coach Hambrick told the batter to put one as close to the warning track as possible, and as he was told the ball was near the right center wall at 370 feet when Joe fielded it. Coach Hambrick watched Joe make the catch and with bated anticipation wanted to see how much arm Joe had and if he would hit the cutoff man. Joe's throw went straight and directly over the cutoff man. With a short step in front of home plate, the catcher snagged the ball at chest level. With that throw, Coach Hambrick called in Joe, Coach Pickup, and Coach Henning to home plate. It was at this moment that Coach Hambrick's unbelief in a player that he had never heard of before, a completely unknown talent that had stayed off the radar, that could emerge out of nowhere on his field, vanished.

The only thing that Coach Hambrick had going through his mind was him praying to God that if Joe could hit the ball barely would be good enough for him. Giving Joe a little time to catch his breath and rest a little, Coach Hambrick, Henning, and Pickup started asking Joe a few questions. They explained to Joe that Coach Robinson and Peter Whyte had asked Coach Hambrick to give him a tryout and asked as a longtime old friend. Without question and the only explanation Coach Hambrick had from Coach Robinson was that Joe did not need his help in telling anybody how good he was. He had said if you gave him a chance, you would find out soon enough.

Well, it was time for Joe to show off his hitting skills, and by this time, Coach Hambrick was really getting anxious. He wanted to know for sure that he, Joe, was a complete package. Coach Hambrick had pulled up a couple of his pitchers that were in the rotation and wanted to give Joe the real deal if he got that far. Coach Hambrick also brought Coach Walker, his batting coach, to watch Joe. If Joe had problems in batting and hitting the ball, he wanted to know if it was something that could be worked on and improved, if at all possible.

As Joe walked up to the plate, batting right, Coach Hambrick and Walker were watching very closely and saw that Joe was relaxed from the moment he got into his stance and had little movements in his legs, arms, and hands, and with this alone, the fears of Joe being able to hit the ball quickly subsided for both coaches. They knew instinctively from the way Joe approached the plate and set in his stance. The first pitch was a fastball in the strike zone. Joe loaded his swing, got separation with his stride as the pitcher released the ball, planted his front foot, started his rotation, and released his swing textbook, and the ball sailed out of the park in right center field. In Joe's mind, he was thankful for Coach Robinson bringing to Stillwater Mike Shelton and Steve Clark because he knew what speed to expect and felt like that experience a week earlier gave him the confidence and the ability to meet the first pitch with confidence and send it out of the park. Throughout the rest of the batting tryout, Joe connected with most of balls that were thrown to him. He batted left and right, took the inside pitches with ease, and impressed Coach Walker with his weight transfer that allowed him to make good contact when jammed. In less than a half an hour, Coach Hambrick said it was enough and went to Joe and shook his hand and told him that this morning's events would last in his memory for as long as he lived and would be a story he would tell to anyone that would listen. Coach Pickup went to shake Joe's hand and told him that his swing and batting was the best he had seen in thirty years of coaching. Coach Pickup continued about Joe's swing saying it was natural, smooth, and extremely powerful and wanted to know if Joe saw the ball as it left the pitcher's hand and if he could see the rotation of the ball. Joe answered yes. Coach Hambrick overheard the conversation between Joe and Coach Pickup, and he knew what it meant for Joe to have that rare ability. Coach Hambrick also told Joe that he had done better than any player he had ever given a tryout to in his career, and if Joe wanted to play ball for him, the job was Joe's to take.

Everyone in the park that day gathered in the locker room after Joe's tryout, and Joe seemed to be the honored guest. All sorts of questions swirled around the room about who Joe was, his family, and his baseball experience. Joe enjoyed the fascination about his background and the compliments about his playing ability. The people present that day were the field maintenance workers and a handful of players that Coach Hambrick had asked to be there for varied reasons and to help with Joe's tryout. When all the excitement and questions had settled down, Coach Hambrick told Joe that he was to report to the general manager and owners in the owners' offices when he had showered and dressed. Coach Hambrick gave Joe the directions through the stadium on how to get there and then walked into his office and told Joe that he looked forward to working with him in the future.

Joe felt good at this point and thanked God for how well the tryout went and that he did not screw things up by being late. In the back of Joe's mind, he wondered what the phone call to Coach Hambrick was all about and why he changed his mind to give him another chance.

CHAPTER 19

San Diego Sand Dogs and a New World

As Joe was showering, the enormity of meeting the owners and the change of his life and of Louise's was about to take his breath away. It wasn't apprehension. It was pure excitement, the excitement of the unknown. In the next few minutes, Joe would be talking with people who would give him an opportunity, which would change most facets of his life to date. Joe's life to this point had been spent within fifty miles of where he was born. The people he knew, the culture, the land, and all his friends were enveloped in an area fifty miles or less from home.

While dressing by himself, in a locker room that was ten times bigger than any locker room he had ever been in before, his thoughts drifted to the fact that the town he would reside in would be ten times larger than any town he had visited before. Joe then had thoughts of Howard and Mary Marshall, his great-grandparents. Joe knew that his experience of the moment paled in comparison to the 1889 Land Rush when Howard and Mary risked their life and everything they owned to live in a place removed from civilization, where their physical toughness and wits would separate them from surviving or dying. The stories handed down to Joe were told from the excitement that Howard and Mary had of the opportunity to start a life anew without regard to the difference or peril that the new life embraced. The next thought that Joe had as he made his way to the owners' offices was that of the four guns that were hung in the living room of the Marshall farmhouse outside of Crescent, Oklahoma. Two Winchester .44-40 carbines, a Browning-designed Winchester lever action twelve-gauge shotgun, and a .44-40 Colt Bisley pistol, the very ones that Howard and Mary carried with them throughout their lives as tools of survival in a sometimes-hostile land. With a picture in his mind of the guns that were needed in his great-grandparents' life, he thanked God that his change of lifestyle and his opportunities were not as life-threatening as his ancestors.

With all the thoughts going through Joe's head, the ten-minute walk to the owners' office seemed to pass as if it were but seconds. There were solid glass walls and a glass door that entered a receptionist's area, and a very pleasant lady with dark brunette hair welcomed Joe in and asked him how she could help. Joe told her his name, and she told him to go right through the door on his right, that he was expected.

Joe opened the door and walked into the office and was surprised to see the two men that he had helped lift the barrels onto the truck a few hours ago. As he walked into the office, Joe had remembered their names and acknowledged them by saying Mr. Jones and Mr. Rodriguez. They responded by asking Joe how his tryout went, did it work out that he was late. Joe responded with a "Yes, sir," and everything came out better than he had expected. Joe was a little perplexed at this moment and did not understand why he and the guys he had helped earlier were in the same room at the same time. Joe stood there without saying a word for a few seconds, trying to think through what he was instructed to do. He thought that he was in the right place at the right time when Mr. Rodriguez asked Joe what he thought of playing in the San Diego Sand Dogs organization. Joe replied that he was excited for the opportunity and could hardly wait to talk to the owners about that possibility.

Mr. Rodriguez then told Joe that he did not want Joe to address him as Mr. Rodriguez, that Benito would be fine with him. Then looking over to CD, Benito asked how he wanted Joe to address him, and the reply was Mr. Jones would be fine for now. Benito told Joe that since the introductions were over, it was time to talk business and about Joe's future in the San Diego Sand Dogs organization. Joe shook his head slightly from side to side with a little squint of his eyelids and told Benito and Mr. Jones that he was confused and did not understand. There were two desks in the room that sat side by side in front of a glass wall that looked over the entire ball field from the third base side. Behind the two desks were executive-style chairs. As Joe was trying to figure out what was going on, Benito and Mr. Jones moved from standing in front of the two desks around to the back of the desks and sat in chairs with the view of the field behind them.

When Benito and Mr. Jones took their seats, Benito told Joe to pull up a chair to talk over some details about Joe playing for the Sand Dogs. Joe, a little stunned, did what he was asked but could not figure out what these two gentlemen were up to. There they sat in their light-tan khaki work shirts and pants with the San Diego Sand Dogs embroidered emblem over the left-hand shirt pocket with well-worn work gloves stuffed halfway in their right-hand rear pocket of their pants. A soiled San Diego Sand Dogs baseball hat laid on their respective desks and a pair of lace-up work boots finished off their attire. At best, the situation was disconcerting to Joe, and Joe finally said again he did not understand, trying to be as polite and respectful as he could be.

After Joe said that, Benito declared that Joe was here to talk to the owners, and that he and Mr. Jones were the owners. Joe sat staring at Benito and Mr. Jones, trying to comprehend the situation and what he wanted to say. Above all, he did not want to say the wrong thing. Joe, thinking someone was playing a joke on him, dispelled that notion and declared to Benito and Mr. Jones that he had just gained a reinforcement of a life lesson, which he was taught years before from his grandfather. Joe said that he wanted to play for the San Diego Sand Dogs organization. Benito said that it was great, and speaking for Mr. Jones and himself, they wanted Joe to play for them. Benito then asked Joe what the life lesson was that his grandfather had taught him years before. Joe summarized part of what his grandfather taught him. "Never assume. Find out the facts before you say or take action" was Joe's reply. Joe said that earlier he had made an assumption when one was not warranted, and that when the facts were brought to light, he doubted their authenticity but did not have any reason for not believing what was being said. Joe then asked where they would start and what he needed to do.

Benito told Joe that he and Mr. Jones had watched his tryout and agreed with Coach Hambrick's recommendation to get him signed as soon as possible. Joe asked Benito and Mr. Jones if they already had a contract, and they said no. For the first time, Joe heard Mr. Jones's voice, asking him if he had an agent, and Joe replied that he did not. Mr. Jones asked Joe why he didn't have an agent. Joe explained that he figured he could represent himself better than anyone he knew. Basically, he would not know who to trust any better than himself. At this point, it seemed to Joe that Benito stopped talking, and Mr. Jones took center stage in asking Joe questions. Joe felt that Mr. Jones was getting a little irritated with Joe from his tone and tension in his voice. Mr. Jones then asked Joe how they were supposed to continue on with preliminary negotiations if Joe did not have representation and an idea of what he wanted in a contract.

Joe then told Mr. Jones that he knew what he wanted in his contract, and he would be glad to tell Mr. Jones the details. Joe then explained what he expected of Mr. Jones and Benito, starting with how much money was needed for the first year. Joe needed enough money for him and his wife-to-be to move to San Diego, rent a modest place in a nice neighborhood, buy basic furniture, and money to get him to his first paycheck. Mr. Jones at the mention of paycheck immediately asked Joe how much that first paycheck was going to be. Joe had a confidence about him that was second to none. He was very comfortable in his own skin and knew what he wanted without asking anyone else.

Joe told Mr. Jones that the first paycheck would be determined by him and Benito. Joe felt and expressed to them that his first year would prove how good Joe really was, and he knew that owners paying for something that had not been tested, put pressure on everyone, and Joe did not want that. Joe suggested that they pay him a first-year salary of the least-paid player on the current San Diego Sand Dogs active roster, and he would leave it to them on how much money they would advance to get Joe and his new wife set up in San

Diego. Joe told Mr. Jones that it was his choice, and whatever he and Benito came up with would be fine with him for the first year. Again, Joe hit a nerve with Mr. Jones when he said first year. Mr. Jones then asked about the second year.

Joe felt that if he was as good as he thought he was and if his playing made the San Diego Sand Dogs better, and they won more games, then Benito and Mr. Jones would quickly know his worth and would increase Joe's pay accordingly. Joe looked at Benito and Mr. Jones and asked them if they had the best player in the majors playing for them who won games and put fans in the stands, would they not pay top money to keep that player? Joe at this moment said there were a couple of things that he wanted Benito and Mr. Jones to agree on. One, he wanted to get paid relative to his worth in winning games, and two, that he wanted to have the final say on when he would give up playing and retire from the pros. Mr. Jones wanted a little clarity. If Joe did not perform and help win games, his paycheck goes down, and even if he was not getting paid because he was not helping the team win games if he was just sitting on the bench, he makes the call on leaving the team. Joe said that he could agree on that. Mr. Jones asked how they would know if he was being paid enough, and Joe replied that if he stayed, it was enough. Joe then told Benito and Mr. Jones they would have a year to decide if he was worth it or not, and that the money spent would be the minimum. Joe went on to explain that as far as the concern for this day, the number they come up with was good enough, so how could they lose?

Joe went further to explain that someday, sooner or later, he would return to the family farm outside of Crescent, Oklahoma, if he made it in the majors or not. Joe wanted to explain to Benito and Mr. Jones that he knew exactly who he was, and in his perception, being a big-time professional baseball player would not change him or his views on life. Where Joe wanted home to be is where it already was, on the Marshall farm. Joe also explained that the money he earned playing baseball was important, but it wasn't the all-encompassing reason that would direct his life.

Today, Joe felt he had met two distinct individuals, like himself, who knew exactly who they were, real men of honor that knew hard work and recognized those qualities in other people. Joe felt familiar with his two new acquaintances, and he had the feeling that he was back home with friends when he talked to Benito and Mr. Jones because they exemplified the same characteristics of people he grew up around and trusted. Joe did not consider it a liability for these new people he had just met to direct his future.

Mr. Jones paused for a couple of minutes, then looked Benito's way, and said that Joe was right. If they didn't like what they see in a year, he would be gone, and if he did as good as expected, then it's their job to figure out his worth. Benito agreed with Mr. Jones, and they told Joe he had a deal. Benito continued telling Joe that Mr. Jones and he would discuss the situation, and that there would be a check in the mail at Joe's Stillwater address within the week. They would be in touch with where Joe was to report to start his career. Joe shook hands with Benito and Mr. Jones and left for his hotel and his return trip to Stillwater.

After Joe left, Benito sat at his desk and Mr. Jones at his. Benito, in private, would always call Mr. Jones, CD, and CD would always call Benito, Rod. The first words out of CD's mouth were asking Rod if he was out of his mind, leaving a deal so wide open and nothing on paper, and this could be the biggest mess that they had ever been in or a part of. Rod didn't say a word for a couple of minutes, and the silence was deafening to CD, so CD demanded that Rod say something. Rod looked at CD and asked if the contract they had between them had worked out over the years. Now there was silence from both of them because there had never been a written contract, only a handshake.

After ten minutes, with their feet on their respective desks leaning back, looking at the ceiling, Rod broke the silence, reminding CD that he was the ex-baseball player and asked CD what he thought of Joe's tryout performance and ability. CD and Rod earlier had hurried from the spot where they were loading the barrels to a place that they could see Joe's entire tryout. CD looked over Rod's way and said that he had never seen that level of raw talent and skill, in the Negro or white league, and if Joe could stay healthy throughout the years, they more than likely witnessed the greatest baseball player of all time starting his professional career. Rod then asked, with his feet still on his desk, as though daydreaming, if that was the case, how much of a chance were they really taking. CD told Rod none at all, and that he understood that this was not something to be fearful of, but a blessing out of nowhere. Rod asked CD not to be stingy, but to send Joe enough money so he and his soon-to-be bride could be totally comfortable starting out in his new career. CD agreed and asked Rod what he thought of Joe's handshake earlier after they loaded the barrels. Rod replied like grabbing hold of a 2×4, and CD agreed.

When Joe returned to Will Rogers Airport in Oklahoma City, he was greeted by Louise, Ron Robinson, and Paul Pixley. Joe had called Louise when he had returned to the hotel in downtown San Diego and told her the good news, and now those present wanted to know all the details from start to finish. Joe relayed the whole story about helping the two guys that he assumed were maintenance workers at the baseball park to eventually talking with the same two about playing with the San Diego Sand Dogs. When they arrived in Stillwater, they went straight to Coach Robinson's house where Jane, Juanetta, the Shells, LaTrenda, Steve, and friends had gathered to greet Joe and have a party to celebrate the good news.

The questions of the evening were about where Joe was going first and how long he would be in the minor league, how much he signed for, and what it felt like to be on the field of a major league park. Joe answered most of the questions about money and where he would be sent by saying that all those details were being worked out, and that he would know those answers later next week. Joe answered all the other questions in as much detail as he could fully explain. Others wanted to know what the big city of San Diego was like and if Joe was intimidated by the big highways and traffic, to which Joe said no. He took a cab everyplace he went. Joe was impressed by the number of friends and acquaintances that had shown up to celebrate his new journey and hoped that he would remember the feeling and this night for the rest of his life.

When most of the crowd had left and only family, Louise, Paul, and the Robinsons were still there, Joe wanted to talk to Coach Robinson about what he knew of Mr. Rodriguez and Mr. Jones.

Coach Robinson said that he had known them both for many years and knew a little about them before they were owners of the San Diego Sand Dogs. Coach Robinson mentioned to Joe the main thing he knew about Rodriguez and Jones was they were atypical owners and didn't follow the conventional path to ownership that most owners of major league teams follow.

Coach Robinson related to Joe the story that was told to him by Benito Rodriguez twelve years ago when Benito owned a minor league team in Southern California, and he was there to check out a player that was on Benito's team where a trade was being considered by the two teams. Coach Robinson said that he had made the trip to see firsthand the player in question and evaluate his worth in the trade.

Benito asked Coach Robinson what his background was, and Ron told him that he was reared on a farm in southwest Oklahoma, and the farm life was all he knew until he left at eighteen years old. Coach Robinson said that on that visit, Benito felt that there was a connection between them, and Benito continued to tell Coach Robinson about his family life. Benito mentioned that he was a first-generation Hispanic, and his parents had emigrated from Mexico just after World War I, with Benito being born in Southern California shortly after they arrived. Benito's folks settled with family members that had been in California since the turn of the century, and they owned their own farms, which was quite unusual for the times. While there, Coach Robinson stayed with Benito and his wife and in conversation had shared their life's journey with each other and found out there were similarities in their backgrounds. Benito had farmed from early in his life until he went into the Marine Corps at the start of World War II. After the war, he started running the conglomerate of the family farms that his dad had organized when Benito was fighting in the South Pacific. Coach Robinson said that Benito did not go into great detail other than shortly after he returned and started managing the farms, he incorporated their holdings, and after incorporating, he started borrowing money to leverage and expand their holdings and crop production by ten times in as many years. Benito mentioned to Coach Robinson that he had integrated their business horizontally and vertically from the early fifties to the late fifties, and that he had gained total ownership of the corporation by 1959. The corporation, at that time, was so vast that he bought a national accounting firm to keep track of things and moved the accounting firm to a multistory building he owned in downtown San Diego to be closer to where Benito lived.

Coach Robinson also told Joe the story of how Benito got involved in baseball, starting with ownership of a minor league team that came about when Benito bought a corporation that was about to go into bankruptcy for a dime on the dollar and, within its holdings, a 51 percent controlling interest in a minor league professional baseball team. The interesting thing about that minor league team was the other 49 percent was owned by C. D. Jones, Benito's equal partner of the San Diego Sand Dogs.

Coach Robinson couldn't tell Joe much about CD because he had never met him. On the trip that Coach Robinson met Benito, CD was on the East Coast brokering some kind of trade with a minor league player to replace the player Coach Robinson was looking over. Coach Robinson did share this with Joe, that Benito and CD shared business duties equally, with the exception of picking talent and the compensation for that talent. CD did that job. Joe had shared his story of meeting Benito and CD, and Coach Robinson found it interesting how it all worked out. Coach Robinson expressed to Joe that his true character showed in his willingness to help, and he knew from talk in the baseball circles that the content of character was more or as important to Benito Rodriguez and C. D. Jones as talent. Coach Robinson also told Joe that Benito and CD knew of his family background of farming, and that was a major factor in giving Joe an opportunity, being an unknown, to try out.

CHAPTER 20

Joe's Professional Baseball Career Starts

Louise and Joe finished their degree work by the end of the second week in May and finished in the top 5 percent of their graduating class and in their respective majors. Joe had received in the mail a check from the San Diego Sand Dogs that gave him and Louise enough money to get a start and establish a home in San Diego. When Joe opened the envelope that contained the check, he found the amount of the check was much more than he had expected or even dreamed it would be. Joe remembered Benito asking CD not to be stingy, and for a fact, he was not. When Louise and Joe considered the amount of money they received, they figured out they could get by a year, buy a basic new car, and have a little left over, not counting the amount of money that would be paid to Joe on a monthly basis.

The next thing on the list for Joe and Louise was to get married. The plan they had was to have everything they didn't want in their respective residences given away or sold, and the things they wanted to keep stored at each of their parents' houses. The items Louise and Joe wanted to keep amounted to a couple of boxes of memorabilia, which they did want to keep but did not want to transport and take up room in the car on their trip to California. Joe and Louise took Nellie Belle back to the Marshall farm where Jane had cleared out a place in one of the barns for Joe to park it. Joe had asked Uncle Steve if once a week he would start up the old girl and take her for a short spin, just to keep everything in working order. Joe also asked Steve if any work or maintenance needed to be done on Nellie Belle, he would pay for it if Steve would arrange the work. Steve agreed to do that for Joe and assured him that it would not be a problem. Joe told Steve that on the occasions that he and or Louise would return home, if they had to fly because of time, it would give them a vehicle to use, and Steve said okay.

Louise's dad had given her an old family car to use when she was at school, and she returned it to her folks to be used by her little brother when he went off to college. This left Joe and Louise without a car, and they decided to buy a new one to start off to California. Joe asked Louise what kind of car she wanted to get, and with a little thought, she said she wanted something that would take them anyplace they wanted to go. Louise wanted a vehicle that could take them into the desert, beaches, or even into the mountains whenever they wanted to go. Joe agreed, and they settled on a 1972 black Ford Bronco. Louise and Joe were both excited to have a brand-new three-door, four-wheel drive 4×4 Ford Bronco powered by a 302 V-8. It made them feel like there was still a connection with Nellie Belle because it was a standard shift, and it had the ability to go where most did not dare go.

Even though their new Bronco was a great-grandchild of Nellie Belle, it rode smooth and quiet, had air-conditioning, and everything worked, even the windshield wipers. Louise and Joe loved their new car, and it gave them the feeling they could go anywhere an adventure would take them. Being the three-door wagon type, it also gave them all the room they needed to transport their belongings halfway across the United States to sunny Southern California. Everyone at home was relieved by the fact that they were making such a long trip, which included going through the desert, in a new car as opposed to an old worn-out used car that would increase the possibilities of breaking down in the middle of nowhere.

Joe and Louise did not possess, while in college, a single piece of furniture that was not a hand-me-down or worn completely out. Louise was happy to know that the money was there to buy what they needed and above all what they wanted to make them comfortable in their new place. They both had small items for the kitchen and bathroom they would take with them, and there would be some wedding gifts they would want to set up house when they arrived in California. Other than that, it would be a buying spree for a couple of weeks for Louise.

Louise wanted to have the wedding in the First Methodist Church in Crescent, Oklahoma, on the first of June at 11:00 AM. Louise liked the thought of a June first wedding because it made it easier to remember and to figure exactly how long they have been married when asked. The only date she preferred to June 1 was January 1 because it made their anniversary date even easier to remember when figuring how long they would have been married, but she didn't want to wait six months to have that date. The 11:00 AM time gave them a twelve o'clock noon reception and a one o'clock departure for the start of their honeymoon driving on Highway 66, following the sunset west, with their first stop in Amarillo, Texas, at seven that evening. Joe's first trip out of Oklahoma was his tryout in San Diego, and that was also his first airplane flight. This was the first road trip out of Oklahoma for Joe and Louise, and it was taking a highway they had both heard about from family and friends throughout their lives, the Mother Road, the fabled Highway 66. Highway 66 was where Louise and Joe would spend their first week of marriage, stopping in and staying the night in little towns whose names they heard many times, but never, until now, had witnessed. For them, it was a trip of a lifetime.

Driving to Santa Monica from Crescent would take two long days with one overnight stay and only stopping for gas with a quick bite to eat while driving down the road. Joe and Louise wanted to see what sights Highway 66 had to offer the first-time traveler, and they did not want to just drive by and wonder what they had missed. They made a list of the sights that family and friends had talked about and had enjoyed seeing on numerous trips back and forth on the Mother Road. Most of their friends and relatives made multiple trips back to Oklahoma to see relatives, normally once a year during the summer. Each time, they would stop at one of the sights, and over a decade, they would have managed to see most attractions along the 1,400-

mile trip at least once, and some sights, they would stop on every trip coming or going.

Louise and Joe both wanted to stop at Blue Hole, Santa Rosa, New Mexico; Santa Fe, New Mexico; Petrified Forest National Forest, Arizona; Meteor Crater, Arizona; Winslow, Arizona; Grand Canyon National Park, and look at the Pacific Ocean from a hotel room in Santa Monica, California, and other stops all along the historic road. They planned a week on the road staying the last night in Santa Monica, then going south along the Pacific Coast Highway arriving in San Diego a week later. This would be their "honeymoon trip" that they wanted to repeat over the years with fond memories as they traveled home to see friends and relatives.

When they left Santa Monica, they traveled along the coast road with the Pacific Ocean to their right side, soaking in the sights all the way to San Diego where they checked into the same hotel that Joe stayed when he was there for his tryout, the U.S. Grant. C. D. Jones had his assistant make the reservation in the Grant for as long as Joe and Louise needed before they found a place that was suitable to them. Mr. Jones had contacted a realtor to show Joe and Louise three properties that he had previewed to make the choice easier on the newlyweds. Joe and Louise were very appreciative and, after looking at all three, picked one that was closest to Eaton Field and had a view of the Pacific Ocean. Mr. Jones had also picked properties that had a clause in the contract for lease to own that would apply their lease cost to the purchase price if Joe and Louise decided to purchase the property at the end of a year, which pleased Joe and Louise immensely.

The U.S. Grant Hotel was by far the nicest hotel or motel that Joe and Louise had stayed in during their trip out and was a nice place to spend the last night or two of their honeymoon because the next day or two would be spent buying furniture and setting up house. They chose furniture for every room and a washer and dryer. Joe and Louise had transformed themselves from country kids looking at rolling hills, prairies, bean and wheat fields, and little country towns to real-life cosmopolitans living in a county that had more people than the state from which they moved. The nice thing for

Louise and Joe was the fact they were experiencing this new life for the first time together, being immersed in a different culture, and having the same experience in adjusting.

After they moved into their new home, they were trying at every moment to take it all in. For the first few days, Joe and Louise would wake up on Oklahoma time at dark thirty and have breakfast sitting out on the back patio, looking at an unobstructed view of the ocean. A dark ocean was slowly being lighted by the rising eastern sun. As they watched the sun rise on the ocean, Louise would say, "This isn't Oklahoma, Joejoe," and Joe would agree.

Joe met with Benito and CD a few times during the two weeks they gave him to settle in after his arrival in San Diego. On his last visit with them, Joe was told the plan for him and where he would start his professional career. Because CD did not think Joe would be in the minors but a short time, he wanted Joe to locate in San Diego. The people in management of the San Diego Sand Dogs handling Joe felt that a triple A affiliate would be the best fit for Joe and his level of talent. They also felt that to move Joe immediately into the majors was a mistake. CD, Benito, and the management team wanted to see Joe perform in a daily competition with some of the best players in the world or next to them. The big question was how long Joe would be in the minors, and that answer would be based on his performance. Benito and CD thought of Joe's stint in the minors as a warm-up or getting up to speed for Joe's confidence. Neither CD or Benito had any doubt that Joe would transition without a problem. They just did not want Joe to have to start his career adjusting to the top level. They wanted him to excel at the top level from his very first appearance as a San Diego Sand Dog.

During the two weeks they had off to get everything in order for Louise and their house, Joe contacted the United States Air Force reserve unit in San Diego to get signed up, enlisted, and sworn in to start his military commitment for the next six years or more. Joe had worked a lot of the details out about his in-processing to the US Air Force reserves through mail and telephone calls long before he and Louise arrived in San Diego. General John Battle had directed Joe while he was in Stillwater on what to expect and had a contact person set up to help Joe through the enlistment process and in-processing. Joe knew beforehand what the steps would be for him to go through officers' candidate school and what would be involved in his commitment. Joe would make his monthly meetings in San Diego until baseball season was over, and then he would report to Maxwell Air Force Base in Montgomery, Alabama, for officer training school and, upon completion, to be assigned to Kessler Air Force Base, Biloxi, Mississippi.

CD and Benito told Joe that he would start his professional career in Seattle, Washington, playing for a triple A affiliate of the San Diego Sand Dogs organization, the Seattle Loggers. Joe was agreeable with any decision that Benito and CD came up with concerning his placement with a team and was very pleased with the team and location that he was assigned to play with. Seattle, Washington, was a great selection for Joe because there were many connections for air flight and train services along the West Coast from San Diego to Seattle. This would provide weekend trips, when the Loggers had a home stand, for Louise to visit Joe for as long as CD and Benito thought it necessary until Joe was called up to play for the Sand Dogs.

Joe was placed on the roster of available players of the Seattle Loggers and worked out with the team for a few days before they listed Joe on the playing lineup. Joe was placed in right field, and they had him eighth in the batting order. The game was scheduled in the early evening, and the lights on the field gave Joe a familiar feeling he had not experienced in a long time. Playing at home, the Loggers took the field first, and as Joe left the dugout to take his position in right field, he felt his heart pounding, and his mind was filled with thoughts of the past and the last game he played in under the lights, the night Walt, his dad, died. No matter how hard Joe tried to focus on the present, he still found himself deep in thought of that evening, how normal things were during and after the Legion game over six years ago. Then the thoughts and feelings of eating supper with his teammates and family, eating fried chicken at Beverly's restaurant in Oklahoma City, where Walt was telling Joe how proud he was of him and that Joe's talent and level of play had advanced so much in the last month while playing Legion ball.

Joe was standing in the right field awaiting the first batter to approach the plate, and he could hear his dad's voice, from that time six years ago in Oklahoma City, in his head as though Walt was standing next to him in right field, telling him that if he desired to, he had the talent to play professional baseball. Now Joe realized what Walt had told him then, that at this very moment what Walt had said, had come to fruition. What Walt and others had thought over the years was actually happening with the approaching batter to the plate. Joe was playing professional baseball.

The sights of the ballpark, the feel of the night air, the smells, the sounds, the voices of players and fans in the stands, and the actual feeling Joe had of being on the field as part of a team that was playing and competing to win a game exhilarated Joe to a point that he was tingly all over his body and felt pins and needles waiting for the first pitch. The batter started his walk to the plate, and as he took his position batting right, the ump yelled, "Play ball!" The pitcher took his windup, came around, and the ball was released. As Joe watched the first pitch, he could see the bat contact the ball, and immediately, Joe knew the ball was going in his direction, and it would be his play. The ball was going to Joe's left, flying deep into right field just a few feet inside the foul line. For most of those present, fans and players, it was thought to be a hit unplayable, out of reach for the right fielder. Joe's instinctive first move and in addition to his blazing speed, he made the play. It was what would be expected in the future of him, a routine rundown play with Joe making the catch, throwing the ball to the first baseman ready for the second batter.

Except for two attendees in the grandstands, all fans, players, and staff thought for sure that was a hit and maybe a hit with extra bases, but for these two, Benito and CD, that was precisely what they had expected and knew that would be the first of many good hits that Joe would snatch and rob from an impressive line of batters over the years to come. Joe had made another indelible impression on a totally different group of people, this time professional baseball.

The crowd was silent for a few moments as they wrapped their heads around Joe's catch, a catch that should not have been made by anyone known to them in or out of professional baseball. Once the play sunk in, the crowd went wild with everyone wanting to know who the new player was and where he came from. Joe was a known commodity on his first play in professional baseball.

For the next two innings, the fans and all those present became anxious for Joe to bat. The first inning was three up and three down. The second inning, the crowd was in hopes of seeing Joe at the plate, but batting eight in the lineup left Joe on the deck with the third out at the bottom of the second inning. Joe had been involved in several plays throughout three innings but none as spectacular as the very first out of the first inning. What the fans and onlookers wanted to know now was how this nobody could handle a bat, and all present could hardly wait until Joe was at the plate.

The score at the bottom of the third inning was zero to zero. Joe would lead off the third inning for the Loggers, and the crowd was hushed as the first pitch was delivered. The pitcher on the mound that day was Sam Turner, a young twenty-year-old kid from Kansas, recruited out of high school, had been in the minors for two years, one in a double A team, and his second year, he was moved up to triple A. Sam had excellent speed and a good breaking ball and was more than likely looking at his last year in the minors. This time next year, he would be moved to the majors. Since Joe was a complete unknown, there wasn't a book on him. The catcher gave Sam a sign for a high fastball inside, and Joe watched it over for strike one. The second pitch was a fastball low and inside that missed, and Joe watched it over the plate, ball one. At this point, the fans had passed from anticipation to anxiety, wanting to know if Joe could hit the ball, for if he could, they might be watching the start of a big-time player and career. The third pitch was a curveball that broke very well, and Joe took a full swing that twisted him completely around where he had to reach around to catch himself from falling to the ground. This big-time swing that missed left the crowd a little disheartened, and some hopes of Joe being the player they wished for, a little dashed. The count was now 1–2, and Sam Turner was feeling his oats. He waved off a sign for another high inside and wanted to see Joe go out swinging at another one of his breaking balls. The catcher relented, and the call was for another curve, and Joe could see it this time the moment the ball left Sam's fingers.

As Joe could see the ball, almost in slow motion, he uncoiled and made full contact with a full swing, and the ball sailed off his bat toward the left center field as high as any Logger fan had ever seen a fly ball clearing the fence by twenty feet, and it was in the record book for Joe's first time at bat as a professional, a home run and batting a thousand.

When Benito and CD saw how far the ball cleared the left center fence, almost simultaneously, they both stood up from their seats and decided they had seen enough and would start back to San Diego immediately. Benito and CD, in discussing Joe's time in Seattle, they found that they were still in agreement that Joe would be there until the first or second week of September if nothing changed with his performance status and refining his playing skills, which would make him more viable when called up to the majors. The main reasons Benito and CD showed up at Seattle was twofold, to see Joe's first game as a professional, and second, to watch Joe bat against Sam Turner. Turner had been on CD's radar for the last two years, and he knew that Turner was a short-timer and would be called up, if not this year, the start of the next season. CD thought that Sam Turner would be one of the top pitchers in the majors and a force to contend with. CD was also considering a trade for Turner, and those thoughts were not diminished by Joe knocking Turner's curveball out of the park on this particular evening. CD knew that Sam Turner would make note on Joe's at bat and the next time, if ever, that he faced Joe Marshall, he would make hitting a home run more challenging. Joe's first game was a huge success and one that would go down in the history books. The fans that night went wild every time the ball was hit in Joe's direction, batting, or on base. Joe's following started on that very Friday evening on June 23, 1972.

When the game was over, Joe and some of the other players returned to the hotel in downtown Seattle. Most of his teammates who returned to the hotel were going out to party and have a good time. They wanted Joe to join them, but Joe wanted to go to his room and call Louise and tell her how his first game went. After that, Joe just wanted to go to the hotel lounge for a burger and a beer.

Joe spent close to an hour talking to Louise and giving her a play-by-play description of how the game went, and she was excited to hear every detail and was very happy for Joe and his debut in professional baseball. After they finished talking, Joe wished that Louise was there with him. Not having someone there to enjoy the moment took a lot out of the experience. Joe had the same feeling after Walt died, and that was a big factor why Joe did not want to play baseball anymore. For Joe, sharing the experience with his dad was equal to the excitement of actually playing the game. Joe left his room and went to the lounge and ordered a beer and something to eat. While he was waiting for his order, he started listening to a song that someone had played on the jukebox. The beat was melodious, and the artist had a strong, soothing mellow voice, and the lyrics made him think of Louise. It was the first time Joe had listened to this song and wanted to know the name of it. Joe walked over to the jukebox, saw the name of the record playing, "Song Sung Blue" by Neil Diamond. The next day, early in the morning, Joe went to a record shop and bought Neil Diamond's album *Moods*. Joe purchased the record and an eight-track tape, two copies each, one set for him and one for Louise. It was at this moment that Joe decided that he wanted Louise with him no matter what the cost. This was the start of the first year of their marriage, and at least for the first year, before Louise started her career, Joe wanted them to be together as much as possible. Joe called Louise, and she agreed. It was settled. Louise would spend the weeks to come with Joe in Seattle or on the road. Joe would always refer to that time with the Loggers as one of the best times of his life, and Louise, likewise.

Joe's playing time with the Seattle Loggers was reminiscent of his first night. Joe quickly adapted to the higher level of play and not only adapted, but excelled. The word got around fast about this great player that came out of nowhere and the immediate impact he had on the team. The Friday night that Joe started for the Loggers was the first of a three-game home stand. The first night had an average attendance, but the second and third night, there was nearly a capacity crowd. They all wanted to see this would-be great player as he started his professional career.

The longer Joe stayed at Seattle, the more he became of interest in and around the baseball world. Somehow the word snuck out that the Sand Dogs might be calling Joe up from the Loggers before the end of the year, and if that occurred, there would be a corresponding change in the Sand Dogs' roster and starting lineup. This speculation of changing players late in the season and bringing a rookie up so soon in the start of his career made for a lot of ink and endless talk within the ranks of baseball analysts, sportswriters, and baseball commentators. Before the first of September, there was more interest about the kid from Oklahoma than there was about the league leaders. Joe had made himself the hottest item in professional baseball, and with Joe's pending move from Seattle to San Diego, the sales of the fifth-place Sand Dogs started climbing with fans, hoping their ticket would be the one where they could watch the debut of Joe and his first game in the majors. For all the other fans, it still would be a good ticket to catch a glimpse of Joe playing in his first season in the majors.

In Seattle after that third game, people would stop Joe on the street and tell him they saw him play and describe his catch or at bats and then ask him for his autograph on anything they had that ink would leave an indelible signature on. Not only his play but his personality brought people out of the woodwork to see, touch, talk, or get his autograph. In just a matter of weeks, and already some half-a-dozen home runs, Joe had metamorphized from a newbie to a sensational personality that people in Seattle wanted to get to know. Every day, in the morning and evening editions of the Seattle newspapers, there would be a new article about Joe and his background. Not everything that wound up in the papers were necessarily true or completely correct. This was all right with Joe because it gave him something to talk about when he was given an impromptu interview. This way, Joe could talk about what he wanted to and was always prepared to do so.

Joe would call his folks back home at least once a week and give them a rundown on what was happening with him, Louise, and baseball. On these calls, Jane would tell him that occasionally, reporters from Tulsa or Oklahoma City would be in Crescent, and the townsfolk would come over the party line, telling her of a few reporters that would ask around about Joe and where his kinfolk lived. Again, like it was in Walt's time, anyone that knew the Marshalls and where they lived also knew that Jane or anyone else in the family did not want to be bothered with a reporter that just wanted a story and didn't really care about Joe's story or her. Those reporters would be given directions that would sooner have them drive off the edge of the world than find the Marshall farm.

One day, early on a clear-sky, sunny September morning, Jane answered a knock on the side door of the house. The early September morning was warm, so the side door was left open with a nonlatched screen door that allowed Jane to see a neatly dressed young man was knocking. Jane asked politely, talking through the closed screen door what she could help the young man with. He introduced himself as Bill Harper, saying that he was a sports reporter for the *Stillwater Gazette*. Jane took a few moments as she gathered her thoughts and asked Mr. Harper if he played baseball with the Kingfisher High School team in the midsixties, and Bill replied with yes, and that he had played against Joe. Jane said that she remembered a Harper kid that played for Kingfisher High School. The kid she remembered was an outstanding third baseman and a better-than-average hitter. "Was that you?" she asked. Again, Bill answered yes. Jane paused again, then asked Bill if he was a couple of years older than Joe and if he had signed to play college ball with Wichita State right out of high school. Again, Bill said yes. At that point, Jane stood to the side and opened the screen door wide and asked Bill if he would like to come in and join her for a cup of coffee. Bill said yes, entered Jane's house, and had a seat at the kitchen table where he was served a cup of coffee.

After Jane poured herself a cup of coffee, she sat down and asked Bill to tell her why he made the trip out to the Marshall farm. Bill said that the first time he had seen Joe play baseball was in a high school game in the spring when he was a senior at Kingfisher High School playing Crescent High School when Joe was a sophomore. As Bill told the story, he watched Joe step up to the plate in the first inning, and on the first pitch, Joe made full contact with the ball and sent it ten feet over the center field fence that was marked 390 feet. Bill told Jane that he couldn't remember anything about that game except watching Joe field, throw, and hit the ball all day long. After that game, Bill told Jane that he knew he had seen a future great of the game and decided he would keep up with Joe's career, even when there wasn't one. Bill also told Jane that he knew where Joe was and what he was doing for the last six years, and when he heard that he was heading to San Diego, knowing that Joe could become one of the greatest baseball players of all time, it was one of the most exciting days of his life, next to his marriage and the birth of his son.

Jane asked Mr. Harper if she could call him by his first name, and Bill said that he would prefer that to her calling him Mr. Harper. So Jane asked Bill how he kept up with Joe over the last six-plus years. Bill told Jane that he had read about Walt's death shortly after the accident, reading about it in the local Kingfisher paper, and that his folks had a subscription to the *Daily Oklahoman*, an Oklahoma City paper. He would look for Joe's name when the *Oklahoman* would report on the local Legion teams. After the wreck that took Walt's life, Joe's name no longer appeared in the baseball reporting. After the end of that school year, Bill told Jane that he had a summer job, but before he left to attend and play ball at Wichita State, he had made the thirty-minute trip from Kingfisher to Crescent early one morning to see if he could find out anything about Joe. Bill continued that on that first trip, it was early in the morning, and he had gone to Dot's, the little restaurant downtown where all the locals go for breakfast. While he sat at the counter, which had swivel stools, he could rotate around and talk with the people sitting in the booths behind him and start up a conversation very easily. If he stayed long enough, there would be another group of folks show up that he could have new conversations with.

Bill explained that after six cups of coffee, a three-egg skillet piled with potatoes, and two biscuits covered with gravy, enough food to last him for the entire day, enough people had come and gone that he found out a lot about Joe. Jane asked Bill how he got the townsfolk and locals to talk about Joe, and she wanted to know how he knew that the information he received about Joe was accurate. Bill explained to Jane that he would start out with asking a question about a kid that was a heck of an athlete that played baseball for

Crescent. He himself played for Kingfisher and if they knew anything about him. Usually, the waitress was closemouthed at first, and then he would tell about this home run that Joe hit at the start of the summer and how he thought it was the longest hit ball he had ever seen. Bill told Jane when he would tell that story, inevitably someone close by, maybe in the booth behind him, would start talking about a ball Joe had tagged that they had witnessed. Bill said when someone would start up about Joe, that he would throw into the conversation that the ball he had seen Joe hit went over 390 feet in the air. Bill said that would ignite the talk with another patron in Dot's that the ball they had seen went over 400 feet and so on, until after two hours, and a new group of customers took the conversation from there until Joe had hit balls to which they would attest, flew in excess of 500 feet.

Bill said that throughout the lengthy café conversations, he would scribble down a few notes on the margins of the local paper he had purchased from the newsstand just outside Dot's before going in, but most of the time, he just took mental notes. As to the accuracy, Bill told Jane that when someone made mention of Joe or the Marshall family and stated somewhat of a fact, someone in the restaurant, who wasn't even taking part until that point and had not said a word, would speak up abruptly, correcting what had just been said with a level of authority. An ensuing conversation between the two locals, where the first that misspoke would eventually stand corrected by stating that they did not actually know the fact, which then corrected what had been said. Bill said that all this was done in a very peaceful fashion with the one corrected saying they appreciated the correction, and they were glad to know the real story. Bill told Jane that it was harmless gossip, mostly local residents that expressed real concern for Joe and the Marshall family, and they all had a desire for the best for Joe and her. At the end of the morning, Bill had enough information to track down Joe to his next destination.

At this point, Bill explained to Jane that he did not desire to pry into private matters, and this gossip knowledge that he had accumulated over six years was all about waiting to know the real story about Joe and to be there when he first made an appearance in major league baseball. The awe that Bill had experienced on that summer evening playing baseball and watching Joe come to bat and hit the ball out of the park and the ensuing play of a talent that far exceeded himself or anybody he knew, that awe he experienced was still with him at this very moment. The bottom line for Bill was to be at Joe's first appearance playing for the San Diego Sand Dogs.

Jane was amazed at Bill, and the thought ran through her head that he might be the first real fan that Joe had outside of family and very close friends. Jane quizzed Bill further, asking him how he kept up with Joe through the years when Joe was at Oklahoma State. Bill told Jane that when Joe left the Crescent area and headed to Stillwater, it became easier for him to keep up with Joe. Wichita State would play Oklahoma State in the start of baseball season in nonconference games. Bill was in his junior year at Wichita State, and the Shockers traveled to Stillwater for a doubleheader with the Cowboys. Bill had heard about the news film of this young kid that was on the practice field making a catch that more than likely saved Coach Robinson's life or, at the least, severe injury, nonetheless, an unbelievable catch that was recorded by a kid nobody knew. At the first telling of the story, Bill told Jane he knew who made the catch.

Bill also knew a couple of the OSU players from the Kingfisher area that he had played ball against or with, and he was able to talk to them while at Stillwater for the games. Bill, while talking to his friends that played for OSU, found out for sure it was Joe that made the catch that was heard around the baseball world. Joe was not at the game that day, but Bill got around enough of the Cowboy players to get answers to fill in all the blanks about Joe, at least for the time being. Bill went on to explain to Jane that he wasn't for sure that Joe would ever play organized ball again, and for a while, he thought that Joe might suit up with the Cowboys. During Bill's sophomore year, it was time that he needed to declare his major while at Wichita State. It was at this point that his desire to follow a baseball player that did not play baseball and the effort it took to follow a student, hoping and anticipating a breakout moment and a start to a stellar career, that Bill chose journalism as a major. He knew without a doubt that it was a good fit.

Bill's job at the *Stillwater Gazette* was not planned but an opportunity that presented itself without any planning on his part. Upon graduation, Bill had an opportunity to play professional baseball at a minor league team, but at the last moment, he came to the realization that he did not have the talent to play at the next level and just wanted to get on with his life. The job at the *Stillwater Gazette* was the only job that was offered at short notice, and Bill took it. Now Bill came to the reason he was at the Marshall farm talking to Jane. Bill wanted to meet Joe and have an opportunity to interview him before and after his first game. Jane told Bill that she understood, and the next time she talked to Joe, she would relate the story, and from there, it would be Joe's decision to talk to Bill. Bill gave Jane his phone number at the *Gazette* and left feeling good about the impression he left with Jane.

Jane did as she said she would do, and in a week's time, Bill picked up the phone at the *Stillwater Gazette*, and Joe Marshall was on the other end. Joe told Bill that he was impressed that a reporter would follow a noncareer and keep up on a player that didn't play. Joe told Bill that his determination and the fact that Bill never approached him and never invaded his privacy about why he did not want to play would get him an exclusive interview if he could be in California for Joe's first game. Bill asked Joe to let him know as soon as possible, and he would meet with Joe at the time and place Joe would choose.

Joe and Louise took life one day at a time while he was in Seattle, and they did not make a lot of long-term plans. They were starting life in new places, and there were endless destinations to see and a wide range of experiences that they could enjoy with each other. At this time, Louise did not look for or desire to find a job until Joe shipped out for his basic training and officer's candidate school. Joe had a military commitment as soon as the season ended, if he remained in Seattle or in San Diego. Louise wanted to spend as much time with Joe as she could before his six-month commitment that the Air Force would require. Joe did not have any extra time between travel, practice, and games while in Seattle. After Louise got their house completely in order and the way she wanted it, Louise decided to travel to Seattle every time Joe had a home stand. On two occasions, Louise took the train from San Diego to Seattle, changing trains in Los Angeles where she boarded the Coast Starlight train for a thirty-five-hour, 1,377-mile, overnight ride to Seattle, Washington. Not changing trains from Los Angeles to Seattle was a new run, and CD and Benito recommended to Louise to try the Coast Starlight at least once of soon-to-be many trips to Seattle. On her second trip to see Joe, she booked the trip by train. When she arrived in Seattle and Joe picked her up at the train station in downtown, Louise could not stop telling Joe how wonderful it was. Louise told Joe about the Pacific Ocean vistas, the snowcapped summits of the Cascade Mountains, hills, valleys, and how breathtaking the scenery was to her. Joe assured Louise that when he was called up to the Sand Dogs, they would take the Coast Starlight from Seattle to San Diego and enjoy all the fabulous scenery together. Louise made all her other trips flying from San Diego to Seattle nonstop because the trip was fast and not very expensive, but Louise never forgot her first trip north on the Pacific coastline while a passenger on the Coast Starlight and could not wait until she made the trip with Joe.

On September 26, Joe received the call from CD and Benito when he was on a road game in Portland, Oregon. He was to report to San Diego on the third day of October, and they were going to put him in the lineup on October 5. He would be starting the game at home in right field against the league leading Chicago. Joe immediately called Louise and told her to book a flight, and he would meet her in Seattle the next day at his apartment. He was heading to San Diego. He got the call. Since Joe rented a car while he was in Seattle, and they didn't have a car to drive back, Joe asked Louise to go ahead and book the tickets for both of them on the Coast Starlight so they could have a couple of days together enjoying the sights, peace, quietness, luxury, and solitude of the train.

The next call Joe made was to Bill Harper with the date of his first start. Joe would have two tickets for him at call waiting. One ticket was for him and a guest if Bill wanted one. Joe also told Bill his home address so that the day before the game, he could have an exclusive interview with Joe, which he could have ready for print the day of the game. Joe also told Bill he could have his first exclusive interview after the game so that all his family and friends at home and in Stillwater could have the news without waiting for the *Tulsa Tribune, Tulsa World,* or the *Daily Oklahoman* to print it two or three days later. Bill told Joe he would be at his house the day before and thanked Joe profusely. Joe also thanked Bill for taking an interest in him all these years.

CHAPTER 21

Sand Dog Joe

The day before Joe's start, later in the afternoon and after a practice session with the team, Louise and Joe were enjoying a sunny seventy-degree day watching the boating activity in the blue Pacific Ocean from their lanai when Louise heard the doorbell. When she answered, it was Bill Harper. Bill was thin and six feet two inches tall and a very pleasant young man. Very politely Bill introduced himself, and before he could say another word, Louise told him that they were expecting him to ring the doorbell for the last thirty minutes. Louise took Bill through the house to where Joe was sitting outside and asked him if he wanted something to drink, and Bill answered that a glass of ice water would be nice.

Bill was excited to finally meet Joe and to be able to shake his hand. Joe was also glad that he had someone to visit with from Oklahoma who came from an area close to home and was presently living in Stillwater. After some chitchat about OSU and people they knew in common, Joe asked Bill what he wanted to talk about and how he could help Bill with the article or articles that he wanted to write. Bill wanted to get Joe's story out, make it as accurate as possible, and write it in such a way that immediately after reading it, all the readers would want to know more about Joe and his exploits on the field. Bill expressed to Joe that the most important thing was to have an article that reflected well on Joe and was the absolute truth, without misrepresentation. Joe appreciated Bill's attitude and was willing to work with Bill to accomplish that goal and give the folks a good read.

Before they started the interview, Joe wanted to know why Bill never looked him up while they were both in Stillwater. The way Joe had it figured, they were both there for the last two years. Bill told Joe that the first day he was in Stillwater, which was two years ago last June, that he checked out the baseball stadium on campus, and from afar, he saw Joe, Paul Pixley, and others going through some batting practice and fielding. Bill said that he watched them for about an hour, and when the group started to finish, he headed back to his apartment. Bill said that it was about every three weeks to a month that he would find out something about Joe's whereabouts and at a distance make a note on what Joe was doing. Bill knew that Joe not playing had something to do with Walt's death. That was as personal as it could get and made it something that was not anybody's business on why or when Joe would ever play baseball again. The bottom line was if Joe had not decided to start playing baseball again, he would have never contacted Joe and would still be looking at Joe from afar.

Bill then told Joe that it was because of him that he chose his profession of journalism. Joe wanted to know the connection between him and Bill being a journalist sportswriter. Bill continued that as he would think about Joe and the possibilities that Joe's talent contained, Bill just knew that Joe would start playing ball again, and he wanted to be the one to tell the world the real story. Investigating Joe's life and finding out real facts gave Bill a rush, and at one point, he realized that finding out facts and not making things up for a story was real journalism, and investigating the facts for the real story was the difference in writing an article and being a great journalist. Bill told Joe that he didn't want to be a good sportswriter; he wanted to be a great sportswriter.

At this point, Joe decided that Bill was a real person, and that he could be trusted with personal details, and how Bill would write about them would be done with total respect to Joe and his family. Joe asked Bill to tell him the story from when he started keeping track of his nonplaying and nonexisting career. Bill repeated the story that he had told Jane starting from the ball game between Crescent and Kingfisher all the way through present day. Joe and Bill went over some details of the past six years, corrected some things about Joe's Stillwater days, details about his tryouts, and some of the dealings between him and the owners of the Sand Dogs. Bill had been very accurate about the things he had discovered about Joe's life and the last few months playing in a farm club of the Sand Dogs.

Joe and Bill parted for the night with the agreement to meet after the game tomorrow and finish up the interview for Joe's first day in the major league. Bill was excited to get his piece finished and called in to the *Stillwater Gazette*, so the readers in Oklahoma would know the real story behind Joe Marshall and his first day in the major leagues.

Now the day had arrived, and Joe was going to have the experience that Walt had twenty-five years ago. Joe had practiced for the last couple of days on Eaton Field and was at ease with the size of the field and the enclosure of the stands that gave Joe a feeling of being small. Through batting and fielding practice, Joe did not give his first day a lot of thought, other than he entertained a feeling that he had arrived at the starting point at the time when Joe felt was supposed to be. The fans slowly started coming into the stadium, and it really did not draw Joe's attention, and the noise was not noticeable because it slowly raised in decibels as the crowd grew. As batting practice concluded, the stadium was a little over half full when Joe left the field. Game time approached, and the team came out of the locker room, through the dugout onto the field. There was a roar that did not compare to anything Joe had experienced before. There was a capacity crowd in the stadium that day to see Joe Marshall, the player that had caught the minds of the Sand Dogs fans, and they were anticipating seeing the start of what they thought would be a baseball legend.

Joe gazed at the crowd while standing prior to the introduction of players and the playing of the National Anthem. He had what he had heard other people describe as "an out of body experience." It was as though time was standing still, and a second seemed to take minutes to pass. Joe literally thought he could feel every nerve ending in his body, the hair on the back of his neck standing on end. He had the feeling that every eye of the forty-thousand-plus fans was looking at him and nobody else. This was like no other feeling Joe had felt before, and it was as though these moments were being etched in stone, not to be forgotten, in his memory to recall at any time. To Joe, this was the ultimate time of his baseball career, and he wanted to soak it all in to the nth degree.

The start of the game was 1:05 PM. The sunny sky was clear and blue as it could be, seventy degrees, and a slight west breeze that made it a perfect baseball day at Eaton Field in San Diego, California. Joe was starting the game, playing in right field and batting next to last in the batting order. Through the top of the third inning, Joe fielded routine fly balls when the bases were empty, and the infield took care of most of the action. For the Sand Dogs, it had been three up and three down for the first two times at bat. Harvey Townsend, the first baseman, was seventh in the batting order just ahead of Joe. On the first pitch, he hit a Texas Leaguer that dropped into right field. Harvey was standing on first base as Joe approached the plate. Joe was given a hit-away sign and, at the moment of the first pitch, watched a fastball whiz past him for a call strike. The moment he heard the ball hit the catcher's mitt, his brain clicked in, and he knew for a certainty that he could have hit the ball soundly, but he couldn't get his body and brain to work together. Again, Joe was at the plate watching the wind up, and he saw the ball leave the fingertips of the pitcher and knew instantly it was another fastball that was heading for the strike zone and yet again heard the ball hit the catcher's mitt, with a call of strike two. For the second time, Joe knew if he had committed to take a swing, he could have connected but did nothing. The third pitch was thrown a high and outside, and Joe felt relieved because he had watched another pitch go by feeling if had it been in the strike zone, it would have been called a strike three, and he would be heading for the dugout without swinging his bat.

Joe backed out of the batter's box before the next pitch, took a deep breath, and told himself to look at the ball. If it looked right, not second-guess himself, pull the trigger, and take a swing. Joe stepped back into the batter's box, readied himself for the pitch. This time, he could see the pitch coming and knew instinctively it was a fastball over the plate at knee height. Joe unwound his body, keeping his eye on the ball. His swing was a little late, and he did not square his bat at contact. He hit a fly ball deep into the right field corner. The right fielder was at a full run in an attempt to catch the ball, but the ball hit the wall high and fair about two feet inside the right field foul line. The right fielder overran the play. The ball had bounced high off the wall over his head and back down the foul line on the far side of the right field. By the time the right fielder caught up with the ball, Joe was getting ready to make his turn at second base when the third base coach waved him on to third base. The right fielder hit the cutoff man, and Joe slid into third base just as the throw from the cutoff man hit the glove of the third baseman. Joe was safe at third with his first triple. Joe started off his career with a triple, batting a thousand and one RBI. The crowd went crazy, and Joe took it all in, wanting to keep these mental pictures, in detail, for the rest of his life.

Through the rest of Joe's first game, he had another two times at bat, with a single off a 3–2 count and a walk off of a 3–1 count and another RBI. The Sand Dogs beat Chicago that day while most, if not all, professional baseball ball world and the rest of the nation asked the question, Who the heck is Joe Marshall, and where did he come from? About the time the game was over, back home in Stillwater, Bill Harper's interview with Joe from the night before just came off the press and into hands of rural Oklahomans. Newspapers from every major city in the United States were getting the story line about Joe Marshall from the country press of the little *Stillwater Gazette* in the backwoods of Oklahoma. It was a tie-in to their article: the debut of a could-be-great's first game. When Joe emerged from the locker room, reporters from all over were there to ask Joe questions about his performance in the game and his past playing experience. Joe was polite and told all the reporters that approached him, that after the next game, he would make himself available and take time to answer most of their questions.

As planned, Joe met with Bill Harper after the game at Joe's house to give Bill an exclusive interview. Bill asked Joe about his thoughts and feelings before, during, and after the game. Bill also wanted to know how Joe felt about the journey he had made from his dad's death to present day, and Joe answered all of Bill's questions as fully as possible. Bill had supper with Louise and Joe, and when finished, he thanked Joe for allowing him to have the two most important exclusive interviews of his career, and that he would do a good job of telling the public about Joe's life and family. Bill headed back to his hotel room to forward his story to the *Stillwater Gazette,* pack up, and get ready to catch an early-morning flight back to Oklahoma City. The two exclusive interviews over the last two days was just the start of a supersuccessful career as a sportswriter and columnist for Bill. In just two days and two articles, the newspaper and baseball writers were also asking, Who the heck is Bill Harper, and where did he come from?

Bill and Joe kept in constant touch over the years. Later on, when Bill moved to Los Angles, California, they became close friends, spending many family days with each other.

The next three weeks, the last of the season, Joe finished as spectacularly as he started. For the 1972 season, Joe finished batting a .444, 9 RBI, and three home runs. Joe, in less than a month, had become an overnight sensation in the baseball world, poising himself for an incredible start for the 1973 season. This also made the Sand Dogs organization an instant success for ticket sales for the upcoming season. Everybody that knew Joe or was associated with Joe became very popular around the newly acquired fans.

One week after Joe finished the season, he was kissing Louise goodbye and heading for officer training school with the United States Air Force at Maxwell Air Force Base in Montgomery, Alabama, where he would spend the next nine and a half weeks. Joe had chosen financial management officer as his field in the Air Force, and upon finishing OTC, he would be assigned to Kessler Air Force Base in Biloxi, Mississippi, to be trained in USAF financing, accounting, and administration processes. Upon completing his training at Kessler, Joe was assigned to Edwards Air Force Base outside of Lancaster, California, in the middle of the Mojave Desert. Edwards was a great assignment for Joe because it was less than a four-hour drive from San Diego. Joe also found it to be interesting because of it being a flight-testing center for upcoming experimental aircraft and top-secret projects.

General Battle instructed Joe to apply for a high-security clearance when he first entered basic training so that when it came time for Joe to be assigned to a permanent duty station, he would have the clearance to take any job that was available, including the top-secret projects. Edwards Air Force Base had the top people in their fields and some of the Air Force's brightest minds working side by side with civilians attempting to develop futuristic aircraft and was a heady place to be. This was a good fit for Second Lieutenant Joe Marshall, and he was excited to be assigned to a base that was using and developing cutting-edge technology. The three-and-a-half-hour drive from San Diego to Edwards was all right with Joe, and it provided him time to be alone and think without any interruptions.

Until Joe was stationed at Edwards, the need for a second car was not an absolute necessity, but in the middle of a desert and three to four hours from home, it became one. Louise and Joe had discussed it while he was stationed at Biloxi and again while he was at Kessler. Louise kept the Bronco while Joe was away because he really did not need a car. His schedule left him little time to leave the base, and going to San Diego for the weekends while in Alabama and Mississippi was out of the question, being more than halfway across the nation. Also, the downtime on a weekend, while Joe was in the Air Force schools, gave him a chance to study because he wanted to graduate these schools in the number one position, and that he did. Now that Joe was at Edwards, he and Louise agreed a second car was necessary. With this in mind, Joe thought that his first weekend he had free, he would catch a ride into Lancaster where he could look at used cars at the local dealerships. The second day Joe was at Edwards, while he was walking from his apartment in the bachelor officer quarters to the building he was assigned to work in, there was a For Sale sign on the windshield of a 1967 blue Corvette convertible. One of the pilots assigned to the base was going to buy a new car and was ready to sell his Corvette because now his needs were more in line with a station wagon instead of a two-seat sports car. Joe walked by at first, not really giving it much notice, but before he reached the door to his building, he paused for a moment, turned around, walked back to the car, and wrote down the contact information that was on the sign. That evening, when Joe was in his room, he called Louise and told her all about the car and told her the asking price. Louise didn't think that it was a very practical car, but it sounded like a fun car to have when living in Southern California, and she thought that it would be fine for now and would be an easy car to sell later when they needed to get something more practical for their family.

The Marina Blue Corvette had a 327 ci, 350hp engine, side-mount exhaust system, bright-blue interior, thirty-six-gallon gas tank, posi-traction rear axle, removable hard top, close ratio heavy-duty 4-speed manual transmission, air-conditioning, power brakes, power steering, power windows, cast-aluminum bolt-on wheels, and an AM/FM radio. The car was perfect without a scratch one and was as nice-looking as the day it was first purchased. The owner of the Corvette was a pilot on the base and had maintained the car to the letter. He was going on to his next duty station, which was overseas and needed to sell the car as soon as possible.

This '66 Corvette listed at six thousand dollars new and was an expensive car when the major bought it, but now with forty-five thousand miles and six years later, plus the Corvette took a design change in 1968, making a '66 Vette less desirable at the time. The major dropped his price to $1,400, and Joe bought it. Joe thought it was a great deal and well worth the purchase price and knew that Louise would like it as well. As impractical as the Corvette was, it was that much more fun to drive, and Joe loved it.

Joe spent the next two months at Edwards and was convinced that this was the best assignment throughout the entire United States Air Force that he could have possibly been attached to and was very thankful to be able to work around the high-caliber people that were at Edwards Air Force Base. Edwards was a testing facility and proving ground for the Air Force and only the top people, enlisted and officers, were assigned there. Joe made many lasting relationships with the folks he met and worked with over the many years he was at Edwards.

Two months passed quickly, and Joe was finished with his six-month active-duty commitment with the Air Force. After Joe's six months' active duty, he would be required to spend two days a month and an additional two weeks a year active for the next five years of his obligation to the US Air Force. With this military commitment, Joe would be able to play baseball and fulfill his duty with the Air Force at the same time. For the last two months that Joe was at Edwards, he made it home to Louise almost every weekend, and those he didn't, Louise went to Edwards to spend the weekend with Joe.

Now Joe was driving home to San Diego after his last day of active military service, for a week's stay, after which he would be traveling to Phoenix for spring training camp with the Sand Dogs. When Joe finished his work at Edwards that last day, it was early evening on a Friday. Joe had the removable hard top on and his gear piled up in the passenger floorboard and seat because there was little room behind the seats when the convertible top was stowed in the down position. As Joe drove along, he pondered about the vastness of the desert and how the landscape died into the mountains ahead of him as he passed by the Joshua trees that populated the Mojave Desert. Joe thought that this would be a great drive to have the top down, push beyond the speed limit, and enjoy the feeling of the open road, and the next time he made this trip, that is exactly what he would do. Driving nearly due south from Edwards to San Diego, Joe left the mostly deserted, peaceful open roads of the Mojave and started seeing more traffic the closer he got to San Bernardino. This alone changed his thoughts to how his and Louise's life would be taking on another change in the next few months, and based on how well his baseball career developed, that change might last for as long as he was old. If the success of Joe's brief appearance at the close of last season was an indication of what his career was to become, this made Joe more eager to start a new chapter to his and Louise's life, and the closer to home he drove, the more excited he became to get started at the first of the season as a listed player on the Sand Dogs' official roster.

It was later in the evening when Joe arrived home, and the sun was just starting to set. The loud engine noise that the Lake Side pipes on Joe's Corvette let Louise know that Joe had pulled into the driveway. She moved quickly to the front door to greet and welcome him home. The moment Louise opened the door, Joe could smell the supper Louise was preparing for him. The smell of fried potatoes and onions was identifiable and unmistakable and could make your mouth water at the first whiff. Louise had fried porkchops to go along with the meal, another one of Joe's favorites and a combination of foods that Joe's mother, Jane, would occasionally fix for Joe at special times. This was a special moment for Joe and would vividly stay in his memory, hopefully for the rest of his life.

When Louise and Joe first arrived in San Diego from Oklahoma, they knew Joe would be unsettled for a few months, and that was fine with them. As the time continued on with Louise and their new home, Joe looked forward to this very moment where they felt they would be for years to come and a routine that would be repeated for many years in the future. This was the "start" of the end of complete lifestyle changes and new experiences and the beginning of establishing their home and future family.

CHAPTER 22

Professional Baseball and Family

Edwards Air Force Base, San Diego, and Scottsdale, Arizona, *biff, bam, bluey,* Joe and Louise found themselves at the start of spring practice, new sounds, and new living accommodations. At the time, Louise and Joe didn't consider how many times this start of spring would repeat itself and how familiar the surroundings would become over the next two-plus decades to them and their family and close friends, but they were looking forward to this being a consistent lifestyle and hopefully each year being as anticipated as the first.

It was back to baseball again, and other than the new park, facilities, and weather being new, the faces and people were familiar, and that eased the tension for Joe and Louise. There were a couple of new players that had replaced players from last year, but for Joe, his time at the end of the season was so brief, he had not made friends with any of them. With a lot of unknowns about Joe and his abilities and being brought in at the end of a season, most of the team, as it seemed to Joe, did not embrace his presence and seemed a little standoffish. This was the most dramatic change for Joe at the start of spring practice. Nearly everyone came up to him when he entered the locker room to greet him and say hello. As other players arrived to the locker room, the moment they saw Joe, they came over, shook hands, and gave Joe a warm welcome. The only one that did not greet Joe in a friendly fashion was Coach Hambrick. Joe didn't take this to heart because he quickly observed that Hambrick did not have a jovial greeting with anybody on the team. This was pleasing to Joe for the fact he was treated by Hambrick just as he treated everyone else. As time passed, Joe started to see similarities in Scott Hambrick and Ron Robinson. In fact, by the end of Joe's first season, he would find himself visiting with Jane and telling her the two coaches might be fraternal twins, separated by birth and time.

Joe did not realize the dynamics in his late arrival to the Sand Dogs' roster at the end of last season. At the time, most of Joe's thoughts were centered around his new surroundings, his time with or without Louise, and what he needed to do at his new job to be successful. When CD and Benito told him to leave Seattle and show up in San Diego and that he would be put on the Sand Dogs' roster for the last two weeks of the season, he did not question the decision. Joe just did what he was told to do, and if there was to be an explanation, it would come in due time. Joe did have the thought, which he never expressed, as late as it was in the Sand Dogs' season, on why the last-minute rush.

At the same time, the team did not understand management's decision to bring Joe aboard so late in the season. The team's standing would not be improved enough to make a difference in postseason playoff, so why bring in what was thought to be a superstar at the end of the season? Give him more time to adjust in the minors for the rest of the season and leave him in Seattle. Another thought the team had was a management move that would place Joe in a more valuable trade before the start of next season. If management could show Joe off, then his value would go up, and it would make Joe a money deal as a trade for the owners, and Joe would be no help to the team. Most of the team felt Joe would be playing against them next season, not with them.

Now Joe had a feeling of acceptance, although the coolness of the team at the end of the season didn't bother Joe. It felt better to be part of a team that saw him as an asset and one that was going to help them win. With the start of spring practice, there was also a start of eagerness and enthusiasm that was not present at the end of last season. When Joe started thinking about the difference on how he felt and how the team played from then to now, it was hard for him to define the ingredient that explained the disparity in the energy levels. After the end of the first week of practice, Joe noticed in the locker room and on the field, there were conversations between his teammates about the end of the season and what teams might have a shot at postseason play. Added in the conversations were questions about the Sand Dogs being in the mix and what their chances were of being winners of the West Division and talk about even playing in the World Series this year. This was when Joe identified the component that was invigorating himself and the team. It was expectation.

The simple added thought of success, or even the expectation of success, was enough to change everything. This reminded Joe of his freshman and sophomore years in high school when winning was a thought his teammates could entertain. It made them do more than they thought was possible of themselves, just to have the chance at victory. They, all to the last man, bought into doing whatever was required of them. Years after when Joe would think of his first season of spring ball, he would marvel at the absence of difference between high school boys, fourteen to eighteen years old, and men, twenty to late thirty years old. Given the chance to win, they would challenge themselves to exceed their limitations and give it all they had, plus, be first to cross the finish line.

Joe had a gut feeling about his first season that it might be spectacular and one for the record books, and it was. At the start of the third week in October 1973, the San Diego Sand Dogs had won 117 games and lost 45, winning the National League pennant 26 games ahead of second place St. Louis and setting a record for the most wins of a major league team in baseball history. The Sand Dogs entered the World Series as a favorite and beat New York five games to one for the 1973 World Series Championship. Joe was voted the MVP of the National League for regular season and the MVP of the 1973 World Series. In 1973, Joe played in 162 games that consisted of 640 at bats, 232 hits, 45 home runs, 70 stolen bases, and 111 runs batted in. Joe was awarded a Rawlings Gold Glove for his performance as a National League outfielder and was voted Rookie of the Year. The most amazing part of Joe's first year was that he never peaked. With each passing week, Joe honed his skills and got better at the game than the week before. The people close to Joe and his teammates saw his improvement from week to week, and by the end of the season, the only thought they had was what Joe would do next season. Literally, the sky was the limit to his abilities.

Bill Harper was always the first to get a story line from Joe. Bill would be at his office, next to his phone, waiting on a call from Joe. Sometimes it would be at 3:00 AM Central Standard Time for a game that started at 7:00 PM Pacific Standard Time before Bill got a call from Joe. All the years that Joe played, Bill was first to get a story line from Joe. Joe knew that the folks and friends at home in Oklahoma kept up on him, and he always wanted them to know the latest scoop first, for those that were interested. No matter where Joe was, Bill knew as soon as Joe could get to a pay phone after a game, he would call Bill and fill him in on all the details. At the end of Joe's first season, one of the largest newspapers in Oklahoma, the *Daily Oklahoman*, hired Bill away from the *Stillwater Gazette*. This really didn't take anything away from the readers of the Stillwater paper because most folks in the rural areas that took the local papers also took one of the major state circulation papers. Around central Oklahoma, the family and friends of Joe Marshall, through the reporting of Bill Harper, would have the privilege of reading it first in the *Daily Oklahoman* as soon as or before anyone else in the entire country.

The personal relationship between Joe, Benito, and CD and their families grew closer with the passage of time. At some point along the way in their budding friendship, CD and Benito asked Joe to call him Rod and to drop the Mr. Jones and just go with CD. Joe agreed. By the end of the first season, Joe met routinely, during home stands, with Rod and CD and after the end of the first season, during the first off season. Not a week went by that the three of them got together to talk about baseball, investments, past lives, current events, and the best places to eat. The relationship very quickly developed to one that resembled a family and less of one of a player/owner relationship. Joe found out a little more about the backgrounds of CD and Rod every time they got together, and they found out more about Joe.

One of the many things they all three had in common was their farming background. CD was third generation from a slave family that, after the Civil War in 1865, settled Peyton Colony just outside of Blanco, Texas. Until he joined the United States Army in June of 1942, CD lived and worked a 2,000-acre farm in Peyton Colony with his parents and his two older brothers. CD's parents owned their farm outright, and like Joe's folks, they were good managers and hard workers, which allowed them to prosper and be successful in good times as well as bad. CD's mother died in 1939 from pneumonia, and both of CD's brothers died in World War II while serving in the United States Navy.

During World War II, CD served and fought with the 333rd Field Artillery Battalion where he was involved in many battles, including the Battle of the Bulge, in Bastogne, Belgium. The 333rd, a black segregated unit with a black headquarters, had been in support of the 105th Infantry Division at the beginning of the battle and was attached to the newly arrived 101st Airborne Division. CD served his country with pride and honor and was a highly decorated soldier.

When CD returned home, he convinced his dad, who had married his mother when she was twenty, and he was forty, now sixty-five years old, to lease the farm and go with him to California. CD talked with his dad about how things had changed in Peyton Colony before and after the war, that many had left and were not returning to farm, and their opportunities would exceed those than if they stayed in Texas. His dad agreed. CD was a junior and had the same name as his dad. His dad, Cardozie Darnell Jones Sr., went by Darnell.

During his time in the Army, CD learned three major things. First, he learned to play baseball with the best of them, and he played baseball all the time he was in the army, from the first day to the last, and made a lot of money while playing (baseball seemed to be the major pastime for most servicemen, weather permitting). Second, he also learned how to play poker with the best of them and also made a lot money at it, and the third thing he learned was not to be fearful of anything. Bastogne left a lifelong reminder of that to him. CD's brothers, at the insistence of their dad, listed each other as beneficiaries to their National Service life insurance. Their dad thought that if something happened to them, the money from the policy would help those brothers that survived to get a new start on life and help them to follow their own dreams, and that was the plan CD had. Each policy had a death benefit of $10,000. The two policies combined, awarded to the surviving brother, CD, totaled $20,000. CD accumulated a large sum of money from his paycheck of four years of service, poker winnings, and betting on baseball. Including the additional life insurance from his brothers, CD had enough money to do whatever he wanted to do.

What Joe knew about CD's background was incomplete, but soon after he and his father left Texas was about the time he got involved with the ownership of a minor league team, where he played and obtained a 49 percent ownership of the team he played for. This was the same team that Rod purchased a 51 percent ownership. This was when Joe surmised that CD and Rod began their friendship and partnership.

Joe learned a lot about his new friends during the many get-togethers they had that first year. Other things he learned about his newfound friends was the separation of their duties in their partnership. All things pertaining to baseball talent, baseball in general, and running the business end of all their enterprises were CD's responsibility. Investments and financing fell under Rod's direction. Joe also knew they had an awareness of all sides of the business ventures that each took care of, but they did not question the decisions each made in their area of responsibility. Joe admired the loyalty and respect that CD and Rod had for each other, and the only relationship Joe had to compare with theirs was his own family.

The moment the season was over, CD and Rod asked Joe and Louise if they would like to sail up the West Coast and back, taking about one week. Joe and Louise talked it over and agreed to go. This trip CD planned was not just pleasure but a business trip to discuss not only Joe's career in baseball, but the off season too. When Joe and Louise showed up at the docks in San Diego, they boarded a Morgan Out Island 41, named the *Sand Dawg*. The *Sand Dawg* was a one-year-old sailboat that did not meet the look of sweet sheer lines, close-to-perfect balance, and classic elegance of the time. The *Sand Dawg* was not the boat a sailing traditionalist would pick at the time because of its pudgy appearance, which sacrificed elegance for volume and headroom in the cabin area. When CD and Rod purchased the boat, it had been in the water for a month, and because a friend of theirs got caught up in a cash flow problem and needed money quick, not having the time to get a loan, looked to CD and Rod to sell the boat and made them a deal they couldn't resist. Rod and CD had sailed for the last ten years and had owned many different sailboats that they bought and sold for a profit, always from somebody that was in financial difficulty and needed to unload their boat before it was repossessed or to cover a bet on the horses. They had established a relationship with a young man that maintained boats, and they were always in the know on a good boat that was moving away from the present owner. Most of the time, they made a good return and enjoyed a nice-sailing craft for little or nothing.

The *Sand Dawg* was an exception because it was new, really nice, very roomy, and comfortable. Added to the comfort of the *Sand Dawg* were separate sleeping quarters for Joe and Louise that afforded them plenty of privacy in a somewhat small area. Added to the unbelievable low-price CD and Rod paid for the Out Island 41, they knew the designer of the boat, Charlie Morgan, who was well-known and highly respected among sailors and boat designers. Charlie Morgan told Rod and CD that his boat would sail as long and for as many years as they wanted to sail it, even if they lived to be one hundred years old. Rod felt that was the best endorsement of a product that he had ever heard and believed it as well.

When invited on the trip, Louise asked Joe if he thought CD and Rod would invite any lady friends along. At that point, she asked Joe what he knew about their past and/or present marital status. Joe explained to Louise they would have told him if anybody else was included, and that he knew very little about their social life that included females, but he knew they were not married and had been single for at least ten years. CD and Rod had both been married before, and Joe knew very little about their wives, except for the facts they were deceased. Rod's wife, Maria, died giving birth to their only child, Ramon, in 1965 and that Ramon lived with his grandparents, Maria's parents, the majority of time. CD's wife died in a car accident while visiting her parents in Louisiana about a year before Maria died.

When Joe and Louise arrived at the docks in Mission Bay, CD and Rod were in the parking lot to help carry their luggage and get it stowed on the boat. Joe and Louise both felt a little apprehensive when they boarded the *Sand Dawg* because it was their first time to be on a sailboat and had never been on a boat of any kind on an ocean. After the gear was stowed and while still on the lower deck, Rod gave Joe and Louise a brief tour of the sleeping compartments, galley, emergency gear, head, radio, and engine compartment. After the lower-deck tour, Rod moved Joe and Louise topside as he continued his walk-through of the boat, from the stern forward through amidships to the bow, explaining port from starboard, giving them the name and function of every item and part of the boat, more or less giving them a sailing 101 course.

While Rod was familiarizing Joe and Louise with the boat, CD was going through the final checklist before getting underway. The final comment Rod gave Louise and Joe was that they would both crew in sailing the *Sand Dawg*. There were no free rides. Joe and Louise listened closely to what they were told because they wanted to get it right and not cause any problems. Their fear or apprehension left when they started to focus on what CD and Rod told them to do, and they were in the coastal waters of the Pacific before they knew it. They found the experience the most exhilarating thing they had ever done. When Louise and Joe left Oklahoma in their Bronco, they wanted to try new things, take new adventures, and take part in as many new experiences as they could. Sailing in the Pacific Ocean with the engine off, being propelled by nothing but the wind had no equal in their lives. They loved it.

The course that CD and Rod set was to sail to Catalina Island, drop anchor, and stay a couple of nights in different bays between Avalon and Two Harbors. From there, they would sail to Dana Point, south to Oceanside, and back to Mission Bay, dropping anchor at different bays as they headed south, spending another five nights staying wherever they wanted to. The first day would be the longest sailing day of the trip, and the rest would give plenty of time to be at anchor and relax. This would give ample time to discuss business without interruption and enough activity in the day for an early respite in midafternoon that would be welcome.

CD and Rod knew about Joe's academic background and had one of their officers from their accounting firm go to Oklahoma State University to visit with Joe's instructors about Joe's accounting, finance, and business acumen and how successful they thought Joe would be in the business world. The feedback was all the same from everyone they met with. They didn't know Joe was a baseball player until they read it in the local paper last August, and from their viewpoint, no matter how good Joe Marshall was at baseball, it might not measure up to his potential in business and finance. CD and Rod felt really good about trying to hire Joe for his off season to work for a position within their corporate offices. CD and Rod looked for corporate talent as much or more than they did athletic talent. They felt that finding a superstar that had the right fit and personality was much more difficult than finding the equivalent in the baseball world. In the baseball theater, you could measure the performance by the end of the day, week, month, or season and could see immediately what corrections could be made. Another big factor in professional baseball, you knew when a player was leaving, other than by injury, and had opportunities to make the adjustment and/or replacement. In corporate business, key people were there one day and gone the next with little or no notice, leaving for a higher-paying job or another company where they thought they could advance faster.

CD and Rod were always looking for business talent that they could develop and bring along to be key people who would fit well into their business plan, and at this very moment, they felt that Joe might be the best recruit they had ever found, not giving any consideration to his baseball abilities or his prowess on the diamond. The first night, they anchored in a beautiful natural bay just a little south of Two Harbors. After supper, relaxing on the deck as the sun was setting, Rod and CD started telling Joe and Louise about their other business holdings, ventures, assets, and investments in great detail. In a very benign manner, Joe interrupted Rod and told him that he had a complete knowledge of most of the holdings and investments of the Jones Rodriguez Corporation. CD and Rod looked a little surprised but told Joe to continue and tell them the extent of what he knew about their business. Joe had studied the Jones Rodriguez Corporation since the first day Coach Robinson had secured a tryout with the Sand Dogs and continued to research the public records and articles about them as individuals and their business. When Joe finished an hour later, CD and Rod had to admit that Joe told them more than they were going to tell Joe.

The four of them sat silent for a few moments, and then CD asked bluntly if Joe would like to go to work for them in a corporate position. Joe asked how it would work with him being gone from his job from April to October during baseball season. CD and Rod looked at each other and had a good belly laugh and then told Joe they owned the business. They would make it work. Joe asked Louise what her thoughts were about taking a second job from the same people that he already worked for, and she replied that if they were as good to work for in the corporate world as the baseball world, it would probably be a dream job, and they should do it. CD asked Joe whether he wanted to know how much he would make before he took the job. Joe's reply was the same as it was when he was offered the opportunity to play for the Sand Dogs. "Pay me what I am worth." Again, CD and Rod looked at each other, laughed, and said it was a deal. Another drink and they all went below for a good night's sleep.

Just before they dozed off, Louise asked Joe if they should be more exact about how much salary they should want when asked. Joe told Louise the way he had it figured, they received much more money than he would have asked for when he signed to play for the Sand Dogs when he asked to be paid what he was worth. If they didn't pay him anything for this second job, they had more money now than they ever dreamed they would have. Plus, he would have a job where he could learn the intricacies of finance and business corporation of big-time players in the business world. Joe and Louise both agreed that they had complete trust in CD and Rod. They knew they would be well taken care of without doubt.

After another day of sailing, they found a bay south of Dana Point to stay the night, and again, after a supper that Rod prepared, they all set on the deck as the sun set, having a drink and good conversation. Rod asked Joe about life after baseball and what he wanted to do at that time. Joe had no hesitation about answering the question Rod posed. Joe said he loved baseball and could hardly think of a time without it. Joe continued that when his dad had died, it wasn't that he did not want to play, but he considered what he needed to do at the farm and felt that he was following his dad's desire to do one thing at time and not divide his focus on the job at hand. Plus, his good friend Paul Pixley always had a game of catch or a game at Wycoff Corner going to keep him involved and not void of baseball. The same thing happened at Oklahoma State. Because of Paul and Coach Robinson, he was able to keep his hand in the game. Joe added that when that time in the future came, when he decided to stop playing professional baseball, he had an idea on how to keep playing for as long as he wanted to. Because of his love of the game, Joe truly never gave a thought to when he would quit playing professional baseball. In his mind, he could see them carrying him feet first on a stretcher off the diamond.

CD and Rod were both interested in Joe's comment about playing as long as he wanted to and asked Joe to expand on his idea. In his reply, Joe emphasized that he wanted to be the one that makes the choice to stop playing at the professional level, and after that, he had a vision of another level of baseball that he called Joeball. CD and Rod wanted to know for sure that this was a real game with live people playing it. Joe assured them it was a real game with real people, and he called it Joeball because he didn't have a better name to call it. It was his idea of a baseball game where players that love the game can continue to play at a slightly diminished level.

CD and Rod asked Joe to continue about this Joeball idea of his and explain how it worked or how different it was than any other baseball game, and Joe went on to explain. First, the players for his team will be retired or ex-professional baseball players of all ages that didn't want to stop playing. They would play at a park that they all owned, and the rules of substitution and limitation of roster would not apply to them but would apply to the opposing team. All other rules were the same for both teams. There would be no road games.

All games would be played at their park and no place else. There would be a winner's purse of a large amount of money that the visiting team could win if they beat the home team of ex or retired professionals, no questions asked. The visiting team had to be a real organized team of any level, with an existing roster, which had played a season or was playing in a season that had a current win/loss record. The team that wanted to challenge Joe's team could be of any age and/or level of baseball and would sell tickets to all events.

CD and Rod thought Joe had an interesting idea and asked more questions about the facilities, and Joe was obliged to answer all the questions they could come up with. They wanted to know if the games were all the park would be used for. Joe explained his idea at present; that it would be a place to hold games, teach lessons, hold baseball camps, have visiting professionals come in for seminars, and a school to teach field maintenance. A complete baseball facility, which would be operated as a nonprofit organization funded by permanent perpetual growth endowments. CD and Rod liked Joe's idea and inquired when this would start to take place, and Joe told them he already had the property back home in Oklahoma, and when he and Louise were more established financially in the years to come and the monies became available, the ideas and plans would start to come to fruition. CD and Rod told Joe to keep them informed of his plans as the years passed because it sounded like something they would like to be a part of, and Joe agreed to do so. This concluded another day at sea, and they went below for another night of being put to sleep by the gentle rocking of the boat and quiet ocean noises.

Three more days and nights on the *Sand Dawg*, sailing south down the California coast, and they would be back to Mission Bay, and the plan was for Joe to have another two weeks off before starting his new job with the Jones Rodriguez Corporation as a trainee in the financial and investments side of the business.

Joe and Louise thought many times on their first time sailing and the week they spent on the *Sand Dawg* with CD and Rod and how a relationship started that week to transform into a lifelong friendship that would become as close or closer than family. Many more trips were taken on the *Sand Dawg* over the next years that started out as a time away from baseball and business, but always seemed to involve a large amount of business and strategical planning. The total lack of distractions while on the ocean and at anchor in a bay or cove seemed to be the impetus for thinking clearly, staying on point, and meshing ideas for current and future plans and decisions. The trips were planned so that Louise could go along because of her razor-sharp mind that brought a lot to the discussions. Rod and CD gleaned and learned invaluable insight from Louise because she approached issues from a different perspective and a different viewpoint than Joe and themselves. Rod and CD felt that Louise brought a balance that was lacking in years past to their long-term planning and direction. On these sailing trips, Joe and Louise really got into the sailing, learning more and more until the day when they were in charge of the trip and the boat while CD and Rod did the crewing and were happy to do so.

In a time period of less than twenty months, from a life in rural Oklahoma, living the first twenty-plus years within sixty miles from where they were born, hardly ever leaving a half-dozen counties that surrounded Crescent, Joe and Louise had now traveled from coast to coast, border to border, all over the United States including most of its major cities. Louise and Joe had decided that when Louise's job didn't prohibit her from going, that they would travel together wherever Joe's jobs took him, and they had a great time doing it. CD and Rod were right about hiring Joe because he was as much of a superstar in finance as he was on the baseball diamond. Joe moved up fast with the Jones Rodriguez Corporation and soon became a major player in the firm. At first, the business world met Joe with a little skepticism because of his stardom in professional baseball. It did not take Joe long to convince his relations and counterparts in the business arena that he was not a professional jock that had a job because of his popularity as an athlete. After the first encounter or meeting with Joe, people realized that Joe had a superior business intellect, and he was, or would be, a force to contend with.

CHAPTER 23

A Great Career and When to Call It Quits

Joe and Louise lived a storybook life, and Joe's baseball career spanned twenty-seven years. During Joe's playing career, he remained active in the United States Air Force reserves and held the rank of lieutenant colonel as an intelligence officer. During his years in the reserve, he was called to active duty three times, first in 1983 during the invasion of Grenada, second in the 1989 invasion of Panama, and the third time in 1990 for the Gulf War. Joe's active-duty service overlapped with his professional baseball two times, but only briefly. In the same twenty-seven years, Joe worked for CD and Rod at Jones Rodriguez Corporation, attaining ownership, making him an equal partner with his close friends. Joe maintained a managing director position with equal responsibilities to that of CD and Rod.

Joe was a very recognizable baseball celebrity who attracted many people who wanted to have a business relationship with such a widely known and popular figure. This made it easy for Joe to have the contacts he needed to be successful in the investment business. Joe was very knowledgeable and savvy of the business world on a national and international level. Over the years, working closely with the great business and financial minds who worked for the Jones Rodriguez Corporation, Joe learned the ins and outs of the financial investment, banking, and stock market arenas. Corporations and financial institutions worldwide knew of Joe Marshall and his work product for the Jones Rodriguez Corporation. Most of his international associations did not know or understand his connection with professional baseball; they only knew of him as a superstar in international business.

The clients Joe enjoyed the most to work for came from his association with the baseball community. This group consisted mostly of baseball players, both current and retired, but also included trainers, managers, groundskeepers, and facilities managers. The connection was baseball. Any and all involved in the game were drawn to Joe for help to them make money. Joe's acuity progressed in his business, investing, and investment counseling abilities each and every year. Joe discovered most investment counselors work hard for new clients for one to two years, after which more effort was channeled looking for new prospects. Joe did not spend his time looking for new clients; they found him.

With his investing business, Joe was able to meet and get to know a lot of baseball players. Most professional baseball players did not make the huge salaries that the general public thought they had, nor did they have long careers. What the public did not see were the nonstarters, but the players that filled out the twenty-five- and forty-man rosters. So many of these players were the same age as starters in their position; they sat in the background only seeing limited playing time when the starting player they backed up was sick or injured. Some very good players could spend their career waiting for someone to get injured, traded, or they themselves get traded, for them to have a chance to be in a starting lineup and garner the bigger paycheck. Players came up through the minors, most stayed in the minors, and a few made it to "the big league." Of those that made it, some stayed for a brief time and some for the rest of their careers. By far, the mass majority of professional baseball players had little or no money, but those that stayed, played for the love of the game.

Some of the players that did not make it to the majors sought Joe out to help them because of his reputation of being honest and really working for the people that trusted him. Joe also helped them invest their signing bonuses, which might be the only big money they would ever see in their professional baseball careers. These were the guys that Joe liked being around the most, the real individuals that played for the love of the game who would never see the big leagues or the big paychecks but played because they had a chance to play.

When Joe would be working with players from all over the baseball world, he would get to know most on a very personal basis. Joe made a lot of lifelong associations that he always kept in touch with, not just a business relationship, but as a friend. One of the questions Joe would always ask his clients and his friends that were clients, "What do you want to be when you grow up?" This was a rhetorical question that those queried knew what Joe was asking. The question was really, When you are through with baseball, or when baseball is through with you, what do you do next? So many times, after asking this question, Joe would get a dazed stare, a stare not really looking at anything or anybody, just a blank stare. After maybe a minute of silence, an oft-heard response was one that said, "I really don't know. I have never considered not playing." Joe found out that most players focus so hard on what they were doing and had focused on baseball since they were a little kid, that not playing never entered their mind. The reality was that the end of playing was going to happen, not if, but when.

On almost every occasion that Joe inquired about life after baseball, the one he asked would ask Joe the same question. Joe always replied with the same response, that when he decided to quit playing, there was a family farm in central Oklahoma, near a little rural town by the name of Crescent, that his great-grandfather Howard Marshall claimed in the Land Run of 1889, which his family has continually farmed ever since. He would return and also farm to the end of his days. Joe would also tell whoever asked that he really never planned to stop playing baseball. Joe would always get queried on how that could be, and Joe would tell them about his plan to play what everyone nicknamed "Joeball." Over the years, Joe made a list of players that told him if he ever got his idea of Joeball going, they would like to be a part of it. Joe told them it might be a while, but when the time came and things were in place, he would give them a call.

Joe and Louise had two sons, Joe and Payton, that were born in 1974 and 1976, nineteen months apart and separated by one year in school. Upon their graduation from high school, they were appointed to attend the United States Air Force Academy and graduated with the class of '96 and '97, serving as pilots.

Rod's son, Ramon, in his midthirties during Joe's twenty-seventh season, had a job working for Jones Rodriguez Corporation, where CD placed him in the public relations department, a job where it was felt that he could do the least amount of harm. Many years back, when Rod's wife died, at the insistence of his wife's parents, Ramon's grandparents, Rod allowed them to take a major part in the rearing of Ramon. Ramon spent most of his time through the week and most holidays with his grandparents, who did not care for or respect Rod. Rod and CD both agreed that Ramon was spoiled, and he was more attuned at spending money than he was at making it. Ramon was the typical ne'er-do-well playboy, with near-unlimited funds at his disposal to spend as he wished. Ramon developed a resentment for Rod's friends because he felt they didn't care for him, and he was right. Ramon wanted his dad, Rod, to treat him and advance him in the corporation just as he did Joe. That was not even a thought for Rod, let alone act on Ramon's desires. When Ramon was around Joe, he would give Joe directions to let everyone within earshot know that he was Joe's boss and not the other way around. Joe very rarely engaged Ramon in conversation and never asked him questions or directed him in any way because it always resulted in a confrontation. Basically, CD, Rod, and Joe avoided Ramon at all costs. CD had two employees that kept track of Ramon from a distance in an effort to counteract any and most actions that Ramon took on behalf of the company. CD did this to help save Rod as much embarrassment as possible, and he did this with Rod's knowledge of the situation. The saving grace about Ramon was that he liked to travel all the time, and when he was in town, he only showed up for work, at the most a couple of hours a day, because he kept time with a calendar.

In Joe's playing time in major league baseball, he was honored with every award there was and held the record for highest batting average for a single season of .428 and the highest career batting average of .368. Of his twenty-seven years of playing, he was voted into the all-star game twenty-seven times and played twenty-five times. Joe's last five years, because of injuries, had its ups and downs with him trying to be in top form for 162 games per year. The effort it took to continue to play proved to be taxing and difficult for Joe to maintain, along with trying only to miss the minimum number of games because of injuries. In Joe's last three seasons, he was put on the fifteen-day disabled list once each season. Joe only played at full speed, and after Joe turned forty-five years old, he found that injuries typically he would have played through at a younger age became annoying and a limitation to his ability to play at full capacity if he did not give them appropriate time to heal and recover. At the end of each of the last three seasons, family, friends, and those close to Joe thought he would announce his retirement, but nonetheless, to their mystification, he did not. Joe, a person that approached all aspects of life with a controlled, direct, and sensible approach, now for the first time, within the confines of people close to Joe, were seeing what seemed to be a fallible segment to his character.

Season after season, Joe's performance on the field was unparalleled, but even the slightest injuries took longer and longer to overcome. Age was playing a factor in Joe's game. An incident in the second week of June, of Joe's twenty-seventh season, proved to be the turning point in Joe's illustrious career. On a sunny afternoon game in mid-June, Joe was running from right field to center, chasing a high-hit fly ball, when he collided with the center fielder doing the same. The collision left them both motionless for a few moments. Joe sustained a shoulder and knee injury with an added mild concussion but walked off the field. The center fielder left the field on a stretcher with a nondisplaced fracture in his right cheekbone and a concussion that left him unconscious for several minutes. After Joe had been examined by the doctors with x-rays, MRI of shoulder, knees, and torso, they found a fractured rib, severe trauma/strains to Joe's right knee and shoulder. Joe admitted to the doctors that he did not remember the collision with his teammate, and he must have been unconscious for a few seconds because he could not figure out how he came to be lying facedown on the field. This lack of memory and momentary unconsciousness gave the doctor reason to believe that Joe also suffered a mild concussion.

The team physician talked it over with Joe and wanted to place Joe on the sixty-day disabled list to give him enough time to recover from the broken rib and other injuries. This did not bid well with Joe. He felt his injuries were minor, and it would take him less time to recover, where his health would not limit his playing or performance. The fifteen-day DL was not an option for Joe because he did not want his place on the roster to be filled with someone else. In Joe's mind, all he needed was a few days to recover, and he wanted to be placed on the day-to-day where the medical staff could evaluate his recovery. Being on a day-to-day evaluation would leave him on active roster, and a replacement would not be called up. Joe also knew if he were to be placed on the sixty-day DL, the sixty days out would go past the August 1 deadline, and he would not be able to return to the active-team roster for the rest of the season. The sixty-day DL would be in effect the end of Joe's twenty-seventh season, and Joe did not want that to happen.

Joe went to Rod and CD and discussed the situation and expressed his desire to continue to play because he did not want to be pulled off the roster for the rest of the season. If this happened, Joe felt that making the team next season could put him in a pre-carious situation where he would be taking his replacement's job in the spring. Rod and CD told Joe it was up to him because their deal was that Joe would make the call when he would quit playing, and this situation did not change anything with the original agreement. Joe was relieved, and he was placed on day-to-day until he wanted to return.

Joe being injured placed the Sand Dogs one man short on their twenty-five-man roster, and it made the majority of the team uneasy with Joe not relenting in giving up his spot. The extra man was important in helping the team win games. When someone had a minor injury where one, two, or three days would give them enough time to recover and be able to play at full speed, it meant the team would be two players short with Joe on the active roster and so on. The team as a whole did not understand the reasoning allowing a position being left open for an extended period of time. This would eventually leave the team at a disadvantage. Some of the young first-year players who had not been around Joe, except for the last few months, felt that Joe was not a team player and were very vocal about their feelings.

Joe did a good job at trying to hide the pain and discomfort of his injuries while he was on the field, but at home, Joe could not continue the charade under the watchful eye of Louise. Louise could see and hear Joe all through the night as he tossed and turned, trying to find a position that would let the pain subside so that he could get some sleep. Then, in the early morning, Joe would finally give up trying to sleep and get up from his restless night. Louise would awaken as Joe got up, and she would see him struggle to stand up straight when he got out of bed and for him to take a herculean effort to make his stiff feet, knees, and legs take the first steps of the morning on his way to the bathroom. As the morning progressed and Joe moved around the house during his daily morning routine, ease of movement and normal flexibility would slowly return.

The first week of Joe's convalescing, not playing or practicing along with the minimal movement needed for him to be on the field, ended too soon with only the slightest, nearly nondetectable, healing and recovery. After the second week, Joe could tell his condition had improved considerably. This improved condition that Joe was experiencing was very welcomed by Joe, but he realized that his healing had not been tested under game conditions, and in the back of his mind, he wondered if the mend would hold up when he gave a maximum effort.

On the fourteenth day, Joe was placed back into the starting lineup. Now it was the middle of the season, and Joe was on the field not because he could contribute to the team, but because of who he was and his insistence that he wanted to play. Uncharacteristic of Joe, over the next few weeks, he became belligerent and surly, and all those who knew Joe gave him a wide berth. People and players in the organization that had been around for two years or less and were not familiar or had not been able, because of time, to know Joe, found the situation and Joe's attitude disconcerting and irritating. What elevated matters to a less than tolerable situation was that Joe's play and production in the games nearly went to zero. Being noneffective at bats and not being able to run down a rookie fly ball made Joe a target, offensively and defensively. Joe became a persona non grata on the roster. This accelerated the bad mood of the entire team, those who knew Joe and those that didn't. Then the short-memory fans turned against Joe while the boos started and did not stop.

Rod and CD knew Joe's feelings from the start of their relationship, twenty-seven years ago, that Joe would make the determination as to when he would stop playing, and they would not even think about mentioning retirement to Joe, let alone asking him about it. Rod and CD only knew respect for Joe and his feelings, and they were not to question Joe about his intentions but allow him to resolve this situation in his own time in his own way.

CD and Rod had introduced Louise and Joe to the card game bridge on their first sailing trip on the *Sand Dawg*, and ever since, they would get together once a month, usually at Louise and Joe's house, sometimes back on the *Sand Dawg*, to have dinner and play bridge. This was an event enjoyed by all, and when Louise and Joe's sons (Payton and Joe) were still living in the house or were home on leave, they would sit in, play a few hands, and sometimes substitute for one of them when scheduling would interfere with the date. During the time that Joe resumed playing and the controversy was going on within the team, one day coincided with their regular once-a-month bridge game. The conversation was light, and everything was normal as usual during the evening dinner and card game, until Rod asked Joe how he was feeling. Rod was innocent in his query and was sincere in wanting to know if Joe was doing okay. Rod and CD had noticed that Joe was a little more intense than normal, and it was obvious that when he stood up, there was a slight limbering-up process before he could take his first step to where he was going. Although not insinuating anything, the question hit a nerve with Joe. Joe went off in a little bit of a heated tirade, of which, in many less words, had the essence of telling everyone present that he was fine, and it was his choice and no one else's business when he retired and/or stopped playing baseball. The rest of the evening, all present knew where the eggshells were but chose not to step on them, and the evening ended well. When CD and Rod had left the Marshalls that evening, they discussed at length how all was not well with Joe and their family. No one in Rod's or CD's families were closer to them than Joe Marshall and his family. Joe was, in all concerns, a son to CD and Rod, and Joe reciprocated the same feeling.

Two weeks had passed since Joe had seen Rod and CD. The Sand Dogs had been on the road for ten days, and the middle of August was fast approaching. The Sand Dogs were in fifth place in the league, about the same place when Joe showed up just a little shy of three decades ago. Joe was struggling but still playing, and the general atmosphere of the team was anything but harmonious. The Sand Dogs had just finished an afternoon game while in Chicago that they lost, 5–1. After the game, Joe and his teammates went in the locker room. When finished, they would board a plane heading back to San Diego to start an at-home series in hopes that they could turn the end of the season around by winning at home. When the team was packed up and ready to leave for the airport, one of the reporters came into the locker room and announced that C. D. Jones and Benito Rodriquez had been killed in a boating accident and wanted the team's reaction to the bad news. Although there was discontent among the players about Joe still being on the active roster, and they blamed him for many of the losses, the Sand Dogs were still a tight-knit group and had no appreciation for reporters in general and immediately threw the guy out of the locker room on his ear. A quick call from many of the players on their mobile phones to the Sand Dogs' general offices in San Diego confirmed that there was a boating accident, and it was felt that Rod and CD did not survive.

The team needed to get to the airport to make their flight, and Joe did not have an opportunity to call Louise until he arrived at their departing gate. A lot of the players on the team had mobile phones which of late had become very popular. Joe had resisted buying one, thinking it was a little foolish to think you had to have a phone on you at all times. On the trip to the airport, one of the older players and a friend of Joe's gave him his phone to call Louise, and she confirmed what they had heard. During that call, Joe asked Louise if she had the time and the stores were still open, being a two-hour time difference, to purchase both of them a mobile phone. She agreed.

By the time Joe arrived at the airport, where Louise picked him up, most of the information had been confirmed, and the search and rescue had not found any survivors, nor had they recovered any bodies. The story that Louise had discovered involved CD and Rod trying out a used sailboat they had just bought through their old friend, the one that sold them the *Sand Dawg* twenty-seven years ago. It was the typical deal where someone got upside down on a boat deal and needed cash money and also get rid of their boat as soon as possible. Rod and CD had not done the boat trading for a couple of years, but they would occasionally help their old friend out. It was one of those deals with a slightly older boat that had some minor fuel and auxiliary engine problems that the previous owner could not afford to get repaired. It rendered the boat hard to sell for what it was really worth in a short period of time. The twofold plan Rod and CD had was to take it out to see if they could determine what it really needed; plus, they wanted to get out to open ocean and enjoy the day at sea. They had started at daylight and had planned a west tack that would take them out as far as possible before returning home while there was still daylight. When Joe first heard the news, he assumed that Rod and CD were on the *Sand Dawg*. Now Joe was wondering why they would take a boat they were not familiar with so far out on a shakedown cruise, where they planned to be in the open, deep seawaters, out of sight of land.

The following morning, Joe contacted friends he had in the military that put him in touch with the US Coast Guard and Navy personnel that had information on the search-and-rescue efforts that were ongoing. Those conducting the rescue had accurate and more information on what really happened to the boat, CD, and Rod. The contact person Joe was given in the US Coast Guard was a Commander Randall Adair. When Joe contacted Commander Adair, he was very helpful and told Joe all he knew about the operation. The commander explained he had obtained the firsthand report from the witnesses aboard the sailboat *Plunger*, who had first reported what they thought was an explosion on the distant horizon. The passengers and crew of the *Plunger* immediately decided to set course to the site of what they assumed was an explosion of a boat to help survivors, if any. Those aboard the *Plunger* estimated the distance of the explosion was six or seven miles away. Commander Adair told Joe that the passengers and crew gave corroborating detailed statements to the commanding officer of the United States Coast Guard MLB 47206. The MLB 47206 (47' motor lifeboat) intercepted the *Plunger* at the incident site, where there was a small debris field floating on the surface. The Coast Guard motor lifeboat was the first vessel on the scene and was soon joined by another MLB and search aircraft, looking for survivors. Both Coast Guard MLBs and aircraft conducted an immediate search of the area for thirty minutes, until it became too dark to continue. The next morning, an extensive grid search began at sunup and continued to the end of the day with no success at finding survivors.

The area where the explosion took place was estimated to be slightly over six thousand feet deep, and at that depth, inspection and/or recovery of the boat was not a viable option. The search continued for three days before all efforts were cancelled. Officially, Rod and CD were presumed dead, and any hope of finding them alive was nonexistent. When the search ended, Joe could not believe he had lost two members of what he considered family. Joe and Louise were devastated.

There were three days before the Sand Dogs' home stand would start, and Joe considered and hoped management would postpone the next two games, and that would give the team five days to adjust to the loss of two of the most important members of the Sand Dogs' team. The second day after returning from Chicago, there was a scheduled practice. Joe decided to go to the field but really did not feel like practicing and was assured that everyone else felt the same.

As Joe and his teammates sat in the locker room not knowing if they should dress out for practice and feeling that it and the next two games would be postponed, the manager walked into the locker closely followed by Ramon, Rod's son. The current manager, Ray Grandstaff, had replaced Scott Hambrick when he retired five years ago. Ray was a very competent manager, and most of the players got along well with him. Ray Grandstaff was a retired professional baseball player and had a great understanding of human nature and knew how to get the most out of his players. Joe had a lot of respect for him and his ability to manage the team. Grandstaff asked for everyone's attention and wanted to make an announcement. He looked at the floor for a few moments as he stood silently. Then Ray looked up and around the room and announced that the scheduled practice would start in thirty minutes, and the game schedule would stay as it is. No games would be postponed. With that, he told everyone, except Joe Marshall, to get dressed and be on the field in thirty minutes. Ray asked Joe to come into his office. There was an issue to discuss. Ramon joined them in Ray's office. When the three of them had a seat, Ramon took the meeting over and told Joe his playing days for the Sand Dogs were over. Joe was confused and looked to Grandstaff for an explanation. Grandstaff looked down and shook his head while telling Joe it was not his call.

Joe knew that over the years, Ramon had a raging dislike for him, and on many occasions, Joe tried to discuss things with Ramon, but because of Ramon's belligerent attitude, Joe could not make any headway in curbing Ramon's feelings and at a point gave up trying. Although Rod never compared or suggested that Ramon be like Joe, Ramon perceived the comparison and felt like Joe was the golden boy in his dad's eyes, that he could do no wrong, and that made Joe an enemy. Ramon was lazy, self-absorbed, and at best, narcissistic. He was the product of his grandparents' rearing, always allowing him to do as he chose without respect or regard to anyone. He was always deserving of something nicer, faster, or better than what others had. Ramon was taught that he was privileged, without regard to hard work or effort on his part, that he should always be the recipient of presents, rewards, or praise, deserved or not.

Ramon had a resentment of all people in authority. Many times, CD was called upon in Rod's absence to call their attorney to bail Ramon out of trouble. When receiving a minor traffic violation, Ramon would react to something the officer said or how he talked to Ramon, escalating the incident from a simple fine to be paid, to arrest and incarceration. There was a saving grace for Ramon. He never involved himself in smoking dope or doing drugs, for reasons unknown to CD and Ramon's grandparents. For this, everyone connected to Ramon was thankful to God. The problematic attitude that drove Ramon was the size of his ego and self-importance. It was large enough to be equally divided among every citizen in San Diego, and even diminished, it would result in an unhealthy level per individual. In Ramon's mind, there was the illusion that he should be the boss of all of Jones Rodriguez Corporation, and now it seemed that he was the heir apparent.

Joe thought he knew how the Sand Dogs' organization was set up, and he told Ramon that he might have the authority in the near future to make decisions for the club, but at this point in time, he did not possess that decision-making ability. Joe continued to tell Ramon that even if he did, there was a long-standing agreement with the ownership, that he could continue to play until he made the choice to retire.

It was at this very moment that Joe had a sinking feeling because Ramon put a smile on his face that reached from ear to ear. This was puzzling to Joe until Ramon read from a document that he pulled from his jacket pocket. Throughout all the legal jargon that the document had in it, the essence was that if CD or Rod would die, the survivor would assume all authority and ultimate decisions for the Sand Dogs' organization. Joe examined the document and found that it was signed by Rod and CD, witnessed with seal thereupon. It also had the approval of the board of Jones Rodriguez Corporation, that upon the death of both Rod and CD, that Ramon would sit on the corporation's board.

Joe could hardly believe his eyes. The existence of a document of this nature that addressed the issue as to who would run the Sand Dogs upon CD and/or Rod's demise seemed convenient for Ramon. It also seemed inconceivable to Joe that it was drawn up and signed two months ago without his knowledge, which made it suspicious and suspect to its authenticity. Ray Grandstaff told Joe that the club's legal department had contacted him late yesterday afternoon when Ramon had presented the document to them. They knew about it because CD and Rod told them to write it. Ray looked Joe in the eyes and said it was absolutely legal and that Ramon was the boss.

At this point, Ramon spoke up and told Joe that he would honor his dad's word and that Joe could continue to play for the Sand Dogs, but he would be playing for their rookie-level farm club, the Elizabethton Zebras, located in Elizabethton, Tennessee. Ramon told Joe that he had a choice: quit and clean out his locker, or clean out his locker, pack his suitcases, and head for extreme northeast Tennessee. When Joe's dad Walt died, he felt extreme anger for the two boys that were joyriding in their grandparents' old truck. At first Joe wanted them to feel what he felt at the loss of his dad. If they could not experience the feeling Joe had, simply put, in his anger, he wanted to beat the hell out of them. Two months after the accident, Joe let the feeling of hate go because he did not want that to be part of his life, and now, for the first time since then, Joe had a similar feeling for Ramon. Ramon was irresponsible, and as he motored through life, leaving in his wake many people that disliked him.

Cleaning out his locker and quitting did not seem to be the right choice at the moment, and Joe considered that if that was what he did, it would be allowing Ramon to change the person he was, and Joe did not want to give Ramon the pleasure of firing him. There was silence in Ray's office for a few moments until Joe asked Ray if he would contact the manager of the Elizabethton Zebras and tell him his new player would be there at the end of the week. Ramon laughed, Ray shook his head slightly side to side, telling Joe he would take care of it. All Joe could think about was how he would explain this to Louise.

CHAPTER 24

The End of Professional Baseball

In Joe's unbridled desire to control his own destiny and in his undiluted thought that time and age did not play a role in his ability to continue to play the game, Joe found himself questioning the actions that just occurred in the heat of the moment. Deep within his being, Joe knew he should have discussed such an outrageous decision with Louise before he accepted the deal to move to Elizabethton, Tennessee. On the short drive home, Joe was hoping that Louise would be out of the house running an errand or shopping because that would give him a little more time to muster the courage and find a better way to explain what he had done.

The garage door was closed. When Joe pushed the button to open the door and pulled his car into the garage, there was Louise's car. Joe knew that the moment he greeted Louise, she would know that something was up because she could read him like an open book. It would be fruitless for him to try to avoid a discussion with Louise or wait to find the exact words that would make this ill feeling go away. He knew to address what had happened as soon as he walked into the house. Already upset at the loss of CD and Rod, the only thing Joe could envision was that Louise, already being distraught, would be angry with him when he revealed what he had agreed to do less than an hour ago, with Ramon.

Joe passed from the garage through the laundry room into the kitchen and found Louise with all the fixings out on the counter to start making turkey sandwiches. As Joe stood there pausing for a few awkward seconds, Louise took the lead and told Joe that she had just placed two beers and two glasses in the freezer to make them super-cold and would he mind pouring an ice-cold beer for both of them. By the time Joe had washed his hands and slowly poured the beers, Louise had finished making the sandwiches, and they were ready to eat. Because he had been so consumed in his own thoughts on how he was going to explain to Louise what he had done, he hadn't realized until the moment he placed the two beers on the kitchen table, as to how Louise knew he was coming home. Joe had not called, but Louise was preparing two beers and sandwiches when he walked through the door. While Joe was pondering his thought, Louise sat at the table, grasped her beer, and told Joe she wanted to propose a toast. This was all a little disconcerting to Joe, until Louise uttered her toast, "Let us drink to new horizons of sunrises and sunsets from the mountains and valleys of Tennessee."

Louise saw Joe's questioning gaze and explained that Ray Grandstaff had called the moment Joe left his office. Ray wanted Louise to know that Joe was provoked by Ramon, and the situation was just short of Ramon physically shoving Joe into a corner. Ray also wanted Louise to know that Joe flat told Ramon that he would play ball for the Elizabethton Zebras rather than to concede to Ramon, resigning from the Sand Dogs' organization. Ray, knowing how Joe normally handled situations, went beyond limits of his relationship with Joe, when he called Louise, but he did not trust his friend to fully disclose a situation where he made a reactionary decision rather than a rational one.

Before Louise and Joe left Oklahoma many years ago, their conversation was to always return to Crescent and the Marshall farm where their roots were, when Joe's baseball career was over, be it one year or twenty-seven years. The return home for the two of them might not have appeared in daily, weekly, or even yearly conversation, but was assured the thought was ever present in the backdrop of their life in California.

After making the toast, Louise explained to Joe that it made no difference to her if they moved temporarily or permanently from San Diego. The decision to leave was present the day they arrived in

Southern California, and in the last few years, Louise had entertained the thought more than once about their departure and return home. Louise assured Joe that in her mind, their returning to Crescent, Oklahoma, and the Marshall farm was never an if but when.

Louise and Joe had made many close friends and associations in their nearly three decades in San Diego through baseball and their combined business careers. Louise did not cherish the idea of leaving a life they had built over the many years, but the thought of them remaining in San Diego after Joe retired from baseball was never an option in their plans. Although Elizabethton, Tennessee, was never in their plans, and the possibility they might return to San Diego before finally leaving for Oklahoma, Louise had nothing to reconcile in her mind and conveyed to Joe she was good to go.

Considering there was a remote possibility of Joe and Louise returning to San Diego because of Ramon's feelings toward Joe and Joe fully recovering from his injuries, Joe and Louise chose not to place their house on the market. They wanted it to be available for Little Joe and Payton to use when they had leave from the Air Force or were passing through San Diego on assignment. Little Joe was stationed at Travis AFB in northern California, and Payton was stationed at Nellis AFB in Nevada and were often in the San Diego area. The house was open for their use, and in the oversized garage that had been added to the original house sat the old 1972 black Bronco and the 1966 Marina Blue Corvette. Joe and Louise had maintained both of these vehicles mechanically, interior and outside finish, in showroom condition over the years, and they were street ready at any moment. Little Joe and Payton both drove the Bronco and Corvette from the moment they got their driver's license, through high school and when they were home on leave from the Air Force Academy. It was a highlight, when they were home, to take either one of the old cars for a spin and a ride around San Diego.

Joe and Louise were very conservative, and when it came to cars, they chose to drive four-wheel-drive Ford Explorers, since the first year of the Ford Explorer in 1991. Joe and Louise purchased two new Explorers every two years. Not having a lot of time to get things moved to Elizabethton because Joe had to report to the team within a week, Joe and Louise decided to pack one of their Ford Explorers with as much needed things as possible and drive across the United States, starting off with retracing their first trip to the West Coast on Highway 66. Joe and Louise could have flown to Tennessee and upon arriving purchased what they needed and rented two cars until the end of the Zebra's season. They thought the road trip would give them enough time to reflect on the recent events that were changing their lives.

The main reason Joe and Louise didn't want to fly was their prized procession, Mofo, Moses IV. They didn't feel comfortable crating Mofo and flying him across the country out of their sight. Joe's dog, Moses, the one his grandfather Howard gave him when he was little, died when Joe was a senior in high school. While Moses was still in his prime, Jane brought home a mate for Moses so that they would have a descendant to continue his lineage. The first female Jane brought home was Indiana, a standard-size Jack Russell, mostly white, with black-and-brown ticking, and it seemed that the energy between the two dogs was unending. Since Joe left home, Jane continued the breed of Moses I Jack Russell. Jane developed a reputation as a good breeder of Jack Russell, and at least once every two years, she would have a litter with all pups being spoken for before they were born.

After Louise and Joe established their home in San Diego, Jane and Juanetta made their first trip to visit them. Jane drove for two reasons: first, she brought some personal possessions that belonged to Joe and Louise; second, Juanetta would not fly. Along with the things Louise and Joe did not have room for on their first trip out, Jane brought along with her a surprise. As Louise and Joe walked to the car just seconds after Jane pulled into the driveway, Jane stopped and turned off her car. As she opened the car door, out jumped at full speed an eight-month-old male Jack Russell that looked just like Joe's Moses. In the time it took Jane to exit the car, the pup made three trips around the front yard and jumped back into the car twice. He came to a stop at Joe's feet, looking at him straight into the eyes. Joe clapped his hands, and the pup jumped up into Joe's arms. As Joe was giving the pup a good rub and squeeze, he inquired of his mom what his name was. Jane said they had named him Moses the second because it would be Joe's second dog, but Joe could name him whatever he wanted to. Joe and the family from the start called Moses, Mo, so Joe asked what they called him, and Jane replied with MoTwo. The name was fine with Louise and Joe, so from that moment on, there were three members of the Marshall family in San Diego: Jane, Joe, and MoTwo.

MoTwo (Moses II) lived for a healthy thirteen-years plus, Mo T (Moses III) lived for a healthy twelve-years plus, and now there was Mofo (Moses IV), the most prized possession that Joe and Louise would take with them on their trek across the middle of the United States. The only planned stop Joe and Louise had was the Marshall farm in Oklahoma. Louise had called the night before they left San Diego to let their folks know they would be there late in the afternoon the day after tomorrow for a surprise visit. Without asking a lot of questions why Joe and Louise were taking a road trip to Oklahoma in the middle of the season, Jane simply agreed that she would see them in two days. All the Marshall clan were excited about the upcoming visit with Louise and Joe. All family members expected to hear Joe and Louise announce Joe's retirement. The only question they had was, Why now?

Together, Joe and Louise made few trips to Oklahoma. At least once a year, Joe would fly out and spend a few days mainly talking with Steve about farm business. Because of the financial success that Joe and Louise had, they were able to fund projects and infrastructure on the farm and had purchased contiguous land when it came available. The Marshall family had added five sections of land to the farm over the last twenty-seven years as neighbor owners died or aged to a point they could no longer work the land. On numerous land purchases, Steve and LaTrenda allowed the older owners, who did not want to leave their home places, to live out their years in familiar surroundings, even though they no longer owned it.

Joe and Louise stayed on the farm from Sunday late afternoon and left at daylight the following Tuesday. They explained the situation in full detail: from the situation with Joe's injury, the death of CD and Rod, to the conflict with Ramon. No questions were asked of Joe about his decisions, and the family wished Joe and Louise the best on their new adventures as they pointed the car to Tennessee.

After a two-day drive, Joe and Louise were very happy when they pulled into downtown Elizabethton, Tennessee. Its location in between mountains and along the banks of the Doe River gave it a Norman Rockwell appeal. It was known for its historical and architectural merits with the most noteworthy structure being the historic Elizabethton Covered Bridge, built in 1882. Joe and Louise's initial plan was to find accommodations in the nicest hotel and stay there for the duration. During their trip from San Diego, Joe and Louise were on the road for four days, and it gave ample time for Louise to talk to Joe about his thoughts, the desire he had to continue playing, and what direction they would take when he was fully recovered from his injuries. Joe finally gave Louise his answer, and it was simply that he did not know. Joe explained to Louise that he did not want to stop playing, but also he did not understand his rationale to continue, given the current circumstances. Joe apologized to Louise for disrupting their lives and embarking on such an injudicious escapade that he compared to going down a rabbit hole. The six years that Joe did not play any organized ball after his dad died was like experiencing two deaths. The last two years of high school, his thoughts about not playing were curtailed by his increased responsibilities on the farm filling in for Walt and helping his mom and his close friend Paul Pixley and getting an occasional game going with other friends at Wycoff Corner. At OSU, studies, Paul Pixley, and Coach Robinson allowed him to continue on with his life without being transfixed on his desire to play. What Joe expressed to Louise as they settled in for their first night in Elizabethton, the thing that would quench his overwhelming desire to play had as of yet not materialized in his mind, and until then, he did not want to stop. Louise told Joe she would stop asking, and she knew that the moment Joe figured out the formula he needed, he would make the right move, and that was good enough for her.

Joe and Louise arrived in Elizabethton on a Friday night. Early the next morning after they had breakfast in a little downtown restaurant next to the hotel, they headed for the ballpark for Joe to check in with the manager of the Elizabethton Zebras. Joe and Louise talked about the lack of attention that they would normally have in San Diego when checking in a hotel, eating in a restaurant, or simply walking downtown. On every occasion, there would be people and fans queueing up for a handshake and/or an autograph. Early on this particular Saturday morning, those interruptions did not happen in this small town, in this little restaurant in downtown of the middle of nowhere, crowded to capacity. Louise and Joe both enjoyed eating breakfast, checking in the hotel, and walking around the town without any interruptions or special attention given to them, not that they wanted it, but it was strange to them that it did not happen.

The directions they were given made the distance to the ballpark from where they were staying less than a five-minute drive, and to them, there was little or no traffic. It was as if they had the streets to themselves. As they drove the few blocks to the ballpark, they passed many people walking on the sidewalks throughout the downtown area, and it seemed they all waved at Joe and Louise as they passed by, yet another strange feeling for Joe and Louise. As they made their last turn that led them to the ballpark, straight ahead was a sign that let them know they had arrived.

As they made a left turn into the parking lot, it appeared to Joe like a nice high school field that he might have played on in the Oklahoma City area when he played Legion ball nearly thirty-five years ago. Joe could tell there was some wear on the field and infrastructure. He guessed it was probably around twenty years old, well maintained, but in need of a few capital improvements. At first thought, Louise and Joe both believed that the real park was someplace nearby, and this small field was what one passed by getting to the real stadium. With that thought still in their mind, they realized they could see a quarter of a mile in all directions from their vantage point, and there was nothing else in sight except for green grass, trees, with a serene parklike atmosphere. They had arrived at the home of the Sand Dogs' affiliate single A team's home park, believe it or not.

As Joe and Louise sat in their car looking through the windshield, they had a recurring thought. There was nothing wrong, but what in the world were they expecting? Not this. There to the left of a gray building with a nearly flat roof was an entrance gate with a sign above that had the San Diego Sand Dogs logo, and at the bottom of the sign painted in red letters the name "Joe O'Brien Field." As Louise and Joe read the sign silently, they knew they were where they were supposed to be.

Joe O'Brien Field had a seating capacity of 1,500 and was a typical field in the Appalachian League. It was built in 1974, twenty-five years ago. The parks in this league were not the drawing card. It was the atmosphere, and for that, Joe O'Brien Field got a nine out of ten. Joe asked Louise if she would accompany him while he looked for the office where he was to report, and Louise obliged him with a smile on her face. As they approached the gate with the sign above them, Louise had the feeling that for the first time in their married life, Joe was second-guessing himself, and he was sure this was not the wisest choice he had ever made. Joe was feeling that his stubborn, hardheaded desire to continue to play and not quit had taken him from the heights of stardom to the bottom level where first-year rookies seldom had the chance to have a second year.

They found the door that led to the locker room, which would in turn take them to the manager's office. The locker room had a concrete painted floor, which was in need of another coat of paint, wooden benches, a gang shower at the far end, one stool, and urinal without enclosures, two lavatories hung to the walls, and small metal lockers that covered the walls. The illumination from the fluorescent lights on the ceiling was not enough to read a newspaper but gave enough light to identify what piece of clothing you were getting ready to wear, and at the opposite end of the gang shower was a large fixed glass window and a door behind which was the office of Bill Lowe, the manager of the Elizabethton Zebras.

Joe knocked on the door and immediately heard a deep, rough voice tell him the door was not locked. Joe and Louise entered the small office, and seated at his desk with his back to the door sat a slightly balding white-haired man. Without looking to see who was in his office, he asked, "What the hell do you want?" Joe sheepishly mentioned that he was Joe Marshall, and he was here to check in with Bill Lowe and hoped that someone from home office had contacted him about his arrival. Not hesitating a second without turning around from facing his desk came the reply, "Where the hell have you been? You're supposed to have been here yesterday. Do you keep time with a calendar?"

Joe and Louise stood there in silence for two seconds, which was way too long for Bill Lowe to wait for an answer. He spun around in his chair and came to his feet in one fell motion, with an angry attitude fixed on his face, to place himself nose to nose with his silent and late new player. As Bill's nose came nearly in contact with Joe's, the first thing that flashed through Joe's mind was, could it be possible that he had encountered yet another carbon copy of Ron Robinson and Scott Hambrick? And in fact, he had. No more than a moment had passed after Bill had risen completely and was standing face to face with Joe. He took a half step back, resting his butt on the edge of his desk, pausing without a word said, staring at Joe for some very awkward ten seconds, then making the statement, "You are Joe Marshall?"

Bill quickly composed himself and realized that there was a woman present and apologized for his speech. He pulled up two chairs so that Joe and Louise could sit. Joe introduced Louise and Bill asked if they could all start over and talk about the odd situation that was before them. Bill asked Joe to explain the whole situation so that he could have a better understanding of what he could do to make things work out better. Joe started with the relationship he had with CD and Rod, then the relationship he had with Ramon over the years, then progressed to the events of the week before and the strange timing and document that Ramon had in hand that gave him the immediate control of the Sand Dogs. Bill figured out quickly that Ramon was grinding an ax against Joe, and according to the original agreement that Joe had with Rod and CD, Joe was operating well within his rights of that agreement. Bill asked Joe if he could speak frankly about the situation, and Joe did not have a problem with Bill saying what was on his mind. Bill asked Joe point-blank if Joe thought he was taking the wisest path by continuing on his current direction, and Joe replied that he didn't know but was committed to his decision.

Bill then asked Joe if the bottom line and answer to his predicament was that he was just not ready to leave the game. To that, Joe simply said yes. Bill then asked Joe to give him an indication of his recovery and if his injuries were still persisting in causing pain, limiting his performance and ability to play. Joe told Bill he was fine until he extended himself, which left him more or less to start recovery all over again. Bill wanted to know how much of an asset he would be to his team, and Joe replied little or none unless he could heal up. Joe also added that every so often he had a good day or two until he would have a setback that took him back to the day the injuries occurred.

Bill told Joe that they had a little over six weeks left in their season, and so far, they were leading the league with the best season they had had in twenty years. Bill, trying to sum up the situation, asked Joe to correct him when or if he was wrong. He then started to repeat what he assessed that needed to happen. Bill began with if Joe can stay on an active roster and play without being put on a day-to-day injured reserved list, make it to the end of the season, then Joe would have the rest of the winter before spring practice started to completely heal and be at top-performance level. Bill continued with if Joe could get his best game back, he would have a chance to get back in the major leagues next season, and Joe agreed that Bill's assessment was accurate.

CD and Rod knew all the management personnel in all their affiliates from the largest to the smallest, and Bill Lowe was not an exception. Bill Lowe, CD, and Rod's relationship went back for decades, and in their history was a bond that Joe was not aware of. Bill explained to Joe and Louise that he owed more to CD and Rod than he could ever repay in his lifetime. Bill went on to explain that this year was probably his last time at bat, and his retirement at age seventy-nine years old had been discussed by him, CD, and Rod at the start of this season. Bill noted that it was he that had approached them and not the other way around. Bill said that Rod and CD both told him that it had always been his choice on when to quit, and it still was.

Bill told Louise and Joe that it broke his heart when he heard what happened to CD and Rod. It added ill feeling upon grief when he received the memo that Ramon had immediate charge of the organization. Bill was totally mindful that Ramon did not possess the ability and experience and could not believe that Rod and CD were in their right minds when they drafted such a document that placed Ramon in charge.

Bill asked Louise and Joe to forgive him for rambling, but he felt that if CD and Rod were sitting in his office at the moment, and he could ask them what to do, Bill knew they would tell him to weigh everything out and try to honor their commitment they made to Joe. Then, Bill, a crusty old dog formed by the same mold that was used for Ron Robinson and Scott Hambrick, told Joe it won't be popular with the fans or his teammates, but he would go along with placing Joe on the active roster. As a side note, Bill explained his astonishment when he realized who Joe was. The memo Bill had received just mentioned Joe Marshall would be added to the team, and he thought it was a coincidence that his new player would have the same name playing in the same organization, at the same time along with the legendary Joe Marshall. Bill continued with telling Joe and Louise that when word got out as to who was here, there won't be an empty seat in the house. Bill also mentioned that there would be high expectations, and if Joe could not play at a high level and help the team win, he had no idea of how the fans would accept such a disappointment. Bill instructed Joe to show up for pregame tonight, and he would introduce him to the team, and while he was here, he would set Joe up with uniforms and a locker. Bill told Joe it would take him the better part of a day to get him registered as being a member of the team, and tonight, there would be a possibility he could be substituted into the lineup, but it would be very unlikely that would happen.

Bill explained to Joe that tomorrow would be different because Joe would have to be in the starting lineup, and Joe understood. Bill told Joe he was going to place him at first and move his new teammates around in an effort to place the weakest of them in a substitute roll, and more than likely, he would take some flak for it from the team, but he would handle it. The game scheduled for this evening was the first of a four-game home stand, and the next four days would give Joe and Louise time to get familiar with their new home for the next six weeks.

Joe was nervous about his first night in an Elizabethton Zebras' uniform. He left early, and when he got to the park, he was the first to show up and the first in the locker room. Joe started to change into his uniform when one of his new teammates, Eddie Lewis, a catcher, arrived early also. Eddie walked over to his locker, which was at the opposite end of the locker room. Joe had his back toward him. Eddie spoke up and inquired if Joe was the new guy that had just joined the team, and Joe told him he was. With that, Eddie redirected his steps toward Joe and at the same time introduced himself as Eddie Lewis. Joe turned around and outstretched his hand to join Eddie's outstretched hand to shake and told Eddie that his name was Joe Marshall. At that moment, Eddie's body and outstretched hand stopped moving toward Joe, and Eddie froze in his tracks with his mouth agape and did not move a single muscle. Joe asked Eddie if he was all right. Eddie did not respond, not even blinking an eyelid.

For a moment, Joe thought he would have to catch Eddie because he thought he was going to pass out. After a couple of seconds, Eddie took a deep breath while never taking his eyes off Joe and finally spoke and said, "You're Joe Marshall." He grabbed Joe's extended hand with nearly a death grip and shook it so fast that Joe nearly lost his balance. Eddie started telling Joe all the games on television he had watched Joe play and recounting games that he and his dad had attended where they watched Joe play. Eddie told Joe that he had followed his career since he could first remember, and he had all of Joe's baseball cards. Joe finally calmed Eddie a little bit and asked him to take a seat on one of the dressing room benches so they could sit and visit a little before everyone else showed. Eddie was so excited he started to sit, then stood back up and repeated that motion three or four times until Joe spoke a little gruff and said, "Take a seat now," at which Eddie with a big smile on his face sat down abruptly. Eddie could not stop himself from repeating over and over again as fast as he could, "I've met Joe Marshall," until Joe gruffly told Eddie to stop talking at which Eddie immediately complied. For a few seconds of silence, Eddie literally vibrating on the bench, a moment of emotional sobriety fell upon him, squinting his eyes and holding his head slightly askew, out popped the question, "What are you doing here?" Joe told Eddie that his question deserved an answer, but it would have to wait until they had a little more time than what they had at the moment. Eddie asked Joe if that meant that he would get to meet and talk to Joe again, and Joe told Eddie they more than likely will have many times to visit in the immediate future, and they can discuss more than why he was where he was. This fueled Eddie's emotions to a fever pitch, and Joe thought again Eddie might pass out, but he didn't.

As other players entered the locker room, Eddie would yell from the other side and tell them that "the Joe Marshall" was in the house and to come over and meet him. The electricity in the air of the locker room, which was generated from the excitement of Joe Marshall being there, kept increasing as the players entered the room, to the point one could feel it on their face as the team gathered around Joe. Not one player, except for Joe, had even started to get dressed out, and everyone present was crowding Joe, attempting to talk or maybe touch Joe until Bill Lowe walked in, and in a booming voice, he told the team they better be on the field in five minutes, or they would all be fined. Joe's popularity then took second place, and everyone raced to get dressed and report on the field in five minutes, including Joe.

That evening, the game turned out to be a disaster. After the game, while in the locker room, Bill Lowe addressed the team and told them they couldn't find their butts with both hands in a well-lighted room and come tomorrow, they had better get their heads in the game. Throughout the game, every player on the Zebras' roster had a difficult time taking their eyes off Joe and gave him more attention than they did the game. While everyone was still in the locker room, Bill told the team that Joe Marshall would be added to the starting lineup and would be considered an active player on the team. Bill also told the team that Joe might not play every game and may not play the entire game, and that decision was his and his alone. Bill also wanted to address questions that might be asked, like why Joe Marshall was on this team. Bill told them if that question was asked, they would already know the answer if it was any of their business, so they shouldn't ask. The entire team stayed in the locker room for another two hours asking Joe nearly every question imaginable, and Joe answered them all.

The next day, Joe was at O'Brien Field an hour early, and to his surprise, the parking lot was nearly full, and the stands were more than half full of fans. Louise planned on dropping Joe off and coming back at the start of the game, but when she saw all the people, she decided to park and go through the main gate with Joe. The moment Joe got out of the car, he heard someone yell his name, and before he could get across the parking lot, he was engulfed by a throng of fans, all wanting to shake his hand and get an autograph. Unlike the day before when Louise and Joe walked across the parking lot when all they could hear were the birds chirping and crickets. Louise looked over to Joe, moments before the crowd descended upon them, and told him the folks around here must have received the word he was in town. Joe agreed.

It took Joe and Louise thirty minutes to walk a mere one hundred feet with all the fans clamoring around them. As Joe and Louise reached the main gate to the field, Joe told the crowd that if they would return after the game, he would spend as much time as needed to sign autographs for all that wanted them. The crowd allowed him to pass through the gate so Joe could get dressed out. An hour early the day before, Joe walked into an empty dressing room, but today, the entire team and coaching staff were already there and waiting. As Joe finished getting his uniform on, Bill emerged from his office and positioned himself in the middle of the room. Bill started telling the team that he wanted Joe to say a few words before the team took the field for pregame and that he had not told Joe beforehand that he was going to talk. Bill also added that he did not know what Joe was going to say, but he might mention things that were important to the team. Joe knew that he needed to address the team, and in Bill's wisdom, this time was as good as any.

Joe had everyone's undivided attention and asked everyone to grab a seat, and he would remain standing so he could see all their faces. Joe started off with explaining that he had been injured during a game a few weeks ago, and not wanting this season to end with him on an injured reserve list, he was kept on a day-to-day, hoping he would recover and be able to play. Joe also told them in light of the events last week and a change in management, to continue to be part of the Sand Dogs' organization, he would be sent to a farm team and would have to maintain a playing status on the active roster for the rest of the season for him to be reinstated. He continued with telling his new teammates that he would not be much of an asset to their team and more than likely a detriment. Adding to his talk with the team, Joe explained how aggressive the leadership was to remove him from the organization, and if that happened, it would be the end of his career because he did not want to play for any other team than the Sand Dogs. The end of his address to the team was that he wanted to choose the time he would retire, and at the moment, he was not ready to make that choice. The locker room was very quiet for a few moments until Eddie Lewis stood up to say a few words. Eddie expressed the fact that he might not make it to the majors, and he might spend his career in the minors, and if the truth was known, that would be the same for the mass majority of the players in the room. Eddie's thought that being on the same team and being on the same field as the great Joe Marshall might not be playing in the majors, but it might be as close as he would ever get. To be able to tell his friends and family that he played as a teammate with Joe Marshall might be the best baseball stories that he would ever be able to tell. Eddie told Joe he would make the best of it to let him continue his career, and at that point, the entire team jumped to their feet and agreed with Eddie in one unified loud voice.

As the team took the field, they found the stands were overflowing with an overcapacity crowd that Joe O'Brien Park had never seen before. The seating capacity of the park was 1,500 and standing in every nook and corner of the park another 1,500. Nearly all citizens of Elizabethton that had ever heard on the radio or had seen Joe Marshall play, came out that night to see a true superstar of baseball.

All the players that made up the roster of the Zebras were the typical talent one would find on a single A team in the pros. Every player had been a superstar on their hometown Legion or high school team, and most continued to be a star at a collegiate level before they arrived at Joe O'Brien Field. The problem all the players faced when they arrived at the pros, at any level, they were all stars where they used to play, and now, there were no average players, just great players that hopefully got better. Basically, if their skill level did not change, management would move them up, down, or out; there was always a new talent to take their place.

That night, with three-thousand-plus fans watching the game, the noise level at a record high, the energy level and the focus of every player empowered the team to play at a higher level than they had ever played. Joe's healing improved considerably over the last ten days of inactivity, and he was cautious not to overextend himself throughout the game. Joe at bat would be the moment he would let his teammates down because he could not fully rotate and bring his bat around full speed and extension without reinjuring himself, nor could he run at full speed. What Joe could do was bunt, make contact with the ball enough to clear the extended gloves of the infielders, and pull the ball in a check swing enough to advance a runner. On defense, if Joe had to extend himself to catch an errant throw, he would run the greatest chance to reinjure himself because of his natural tendency to field the ball and not be able to check his move. Everyone knew that their throws had to be on the money and that they were. In the locker room after the Zebras won the game, Bill Lowe addressed the team by telling them that he had just witnessed for the first time in his career, a single A team play absolutely flawless major league defense.

Bill Lowe was masterful in the way he played Joe through the lineup, working with him every day not to reinjure himself. Joe would sit next to Bill when he was not on the field and listen intently to every word of instruction that Bill gave him. After every practice and game, Joe would stay in the locker room as Bill would give Joe a rubdown and massage with some kind of liniment that Joe was sure Bill used to use on horses in his younger days when he worked in the Thoroughbred racehorse stables. Joe felt the heat from the liniment was nearly intolerable at first, but the longer it was on his skin, the more relaxing and soothing it became. The smell was the real issue not so much for him as it was for Louise. Bill gave Joe strict instructions not to wash it off until the next morning. It became an easy fix for Louise. She just rented another room so she could sleep at night.

Bill spent many hours a day with Joe going over complex stretching exercises and a series of slow-motion moves that Joe had never seen before and, at first, thought was weird. Bill told Joe that there was not an explanation and for Joe to do what he was told, and the benefits would give all the explanation necessary. At first, the contortions Joe put his body through in the stretching exercises were painful, but as the hours, days, and weeks passed, the pain passed and was replaced with an exhilarating euphoria that left Joe with a desire to tie himself in an even tighter pose. After the stretching, Bill would instruct Joe in these slow-motion exercises that had odd names like Patting Horse's Mane, Catching Bird's Tail. Joe asked Bill where he came up with all these exercises, and Bill told him he didn't. A Chinese guy he met in San Francisco forty years ago taught him how to do these things. Bill told Joe these exercises promoted healing and, when not injured, physical well-being, especially extended motion and balance. Over the days and weeks, Joe became intrigued about this process that Bill called tai chi and wanted to know more about it. Bill explained that when he played ball in San Francisco, he had an injury that persisted and would have prematurely ended his playing career if he could not get over it. The Chinese Sifu that helped Bill was Master Minghan Luo, and he was alive and well, still teaching in San Francisco.

The liniment, massages, stretching exercise, and the tai chi had Joe in the best shape he had been in for years. Bill slowly led Joe into a full swing over the three weeks of his conditioning program, and Joe was back to his old self, ready to knock the ball out of the park, and that was just what he did. After Bill gave Joe the green light to play all out, Bill realized that Joe's talent overwhelmed the skill level on the Zebras and every team in their league. Bill continued Joe's rehabilitation, and during one of their early-morning sessions, Bill explained to Joe that it was just a matter of time before Joe would encounter another injury, and as time went on, recovery would be elusive and maybe impossible. Bill explained to Joe that one didn't run a great racehorse past his prime until he broke a leg, and one had to put him down. Bill explained to Joe a great trainer knew when to let a great racehorse go to pasture and enjoy his life. Bill's comments hit a nerve with Joe, and Joe replied that he understood the analogy, but the horse couldn't tell the great trainer how he felt about being put out to pasture. Bill had an understanding of players not wanting to give up the game and fully understood Joe's feelings and knew that if Joe did not know when to quit, time and age did. For this moment in time, Joe was back on top with his game, enjoying every moment of it, and he had the feeling it would go on forever.

As the last two weeks of the Zebras' season approached, Joe seemed to be unsettled when he was alone with Louise. As Louise and Joe talked things over, Louise found out that Joe had come to a reality check. He explained to Louise that his recovery and ability to play in the majors was not in question, but he did not know of another team who would take on a player of his age, and even if he could sign with another team, he only wanted to play for the Sand Dogs and nobody else. Joe felt that his only decision was to play another season in Elizabethton, and since he was not ready to retire, that was what he would do. Louise wanted Joe to do what he felt was right, but if they were to be in Elizabethton for a full season, they would have to find a house, and Joe was okay with that.

The last game of the season was an away game in a small town in Kentucky. The Zebras had won twenty-two of their last twenty-five games, an all-time record in their league. After Joe's arrival with the Zebras, they would pack the stadiums to capacity for home games as well as away games. Most of the fans of the Zebras' opposing teams just wanted to see Joe Marshall play, like it was an exhibition game. Hundreds of fans came to the game to see their team play and have an opportunity to get one of Joe's baseball cards signed or his autograph. Joe made himself available before the game and after the game to give any and all fans his autograph. The Zebras were in first place, and the team they were playing, the Bowling Green Road Runners, were trailing the Zebras by four games. This was the last game of the regular season for both teams, and the outcome of the game would not change the league standings.

There were some diehard Road Runner fans that followed their team closely and had expected the Road Runners to finish the season in first place. With Joe Marshall on the Zebras' roster and the inspiration he gave the team to play beyond the normal level, they took the lead in the last two weeks of the season and never gave it up. For some of the Road Runner fans, it caused some ire and bad feelings that a rival team have a ringer like Joe on their roster. It seemed to be an unfair advantage to have the greatest baseball player of all time playing at a single A team against talent, for the most part, far below his ability. This resentment boiled to a level that some inebriated fans were a little hostile and vocal about Joe playing on the Zebras' team.

It was the top of the ninth inning, and the game was tied four all with the Zebras at bat, no one on, one out, the batter with a 0–2 count and Joe on deck. Half a dozen Road Runner fans that had way too much to drink decided to heckle Joe through the fence. They had started on Joe as he approached the on-deck circle, giving him insults and telling him that he wasn't good enough to play major league ball anymore, so he was down in the minors showing off. They yelled at Joe and told him he was washed up, and he should go back to where he came from. Joe took it all in stride until they decided to pitch their half-full cups of beer all at the same time. Joe was covered with beer from head to toe. This enraged Joe, and he charged the fence, ready to rumble when simultaneously, fans from the stands surrounded the offenders and pushed them out of the park. Teammates from both teams surrounded Joe to calm him down and protect him from doing something he would regret, no matter how provoked. The drunks were removed from the park and taken to the local lockup, and the game was delayed for a few minutes.

While the game was delayed, Joe went into the dugout and with a wet towel wiped his face and clothes down to remove as much of the beer as possible and started back on to the field still red hot with anger. When he emerged from the dugout, everyone in the stadium stood to their feet and gave Joe a standing ovation that continued and did not stop. The game resumed, and the batter hit a straight shot over the head into the outreached glove of the first baseman for the second out. The cheers and applause intensified as Joe approached the plate, and before stepping into the box, Joe took a few moments for a long hard look at the fans standing and continuously cheering him from the first base side, rotating his head to see the folks behind home plate and down the third base side of the stadium. In but a moment, Joe saw his whole career, from Crescent to now, and realized how blessed he was. In that moment, Joe prayed to God to give him a hit that he could be happy with for a lifetime and stepped into the box. The young pitcher Joe was facing had a good sinker, and he had worked it well for the last two innings after he had replaced the starting pitcher. Joe's first pitch was a slider that dropped perfectly to the inside, and Joe took a full swing for strike one. The next pitch was a high and outside ball, count 1–1. The next pitch was a sinker, but this time, it stayed up and flattened out, and the ball was coming over the plate. Joe got his hips moving, kept his hands back, took his swing, and stayed through the sinker. He drove the ball right up the middle. It sailed over center field and out of the stadium. Joe was trotting to first base as he watched the ball clear the stadium and literally go out of sight in the dark of the night at which time, he thanked God for a hit he could be happy with for the rest of his life.

The parking attendants marked the place where the ball landed in a grass area on the edge of the parking lot, and when measured, the ball traveled 658 feet. As Joe stepped on home plate, the crowd was still cheering and applauding.

The Road Runners went three up and three down, and the ninth inning was over. The Zebras won the game and league. The league president and representatives from the Zebras were there to accept the award. After the ceremonies, the announcer asked Joe, as a player and a celebrity, to take an interview and make some comments about his playing time and his home run that he had hit just moments before. The microphone Joe was using was connected to the public announcement system of the park when Joe was asked to make his comments. He paused for a few seconds before he spoke. Joe started off saying he appreciated all the fans, teammates, and family that have supported him for the nearly three decades that he had played baseball, and that he was going to take this opportunity tonight to announce his retirement from professional baseball. After

Joe made his announcement, he handed the microphone back and walked over to a gate just past the dugout where people were waiting to get his autograph and talk to him. Joe stayed there for an hour until every fan that wanted his autograph had it.

Louise sat in the bleachers on the front row until the last fan walked away with autograph in hand. Louise was the last person sitting in the stands, except for two bearded homeless-looking old men sitting seven or eight rows above her. Joe went to Louise to sit beside her and ask her what her thoughts were about the events of the evening. Joe knew that he had not discussed his departure from baseball to be announced this evening with Louise, but he was sure that she would say it was up to him, and sure enough as Louise looked into Joe's eyes before he could say a word, she told him it was his choice and his alone.

In the few minutes that Louise and Joe were discussing the recent events of the evening, the two bearded men sitting above them had made their way down the bleachers and positioned themselves, standing directly in front of Joe and Louise. From their appearance, well-worn clothes and heavy beards, they appeared to be homeless, and Joe thought they were getting ready to ask them for a handout. As Joe looked more closely, he discovered they were both wearing new unsoiled official team baseball hats of the San Diego Sand Dogs. The two old men stood silently, and Joe looked more closely at them when he noticed that on the left wrist of the one on the right there was an Omega Speedmaster 105.012 wristwatch. The only person he knew that wore that particular watch was Cardozie Darnell Jones. Joe very slowly stood up and closely looked at the two faces that stood before him. In a flash, he knew that it was CD and Rod, and he could not believe his eyes. They took off their hats and told Louise it was them, and Louise nearly fainted. It was Rod and CD back from the dead.

CHAPTER 25

Wycoff Corner and Walt Marshall Field

Joe retook his seat next to Louise, and there they sat, motionless and silent, until Rod asked Joe if he meant what he just said from the field about retiring. Joe took a few seconds before he said yes. Then Joe regained his composure and started asking questions as fast as he could talk without giving Rod or CD a chance to answer. Joe was about to hyperventilate when Louise told Joe to take a seat, and with a stern voice that a mother would use when getting ready to punish her four-year-old, she told Rod and CD they owed them an explanation, and it better be a good one.

Rod told Louise that she was right, and it would take awhile to give the full explanation. It would be better if they explained themselves on the way back to Elizabethton. Louise had ridden the team bus and stayed in the local motel with Joe for the final away series. Louise told Rod and CD that riding on a team bus and explaining this situation wasn't going to work. Rod told Louise that they had a rented car that they would drive to the local airport where they had pilots and a private plane waiting that would take them back to Elizabethton tonight. Joe explained to Bill Lowe what he and Louise were going to do and did not mention anything about Rod and CD being alive. Joe did not understand what situation caused Rod and CD to do what they had done and was anxious to hear what they had to say. Rod and CD dropped Joe and Louise at the motel where Joe was able to shower while they made a run to pick up something to eat on the flight back to Elizabethton.

Rod and CD arrived back at the motel with a sack full of Sonic Drive-N hamburgers, cheeseburgers, fries, and onion rings, enough for the four of them and the pilots. It was a short drive to the airport, and in a matter of a few minutes, they were in the air, wheels up and heading to Tennessee. While they were eating, Joe kept on thinking how happy he was that his friends were alive and well and didn't really care if he ever knew the reason or the why of what they had done. Louise, on the other hand, was glad they were all back together, but there had better be a good explanation for this shenanigan Rod and CD had pulled, or there would be hell to pay for the two of them.

The moment they finished eating, Louise told them to start with the boat and why they had not blown up with it. Rod explained that a week before, right after they had bought the boat, when they were trying it out, they were about ten miles out, and a fire had developed in the engine compartment. Two things were wrong, an electrical short and a fuel leak and then a subsequent fire. Rod said that they were lucky they found the fire shortly after it had started, and they had plenty of fire extinguishers to put it out. They were able to make safe repairs and make it back to the harbor. When they were back later that evening, sitting in a marina bar having a drink, the main discussion was how fortunate they had been not to have been blown to kingdom come. They started thinking about how things would work out if all of a sudden, they had been killed. Joe, Louise, Ramon, and everybody else that they were associated with would be affected. They wondered how it would all work out. Rod said that as he and CD continued to drink, the more scenarios came to mind, and the funnier they got. The situation of how Joe and Ramon would get along was the funniest of them, and it grew funnier as the evening moved into early-morning hours.

Rod said they were so drunk by the time the bar closed, they chose to stay in a nearby hotel for the evening and planned on sleeping it off in the morning. During a late breakfast at the hotel the next morning, CD and Rod kept talking about how Joe would deal with Ramon or how Ramon would deal with Joe. At that moment, CD told Rod he had a plan: CD explained to Rod they needed to go away and let everyone believe they were dead so they could witness what would transpire as if they had been blown to pieces the day before, and from that moment, a plan was hatched.

The plan involved getting a directive for Ramon to run the Sand Dogs immediately upon their absence. Rod and CD thought if they had died suddenly without a directive, Ramon would get control of the Sand Dogs soon enough and only after a lot of money had been spent on lawyers, to give him control immediately. All the other business concerns had directives, and people were already in place to deal with the demise or absence of Rod, CD, or both. The Sand Dogs' organization was the only business concern they owned, at that time, that did not name the person to run things if something did happen, but now it did. Rod and CD also had their lawyers draw up a codicil to the directive that Ramon did not know about. The codicil would not allow Ramon to sell or liquidate any assets for a period of three years. The directive gave Ramon the power to conduct ongoing business for the time period that Rod and CD were on their sabbatical. Rod and CD also wanted to see how their relatives and all the other people that surrounded them would act if they thought they were dead.

The details of the plan: take out the same boat the next week, make sure they were far enough out and there weren't any other crafts in harm's way, restart the same fire they had extinguished the week before, tow a small outboard motorboat with them for an escape, get a safe distance away, and watch it blow up with them supposedly aboard. After the boat went down, they made their way back to a more southern harbor where they had positioned a car with clothes and some supplies and went under the radar where they could watch the show. Rod explained that the boat was beyond repair, they owned it outright, no insurance, and it went down in six thousand feet of water. They basically scuttled the boat.

The plan also took into consideration that without their bodies to confirm their death, all business activities would continue regardless of a will, and the trust would govern itself with the trustees that were appointed. This would have continued for years if in fact they were truly missing or dead.

Louise at this point expressed her feelings that when they heard the news that both of them were presumed dead, it broke their hearts, and the pain was almost unbearable. Rod and CD both apologized because they knew that something like that would happen, and it was the downside of the plan, but the fact was that if the pain of losing them was that great, how much greater it was that they came back to life, so to speak. Rod and CD both agreed that it was everyone's assumption and that they did not do or tell anybody anything. They just left.

CD, not having any offspring or heirs, was just along for the ride, but Rod's in-laws and Ramon had all their attention. CD thought it was amusing when Rod's in-laws went to his house and took things, claiming it was theirs to take. Rod didn't think it was all that funny but was glad that he had the foresight to remove the items that had meaning to him and have those items stored in undisclosed locations before his staged untimely departure. Both Rod and CD admitted that Ramon's action toward Joe was surprisingly different than what they had guessed would happen. They thought that Ramon would just fire Joe the moment he had the chance, but when he chose to honor the original agreement and allow Joe to continue to play within the Sand Dogs' organization, although at their lowest level, it was a move that pleased Rod.

Joe, at this point in the conversation, expressed his feelings that he did not necessarily agree with the outcome and their actions. Rod and CD both looked at Joe and asked what part they played in his choice to retire. Weren't they dead when he announced his retirement? This made Joe think for a moment and reanalyze the process from which he came to his decision, and the fact of the matter was CD and Rod completely removed themselves. They did not sway his thoughts in either direction simply because they weren't around. Joe again disagreed saying the plan they had was way too painful, and in his opinion, all CD and Rod had to do was ask him about his retirement, and the subterfuge that CD and Rod went through was not necessary. Rod asked for Joe's help in understanding that a guy who wanted to continue to play with a shoulder injury, a knee injury, broken ribs, and a mild concussion, who did not want to be put on injured reserve and demanded on trying to play on a day-to-day injury list, and at forty-nine years old thought he would be completely recovered in a week or two, could be reasoned with that it was time to retire. Rod and CD stood their ground with Joe and reminded him they did not play a part in his decision to retire. Joe thought a little longer then acquiesced that Rod and CD were right. They could not have convinced him that it was time to give it up. It was his decision, and he was glad it was done. Joe made CD and Rod promise that in the future, they would exhaust any and all possibilities before pulling a shenanigan like this again, and they agreed.

After they landed in Elizabethton, Rod and CD checked into the same hotel where Joe and Louise had been living because it was late, and there was more to discuss between the four of them. Before they went to bed, they agreed to meet for breakfast at the little restaurant down the street from the hotel at nine thirty in the morning, and they would discuss in greater detail what needed to be done when Rod and CD turned up in San Diego alive and well.

The next morning, Louise and Joe were at the restaurant at 8:50 AM, and by 9:15 AM, they started to think they had dreamed that Rod and CD were alive. At that moment, they walked into the restaurant clean shaven, short haircut, dressed in their khaki work pants and plaid shirts just the way they normally always dressed. As they were sitting, the conversation went straight to business. Rod and CD had monitored all their businesses from a distance. CD had with him all the reporting for the last two months for the ranch, land development, fruit farms, Jones Rodriguez Corporation, and the San Diego Sand Dogs. Everything had been operating smoothly in their absence, except for the Sand Dogs.

It was no surprise to the group that under Ramon's leadership that the operation was going amok. From the first day, Ramon had conflicts with nearly everyone in the ballpark from the maintenance workers to the chief operating officer. Ramon went from micro-managing to absentee management. Within two months of running the organization, most of the key personnel who had been hand-picked and groomed by CD had been fired. Ramon's narcissistic, acidic, know-it-all, arrogant attitude separated Ramon from working with someone to get a job done. The bottom line was knowledge-able people could not stand working with Ramon, so they were fired or simply quit. The people that did work for Ramon were typically incompetent, and when things started to go to hell in a hand basket, Ramon just walked away and left things in disarray. This mode of operation had been repeated many times. This was the work product that Rod had come to expect from Ramon, and his handling of the Sand Dogs was no exception.

Rod and CD had closely watched Ramon, without him know-ing it, from the get-go. When they saw the calamity he was causing, they took measures to safeguard the employees and personnel of the Sand Dogs by having a third party secretly guarantee their job and salary in their absence. This would assure CD and Rod that the peo-ple they had groomed and their replacements would be ready to go when they regained control of the Sand Dogs. The season was all but over for the Sand Dogs, and CD and Rod would have plenty of time before next season to get things back in order. Rod and CD had a news flash while at this business breakfast meeting with Joe and Louise. They too were going to retire, and part of putting things straight with the Sand Dogs was replacements already in mind for themselves and the process of moving these people in and promoting others before the start of the next season. Come next season, some-one else would be at the helm of the Sand Dogs, and they hoped they would only be in San Diego part of the time in the years to come.

Joe asked Rod if he knew if Ramon was still in San Diego and what his status was since he left after trying to run the Sand Dogs. Rod said it wouldn't take very long to find Ramon. All he had to do was find out what hotel room Ramon last charged on Rod's credit card, and it would only take the time to drive or fly from San Diego to that hotel to round him up. Rod said that every time Ramon was given an opportunity to handle responsibility, he typically deserted and tried to hide from everyone like he didn't exist. The credit card charges became the informant and locator of Ramon's nullibicity, and he was easy to find because he had no income of his own. For Rod, this was the last straw for Ramon. Rod had a new plan for Ramon that he was going to implement whether Ramon liked it or not, and Rod was absolutely sure he would not like it. Rod's plan for Ramon was to set an allowance for him, which would meet all his expenses for a month. The ensuing month, it would be 2 percent less, and every subsequent month, 2 percent less than the previous month. This would go on until Ramon's allowance would be pennies, and when that happened, if Ramon wanted any money from Rod, he would have to do a job that Rod dictated and do it in a responsible manner or be fired. Ramon had always argued with his father and CD that if they would just step away, he could do a better job at running things than they could. Part of CD and Rod's master plan was to allow Ramon to have a free hand at being the sole boss of the Sand Dogs, giving him the opportunity he had always wanted. Rod and CD felt they knew the outcome, but they were not the ones that needed convincing. At the end of the day, Ramon would not have any room to argue his case. He had the chance and botched it.

The discussion then went to Joe and Louise's plans and if they had given any thought on what they were going to do in the near future. Joe said, without hesitation, that it was Louise's turn to call the shots for as long as she wanted to do so, and then Joe asked Louise what was next. Louise paused and then told those present that they were going to take an extraslow ride back to San Diego, giving Mofo plenty of bathroom breaks, and there could possibly be an extended stay in Oklahoma for most of the winter. Joe liked the sound of that and was eager to spend the winter on the Marshall farm.

The breakfast meeting was over now, and it was time to move on when Joe asked Rod and CD if when they finished correcting the mess that Ramon had created, if they would be interested in spending some time in central Oklahoma this winter. Joe's question was met with a big laugh from both of them. They answered by asking Joe if he remembered old man Johnson who owned the section just south and contiguous to the Marshall farm's south property line, and Joe replied that he remembered old man Johnson quite well. CD told Joe that Johnson was no longer his neighbor, that his new south neighbors were talking to him now. With that news, Joe's smile reached from ear to ear and told Rod and CD that he would see them in Oklahoma before the first frost, and they agreed that they would be there soon.

Before Joe and Louise left Elizabethton, Joe met with Bill Lowe and explained all that had happened over the last few months and how he appreciated all that Bill had done for him. He gave Bill the address and directions to the Marshall farm with his mother's phone number because he was sure there was not coverage in rural Crescent, Oklahoma. When Joe was going through his explanation and CD and Rod's plan, Bill interrupted Joe and told him that a day before he arrived in Elizabethton, he had received a phone call from an old friend, C. D. Jones. Bill explained to Joe that he knew what was going on the entire time, that CD had asked him to look after and help Joe as much as he could. Friendships had very deep water flowing through them was Joe's reply to Bill, and Bill agreed.

Before Joe left Bill's office to start his journey to Oklahoma, Joe asked Bill if he would be interested in taking up roots in Oklahoma and getting involved with an unusual kind of baseball and baseball team. Bill said he would be interested if Joe was part of it, and Joe said he definitely would be. Bill said he would be waiting on the call to relocate, and he would be good to go, but he had one question if Joe didn't mind. Joe told Bill to ask whatever he wanted. Bill wanted to know if this unusual kind of baseball resembled traditional base-ball and if it was called baseball. Joe told Bill not to worry, that it was the same game except for a substitution rule, and that he had given it a nickname, "Joeball." Bill told Joe to put it all together, let him know, and again, he was good to go. Joe knew that Bill Lowe was a quiet, nonassuming, and trustworthy individual, the kind of person that Joe wanted to surround himself with and the kind of person he would build his program around.

Joe and Louise had the Explorer packed with Mofo sitting in the back seat ready to go the minute Joe left Bill's office. From the first mile of going due west, Joe experienced an old feeling of excite-ment that he had not felt in a long time, returning home to stay, not just a visit. Joe kept the speedometer about five miles over the speed limit and decided to drive the fourteen-hour trip in one day with-out staying on the road overnight. Leaving Elizabethton at 9:00 AM, gaining an hour from time zone change, would put them in Crescent, Oklahoma, about 10:00 PM, and at the first fuel stop, Joe would call Jane and tell her to expect them later in the evening. Although Louise had plans on a leisure drive with extra stops, she was all in and really excited about getting to the farm and seeing the family without delay.

As Louise, Joe, and Mofo turned off the highway outside of Crescent onto the dirt/gravel section line roads on their way to the farm, they noticed it was a moonless, clear night, and the sky was so full of stars that they seemed to nearly touch each other. Even with the starlit illuminated sky, the absence of city lights and only the occasional utility light found between the house and barn of the three or four farms they would pass to get home, the night was pitch-black. Ahead of them, the headlights from their car seemed like searchlights with a well-defined beam that produced a striking contrast against the dark of the night. Behind them, darkness prevailed with the plume of dust blotting out all light except for a slight red reflection from the car's taillights. The darkness hid all the reminiscent likenesses that would tell Louise and Joe that they were nearing the old home place until they saw the two porch lights of the Marshalls' home welcoming them to turn on the approaching driveway.

The moment they heard the rumble of a car on the rough old gravel/dirt road, Jane, Juanetta, LaTrenda, and Steve quickly moved from the living room to the front porch, and there they all stood as the lights of Joe and Louise's car turned into the driveway. By the time Joe had pulled up to the side of the house and put the car in park, the family was already at the doors of the car, anxiously waiting for Joe and Louise to get out and give each other a welcome-home hug. Mofo was the first to exit the car, and before he could take care of his business, he was met by Moses V for the start of the most rambunctious thirty minutes of play ever known to man.

On every occasion that Joe had returned home for even a brief stay, he thanked God that all the family members were doing fine, and the farm was still there for him to return to. This night, he thanked God that home and family were still there, and that on this return home, he could stay. Jane had homemade peach cobbler, made with peaches that she had canned this past summer, and two half-gallon cartons of Braum's vanilla bean ice cream ready to serve the moment everyone took a seat in the living room. Before the bowls were in hand, the question and answer started for Joe and Louise to comment on, answer, and on a few totally avoid. The conversation went on for three hours until everyone was satisfied they were all caught up with the direction Joe and Louise would be taking from this time forward. With the last question answered, they all headed for a good night's sleep.

Joe had a short but good solid sleep. The windows were open to a cool October night, and in the morning, the sounds and smells instinctively woke Joe up at 5:00 AM. Joe started the morning out as if he were still in high school, started getting dressed in his work clothes and work boots that over the years he maintained in his old room. Going downstairs, Jane and Juanetta were cooking bacon and eggs, and at the same time Joe was getting a cup of coffee, LaTrenda and Steve were entering the side door. LaTrenda had a tin box lined with tinfoil, filled with fresh baked buttermilk biscuits, and within a couple of minutes, they were having a grand breakfast that would be the start of a workday on the farm. Nobody asked where Louise was, for they all knew that Louise would wake up at 8:00 AM, and if she was hungry, she would eat leftovers or fix whatever she wanted and would clean up after herself. If Louise did not work with Joe on the ranch and in the fields all day, that evening, she would prepare the evening meal. Everyone helped on the farm; work was not scarce. There was always something to do and usually barely enough time to do it. Throughout the years, everyone in the family learned every job that needed to be done on the farm, men and women. When someone was hurt or sick, things still needed to be done. Women in the field and men in the house if necessary, all jobs had a backup to perform the duties at hand. Juanetta and Jane got along well in the kitchen; plus, they worked well together in the garden, the chicken coop, hogpen, milking, and various and sundry farm chores. Over the years, they had learned each other's ways, which made for a good working relationship; plus they were each other's best friend. Louise had learned early on that Juanetta and Jane had their way of doing something, and it seemed to Louise, they thought it was the only way to do it. During Louise's brief stays on the farm over the last three decades, she endeavored to learn most of the jobs that needed to be done on the farm. She did not possess the skill level that the others had, but all regarded Louise as a top-notch hand and a hard worker. Jane though Louise was a great cook, but Juanetta thought it was arguable.

Steve was now in his early eighties and was solid as a rock without any medical problems or medications. Because of Joe's financial well-being over the years, he was able to supply the farm with the needed equipment, infrastructure, and tools to make the Marshall farm a first-class operation. Steve would supply Joe with the information about a piece of land that was close by or next to their property that would come up for sale, and Joe would provide Steve with the funding to make the purchase. Sometimes Steve would get Joe to purchase a piece of land that was not a good fit for their purposes at the time but would be a good piece to trade with on a section of land they did want. Over the last thirty years and because of Joe's tremendous financial success, Steve and Joe had grown the Marshall farm to a mostly contiguous, twelve-plus sections of land, nearly eight thousand acres. The work was taken care of by three foremen that lived on the farm in houses provided by the farm. In addition to the foremen, there were ten hands that worked full and part-time doing all the things necessary to keep the herds and crops in shape to make a profit.

Joe was pleased how the farm had grown under Steve's leadership and management. Without debt, the Marshall farm made good money and was financially strong and had a great future-earnings potential. Now Joe would be around to relieve some of the burden and let Steve have more time off. The farm required attention from Steve, but the foremen that worked for him ran the farm, and these men were carefully chosen by Steve and did an excellent job. For their work, they were well paid and highly respected by all on the Marshall farm.

A few weeks passed, and winter was fast approaching. Day-by-day work was settling in on maintenance issues all over the farm and on equipment. Joe and Louise had decided to keep their home in San

Diego for a number of reasons. They wanted a place to escape to from Oklahoma in the dead of winter, and while their sons Payton and Joe were still in the United States Air Force stationed on the West Coast, it was a retreat for them. Joe would also have to make business trips to San Diego with his involvement in Jones Rodriguez Corporation and the many different investments that he was involved in with Rod and CD.

During the first winter back on the farm, Louise made many trips to San Diego, packing up a lot of personal things and sending them to the farm. Louise also coordinated many of her trips where she could spend time with Payton and Joe. Payton and Joe were not strangers to the Marshall farm and the extended family. Most of the vacations that Joe took with his family involved coming through or staying on the farm. Ever since Payton and Joe were four and five years old, they would spend a month of their summer break on the farm, without Louise and Joe. For Steve, LaTrenda, Juanetta, and Jane, the highlight of the year was the month that Payton and Joe stayed on the farm. The older Payton and Joe became, to spend an uninterrupted month on the farm was more difficult to do because of sports. Often in their high school years, their time on the farm was split into two trips a summer. Payton and Joe were smart and worked hard when helping on the farm, and as years went by, they became dependable good hands on the Marshall farm. Now when Payton and Joe had extended leave from the Air Force, they would head to Oklahoma to spend time on the farm and with their dad and mom.

There were two houses on the property that Rod and CD bought contiguous to the Marshall farm. They had the houses remodeled to fit their needs and let Joe incorporate their land into the use of the Marshall farm. Rod and CD both were happy to be away from the congestion of people and cars on the West Coast and enjoyed the quiet, small-town life of rural Oklahoma. They kept their corporate jet at the airport in Stillwater, and it was available to Joe and Louise anytime it was needed. About three or four times a year, when CD and Rod got the urge to sail, they would fly with Joe to San Diego, and while Joe was taking care of business, they would spend time on the *Sand Dawg* cutting a wake through the Pacific Ocean. Before returning, Joe would take an extra day to join Rod and CD on the old *Sand Dawg* and enjoy every minute of it.

At the breakfast table in the kitchen of the Marshall house, on an ice-cold snowy day, Joe laid out his plans for the proposed baseball stadium and field to be built at Wycoff Corner. The entire family was there that day, including Rod, CD, Payton, and Little Joe. Joe had been working with an architect for a couple of years planning and drawing out detailed plans for the ballpark. The architects and engineers had made many trips to Wycoff Corner over the last two years without anyone in Joe's family and close friends knowing what was going on. Joe had not shared with anyone what he was doing and had thought that he had a few more years to get the ballpark and facilities built before he retired from baseball.

As the plan was explained to all present, there would be a field, a stadium that would seat about 2,500 fans, dressing facilities, dormitory-style housing, equipment buildings, and apartments, all to be built on Wycoff Corner. Joe revealed his plan to have the dormitory for summer camp baseball, where the kids would be housed for their one or two weeks they spent in camp. The apartments would be housing for the players that would compose his Joeball team. The field would be named Walter Marshall Park.

Joe's Joeball team would be comprised of ex-professional baseball players that never wanted to give up the game. All these players had their reasons for stopping their play, be it age and injury, the leading causes that halted a professional's career. Some players caused their own demise, by drugs, alcohol, or in some situations, incarceration. A lot of players just wanted to end their careers, but most loved the game and never wanted to stop. The money had very little to motivate their desire to play. They just enjoyed playing the game and took the money as an added benefit. These players, of all ages, were the ones that would make up the roster of the Joeball team.

Joe's plan was to develop a team that would let players extend their playing time, albeit limited, past their prime years. The players that kept in shape after their playing days still had a little to give that resembled their peak playing days. They might have enough gas left in their tank to pitch to one batter, play one or two innings in the infield or outfield, or one time at bat. Joe figured it would take sixty to seventy players to make a Joeball team. This team would change from year to year as time took its toll in health and physical ability.

Joe's idea was to develop a team that would take on all challengers. The challengers would be limited to an active roster of eighteen players with standard substitution rules, but the Joeballers would have an unlimited roster and unlimited substitution with only one rule. Once a player had played and been substituted, he could not reenter the game. The challengers would get to play the old pros, and if they won, they would receive $100,000 prize money. The challengers would also be required to have a $1,000 entry fee that was not refundable if they wanted to play the old pros. If some kind of a pro baseball team wanted to play the Joeballers, they would have only one rule, no substitutes, unless there was a bona fide injury that would not let a player continue.

Everyone that was connected with the Joeballers had more than one job. Playing was just part of the duties if you were part of Joe's team. Teaching young players at camp, groundskeepers, maintenance, concessions, ticket sales, playing, coaching, and janitorial duties, just to mention a few. A team member could live at the park year-round, could come and go, or just stay during the season. Some of the guys Joe invited had taken wrong turns in their careers and life and were down on their luck. For those that needed a helping hand and wanted a chance to get back on their feet, Joe was there to help as long as they stayed clean, sober, and didn't revert back to their old life they were trying to move forward from. Joe had a hard rule: there was always a second chance, not a third. For those who could pay for their housing, a reasonable rent was collected. At an area a little removed from the ballpark, Joe added an RV park for players, family, visitors, and folks coming to the games.

The park was designed as a total teaching facility for players of all levels. Joe would develop a staff that could help anyone improve their game at any level. If a talent came in that needed a higher level of instruction, or the individual had a peculiarity that needed an expert coach or instructor, that person would be located and flown in on an as-needed basis. The complement of experience and expertise, which Joe would assemble, rarely needed help, but if so, it was located and provided. Pitching, fielding, batting, strategy, and management would be taught at all levels, from little league to professional at Walt Marshall Field.

Joe's plans were to have the entire entity be a nonprofit endeavor, which would have revenue from concessions, camp, instructions, banquet venues, and the big revenue from ticket sales. The sustaining part of Joe's plan was a specified, perpetual growth, permanent endowment for capital improvements that Rod and CD funded. The net from all the revenue activities would fund all the operating costs.

As plans pushed forward, architect designs came into reality as the contractors moved dirt and built the structures that were in Joe's mind, and after a year of work, Walt Marshall Park was completed.

CD, Rod, and Joe wanted a world-class teaching and playing facility, and the end product was just that. The baseball park had a quaint old-park look of red brick and dark-green trim with an outfield that was delineated from the left field foul line to the right field foul line with a billboard fence that had all sorts of advertisers and colorful advertisements. A tall red brick fence enclosed the field and grandstands, and admission was necessary to watch a game. Most of the bleachers were covered, and just like in old baseball parks, there were a few seats that had an obstructed view. When you purchased your ticket, the salesperson would let you know that your ticket was marked with "OBV" to let you know there was something you had to look around part of your time while play was going on.

The old-time baseball park look was the designed look, but the facilities were the best money could buy. From the dressing room, through the dugout, and onto the field, there was not a professional or collegiate facility in the country that would measure up to Walter Marshall Park. In addition to the main stadium, there were four practice fields. Joe owned the entire section that Wycoff Corner was located on, and about one hundred and sixty acres were in use for the complex. During the land rush in 1889, Wycoff Corner was in the middle of nowhere, and over one hundred years later, not much had changed, except for now from a considerable distance in the daytime, you could see the light standards, and at night, when the lights were on, it was as if a beacon were shinning in the middle of an ocean. Walter Marshall Park at Wycoff Corner now defined the area, a destination of definition.

The ballpark nearing completion, the management group, which had their offices in a building connected to the complex, started booking dates with various teams from all around the country that wanted to play against the old pros, and the response was amazing. Nobody really knew the absolute success that the venture would have, but the market research and feelers that went out told the management group that there was a healthy interest in all levels of the facility including teams that would want to play and challenge the old pros for the prize. What Joe and his management team didn't know was the response by teams all over the nation would exceed any and all their expectations. They were able to book the entire season within a week of logging the first date. The other surprise was the level of players that wanted to try out the old pros. Company teams, Little League teams, high school teams, junior college teams, college teams, and club teams all wanted the chance to be on the same field and play against the great names of the game. Along with the huge number of teams that wanted on the field to play, the fan base that followed the teams would purchase most of the available seating in the stadium.

Bill Harper and Joe were steadfast friends, and their relationship had endured over the years. Bill was always the first to know about Joe's career and issues over the last season. Bill had discussed his departure from San Diego and decided to play Joe's move to the minor league as a convalescing issue that would eventually lead to Joe's return to the Sand Dogs. Bill knew Ramon's relationship with Joe and felt that it did not need any fuel from the press and more pointedly not from him. Most of the other beat writers knew the connection between Joe and Bill, with Bill having an exclusive "in the know" reporting about Joe that they would seldom, if ever, contradict with their writing and coverage. When Bill took the lead that Joe was recovering, the rest of the sportswriters followed suit.

Bill was now a syndicated columnist living in Stillwater, Oklahoma, and was the first to break the news that the legendary Joe

Marshall was retiring, moving back to his hometown, and starting a whole new concept in playing, teaching, and coaching baseball. Bill stirred the pot to the boiling point. The more interest that evolved in Joe and his project, the more Bill wrote about it. During the year of construction, travelers would take a detour from their destination and drive from the interstates down two-lane highways and section line roads just to see the park in the different stages of development. Not that he was comparing his project to anything else, Joe imagined what it must have been like when people would visit Mount Rushmore in the isolated Black Hills region of South Dakota while they were carving the images in the solid rock hillside, long before the memorial was ever finished. Joe would marvel at the number of tourists and traffic that arrived on a daily basis, regardless of weather conditions, just to see the ongoing construction.

At the end of a day, on many occasions, when Joe and his extended family would gather at the Marshall farm for supper, there would be a time when everyone was finished eating, that part of the group would retire to the front porch. The porch wrapped around the southeast corner from the front of the house and ran down most of the south side of the house. When sitting at the corner of the porch, one could see south, north, west, and east. The land had a gradual decline to the west, and from the porch corner, there was a grand view looking south and west that stretched past the river and on for several miles. Depending on the weather and who decided to retreat from the house to the porch after their meal, there could be lively discussion or sometimes silent reflection.

As the opening day of Walter Marshall Park neared, Joe found himself more times than not, in silent reflection, sitting in the southeast corner of the porch of the Marshall house, thinking about what brought him to this moment in his life. Often his thoughts would go back to his great-grandmother and great-grandfather, Howard and Mary Marshall, who risked their life and all the belongings that they took, to settle the very place where he was sitting now. Joe would let his thoughts linger with them as he tried to compare a similar risk in his life and could not come up with anything near its equal. The reminder for Joe of how dangerous Howard and Mary's plight was in

1889 hung on the wall of the living room not twenty feet from him, the two .44-40 Winchester 1873 rifles they carried and kept by their side night and day for most of their lives.

In these times of reflection, Joe thanked God that his family was intact, and all his family and his close friends were with him in Oklahoma, except for Payt and Joe. Paul Pixley was a major general stationed at Tinker Air Force Base just an hour drive from the Marshall farm. Joe, still active in the Air Force reserve, was now assigned to Tinker AFB due in large to his close friend, General Pixley. Over the last two years, Paul and his family were frequent visitors to the construction site of Walter Marshall Park and the Marshall farm. Paul and Joe had stayed in close touch with each other over the last twenty-eight years since leaving Oklahoma State University. Now living in close proximity to each other and Joe's frequent trips to Tinker, it was just like old times, and they still enjoyed each other's company as much as when they were kids.

The feel of being back on the farm and close to the land where Joe was the fourth generation of Marshalls to live, work, and experience life was purely intoxicating to Joe. The extreme change of four seasons that gave life a certain cadence was also a special feeling to experience again. Family, friends, and farm gave meaning to life for Joe, and the added fun of still having baseball in his life was the icing on the cake.

The opening day of Walter Marshall Park finally arrived. April 4 was a sunny day, and the temperature at one o'clock was seventy degrees, with a slight wind from the south. Most of Joe's friends attended the festivities including Ron Robinson, still active and past ninety years old. Ron had retired after twelve years as coach of the Oklahoma State University baseball team, a job that he expected to spend one year at. All his Crescent High School acquaintances and classmates that lived in the area showed up to give their support for Joe and the complex.

Bill Lowe had booked an exhibition game with the Oklahoma State Cowboys baseball team, and the stands were full with people standing in every nook and cranny of the park. The roster for the Joeballers listed over sixty players from ages of thirty to seventy. Some of the old pros lived at the park all year round out of necessity, and a large number would come and go depending on what game was scheduled. Then there was a group that showed up at the beginning of the season, stayed in their RV or in one of the park's apartments, and left at the end of the season. All these were special players that still wanted to be involved and play a competitive level of ball. Like Joe, they were not ready to give the game up to sit in the stands and merely watch.

Most of the Joeball players had jobs in the park, plus their playing duties. Some might be working in the concession stand, taking tickets, or a myriad of other jobs. During that first game the Joeballers played, Allen Walker, one of the greatest left-handed pitchers of all time, at the age of fifty-two, was selling cold drinks in the stands, in uniform, when Bill Lowe called him from the stands to the field to warm up and pitch an inning. After Allen pitched the inning, he resumed selling cold drinks in the stands.

In that first game against the OSU Cowboys, Joe played most of the game until he was replaced at the end of the sixth inning. When Joe left the field, he joined Jane, Louise, Steve, Margaret, Paul, CD, and Rod in the grandstand to watch the rest of the game. Everything was as Joe had envisioned it, and the crowd was excited, and electricity filled the air.

After the game, everybody was going to meet at the farm for a huge party and celebrate the success of the park and opening day. Joe, CD, and Rod stayed behind to help the staff to close the park and do whatever was necessary. CD and Rod told Joe they would meet him at the exit of the dressing room in two hours, and Joe agreed. Joe just sat and watched as the crowd dissipated. Many in attendance stayed after the game to get autographs from most of the old pros, including many of the OSU Cowboys that just finished playing them, even though they lost 8–2.

Joe took special notice of a large group of young kids that were running up and down the fence line unattended while their parents were standing in line to get autographs. The team mascot was a big baseball with short legs and short arms. The baseball part of the costume covered the person inside from their midthigh up, and the arms' holes were at shoulder level of the occupant. From the outside, because of the diameter of the baseball, the person inside, their arms only exceeded the ball from their elbows, making like the mascot had very short arms that stuck out of the baseball head/top, just below the midline of the baseball.

Like all other sports mascots, they were there to entertain the fans, especially the young fans. Joe had noticed that the mascot named Joe-B-Ball a few minutes after the end of the game stopped running and basically stopped entertaining the kids at the fence line, much to their disapproval. As Joe noticed this, he stepped from the grandstand and positioned himself at the netting behind home plate and yelled at Joe-B-Ball to get his attention and made a gesture for him to come over to Joe. When Joe-B-Ball made it over to where Joe was standing, Joe asked the mascot to open the door in the front of the costume so they could talk.

Joe-B-Ball opened the front hatch of the big baseball and asked Joe what he wanted. Joe paused while looking directly into the mascot's eyes and explained to Ramon that he already knew what his job was and reminded him while the fans were there, that Joe-B-Ball entertained them until they were gone. With that, Ramon closed the door and ran back to where the kids were yelling for him.

Joe looked around knowing his dreams had become reality and knew in his heart that Walt would have enjoyed every minute of the day and the days to come.

End

ABOUT THE AUTHOR

Ray Akin is a fourth-generation Oklahoman. He and his wife, Jane, were born, reared, and still live in Claremore, Oklahoma. Ray and Jane have two sons and four grandchildren. His previous work, a short story "Death of a Gun," was awarded second place in the 2016 creative writing contest sponsored by the Oklahoma Center for Poets and Writers at OSU Tulsa.

CPSIA information can be obtained
at www.ICGtesting.com
Printed in the USA
BVHW071300050819
555095BV00003B/261/P

9 781684 563876